THE CHERUB'S SMILE

Pamela Gordon Hoad

For James Gordon,
assiduous proof-reader, mediaeval historian,
computer-literate adviser and fount of all kinds
of unlikely knowledge

Acknowledgements

I should like to record thanks to the friends who have supported me during the process of writing and preparing *The Cherub's Smile* for publication. I owe a particular debt of gratitude to Iona McGregor and Oliver Eade, who both read the draft and advised on innumerable matters. They introduced me to Mauve Square Publishing and I am pleased to have joined the authors whose writing has been supported through this facility. In particular Annaliese Matheron has given enormous help in preparing for publication. My son, James Gordon, to whom this book is dedicated, also ran his eagle-eye over the draft and raised many useful points, both as proof-reader and historian.

I am particularly grateful to readers of my first two books in this series – *The Devil's Stain* and *The Angel's Wing* – who have expressed their enjoyment of those stories and encouraged me to continue the tale of Harry Somers. My thanks go to Kit Foster for his work on the cover and, as always, to my husband, Peter Hoad, for his support and patience.

Any errors are of course my own.

CONTENTS

Principal Characters in *The Cherub's Smile*

English characters and friends in order of appearance

Harry Somers, physician
Rendell Tonks, his servant
Leone, apprentice apothecary (originally from Padua)
Lord Walter Fitzvaughan
William de la Pole, Earl of Suffolk
Andrew Cawfield, Suffolk's secretary
Lady Maud Fitzvaughan, Lord Fitzvaughan's wife
Marian, Lady Fitzvaughan's attendant
Gaston de la Tour, Lord Fitzvaughan's companion
Thomas Chope, master carpenter serving Humphrey, Duke of Gloucester
The Prioress of St. Michael's Priory, Stamford
Bess Willoughby, wife to Robin, Lord Fitzvaughan's bailiff
Master John Webber, apothecary in the City of London
Mistress Jane Cawfield, Andrew Cawfield's wife
Jack Cawfield, his son
Grizel, wife to Thomas Chope, sister to Rendell
Gilbert Iffley, factotum to Humphrey, Duke of Gloucester
Bartholomew, Iffley's assistant
Master Edwin Drewman, goldsmith from London, in Rouen
Ralph Egremont, Earl of Stanwick
Humphrey, Duke of Gloucester, uncle to King Henry VI
Father Wilfred, chaplain at Wingfield Castle
Sir Hugh de Grey and Lady Blanche de Grey of Danson, Kent
Stephen Boice, merchant
The Abbot of Peterborough

French characters in order of appearance

Margaret of Anjou, later Queen of England
The comte de Langeais
The Seigneur de la Flèche
Henri Charpentier, follower of the Seigneur de la Flèche
Jeanne, prostitute at the house of the white arrow in Blois
Madeleine, prostitute at the same house in Blois
The comtesse de Langeais
Jeannot, boy at the inn in Chartres
Bonne, a draper's daughter in Tours
Matthieu, a musician in Tours
Master Francisco, physician
A dog keeper in Tours
Berthe, attendant to the comtesse de Langeais

Others
A swarthy man in France
A man with a scar in France and England

Part I: France 1444
Chapter 1

When we made landfall at Marseilles, our vessel limping into harbour, its decks awash, I was on my knees beside the sailor who had lost his footing during the previous night's storm, cracking his head open on a spar. There was no other physician on board the French galley so it fell to me to administer what relief I could to the dying man, alongside the priest who had accompanied us from Livorno. Father Jacques had run us to earth in Urbino in order to deliver the message which changed our plans, diverting us from an intended journey to Rome and saving us from a longer sea voyage direct to England. I had mixed feelings about this intervention but resigned myself to travelling with Lord Fitzvaughan across France to join the Earl of Suffolk's embassy. It would be interesting to observe the negotiations for peace, on behalf of King Henry, Sixth of that name, at close quarters; and I was in no hurry.

It was more than two years since I fled from my homeland, under threat of execution, but Lord Fitzvaughan had brought with him to Italy a pardon, bearing King Henry's personal seal, which directed me to become part of Suffolk's household and to resume the practice of medicine among my fellow countrymen. It was as if the dangerous adventures of my exile had never happened. The trickery and misjudgements, the villainy and sadness, the true friendship and love betrayed: all were behind me. Yet, although there were those I longed to see again in England, I had no hopes of finding joy there. I knew that, whatever route we took by land or water, I could not hope to arrive until well after Easter and Bess was to wed on Easter Day.

I closed the dead man's eyes and consigned his body to the priest to conduct the proper obsequies. Rendell had arrived at my side carrying a bundle of my possessions, ready to disembark, and his face was shining at the prospect of unlooked-for opportunities in our change of plan. The

1

cheeky London boy who had journeyed with me as my servant was now a youthful warrior, trained in military skills, whose bravado had killed a man and saved my life. He was not to be trifled with and I had come to rely on his natural ingenuity.

'Come on, Doctor. His lordship's already gone ashore. I've got your clothes. Leone's taken your tools.'

'Instruments, not tools.' I repeated my habitual correction.

'Yeah, yeah. Hey, watch out!' The rope flashed in front of my feet as I reached the top of the gangplank and I went sprawling but Rendell had seized my heavy gown and he hauled me back from tumbling into the deep water of the dock. 'Blithering idiot! Christ, are all Frenchmen so clumsy? Vous êtes chien sale...'

'Pardon, pardon, monsieur.' A man with a hood hiding his face scuttled off along the quay. The rope was drawn back and neatly coiled while I trudged onto dry land. My cap was askew and the front of my gown filthy but I had reached French soil.

Rendell winked at me. 'Been learning the lingo from the Frenchie sailors. Useful, ain't it?'

*****

In the garret of the grain merchant's premises, where members of Lord Fitzvaughan's party were billeted that night, I examined the bundles which contained my possessions and was content that nothing of significance had been damaged on the voyage. My quarters were above the granary and a film of dust covered every flat surface, making us sneeze, so while I was repacking my baggage I sent Rendell to fetch a jug of the cheapest wine to moisten our throats. I imagined his lordship was more fittingly accommodated in the lavishly furnished rooms we had glimpsed inside the main house. As soon as Rendell had left the room, Leone crossed to the door and ensured that it was firmly closed. Leone was my invaluable assistant, once an apothecary's apprentice in Padua and Verona, but now intent on becoming a physician. The youth, who was three or four years older than Rendell, had used his intelligence and hardiness on my behalf in numerous ways and the fact that I had not met my end in a Venetian torture chamber owed much to his initiative.

He knelt beside me and spoke in a low voice, using his native Italian. 'You may not want Rendell to know but that rope which brought you down was not thrown by accident. It was aimed carefully and designed to topple you into the sea. If Rendell hadn't caught you, it would have succeeded. Your thick gown would have dragged you down.' He saw disbelief in my eyes and continued. 'I was loading the packhorse with your things and happened to turn round when the wretch took up his position on the jetty. He angled the hawser with skill so it cracked across your ankles.'

'Why should he do that? He couldn't have known me from Adam.'

'Don't be too sure. He wasn't a regular dock worker. I made enquiries afterwards because his action looked so intentional. None of the other men had seen him before and he slunk away quickly when you stood up unharmed.'

'How strange. It must have been a case of mistaken identity. You were right not to tell Rendell or he'd have been chasing the fellow round the town with a drawn sword.'

'Maybe he should have. I'd swear the rogue knew exactly what he was doing. Someone's after your blood. We must be wary.

'That's ridiculous. I've no enemies here. Scarcely anyone knows I'm in France. What did he look like?'

Leone looked me straight in the eye. 'Olive-skinned, darker than I am. Maybe not from round here.'

At the sound of Rendell's footsteps on the stair we did not prolong our conversation and I tried to act as if I

3

took Leone's warning lightly. Yet I could not deny to myself that I felt a degree of discomfort, for I had left enemies enough in Italy, some men of rank and power, and if they had discovered that I was not returning home to face execution but had been freed under King Henry's pardon, they might have employed an assassin to give me what they considered my just deserts. If that was so, there could be other attempts on my life but, I argued silently, it seemed improbable I would be pursued across the wide domains of the King of France. Surely it was more likely that Leone had been mistaken in his interpretation of what he had seen?

*****

It took us nearly two weeks to reach Tours, far north from Marseilles, and as every hour passed I strengthened my belief that I was in no danger. I was far from comfortable but my aches were merely physical for, although I had become used to hard hours in the saddle, I was never an accomplished horseman. Each night I was sore and tired, regretting the necessity of enduring long ceremonious dinners and entertainments which were arranged for us wherever we stopped. Lord Fitzvaughan was well known in France and he was welcomed on his own account, besides being honoured as his King's representative. He did not have time to waste in conversation with the troublesome physician he had been deputed to retrieve in Italy and there was more than enough ambivalence in our past relationship to make me reticent about approaching him. Our exchanges of distant courtesy suited me.

On Easter Day we lodged at a hospitable monastery only a day's ride from Tours, joining the abbot and all the members of his house in the chapel for their reverent ceremonies. The gilded screen and jewelled chalices gleamed in the candlelight and the chanting of the brothers was deeply moving but, despite my best intentions, I could not

4

fix my wayward thoughts on God's bounty and the glory of the risen Christ. I could not forget that far away, across the Narrow Sea, in some humble Norfolk church, the young woman I had truly loved was binding herself to a man I had never met. By my own actions I had forfeited any claim to Bess's affections, although she could not know this, but now that my infatuation with another had proved painfully worthless and Bess herself was lost to me, my mind was filled with fancies of what might have been if I had not left my native shores. My despondency was ill matched to such a joyous day and I was glad of any diversion, so when I received a summons to attend Lord Fitzvaughan in his guest-chamber I welcomed a circumstance I would otherwise have preferred to avoid.

Stylishly clad in silk brocade, he held out a goblet of the monks' finest produce and beamed at me. 'Exquisite wine. Quite as good as that from Gascony. Are you now restored in body, mind and soul, Harry?'

'I can't speak for my soul, my lord, but I am well.'

'It's your mind we'll need, when we reach Tours. A messenger has come to me from the Earl of Suffolk. He has a commission for you.'

'Someone in his entourage is ill?'

Lord Fitzvaughan crossed his legs with nonchalance. 'Not exactly. One of his close henchmen is dead. Stabbed and robbed outside a brothel he was fool enough to frequent.'

I could not follow where this exchange was leading. What he described was a familiar enough occurrence.

'It wasn't a random killing, Harry. Or so the Earl believes. He wants you to investigate what happened – with supreme discretion. He fears there are parties at work whose interest lies in preventing a truce between England and France. He'll tell you more himself.'

'I hoped I was to be his physician, not his inquisitor.'

'Your reputation goes before you. Earl William remembers how well you served King Henry in the past.'

I bit my tongue on a protest that the Earl and his Grace, the King, had taken two years to recognise my service and revoke the trumped-up charges against me.

'Don't look so glum, Harry. This could make your fortune. By the way, we have delightful reunions to look forward to in Tours. My sweet Gaston will re-join me.'

He paused and I wondered how his lordship intended to juggle the affections of his longstanding companion, until now detained in Normandy on family matters, with those of his new friend, Bartholomew, who had travelled with him to Italy. He gave a thin, melancholy smile. 'My beloved wife, Lady Maud, has also journeyed from England to join us, at my command. She will doubtless greet you with radiant pleasure. You will give her no encouragement, is that clear?'

I swallowed hard. Lord Fitzvaughan was a fastidious man and this was as near as he would come to challenging my liaison with his wife, both before and, on one occasion, after her marriage. 'Absolutely, my lord. You have my word.' When he did not respond I felt I should say more. 'I understood she was in Norfolk.'

Walter Fitzvaughan sighed. 'She was, but when we were summoned from Urbino to meet the Earl of Suffolk I sent a messenger requiring her presence in France. I don't know how long we shall be detained in this realm, while negotiations for peace ramble on, but my business with her brooks no further delay.' I said nothing, concluding this was something that did not concern me, but he leaned forward as if determined to tell me more. 'It's incumbent upon me to fulfil my conjugal duties speedily, however distasteful,' he said with deliberate emphasis.

I stared at him in astonishment, perplexed by this embarrassing personal confidence, but he continued unabashed. 'You know which way my affections are engaged and that I married only because pious King Henry prefers his advisers to take their matrimonial vows, even if their observance is merely lip-service. I had no thought of any other commitment and was content that my younger brother should remain my heir. Unfortunately, in Urbino, I received news that my brother has died of a fever and my situation is changed. There's no other near claimant and I have no intention of letting the Fitzvaughan estates fall to the crown on my demise. I require an heir, Harry, and must attempt to get one on Maud. She has the appearance of a lusty mare well shaped for breeding, so I must set aside my preferences and lie with her. I have taken a woman before and I imagine she will be compliant.' He slapped his thigh and gave an angry guffaw. 'As a physician, Harry, you may be able to advise what will boost our chances of a fruitful union.'

I felt my belly somersault. 'My lord, old wives have simples aplenty which they claim will cause a woman to conceive. I can't promise you that any bring certain success. Such matters are in God's hands and I fear some marriages are destined to be childless.'

He bit his upper lip. 'You're hardly encouraging but I won't accept that fate. Although the act does not please me I shall serve the woman as well as any man and she shall bear my child. I don't take kindly to being thwarted.'

I bowed my head in anguish, wishing I did not know what I should never have been told, and he noticed but misread my distress. 'I knew others had bedded my bride before I took her,' he continued, 'but it seemed of no consequence to me. Perhaps I should have been suspicious that she had no bastard at her skirts. Still, I will not contemplate defeat and intend to keep her constantly by me until my seed ripens in her maw. I wished you to understand this, Harry, in view of your acquaintance with my household.'

'I'm honoured by your trust, my lord.' I said with shocking insincerity, 'and I wish you good fortune.' A stupid hope flickered in my mind momentarily: that if Lady Maud had come to France, perhaps her attendant's nuptials had been postponed so that Bess might accompany her – but I would not allow myself to dwell on that possibility.

Lord Fitzvaughan stood up and shrugged, as if brushing aside the intimate anxieties he had shared with me. 'There's another subject I should mention. In three days' time, the Earl of Suffolk and all his entourage, which will by then include our party, are to be presented at the French court. I'm advised sufficient progress has been made in the preliminary exchanges with King Charles's understrappers to justify commencing negotiations for a lasting peace in earnest and among the terms under consideration is the marriage of our own beloved King Henry to a French lady of royal lineage. Hence the delicacy and importance of the commission you are to undertake, if someone is trying to vitiate these plans. Accordingly you will meet the Earl in private so that he can tell you his concerns but you'll be wise to take precautions before and after that conversation, to secure your own safety.'

His words jolted me back to reality. 'Are you suggesting I am in some danger?'

'It may be so. If the disaffected among the French nobility have infiltrated the negotiations, they may be aware that your role on Suffolk's staff will not only be that of physician.' He held out a manicured hand and examined his nails. 'I'm told some ne'er-do-well has already been enquiring where you will be lodged in Tours. I don't imagine his purpose is to foster your health and prosperity.'

'Is there a description of this fellow?' My voice sounded to me oddly constricted.

'A swarthy man, I'm told, probably from the south. Watch yourself, Harry, and tell those lads who serve you to keep their eyes open for mischief. We don't want to lose you after going to such trouble to bring you back, do we?'

With his sardonic quip he waved a hand to dismiss me and I plodded along the passage to the monastery's guest-house where Leone and Rendell were awaiting my return with curiosity.

'Cor' blimey,' said Rendell by way of greeting. 'You look as if you've seen a ghost.'

'Several ghosts and assorted unknown spectres,' I replied, failing to instil my voice with adequate levity.

I had misgivings about telling my fiery serving lad that I might face peril but it seemed necessary. His reaction was predictable and, while Leone stayed silent with a deepening frown, Rendell stomped about the room furiously.

'I'll skewer the fucking Frenchie, whoever he is, see if I don't.'

'You're to keep calm and do nothing to make anyone think we're on our guard. This may be linked to affairs of state, at the highest level.'

Leone looked up. 'You don't think it's the same man as...' His voice tailed away as he glanced at Rendell.

'What same man?' The boy sounded truculent.

'Just a silly idea we'd laughed about,' I said quickly. 'Lord Fitzvaughan was clear this is related to the negotiations.'

Rendell pursed his lips but he did not develop his suspicions. Perhaps he was acquiring some discretion, I thought, but I did not care to put his maturity to the test.

Leone judged it prudent to change the subject and he drew out a paper from the pouch at his waist. 'This letter was delivered for you. The messenger from Tours brought it with communications for Lord Fitzvaughan – from the Earl of Suffolk.'

'Is your letter from the Earl?' Rendell asked.

I stared at the handwriting. It did not look like a clerk's hand and it seemed distantly familiar but I could not place it. I broke the seal and unfolded the missive, struggling

9

to suppress the shudder which ran through my body as I read the short message. 'No, it's not from the Earl. It's of no consequence.'

'It's not a threat from your enemies?'

'Sorry to disappoint you, Rendell. It's not a threat, nothing sinister.' I thrust the letter into my gown with a silent prayer that my words were true. It was not the kind of threat the boy meant but its implications were nonetheless alarming.

Much later, when the lads were soundly asleep on their pallets, I crept outside into the lay-brothers' cloister where the moonlight shone down on the careful script and the hairs on the back of my neck prickled as I re-read what it said.

For the sake of what once was between us, Harry, I beg you to wait upon me in Tours. I am in desperate need of your help. M.

How dare she, I thought angrily. All that had been between us was boyish lust, which she had cynically inflamed, and the machinations of an evil man who brought us together for his own malicious purposes. I owed her nothing and her husband was my benefactor who had ordered me not to renew our acquaintance. Yet I could understand very well what frightened her and the cruel dilemma in which she was placed. Besides, it was possible Bess was with her mistress and this would give me the opportunity to see her and, if she was still free, discover whether I had any chance of renewing my suit with my first love. How easy it was to persuade myself to do what, even then, I knew was foolish.

Chapter 2

From the moment we rode into the town from the south it was clear that Tours was bursting at the seams with the supporters of the French and English negotiators and the multitudes of lawyers, clerks, shopkeepers, street vendors, entertainers, whores and tricksters who hoped to profit from their business. We were a sufficiently impressive company, attended by the French guards who had met us at the gate, that we were able to keep the throng of pedestrians at bay in the narrow thoroughfare, but hawkers held up their wares for us to inspect, over the heads of gawping bystanders, and women on balconies called out to us with invitations which we could interpret even if we could not hear their words in the hubbub. I was amused to see Leone blush when a spray of lilies of the valley landed on his saddle and my first thought was that it had been intended for the soldier riding at his side but then, with a shock, I realised it had been truly aimed, when a forward minx stretched out from an overhanging window and stroked his cheek. It had not occurred to me that the bright lad who had become my faithful follower was grown into a handsome young fellow of potential romantic interest to women.

Rendell, as always more alert to such matters, leaned across from his pony and winked. 'I reckon he won't stay a virgin for long in this place. Might try a bit of skirt myself, eh? Gotta start sometime, ain't I?' He ducked away from the cuff I directed towards his ear.

We processed behind Lord Fitzvaughan past the west front of the great cathedral church, which was under reconstruction and covered in scaffolding, to the entrance of the castle just beyond it. As we turned to the right I glimpsed the wide river running on the far side of the citadel but the view was soon blocked by the cluster of towers behind the encircling walls. When his lordship and his personal retinue rode under the raised portcullis, we were made to wait in the

11

roadway while our restless horses pawed the ground and our grumbling stomachs reminded us that it was well past the hour at which we should have dined. It was no surprise to be told at last that we could not be housed in the castle precincts but were to lodge with a cloth merchant half a mile distant, in the centre of the town. At least, I thought, a draper's residence should not be as dusty as that of a grain-dealer and I hoped he could furnish me with material to replace the travel-worn gown I was wearing.

We were hospitably received by our host and, as darkness fell, given the hearty meal we would have welcomed earlier. I rose from the board, stiff and aching from too long on horseback and returned to the chamber we were to share with three musicians who were engaged to play during the ceremonies in two days' time. I trusted these performers were also tired and would not keep me awake but my sleep was to be long deferred – and not by melodious diversions. Outside our room a liveried servant was waiting, wearing the device of three leopards' heads, which I vaguely remembered but could not place, until he informed me that a posse of men at arms had been sent to escort me back to the castle where I was required to present myself without delay to William de la Pole, Earl of Suffolk. I had not expected such a summons until the following day and my head was muzzy with weariness and wine but there was no question of disobeying this command. I wished Rendell and Leone good rest and prayed that the chill night air would refresh my senses.

*****

It was obvious that sleep was far from the thoughts of the castle's residents. As I was led along passages and across courtyards the sounds of citoles, fiddles and laughter echoed from the great hall and a bevy of squealing maidens scurried out of one door, pursued by a red-faced youth

12

wearing a blindfold. The route we took, leading away from the principal rooms, suggested that we would not find the Earl taking part in these festivities and at last we entered a corner tower where an English guard waved us through and thick walls reduced the external sounds to a whisper. We mounted the stairs to an upper floor and I was admitted at once to Suffolk's bedchamber.

I had seen him before on only one occasion and did not remember his features clearly. He must have been in his mid-forties, hardened by years of warfare but with chiselled good looks, and I was struck by the air of authority he conveyed which I fancied was new since I met him over two years previously. I sensed he could be an intimidating presence and was relieved to find that Lord Fitzvaughan was standing beside him.

'Doctor Somers, I recall meeting you. I trust you have benefitted from your sojourn in the Italian states. I understand you've studied at the University of Padua. That must stand you in good stead and I welcome you to my household.'

I noticed he voiced no regrets about the injustice I had suffered and my long exile but I bowed and acknowledged his words politely. I was disappointed that, after bending to speak quietly in Suffolk's ear, Walter Fitzvaughan then wished me well and left the room. The Earl continued to look at me in silence, while I tried to hide the awkwardness I felt, until he seemed to come to a decision and indicated that I might sit on a bench by the window.

'I have a high regard for his lordship's judgement,' he said as if barking out an order on the battlefield, 'but it's important that I can place my trust in you. Before you fled from England you served the Duke of Gloucester.'

I realised I needed to tread carefully on this subject. 'From boyhood, my lord, as my parents had, and I owe much to his favour in sponsoring my education.'

13

'You're honest at least. Humphrey of Gloucester has forfeited the esteem of his royal nephew, King Henry. You know well how that came about and the disgrace brought on the Duke by his wife's treasonable acts. He is no longer of account as an adviser at the court. Times have changed. The great Cardinal, Henry Beaufort, and his supporters now have the King's ear and, since the Cardinal has yielded to the impositions of increasing age, I have the honour to act as chief counsellor to the King. If you are to serve me I must be satisfied that you retain no sentimental loyalty to your former patron.'

I took a deep breath. 'My lord, I am ready to pledge my service to you in all sincerity. I won't play falsely with you or do anything underhand to promote the interests of Duke Humphrey against you or the Cardinal; but I'm not willing to be employed to do him harm. He has my gratitude for his past indulgence towards me and I will not act in any way that is detrimental to him.'

Suffolk smiled thinly. 'You think you can bargain with me? Isn't that reckless? I could have you squashed like a fly, if I so choose.'

'I've seen the King's pardon for my alleged offences. If my life is snuffed out at your behest, my honour won't be sullied by your spitefulness.'

'A physician's honour! An interesting concept. You've become a bold man.' He sat back in his chair, appraising me again, and I held his gaze. 'I like your candour, Doctor Somers, and applaud your virtuous sentiments although I find them impractical. I have a commission for you and it involves no injury to Humphrey of Gloucester.'

'I'm honoured, my lord,' I said uneasily. 'Lord Fitzvaughan mentioned the murder of a servant.'

'Rollo was my closest henchman and carried out confidential assignments for me. That's why I'm convinced his murder was premeditated and intended to damage the negotiations for peace in which I'm engaged.'

14

'Those are high stakes. Will you tell me more of the circumstances?'

He straightened his back and thrust aside a cushion. 'I've been negotiating with the French King's underlings for a month, based in Blois until I came here last week. Naturally it's been necessary for me to send reports of our progress to King Henry and, when consulting him on some sensitive issues, I've chosen to do so surreptitiously as well as using more open channels through royal messengers. Even my secretary, Master Cawfield, remains ignorant about such confidential matters. Rollo contrived to pass on my private messages and three times previously had met trusted couriers, as if by chance, in a house of pleasure he frequented, at the sign of the white arrow. This method of communication has been so successful that I've already received the King's replies to my earlier missives and, if all was well, I'd expect an answer to the last within two weeks. Just before we left Blois to come to Tours, Rollo had an appointment to meet another of his private envoys and the papers I entrusted to him to pass on contained news of extreme delicacy and importance. It related, of course, to the prospect of the forthcoming talks with King Charles in person.'

'Did Rollo intend to use the same meeting place for this last encounter?'

'He did. I wasn't entirely comfortable because his whore might have had some inkling his contacts in the bawdy house were not coincidental but Rollo was confident his arrangements were secure. I didn't challenge him and now I regret my omission. The night watch found his body outside the building around midnight. His throat had been cut.'

'Do you know if he had met his contact before he was murdered?'

'There were no papers in his pouch and no money either. I concede a common thief could have set upon Rollo after he'd passed on the papers to his contact but it would be a remarkable coincidence. I sent a fellow at once to question the whore and others at the brothel but the woman was not to be found and he discovered very little. You'll understand that I couldn't explain to this man what my concerns really were and so I accepted he was unlikely to make thorough enquiries. Moreover, I was bound to leave Blois the following day and dared not allow King Charles's escort to become suspicious. That was when I sent my message to Walter Fitzvaughan and, remembering your prowess as an investigator, I am now placing the matter in your hands.'

I stifled a sigh. 'My lord, I appreciate the significance of what you've told me. You wish me to go to Blois?'

'Immediately the ceremonies have been concluded the day after tomorrow. You need to appear in my train when we are presented to King Charles, to confer some regularity on your position. Public acknowledgement as my physician will give you impeccable reasons for being closeted with me from time to time and enjoying a familiarity I offer few of my household.'

'Thank you, my lord. If your instinct is correct and the murder was linked to the peace negotiations, do you have suspicions as to the instigators?'

'There are those among the French nobility who don't favour a truce. They believe King Charles's men had military ascendancy at the time we began the talks and they'd prefer to follow up their successes in the field by inflicting an overwhelming defeat on the English. Perhaps such men sought to steal my private letter to King Henry in order to disrupt progress and Rollo's death was incidental to their plot.'

'You won't know for a week or so whether King Henry received your letter?'

The Earl nodded. 'The time taken to exchange letters with England can vary according to the ease of crossing the Narrow Sea. In the meantime I must undertake discussions at the highest level without knowing whether my efforts are being undermined and if my royal master approves my actions.'

'Who are the French nobles you mistrust?'

'There may be others but the names I can give you are the comte de St Benoît, the comte de Langeais and the Seigneur de la Flèche. They are cautious in my presence but I've gleaned enough from well-wishers to know they are disaffected.'

'It may be necessary to enquire further into their activities but Blois is the obvious first objective. I'll set out directly after the feast in two days' time and report to you on my return.' I was pleased to hear the firmness in my voice now I was clear as to my task.

'I'm obliged, Doctor Somers. I'm obliged.'

He rose and I took this as a signal to depart, reflecting as I bowed at the door that I had not dreamt I should find myself embroiled in matters of state, on behalf of King Henry's chief negotiator, and wishing devoutly it was not so.

In the passage outside the door a man with greying hair and a surly expression bowed to me. 'My name is Andrew Cawfield. I am the Earl's secretary and deal with all his affairs. You are now his physician, I understand, and I respect that calling. You will of course inform me if he should happen to mention anything outside your professional remit.'

I inclined my head. 'Unless the Earl forbids it, I'll be happy to share with you anything outside my physician's role.'

He glared but must have decided he could not challenge the terms of my undertaking and after a moment he stood back to let me pass. His hostility was evident.

*****

Next day I rose late from my bed and found that Leone and Rendell had been taken by the draper's son and daughter to explore the town, leaving a serving lad from the household to attend me. My immediate reaction was one of relief that I would have leisure to rest before setting out on horseback again, the following day, but the boy held out a sealed letter, very like the first I had received, and I knew my relaxation was to be short-lived. I read Lady Maud's message with a sinking heart.

Wait on me at the castle after the talks resume this afternoon. Lord Fitzvaughan will be in attendance on the Earl of Suffolk and we shall not be disturbed.

I shuddered. Who else but Maud would be so careless of her reputation as to send such an indiscreet communication? If I interpreted it as any other reader would, I must refuse her bidding but, in the light of what her husband had told me, I suspected the purpose of the assignation was not sinful congress. There was little chance that I could offer her useful advice but, because she had confided in me once before, I could not reject her cry for help. While I dressed in my tattered gown, the draper's servant assured me that a new one would be ready for the ceremonies next day. I regretted my shabbiness, not for Maud's sake, but because the hope of meeting Bess in attendance on her filled me with sudden and irresistible excitement.

I went on foot to the castle and, in response to my request to be shown to Lord Fitzvaughan's lodgings, I was led once again to the tower where the English party was accommodated. An elderly serving woman received me and ushered me into her mistress's chamber, where she then seated herself in a window embrasure and took up some embroidery. I was relieved the meeting was to be chaperoned but a wave of disappointment spread down my spine because there was no sign of Bess. Her ladyship was standing by a table, with her back towards me, but as my name was announced she turned slowly to face me and I shivered to see her half-forgotten beauty.

'Well, well, Harry Somers, two years in the Italian states have brought you a look of maturity you didn't have before. Some black-eyed seductress has made a man of you, I'll be bound. I trust all I taught you served to win her affections.'

I glanced towards the serving woman, bent assiduously over her sewing. Maud's words were uncomfortably acute but I would not allow myself to be led down the path of confession and miserable recollection. 'Two years have in no way impaired your appearance, my lady.'

'Gallantry too, Harry, how delightful! Don't trouble about Marian. She's deaf as the stone slabs beneath our feet and won't register a word we say. If you attempt to ravish me, however, she will scream the rafters down.'

'I assure you I shall give her no cause to scream.'

'I'm not quite certain what she would do if I opened my gown and offered myself to you in my shift.' Maud purred with amusement. 'Don't worry, Harry, I shan't do so – although I have joyful memories of your randy manhood.' I felt myself redden and she turned away, swirling her skirt until she sat in the room's single chair. 'Unfortunately this meeting has a more solemn objective. I spoke to you once of a child I bore when I was a young girl and the second infant who died in my belly and was torn from me.'

It was as I expected and I wanted to spare her unnecessary embarrassment so I responded quickly, despite my own uneasiness. 'Lord Fitzvaughan has told me of his hope that you will conceive. He's anxious for an heir. He's obviously ignorant of your misfortune and that you can't bear another child. I'm sorry.'

She folded her hands in her lap and fixed her gaze on my face. 'You don't need to waste your sympathy on Walter or me on that account. He took me knowing I was no

19

maiden, while I was foisted, all unknowingly, with a lord who lusts for other men. We are destined to be childless but so are others, far more worthy of fruitfulness. Unless you tell him my secret, he will never know what I suffered and the reason for my barren womb. He'll have to accept God's will, as others are compelled to do.'

'I'll never break your trust. But if this isn't the cause for your concern, what else is troubling you?'

She rose, steadying herself with a hand on the table-top. 'The child I bore is called Eleanor. A wet-nurse took her from my birth-bed and she was placed in a convent where she has been cared for by the lay sisters and nuns. She reached her eighth birthday last Michaelmas.'

Her voice trembled and I thought I understood her anguish. 'The child has died?'

'No! Dear God, I pray not. But I don't know if I fear that more than the prospect of her serving the appetites of perverted men, as I was made to do. She has been taken from the convent, abducted. Some trick was played upon her guardians and Eleanor was carried away two months ago. The Prioress was distraught when she wrote to me.'

'I didn't know you'd kept contact with the child.' My comment sounded inadequate.

'For all my waywardness, I find I have a mother's heart and I've never forgotten the cherub who looked up at me before they snatched her from my arms. I've not seen her again but I've been given news from time to time that she was well. Until now! Harry, I beg you; this is why I sent for you. Find Eleanor; bring her safely back to the sisters who have nurtured her. Rescue her from whatever dreadful fate she faces. Promise me that when you return to England you will do this.'

I stared at the tears streaming down Maud's crumpled face and heard her voice, which had always been so imperious, pleading in desperation. Her request was preposterous but compassion for her misery overwhelmed good sense, although I prevaricated. 'I don't know how long I'm to stay in France.'

'Walter says we should all return within the month. I implore you to go at once to Stamford, to the convent of St. Michael, and find out where my angel has been taken. Please say you'll do this.'

'My lady, I serve the Earl of Suffolk as physician and I don't know what duties he'll place upon me. I may be confined to his estates but if I can contrive it, I'll go to Stamford and make enquiries. I can't hold out hopes that my quest will be successful. You must understand that.' I knew she would interpret my hesitant words as suggesting more confidence than I felt.

She dabbed her eyes with a kerchief. 'I do. But I can't rest until I've tried to find Eleanor and you are my best hope, Harry. I have faith in you.'

There was pride and defiance in her words and if the deaf duenna had not been watching I would have been tempted to put my arm around Maud's shoulders to comfort her. 'I'm truly sorry for your distress. I will do what I can.'

She swiftly regained her self-possession and stroked the brocade lappets of her headdress. 'And I am sorry for your sadness about Bess. But perhaps your affection had waned amid the fascinations of Padua and Verona.'

'What do you mean? What has happened to Bess?' My voice cracked as I spoke.

'Oh, she is well and I think she's content, although she did fancy herself in love with you. But we heard that you were affianced to an Italian girl, more than a year ago, and after that Bess was willing to listen to the addresses of Walter's bailiff in Norfolk. He's a good man and will treat her honourably. They were to be wedded on Easter Day so Bess is now a new-made wife. But sadly, not yours, Harry. That's why, if you are mournful, I am sorry for your loss.'

I bowed and let myself be escorted from the room by the expressionless attendant. I walked in silence but I wanted to scream as loudly as the old woman might have done if I had laid a finger on her mistress. How had they heard of that stupid, rash betrothal I entered into when I had been miserable and lonely in Padua more than a year ago? Later I had been extricated from this foolish commitment but, it seemed, that news had not reached the Fitzvaughan household or, at least, not in time. Now I knew I had been repaid in full for my unfaithfulness to Bess during my exile and I must reconcile myself to having lost irretrievably what I had not treasured enough.

Chapter 3

I had no experience of formal court ceremony and was overawed by the flamboyance of the reception prepared for the Earl of Suffolk's party when we were admitted into King Charles's presence, leaving our humbler attendants in the courtyard. We entered at the far end of the great hall and processed between the ranks of innumerable French dignitaries, robed in vivid rainbow colours, a blur of silks and velvets, fur trims and glittering medallions. These nobles and their attendants were packed so closely together that the sunlight streaming through the high lancet windows shone mainly on the uneven canopy of heads, some bare, some topped by coronets and others encased in elaborate folds of drapery pinned with rich jewels. In front of me the column of English lords blocked my view of the dais where the royal party sat but the awning over the throne gleamed with cloth of gold and lapis lazuli. There could be no doubt that the display of magnificence was designed to awe every onlooker.

Side by side with the morose Andrew Cawfield, I came at the back of the Earl's train, following Lord Fitzvaughan, and I was primarily concerned not to trip on the over-long hem of my new physician's gown. I walked with care, trying to disguise my uneven gait, the result of a boyhood accident, but not to stare at my feet all the time. I risked a rapid glance up at the gallery above our heads, as the trumpeters sounded their fanfare to greet the English guests, and I glimpsed the blue hangings along every wall, decorated with gilded fleurs-de-lis. Then we came to a halt, crowded together, while the orators exchanged courteous greetings on behalf of their overlords.

William de la Pole was sumptuously dressed, as befitted the occasion, yielding nothing in grandeur to his hosts, and I felt a frisson of pride to see my new master holding himself regally before King Charles and Queen

Marie. I welcomed the prospect of peace between our warring kingdoms but I could not feel warmly towards the enemy who had killed my father in battle when I was still a lad. While proclamations were read and the orators droned on, I looked along the line of Frenchmen flanking us and caught in the expressions of some the same ambivalence I felt and, here and there, an angry frown which hinted at less charitable sentiments. One wizened veteran eyed me directly, scowling, and I had no doubt he did not view the truce which had been negotiated with enthusiasm.

I had lost the drift of the speeches when my companions started to move forward and I realised we must all be presented, in pairs, to royal scrutiny. Master Cawfield and I shuffled through a narrow space and made obeisance to the French King who looked bored and acknowledged us with a languid wave. Then we were required to edge past our principal negotiators and take positions against the wall while the main business of the day was accomplished. A murmur of expectation grew among English and French alike as a portly, middle-aged gentleman advanced from the throng of nobles to stand in front of the dais. The multiple rings on his chubby fingers gleamed as he clasped his hands to his velvet-clad breast and bowed.

'René, Duke of Anjou,' Cawfield whispered, 'Duke of Bar, Count of Provence, and titular King of Sicily, Jerusalem and Naples, no less; although I'm not sure he persists in his empty claim to the manifold kingships.'

'A patron of culture and learning, I believe,' I said, anxious to show Suffolk's secretary I was not entirely ignorant of state affairs.'

'No doubt why his debts are enormous. There'll be no dowry with this marriage.'

A herald banged his staff on the floor for silence and an official recited all of Duke René's honours before the Earl of Suffolk stepped forward and knelt to ask publicly, on behalf of his sovereign lord, King Henry, for the hand of the

Duke's second daughter, Margaret. Then the French Duke embraced the English Earl and King Charles beckoned a bishop to pronounce a blessing, after which a herald announced that the formal betrothal would take place in a month's time and the marriage would be celebrated the following year.

'It can't be any sooner. They'll have to get the Three Estates to vote the money to meet the girl's expenses,' my companion said. 'King Henry's already had to agree to pay for her trousseau and the cost of her travelling to England. She'd better be worth it, this Margaret. She's from a well-connected family, I'll say that, with Duke René's sister married to King Charles. Queen Marie is the girl's aunt.'

'Look,' I said, 'touching his arm lightly, 'the great doors are opening. Are we going to see her?'

Master Cawfield and a hundred others drew in their breath as the procession of ladies appeared, led by Duke René's wife, Isabelle of Lorraine, opulently arrayed, and at her side the fourteen-year-old bride who needed no adornment to capture universal attention. Princesses are commonly spoken of as beautiful, I reflected, but Margaret, with her refined features and cascading auburn hair, needed no flattery; her appearance would win many hearts. Yet I noted that she was well aware of the impact she made, her head held high with no hint of timidity in her bearing. She would be more than a match for the gentle English King. I turned my eyes from this regal paragon and glanced at the women following her, who, I surmised, might have no easy task to please her exacting standards. Several looked down modestly as they approached the throne but one, a taller, frosty-faced but attractive young woman, walked with arrogance to equal her mistress's. She scanned the group of Englishmen, seeming to peer towards me; then she tossed her heavily caparisoned head, with its net of gold and flowing veil, and looked away.

Suffolk was apparently as deeply moved by the sight of Margaret of Anjou as most of the other men, bowing low before dropping once more onto one knee. I could not hear the words he spoke but she was scrutinising him carefully and permitted the flicker of a smile to soften her features for an instant. After this King Charles rose, gave his arm to his wife and led the procession out of the hall, followed by Duke René, Duchess Isabelle, their daughter and the principal English guests. They would be entertained in the private apartments while the trestles were set up in the hall for the ensuing feast. The immense crowd of lesser nobles and their acolytes jostled each other to get out of the way of servants bearing boards and benches and, in the mêlée, the hostile-looking old Frenchman brushed against me, muttering something which sounded like 'deformed English pig'. I pretended not to hear but Andrew Cawfield showed open annoyance.

'Treacherous swine! He's one of a clique trying to undermine the negotiations, loses no opportunity to antagonise the English and stir up dissension among King Charles's courtiers.'

'Who is he?'

'The comte de Langeais.'

I nodded, recalling he was one of those Suffolk had named, and I allowed myself to be hustled into an antechamber where we were to wait for the tables to be prepared. A moment later heads turned towards the door to the courtyard when we heard angry shouting and then, briefly, the clash of metal, whereupon several French guards hurried outside. While calm was being restored I identified with alarm Leone's voice calling for me and, regardless of courtesy, I pushed my way through the throng to reach him.

'Thank the saints, Doctor Somers.' He ran forward to seize my arm. 'They've arrested Rendell for affray.'

A sergeant of the guard was holding my wretched servant by the neck of his jerkin and the boy was cursing foully in English. A liveried Frenchman, clasping a bloodied wrist, exchanged insult for verbal insult and a second guard stood beside his colleague, holding a small dagger and a slender poniard.

'What has happened, officer?' I tried to sound as if I carried some authority.

'This lout attacked me,' the injured man roared. 'Is he your servant, Englishman? I demand restitution.'

'I bloody never did! He elbowed me first and called the Earl of Suffolk a filthy name. Then he drew his knife so I got mine out. He didn't expect I'd be so good with it. Gutless poltroon!'

'That's enough, Rendell.'

'I'm taking both these fellows in charge,' the guard said. 'Everyone knows there's to be no fighting in the castle. Excuse me, physician, I must obey my orders.'

'Your orders cannot be intended to foment ill will between the Earl of Suffolk's supporters and the French court.' I turned at the sound of Cawfield's haughty tone. I had not realised he had followed me. 'Such a minor dispute mustn't be allowed to imperil the harmony of this day. I am the Earl's secretary and I require you to free both assailants in the interests of the accord which has been agreed with his Grace, King Charles. The boy is servant to the Earl's physician. Whom do you serve, fellow?'

The Frenchman glowered. 'The Seigneur de la Flèche, God save him.'

The sergeant stiffened. The Seigneur's recalcitrant attitude towards the truce was obviously well known. 'I have no wish to offend the Earl Suffolk.' He fingered his leather belt and turned to me. 'Will you take responsibility for your servant and keep him out of trouble?'

Where Rendell was concerned that was an unreasonable demand but I grasped the boy's arm. 'Yes, officer, and I'll take him away from the court for a few days.

27

I have a journey to make, out of Tours, and he will accompany me.'

The sergeant bowed to Master Cawfield. 'In the circumstances I can accede to your request, sir. The Seigneur's man displayed unjustified force in drawing his weapon against a mere lad. Be off with you, fellow, and tell your master goodwill towards our English guests will not be so easily undermined.'

The second guard conducted the aggressor from the courtyard and I instructed Leone to take Rendell outside the castle and have our horses harnessed ready for departure within the hour. Then, with genuine gratitude, I hurried to catch up with the Earl's secretary who had re-entered the antechamber. 'Master Cawfield, that was generous of you.'

He gave me a frosty stare. 'What you call generosity owed nothing to any concern for you or your foolish servant, Doctor Somers. My duty is to the Earl and to the success of his business, solely. I bid you good-day.'

He strode into the hall without a backward glance and I took my place at the bottom table from where I could slide out unobtrusively after the first platters had been served. I was not good company for my neighbours, although they seemed happy to converse across me, because my thoughts were absorbed by a conundrum. Was it simple bad luck that Rendell's fiery temper had roused the anger of that particular serving-man? Or had he been singled out by the adherent of a dissident French noble with the intention of instigating violence between the English and their hosts? Whatever the cause of the incident, I feared it had sparked hostility which would not quickly subside.

*****

Two hefty men at arms in Suffolk's livery escorted us on our journey and would have been quite capable of riding the full distance in one day but, in deference to the slower

28

pace which I preferred on horseback, we broke our journey overnight in Amboise and arrived at our destination before noon next day. Lodgings had been secured for us in the shadow of the castle at Blois and I left Rendell and Leone there while I set out, in my doctor's gown and cap, to find the bawdy house, at the sign of the white arrow, which the unfortunate Rollo had frequented. I appreciated the irony of my destination, for I had lived like a monk since I left Verona and suffered the perfidy of the woman I loved there but at least, I thought, I could deal with matters objectively.

Following instructions, I found the entrance to the shabby premises down some steps, signed by an arrow chalked on the roadway. It was a quiet time of day for commerce but, at the sight of a potential client, the proprietress chuckled affably and bade me welcome. In an alcove at the back of the room a brawny ruffian stirred from slumber and peered at me but at a gesture from his mistress he closed his eyes again. Clearly I was not seen as posing a threat to the good order of her house.

'Physician, are you, sir? I've the very girl for you, just come from the country, quite unspoiled. I'll call her.'

I cut in with the story I had prepared. 'Forgive me, madame, but I had an old friend from England who met a sad end near here. His name was Rollo. He'd mentioned a particular girl in this house who gave him pleasure and recommended me to see her if I was in Blois. If she's still with you, I should like to follow his advice.'

The woman pursed her lips but did not deny that Rollo's whore was in the house, which was encouraging, so I took out a handful of coins from my gown and jingled them. She put a hand to her bosom and assumed a solemn expression. 'Jeanne had a liking for your friend and his death upset her more than was sensible in her position. She took ill and wouldn't work for days. I was compelled to tell her to leave the house. I can't provide charity for those who don't bring income. Luckily for her she pulled herself together and recovered her charms. I don't want her upset by remembering Rollo.'

I coughed to cover unease at my hypocrisy. 'Madame, your concern does you credit. I'll be considerate. I have charge of Rollo's affairs and I know he would wish me to be generous in dealing with your house.'

She followed the movement of my hand as I took out another coin. 'After all,' she said with an ingratiating smile, 'you're a physician, aren't you? I can see from your gown. You might give her good counsel. I'll take you to her.'

I followed the woman upstairs to a narrow passage which ran between two lines of worn hangings fixed to a ceiling-rail. She grinned at me, exposing her sparse, discoloured teeth. 'You have privacy in this house, you see, sir, not like the common sort.' When she drew aside one piece of drapery for me to enter, I saw that the compartments were separated from each other by similarly flimsy cloth, and she ushered me into the narrow cubicle.

As soon as I entered Jeanne stood up from a stool and began to unlace her bodice. She was tiny, with very fair hair and enormous blue eyes and, despite my resolve and the seriousness of my mission, I felt a surge of desire. I picked up the wrap she had dropped and held it out. I kept my voice low. 'I need to speak to you, Jeanne, before... anything else.'

She sat down again with a sigh, doubtless accustomed to humouring the quirks of assorted clients. 'As you wish. Are you English?'

'You can tell by my accent. I know of you from my old friend. You were kind to him. I think we are both sorrowful to lose him.'

'Rollo? That's in the past. Will you take wine?' She spoke mechanically as if reciting something she had rehearsed.

She poured two glasses and I went to her side. 'I'd like to know a little more about what happened that night. Can you bear to tell me?'

'There's nothing to tell. It was the same as usual. He came to me and we lay together, then he left. He was a client like any other.' Her attempt at defiance did not ring true.

'He used to meet colleagues while he was at the house, didn't he?'

She started to tremble and the wine slopped from her glass. 'I never saw them. I was in my room.'

'But he told you about them. He trusted you.'

Tears filled her eyes. 'It was some business he had with them. That's all I know.'

'I serve the Earl of Suffolk, Jeanne, and he believes Rollo may have been killed because of the contacts he made here. Do you know if he met anyone that last night?'

I put my arm round her shoulders and she nestled against me, her voice no more than a whisper. 'Yes, he did. I heard them speak in the passage, not the words just a murmur. He had a packet of papers in his hand to give the other man. That was usual.'

'Did you see the other man?'

She shook her head. 'I never saw who he met but that night the fellow had been with Madeleine. She grumbled afterwards because he'd been rough and left her with bruises.'

'Is Madeleine still here?'

Jeanne clutched the loose edge of my gown. 'Stay with me. Don't go to her. Madame will be angry if you leave me too soon and ask for another. She'll beat me for disappointing you. Don't let her think you only came to ask questions.' The wrap had slipped to the ground and she pulled open the remaining laces. She was naked beneath her robe.

What she said made sense and I recognised that I should spend longer with her to avert suspicion but I need

31

not have done what I did next, which was outside the brief I had set myself. I had resolved that I would be dispassionate in questioning Rollo's doxy, that I would be unmoved by her wiles, that there was no possibility of using her, as he had done, for my own pleasure. Yet, when she reached up to draw my face towards her and my lips met hers, my good intentions dissolved and I lifted her feather-light body and carried her to the bed, where I at least found comfort in our congress.

*****

While returning to my lodgings, I pondered the difficulty I had created for myself. If it was the case that Rollo made contact with the man he went to meet, the likelihood was that Suffolk's letter had been carried safely to England and Rollo had been the victim of a casual attack on his way back to his master. If so, there was no more to be done; but I was not satisfied this was the whole story. I had concocted a different theory, although it seemed improbable, but it must be tested and for this it was essential to question Madeleine about the man she had entertained on the night of Rollo's death. Herein lay my problem: for I could scarcely return to the house, asking to see Madeleine, without implying that Jeanne had not met my expectations and I had no wish get her into trouble. I cursed myself for not realising this earlier and, in my annoyance, I began to consider whether I could devise a different plan. To my shame, I thought of persuading young Leone to go to the bawdy house to question Madeleine, although I knew he would be deeply embarrassed to be sent there. It was as well that he and Rendell were not at my lodgings when I returned and I went early to my rest.

Next morning I had thought of no better scheme and, when Leone brought me food to break my fast, I asked him to sit down and eat with me. 'Is Rendell not here?'

'One of Suffolk's men at arms has a friend at the castle and yesterday he showed us the grand buildings. He invited us to go again this morning, for the soldiers were to play at dice and he said we'd have a merry time. Rendell was keen to watch so I told him to go and I'd stay in case you needed attendance.'

'You're not my servant, Leone.'

He gave a sheepish grin. 'I hoped you'd tell me what you found out yesterday.'

I had told him little about my mission in Blois but Leone had shared adventures with me before and could read the signs. 'I'm looking into the circumstances of a man's death for Suffolk. I made enquiries at a house he used to frequent and discovered something of his last movements before he was slaughtered in the street. There's more to look into and another person to see.'

Leone's eyes were bright with interest but he blushed as he spoke. 'You went to a whore-house?'

I nodded. This was my opportunity to suggest he might become involved but I hesitated and in the silence there came a knock at the door of my room. 'See who's there, please,' I said with relief.

He returned quickly. 'It's a woman, Doctor Somers, asking to see you.'

I thought at first it must be Jeanne, though how she could have found my lodging I did not know, but then I saw the hooded figure in the doorway was too tall. I beckoned Leone to follow her back into the room but, hearing his footfall, she looked at me anxiously. 'I would be private, sir.'

'My assistant knows all my business. Who are you?'

'My name is Madeleine. I come from the house of the white arrow.'

I indicated a bench for her to sit. 'How did you find me here?'

She lowered her hood, revealing hard, weary features, smudged with traces of paint, and I was aware of

Leone studying her. 'I thought you might be lodged at the castle so I went to the gatehouse to ask. As luck would have it there was a boy with the guards who told me you were here.'

Leone winked and I shuddered at the prospect of Rendell's taunts about the hussy who had come seeking me. I was cautious and stilted in addressing her. 'Jeanne mentioned you. Why have you come?'

'She said you had questions for me.'

'I do. I'm grateful you've come. I didn't expect it.'

'Jeanne said you wouldn't want to ask for me at the house.'

'That was shrewd of her. Do you know why I want to see you?'

'Because of that English brute who hurt me.'

'Had you seen him before?'

'No. A month earlier another Englishman took his pleasure of me before he went off with Rollo. There was nothing odd about him but this man was a villain.'

I remembered the burly attendant in the alcove when I arrived at the house. 'Couldn't you call for assistance? Doesn't your mistress keep someone to deal with trouble-makers?'

She gave me a withering look. 'When the bastard held a dagger to my throat I dared not scream. He said he liked a woman to be terrified when he took her. There are men with such tastes.'

Leone was staring at the floor and I was sorry he had to listen to this tale. 'Can you describe the man?'

'There was nothing remarkable about his face, except a scar above one eye, the left one. Brown hair, I think, not very dark. It was the sneer that I remember and the cruelty.'

'Was he dressed in livery?'

'Yes, like the other man, with the crest of some animal's head.'

Suffolk's arms bore three leopards' heads and this man was one of his personal couriers. 'Jeanne told me he met Rollo as they were leaving. Did you hear them talking?'

Madeleine pouted and opened her hand. 'You will be generous, won't you, if I speak out?'

Although I did not feel comfortable, I had no option but to trust this woman and I reached for my purse. 'I want only the truth, Madeleine, no embellishment. Even if you heard little, tell me what it was.'

She took the coin and ran her finger round its edge. 'They were already at odds before they went downstairs. Rollo asked him something and didn't like the answer. I heard the wariness in his voice, though I couldn't make out the words because of their boots thudding on the treads.'

'Did you gather any of what Rollo had asked?'

'Something about the River Thames. It made no sense to me.'

'A password!' Leone exclaimed. Could it have been a question needing a password in reply?' I grinned at him, welcoming his intelligence.

'I don't know,' Madeleine said, 'but whatever it was, it angered Rollo. They were still arguing when they went into the street.'

'You could hear them outside the house?'

'Jeanne's room overlooks the yard behind the building but mine looks out to the side street. I'd seen what a temper that man had and I wondered what would happen. I peeped out and saw them turn towards the alley. They weren't shouting so much then.'

'Did you see either man draw a weapon?'

'No. If anything, I thought they'd stopped quarrelling and I didn't stay to watch. That's all I know, sir.'

'You didn't tell this to the officers investigating Rollo's death?'

'No one asked. They'd hardly take notice of a whore's word. It wasn't my business anyway. I know better than to get involved in such affairs but Jeanne was upset after you saw her, so I said I'd come and tell you.'

'I'm very grateful.' I pressed another coin into her hand. 'Don't speak to anyone else about this and don't be afraid. I'm certain that man won't come back to threaten you. He'll have sailed across the Narrow Sea by now. Did he say how he'd travelled to Blois?'

'He didn't say whether he'd come direct from England but he mentioned staying in Rouen. He said the whores there were prettier.' Her expression softened as she stood up. 'I'm pleased to know he won't return.' She gave a bob and moved towards the door, pausing as she reached Leone. She raised her hand and ruffled his thick black hair. 'Here's one I'd be glad to entertain. Don't let your master have it all to himself. Come and see me, lad. I'll show you things you've not yet dreamed of.' She ran her fingers down his chest but he backed away as they neared his crotch. 'Bring him to me, Doctor, when you visit Jeanne again. There's much he has to learn.'

Leone's arms were clenched tightly around his middle as if to ward off probable assault and his face was pale but we stayed silent until we heard her leave the house. 'Our minds were working in the same direction when you mentioned a password,' I said. 'It could have been a plot to intercept the Earl's message – by persons unknown. Yet it seems Rollo might have been reassured about his contact by the time they left the house, if they'd stopped quarrelling. In that case Rollo's murder could be unconnected with the Earl's business.'

Leone did not change his stance. 'Will you go again to the brothel?'

'I've no intention of doing so.' He breathed out and dropped his arms but he still looked worried so I grinned. 'Unless you'd like me to take you for lessons from that instructress?'

He shuddered but smiled happily at my raised eyebrow. 'I'm not ready for that honour. I leave that to my elders.'

'What's he not ready for?'

We had not heard Rendell creeping up the stairs and he broke in on us with a yelp of mischief. 'Christ, Doctor, did you tup that old bitch who came asking for you at the castle? Is that what he's offering you, Leone? Don't listen to him. He's a bloody corrupting influence. You should've come with me. Look what I won at dice!' He held out a handful of coins almost corresponding in value to what I had given Madeleine and he adopted a sanctimonious pose. 'Look after your purse, Leone, and keep away from randy physicians who'll lead you into the paths of vice.'

Leone charged at him, laughing, and they rolled on the floor in a mock brawl while I struggled to suppress the shame I felt at the near accuracy of Rendell's assertion.

Chapter 4

We left Blois next morning, without making any further excursions into the town, and once more we broke our journey overnight at Amboise. This gave us a comfortable distance to travel on the second day and we trotted along the track, which followed the River Loire at a slightly higher level, enjoying the warm spring sunshine. I was pondering what I would report to Suffolk, for I had discovered no evidence of a conclusive nature and had developed a rather extravagant theory which would cause more trouble than it was worth if it proved wrong. I had best keep silent on that possibility, I decided. The rooftops of Tours were already in distant prospect when we rounded a bend and caught sight of the group down by the waterside: the escort of well-armed soldiers drawn up in a semi-circle around their charges, the dogs and pages splashing in the river and the bevy of young ladies on horseback urging them on and squealing with delight as the boys ducked into the reeds. Someone was throwing stones into the river, skimming them across the surface and making the dogs bark with excitement.

Rendell was riding beside me and I slowed as he reined in his pony, pointing to the merry party below us. 'She's a cracker, no mistake. Christ, look at the colour of her hair.'

I composed my face into solemnity. 'That, Rendell, is the future Queen of England.'

'Bloody hell! They say King Henry lives like a holy man. How will he cope with that?'

Good question, I thought but did not voice. Some of the French guards had turned to scrutinise the troop riding above them, frowning at first but then, recognising Suffolk's livery, one raised a hand in greeting which our escort returned. 'Come on,' I said, 'or they'll arrest you for disrespectful staring.'

'No harm in admiring.' Reluctantly Rendell twitched his reins and we moved forward.

We had ridden past the royal party and were about to enter a wooded area on a small promontory when we heard the cries and inevitably looked round to see what had happened. 'I think there's a boy in difficulty in the water,' Leone called. Rendell leaned forward in the saddle and looked as if he was about to gallop down to perform heroic deeds.

'They've plenty of men to do what's needed,' I said. 'We'd best be on our way.'

The shouts and shrieks continued but we had not gone far before there was a cry nearer at hand and, in a moment, I was confronted by a wild-haired but imperious young horsewoman brandishing a switch which she waved towards me.

'You are physician? Yes? Come!' Her command required obedience.

As I raced behind her, down the slope, in a state of confusion, I realised she was the austere looking lady I had noticed at the court among Margaret of Anjou's attendants. None of the other women had moved and, furthest from the drama, the princess sat motionless, while a servant held her horse's bridle. I soon realised why I had been summoned when I saw a guard, wet from the waist down, kneeling on the shingle beside the apparently lifeless body of a little lad whose clothes were saturated.

'I think he's gone, sir,' the man said.

I dismounted and felt the base of the boy's throat, detecting a faint pulse. 'Not quite.' I pressed on his chest. 'What happened?'

'He caught his foot in the reeds and went under. I managed to disentangle him but he'd swallowed water by then.'

Other pages had clustered round us, anxious to add to the account. 'He'd gone in to rescue a dog which seemed to be in trouble, swept along by the river.'

'The dog got out safely though.'

'It trotted ashore downstream.'

'I don't understand. He's a good swimmer.'

I raised the boy slightly, with my hand under his head, intending to thump his back, and found my fingers slippery not with silt but blood. 'He's injured. He's hit his head. That's why he couldn't swim.'

'They were throwing stones. One must have clouted him.' Rendell was kneeling beside me and his words caused much shuffling of feet among the pages.

This was not the time to attribute blame. 'The wound's not deep but the blow has knocked him out. He needs to expel the water too.'

I turned him gently and laid him on his chest, ready to exert pressure on his back, when something crashed on the ground a yard from me and the shock hurled me forward onto the victim more sharply than I intended. Shouts and whistles followed but I was busy with my patient because the force of my fall had caused him to vomit mouthfuls of grey liquid and he opened bemused eyes on the scene of confusion.

'You're all right, don't be afraid. You've a cut on the head and need to lie still while I bind it. But you'll be fine after a good rest.'

The boy gave a feeble smile and one of the humbler attendants ripped a strip from her shift to serve as a bandage. Leone had joined us and helped me tie the cloth in place. 'Rendell's not badly hurt,' he said as if in reassurance.

Puzzled, I looked sideways and saw Rendell rubbing his arm and, lying at an angle among the pebbles at his feet, there rested the bolt from a crossbow. 'Great heavens!'

Rendell and Leone started to speak at the same time.

'It only grazed me elbow. Lucky my jerkin's padded.'

'We saw him just in time, from up on the track. He crept out of the copse as you rode down to the river. We shouted and one of the guards shot an arrow at him. They rode after him but he had a head start and probably got away.'

'The guard's quick reaction must have put him off his aim and his bolt went wide.'

I ignored their chatter and helped one of the Angevin soldiers lift the wounded page onto his saddle. 'Go slowly with him so as not to agitate the bleeding. Get him to bed and ask Duke René's physician to check how he's doing.' I stood and bowed to Princess Margaret who remained exactly as she had been before the attack, her face impassive. She acknowledged me with a curt nod.

Leone was holding my horse and I was about to remount when a resonant voice addressed me. 'We are grateful for your services, English physician.'

I faced the tall, sour-faced lady, upright in the saddle and flushed from her exertions. 'I'm honoured to have been of assistance, mademoiselle.'

'I am the comtesse de Langeais.'

'Your pardon, madame.' I struggled to give no hint of my disgust at the thought of her shrivelled, disagreeable husband, many years older than her, and, although she glanced down at me with haughty disdain, I felt a momentary wave of pity for her. Then it occurred to me that she filled an ambiguous position, married to a man who opposed peace with England, yet serving that country's future Queen.

As she rode off I turned to Leone. 'Why did you think the bolt was aimed at me? Surely Margaret of Anjou was a more likely target. There are known to be Frenchmen angered by the marriage plans. I'm surprised her escort weren't more agitated. They haven't even pursued the rogue.'

'They knew it wasn't aimed anywhere near her and we told them it was meant for you.'

'Why on earth should you think that?'

Leone spoke softly so Suffolk's men would not hear. 'I saw him first, stepping out of the wood, and I gave the alarm as he wound his bow. He was a swarthy man, more likely from the Mediterranean than the north, and his eyes followed you as you went down to the river. He reminded me of that olive-skinned fellow on the quay at Marseilles.'

'Oh, that's fanciful, Leone! Don't let your imagination run away with you.' I laughed, hoping to disarm his suspicions although I guessed I would not be successful. I was glad I had never told him that Lord Fitzvaughan mentioned a swarthy man asking where I was to be lodged in Tours. It was inexplicable and unsettling.

*****

I had not long returned to my lodgings when a clerk presented himself at my door conveying an invitation from the physicians at the French court to meet them and expound the latest medical instruction I had received at the University of Padua. I was anxious to resume my professional role but found the prospect of addressing the assembled doctors who served King Charles intimidating. As a preliminary, I needed to replenish my supplies of medicaments, in case I needed to refer to particular remedies and treatments, so I asked Leone to find a respectable-looking apothecary from whom to purchase samples. In view of his apprenticeship to that trade he could be relied on to obtain good quality ingredients. Then I set out for the castle to call on the Earl of Suffolk.

I did not say where I was going and I did not take Rendell with me as I had no wish to increase his interest in my commission from William de la Pole. Yet, while I hurried through the bustle of the streets, jostled by panniers, ducking aside from careless riders and avoiding barrows loaded with produce from the countryside outside the town walls, I wondered if I had been wise to walk alone. If it was true that the crossbow bolt had been intended for me, I should be wary wherever I went. In such a throng it would not be difficult for a villain to drive a knife between a man's shoulder blades and make good his escape in the ensuing confusion. I glanced frequently behind me and was relieved not to spot a swarthy man from the south but, even so, when I entered the castle gates I breathed more easily.

Andrew Cawfield met me, with formal courtesy, at the entrance to the Earl of Suffolk's rooms but I detected annoyance when he told me he was not to be present at our conversation. 'Your other noble friend is absent from Tours for a few days,' he added as if relishing knowledge he possessed which I did not.

I pondered briefly who he meant, being unaware any nobleman could be accounted my friend, but it came to me that he was referring to Lord Fitzvaughan and I asked if he was to be away for long. Master Cawfield moistened his lips. 'He has taken his lady to a quiet retreat, which Duke René placed at his disposal. They have no children, I understand, and have been often apart since their marriage. I envy his lordship the fulfilment of his matrimonial duty.'

I fought to control the flush which I knew would come to my cheeks and to stop the panic which threatened to sweep over me. I told myself Cawfield's snide comment must be entirely innocent of malicious implications. He could not know of Lady Maud's sad history, nor of my own regrettable involvement with her. Nevertheless I was glad to be summoned into his master's chamber.

The Earl of Suffolk listened thoughtfully to my account of the events in Blois and narrowed his eyes when I suggested that there was a chance his latest letter had been intercepted, although most probably it had been taken safely to England. He drummed his fingers on his desktop before speaking and the anxiety behind his frown was obvious. It reflected my own continuing unease.

'I cannot expect a reply from King Henry before the end of the week, even if conditions on the Narrow Sea are at their most favourable. I wish for his endorsement to the final details of the agreement with the French before the betrothal takes place but I can reasonably delay progress for a few days by seeking clarification of various terms and quibbling over trivia.'

I could not justify undermining his hopes without stronger evidence and if the King's response came speedily all would be well. 'I trust a royal messenger will arrive promptly. Will he will be travelling to you openly or as a confidential emissary?'

The Earl smiled. 'His mission will be openly acknowledged, although I expect him to deliver a private communication by word of mouth as well as bringing official papers. I confess I'm eager to receive him. Rollo's murder has been disconcerting. I'm grateful for your efforts on my behalf. You'd best assume your professional position in my entourage now but I can't rule out calling on your additional services in the future.'

'My lord,' I said tentatively, 'the woman, Madeleine, said the man she entertained – your messenger – had come from Rouen. I suppose that would be the most likely route for any royal messenger to follow.'

The Earl looked at me sharply. 'It would be usual. Whether landfall is made at Harfleur or Dieppe, riders from England make a stop at Rouen, in the lands of Normandy which his Grace, King Henry, still holds. Then they go on to Evreux, I believe, and so to Chartres and the French King's domain. Why?'

'I wondered if you'd spare me for a few more days so I could ride to meet the man who we hope is coming. I should welcome reassurance that he is on his way and, if you'd permit me to take a small escort, your soldiers can

44

ensure he reaches Tours without mishap.' It sounded a feeble argument but I baulked at the idea of enduring days of inactivity and uncertainty.

William de la Pole considered my request, his eyes searching my face as if he sought some hidden meaning, while I attempted to look bland and to conceal what was in my mind. He drew breath and I feared he was about to challenge my intention but then he shrugged. 'It's several days' journey to Rouen. He will travel much faster than you.'

'So if he makes good time, we'll meet him on the road. It's a well-used route, I imagine, with accepted resting places. If we fly your banners, he'll recognise them, and if he's wearing King Henry's livery, we can't miss him.'

'You're restless, Doctor Somers, and I share your disquiet until the fellow is safely here in the castle. Do as you wish, but if you've found no sign of him within four days, I require you to return, for there's a chance you may miss him, if he changes his route, and if he doesn't come at all I may have urgent need of your services.'

'Thank you, my lord. I understand. If your men can be ready I'd like to make a start before nightfall.'

'So be it. They will be at your lodgings within the hour.'

*****

The streets were less crowded by the time I left the castle, so I had a more comfortable walk back through the town. While I made my way at a leisurely pace, I resolved to take Leone with me on the journey, as a confidant whose discretion I could trust, but to leave Rendell in Tours. I might need to fabricate a story about a commission that would call on my physician's skill and therefore benefit from Leone's assistance, but I could sweeten the potion for my servant by assigning him, during my absence, to secure a complete outfit of new clothes for me to wear at the betrothal celebrations in the French court. Rendell would feel a sense of importance at being allowed to choose the material and style of my tunic, while I was prepared to take the risk of his preferences because I could keep my physician's gown tightly clasped over anything I considered gaudy. I was pleased with my plan but felt guilty at my intended deception, however justified the circumstances.

When I turned into the road where the draper's house was situated, I saw there was a disturbance ahead, with a boisterous crowd milling around two figures, and my stomach churned as I realised that anxiety about Rendell's reliability was well merited. The boy was at the centre of the group, flushed and furious, flourishing his short sword, and I rushed forward all the more desperately when I recognised his opponent. The fellow he had antagonised before, who served the Seigneur de la Flèche, was similarly armed and irate, and it was clear from the Frenchman's expression he would make no concessions to Rendell's youthful inexperience. I knew my servant was full of rash bravado but it was obvious he must soon fall victim to the other swordsman's practised skill and longer arm.

It was not easy to penetrate the ranks of the excited onlookers, as they surged to and fro when the adversaries engaged their weapons, and my shouts were ignored. While I buffeted my way between unfriendly observers, I glimpsed the boy ducking to avoid a sweeping lunge which, amid laughter, whipped the cap from his head. The Frenchman twirled his booty on the tip of his sword in triumph but this disrespect only antagonised Rendell and in an instant he had crouched and launched himself under the guard of the older man. They span round twice in a circle before their swords clashed to the side but, as they did so, Rendell twisted and drove his dagger towards his opponent's thigh, a blow parried only just in time by a French poniard. The impact drove them apart and a ripple of displeasure ran through the prejudiced bystanders at seeing their champion

46

momentarily worsted. To my horror someone hurled a loose cobble at Rendell's head, albeit failing to hit its target, and when I tried to grab the boy's jacket and restrain him, my arms were seized and forced behind my back. It seemed I was to witness the slaughter of my loyal and irrepressible servant, whether by fair fight or foul mischief. My agonised protests were lost in the hubbub as the swords clattered against each other once more and this time Rendell failed to dodge away quickly enough. The sleeve of his jerkin was slashed below the shoulder and, although he did not appear to be wounded, I took it as a sign that he could not hold his own much longer against superior ability.

'Put up your weapons! Stop this affray.'

The command came from behind us and heads turned to catch sight of a posse of horsemen, some wearing Suffolk's crest and others the insignia of the castle guard. The crowd parted abruptly, as if a battering ram had been driven through it, allowing the captain of the soldiers to ride between the assailants. 'Henri Charpentier, you are under arrest. You are a coward to attack a stripling and have flouted the royal decree that our English guests are to be treated with courtesy.'

'The brat provoked me with his insolence. For the second time.'

'That's a bloody lie! I'd just left our lodgings on an errand and found him lying in wait. I never said a frigging word before he whipped out his sword and went for me.'

'That's true, officer. I saw it all from the window.' A girl I recognised as the draper's daughter had come into the doorway of the house accompanied by one of her father's apprentices who wielded a measuring rod. 'This man was intent on causing trouble and brought a crowd of cronies with him. They tried to prevent the boy's master from intervening to stop the fight.'

One of the musicians who shared our quarters joined her from inside the house, still clutching his lute, and he echoed her words.

I moved forward, unmolested as the crowd began to scatter. 'I am Harry Somers, physician to the Earl of Suffolk, and it is the case that, when I arrived, the supporters of Monsieur Charpentier held me back in their excitement to view the fight.'

The sergeant of Suffolk's troop had ridden forward. 'We are come to escort Doctor Somers on a journey at the Earl's behest. It would not be the Earl's wish that this incident should foster ill will with the citizens of Tours.'

The French officer inclined his head in acknowledgement and directed that Henri Charpentier be conveyed to the castle. Then he turned to Rendell who was rubbing his arm but looking truculent. 'You have the makings of a good swordsman, young fellow, but I counsel you to keep out of the way of the Seigneur de la Flèche's henchman while you remain in Tours.'

I had already concluded what I must do but I spoke with a heavy heart. 'My servant will be accompanying me on a journey out of the town once more. We are about to depart. I'm grateful for your help.' When the French guards rode off I went over to Suffolk's men. 'Give me a short time to collect my baggage and we'll be ready to leave.'

Rendell frowned at me as he collected his battered cap from the gutter. 'Pompous shit, that French officer!' he said. 'Makings of a good swordsman, have I? Taught by Venetian experts! I'll show that Henri Charpentier next time.' He recognised my look of disapproval and grinned. 'Are we really going off again?'

I nodded and looked up, suddenly conscious of someone staring towards me, and at the back of the dispersing crowd I caught sight of an olive-skinned face and dark eyes which held mine for a moment. The man's right arm was strapped across his chest and from his tortured expression I guessed he was in pain from an injury. He moved away and disappeared while I shrugged off my foreboding, telling myself I would become nervous of my shadow if every dark complexion made me uneasy. If there truly was a potential assassin determined to bring about my demise, he would have had a better opportunity while I made my way to the castle, when I was confident I had not been followed.

Leone appeared, carrying a bundle of what I took to be his purchases from the apothecary, and he moved purposefully towards the draper's daughter and the lutenist, standing together at the door to the house. He seemed intent on hearing a more detailed account of what they had seen. With Rendell in tow, I went to them, full of regret that I must change my plan to take Leone on my mission, but I had scarcely started an explanation of what I intended when he interrupted.

'You won't need me to come with you, Doctor, will you? I said I'd go back to the apothecary to collect the other phials tomorrow. Then there'll be your outfit to order for the ceremonies. I'd be happy to arrange that and I'll sort out what you'll need for the presentation to the French physicians. I'll have everything in order for your return.'

It was unlike Leone to forego the chance of an adventure but I was so relieved by his eagerness to remain in Tours that it never occurred to me to ponder his motives. He beamed at me when I gave permission for him to stay and, unwittingly, he slapped Rendell on his bruised arm. 'You behave yourself while you're with the Doctor, you scallywag. You can tell me all about it when you get back.'

Rendell winced but returned a friendly punch. 'You watch what you get up to as well, mate. I'll want a full account, remember.'

I couldn't imagine what Rendell meant but I sighed happily, for what I thought a difficulty had been so conveniently resolved, and Leone joined the lutenist, chatting in animation as they went back into the house. Within the hour, accompanied by Suffolk's men at arms, Rendell was at my side as we passed through the gates of the town and headed to the north-east. He took up the rather vulgar refrain of a ditty the soldiers sang as they rode and I noted that he knew every word.

Chapter 5

By the third day of our wretchedly wet and windy journey I thought myself a fool for embarking on such a chancy expedition. The weather had changed on the morning after our departure from Tours and through the driving sheets of rain it became difficult to make out the travellers we passed on the road. I feared we would fail to spot King Henry's messenger but I also conjectured that, if the fellow had not crossed the Narrow Sea before the storm broke, he might well have been prevented from leaving the English shore. The saving grace of our ill-conceived escapade was that battling conditions on the road required all my concentration, so that by nightfall my aching body numbed my mind and I fell asleep without pursuing fanciful theories concerning Rollo's fate. Yet it was with the hope of testing such a theory that I had set out, not simply to calm my restlessness as I had declared to Suffolk.

I enquired at all the hostelries on our route to check whether they had seen King Henry's man, and everywhere received negative replies, but I also took the opportunity to ask if they had observed riders in Suffolk's livery on previous occasions and, at the inn in Châteaudun, the landlord remembered seeing such a courier a fortnight or so earlier.

'Did you notice in which direction he was travelling? I tried to sound casual.

'Oh, he called here twice, three or four days apart. First he was on his way to Blois and then he was returning to England – carrying messages to and fro no doubt. There's been a fair amount of such traffic since the English embassy arrived. Good for business.'

It was encouraging news. Assuming this was the man Rollo had met, and Madeleine had entertained, it seemed likely he had received Suffolk's secret letter to the King and made good his return journey in ignorance of his contact's fate in Blois. If that was the case, the messenger we were expecting would bring the royal response and the confidential line of communication remained intact. The unfortunate Rollo's death would be unconnected with his master's affairs and the Earl's worries were unfounded. Finding evidence to reassure Suffolk would justify extending my journey so I resolved we should continue to Chartres, stay there one night and then retrace our steps to Tours.

Before midday we arrived at a hostelry just inside the town's walls and I made my usual enquiries. I hadn't explained the reason for these to Rendell but he had shown good sense in listening quietly to my exchanges and I did not exclude him from them. The landlord in Chartres was a surly wretch and seemed disinclined to speak about his clientele but the potman was more cooperative and, after drawing me out into the yard, told me he had served men wearing a badge with three leopards' heads on several occasions. Rendell followed us and, although he seemed to be absorbed in watching an urchin chasing some hens, I knew he was listening to our conversation.

'I call to mind the crest, sir,' the potman said, 'because it wasn't familiar when I first saw it. After that I recognised the faces of the beast and learned the messengers belonged to the English Earl. Came from Rouen, often enough, and usually the same man stopped here again on his way back north to cross the Narrow Sea.'

That accorded with the arrangements Suffolk had described. Rollo must have summoned his trusty couriers from Rouen when they were needed. But I noticed the qualification the man had added and thought I should check whether it had any significance. 'Not always?'

'Funny thing, that. Got a good eye for a face, I have. Useful for spotting known troublemakers at the inn. The last man who came in the Earl's livery wasn't the same fellow who'd stayed a couple of days before.'

I froze and struggled to keep my voice flat. 'That was different from the normal pattern?'

'Yes, and he wasn't keen to have anyone look at him too closely, kept well muffled, but I saw the badge on his jerkin when he reached for his purse to pay for a stoup of wine. He only called here for a fresh horse because his own was winded. He didn't stay the night.'

'He was in a hurry?'

'That's for sure. Different from the man who'd come from Rouen on his way south. He was a companionable type, bought drinks for others in the pot-room – including me. Then he enquired about the best whore-house in the town and went off to sample its delights.'

Although this news could bear an alarming interpretation I was anxious to deflect any suspicion on the potman's part. 'Maybe the Earl of Suffolk decided he wasn't the right man to carry his messages to the English court,' I said with a grin and put a coin in my informant's hand. 'I mustn't keep you from your duties any longer.'

I waited while the man disappeared into the inn and saw that Rendell was helping the scruffy boy whose task, it seemed, was to round up the hens and drive them out of the yard. They were chatting in friendly fashion but, when he saw I was alone, my servant came to my side. 'Heard something interesting, have you, doctor?'

'Possibly. I'm going to take a walk and think about it. The great minster church in Chartres is renowned so I must take my chance to visit it. Come with me, if you want to stretch your legs.'

Rendell looked up at me and rubbed his nose in a manner I associated with mischievous intentions. 'Nah, I'll stay and help young Jeannot here with the hens. There are eggs to be collected and he's already had a beating for letting them get into the yard.'

'Fine,' I said and set out on my walk but I was bewildered by Rendell's unusually charitable inclinations. Perhaps, I speculated, he recognised in the younger boy a kindred spirit, a put-upon inferior such as he had been when

I first met him in the household of Humphrey, Duke of Gloucester. I smiled benignly but my mind was troubled by what I had gleaned from the potman.

At one time in my youth, when I had no thought of receiving an education, I had been attracted by the idea of becoming a mason and it gave me pleasure to admire the huge blocks of stone, so skilfully laid, in the frontage and towers of the minster. I knew rough-hewn slabs had been dragged from the quarry by devout country folk, who yoked themselves to carts in their eagerness to rebuild the church after it had been ravaged by fire. They must have been proud of the impressive building the masons created and I appreciated its calm dignity. Yet I had to admit that I would have admired the figures decorating its façade more greatly had I not become familiar with the fluid grace of statues by Italian masters. Those in the doorways at Chartres were stiff and severe, more similar to work I had seen in English churches, and I realised with a pang of regret how much I had learned to treasure in the stylish artistry of Padua and Verona, which was now lost to me. Inside the minster, however, the glory of the coloured glass was overwhelming and, after staring at the dazzling wheel window at the west end of the nave, I dropped to my knees in wordless contemplation.

I returned to the inn in a peaceful frame of mind but had no sooner entered the yard when Rendell erupted from the entrance and dragged me aside, grinning ominously. 'Here, listen, I've found out something you should know. It might be important and link with that bloke you was asking about. Jeannot told me.'

Reluctantly I rallied my thoughts from calm respite and enquired what seemed so interesting.

Rendell puffed out his chest, enjoying his moment of superior intelligence. 'You know the potman said a different fellow came here last time on the return journey, different from the one who'd come from Rouen? Well – of course it might be coincidental – but it don't seem likely, given you obviously thought it suspicious. So I reckon it needs looking into.'

'What on earth are you talking about?'

'A body, Doctor, a body found the morning after the first bloke was supposed to have set off for Blois. Floating in a vat of dye in the tanneries. His face was all smashed in and he was stark naked. It don't seem anyone made the connection. No reason they should have done, mind, as they didn't know the messenger might have gone missing. But I've made the connection and I'm right, ain't I? The proper man who rode from Rouen could have been done in and his livery pinched by the villain who went on to Blois and pretended to be him.'

I tried to suppress the panic I felt. 'It's ingenious. But in towns like Chartres there are bound to be murders from time to time. Here's nothing to connect this body in the dye vat with Suffolk's man.'

'It ain't usual to strip all the clothes off a victim, is it? And bodies are usually left in the street or down an alley, ain't they? Jeannot says this one was never identified so he's likely to have been a stranger in the town.'

I adopted a sceptical expression. 'How does Jeannot know all this?'

'His brother works in the tanneries. He spotted the body. He knew it weren't there the day before. You think I'm right, don't you, Doctor? You look worried.'

I struggled to sound judicious. 'I'll grant you it's plausible. But there's no proof. We mustn't let our imaginations run away with us.'

'Yeah,' Rendell said with a wink. 'But you believe it. I can tell. Don't worry I won't breath a word to anyone at the inn. Jeannot can go through it all with you himself if you want. I told him you'd give him a coin or two – but only if he told the truth. Reckon I done all right, don't you?'

'Far too well,' I said and did not disguise my dismay, for if the boy's surmise was correct it substantiated my most sinister speculations and shattered my attempted optimism.

*****

Before we left Chartres Rendell persuaded Jeannot to take me to his brother who confirmed the details of what I had been told. After this it was clear that we must make all speed to Tours, for I was bound to advise the Earl that the man summoned from Rouen, to meet Rollo and take a secret message to King Henry, could well have endured a gruesome end in Chartres. It was easy to speculate that Rollo had then encountered an impersonator at the bawdy house in Blois and, when he became suspicious of an unfamiliar courier who did not know the correct password, he too had suffered the cruel consequences. Where the intercepted letter had been taken, or whether it had simply been destroyed, was more difficult to guess. If one of the dissident French lords had acquired it, there was no indication as yet that he had gained advantage from any private information – but, of course, I had no notion what that information might be. On the other hand, Suffolk might wait in vain for the King's response to his enquiry if the message he sent never left France. I could imagine that any resultant delay in concluding the royal betrothal and ratifying the truce would be taken badly by the French negotiators and I wondered whether this might be the intention: to sour relations irretrievably by claiming bad faith on England's part.

When at last we reached Tours, as darkness was falling, I rode straight to the castle and asked to see Suffolk but I was told this could not be arranged until the following morning because he was closeted in discussions with his principal advisers. I pondered whether this was linked to some dreadful revelation which had come about since my departure but no protestations of urgency could prevail on his guards to admit me. Helpless before an intransigent sergeant-at-arms, I was forced to comply with his orders and return to my lodgings.

With Rendell adding vivacity to my matter-of-fact account of our journey, I outlined to Leone what we had discovered but he appeared abstracted and made no comment. I was disappointed not to provoke his interest but I noted he was pale and thought he might feel unwell. I packed him off to bed and soon went to my own pallet but I spent a restless night, turning over in my mind the conjecture which had grown into near-certainty, and I did not relish the prospect of sharing my theory with Suffolk. If it was true that the genuine messenger had been killed in Chartres, someone had organised this with the intention of tricking Rollo and acquiring the secret letter but surely that could only be a person with extensive knowledge of Suffolk's arrangements? My suspicions immediately fell on Andrew Cawfield as the probable informant. Although the Earl had said his secretary was unaware of his private correspondence with the King, I judged the man quite capable of discovering what was being kept from him and he might even be in the pay of a French nobleman. The idea of a traitor embedded in Suffolk's household was disturbing and it drove away all hope of sleep. I rose at length to a dank morning and, as I retraced my steps to the castle, my spirits descended further into matching gloom.

This time I was ushered at once to the Earl's outer chamber where many attendants and pages were waiting for their masters. Among them was Lord Fitzvaughan's favoured companion, Gaston de la Tour, whom I had not seen since I left England and who had been detained in Normandy while his lordship journeyed to Italy. Our previous dealings had been chequered, although I was grateful for his role in my escape into exile, so when he nodded but did not move towards me I was glad I would not be compelled to make uncomfortable small-talk with him.

Cawfield was not party to the discussions inside the Earl's study but stood directly outside the closed doors, with a supercilious air, as if he was well aware of their content. Taking a deep breath to quell my distaste, I started to sidle through the press to reach him.

I was only two steps from the doors when they were flung open and a group of nobles spilled out, their faces flushed with excitement. Cawfield shot away from me, into the inner room, but Lord Fitzvaughan, exiting past him, acknowledged me briefly as he embraced Gaston.

'The main point is conceded,' he said softly to his confidant. 'Arrangements for the betrothal are to be expedited.'

For some reason I registered this news with pedantic precision, wondering what less significant points were still disputed, and so the recollection stayed with me afterwards. At the time a ripple of pleasure spread through the room as the news was whispered but I had no time to reflect on it because the Earl's voice rang out and Cawfield bustled back to the door looking less self-satisfied than before.

'Doctor Somers, you are welcome. Come in. Leave us, Andrew. You are not required at present.'

In an instant I was alone with Suffolk who was perched sideways on the edge of his desk, holding a sheaf of papers and looking jaunty. He beamed at me. 'I'm sorry to have wasted so much of your time, Harry Somers. I appreciate the dedication you've shown, although perhaps I shouldn't have imposed on you so greatly. Have you heard it was all unnecessary? I concerned myself quite needlessly. You must have missed King Henry's messenger on the road. He arrived yesterday afternoon and he's brought royal agreement to the issues I raised in my private letter. So, you see, my anxiety was unjustified. Poor Rollo safely passed on my letter and it was taken hot-foot across the Narrow Sea. Rollo's sad fate was quite unconnected with his duties on my behalf and my confidences with the King were never put at risk.'

I stared numbly, astonished and perplexed because these tidings did not accord with the history I had constructed in my mind and they did not answer several questions I could have posed. Yet, what grounds had I to challenge the Earl's conclusions? His communication had travelled to its intended recipient and he had received King Henry's reply giving the guidance he sought. Whatever the explanation for various happenings, there was no evidence that the security of his private correspondence had been breached, no reason indeed to suspect Cawfield of treachery. The path to conclude a truce between the former enemies now lay open: peace could be established between France and England, swords replaced by ploughshares, lances and long-bows oiled and set aside; the fields of northern France could grow their crops without fear of wilful destruction; labourers on their lords' domains both sides of the Narrow Sea could bide by their own hearths with their families and sons need not lose fathers in battle, as I had done. That petite and pretty Angevin princess would personify this accord and I hoped she would bring marital delight to England's King. There was nothing in this prospect I would wish to change, nor did I have any serious basis on which to raise doubts. My misgivings must come from too lurid an imagination and it was my own arrogance which clung to them with ill-judged doggedness.

I bowed my head. 'I'm overjoyed, my lord,' I said.

'You sound weary, physician. I appreciate the diligence you've shown. Here's gold to recognise your efforts. Use it to enjoy your remaining stay in France. As soon as the betrothal has been celebrated, we leave for home and you can set up your practice in my household.'

I took the bag he offered with thanks. It was no more than my due, to cover the expenses I had incurred, and it was an effort to force a smile of gratitude. We exchanged pleasantries for a few moments, while I remained torn by indecision whether to douse the flames of his joy, and then I was courteously dismissed. The captain of Suffolk's guard was waiting to join the Earl but otherwise the outer chamber had emptied. I imagined the horde of attendants and acolytes who had filled it previously surging through the English quarters in the castle, spreading the news that King Henry had endorsed the proposed concord and there was no obstacle to peace. I wished I could feel such unequivocal delight.

I made my way along the corridor towards the stair leading out of the tower when a page in Fitzvaughan livery begged me to spare a minute and led me round a corner towards his master's chamber. As we approached them two men in conversation, further along the passage, separated swiftly and Andrew Cawfield, red in the face with annoyance, acknowledged me with a brisk nod when we passed. He must have hoped that I would not know the Frenchman to whom he had been speaking but I had reason to recognise Henri Charpentier as he hurried in the opposite direction. It seemed that Rendell's tormentor had not remained in custody for long but the idea that the Seigneur de la Flèche's retainer had business with Suffolk's secretary was mind-boggling. My heart thudded with renewed anxiety and I cursed myself for wasting the opportunity to tell the Earl of my wild fancies.

I was not allowed to dwell on these worries for I was shown into the Fitzvaughan chamber where, unexpectedly, I was greeted by deaf Marian. There was no sign of his lordship or Gaston de la Tour but, at the sound of the serving woman's voice, Lady Maud entered from an inner closet and I began to tremble. She gurgled, as I quailed, dismissing the page and banishing Marian to the far corner of the room; then she glided across the floor to stand beside me and clasp my wrist.

'Alas, there is no time for me to seduce you, Harry. I must speak quickly before Walter returns.' She gave me a radiant smile and placed one hand on her low-cut stomacher. 'See how my breath comes rapidly. I fear I may faint with emotion.'

'My lady, I should not be here. Is there something you wish to say to me?'

'So callous, physician? Isn't it your duty to give succour to the afflicted?' Her voice was caressing and she leaned towards me, thrusting out her heaving breast. Against my will, I knew she still possessed the power to entice me.

'Excuse me, my lady. I must leave.' I stepped back, ignoring her wail of assumed pain.

'Have you forgotten the cause of my distress?' The charade of helplessness was abandoned as her eyes flashed and her voice hardened. 'I have charged you with a commission. Have you so little respect for me that you dismiss all thought of it?'

I dared not let her suspect how near the truth that accusation was, with my thoughts fixed on the strange circumstances of Rollo's death. 'Not at all but I've had duties to fulfil in France and you know I can do nothing on your behalf this side of the Narrow Sea.'

She swirled away before turning to face me across the table in the centre of the room. 'I've had tidings from Stamford,' she said with an air of triumph. 'The Prioress has written. She is compelled to do so somewhat cryptically in view of the subject matter but I understand her message. She is hopeful Eleanor is unharmed.'

'That's good news. Does she indicate that she knows where the child is or who took her?'

'I shouldn't need to retain your services to find her, if it was that straightforward. I merely wish to emphasise the importance of your early attention to my directive. I require you to present yourself in Stamford as soon as you have crossed the Narrow Sea.'

I was exasperated by her persistence and answered more brusquely than was sensible or courteous. 'I've explained my position. I serve the Earl of Suffolk. I may not be free to travel there.'

Her look was full of venom. 'In years gone by you and I fell into the power of an evil man who directed our actions. He brought us together and embroiled you in the plot which nearly destroyed you. I've learned my lessons well from Roger Bolingbroke, how to control and manipulate lesser creatures. You are minded to evade my commission, I can tell, but if you do so, I shall know what action to take.'

'What nonsense are you talking? I'm sorry for your child's predicament but I can't promise to solve the mystery of her disappearance. I may not be at liberty to go to Stamford.'

Her mouth twisted into a hateful smirk. 'If you do not, sweet Bess Willoughby, as she now is, will be assaulted by ruffians and violated with brutal force.'

I stared at the termagant in front of me, unwilling to credit my ears with the vile threat she had made. 'God forgive you, Lady Maud, for this obscenity. I shall treat it as a measure of your motherly anguish that you speak in this foul manner but I counsel you never to repeat those words.'

'It's no idle warning, Harry Somers,' she snapped. 'I bear no love for the winsome maid who won your heart and I could have wished a less gentle husband for her than Walter's besotted bailiff. If you choose to resist my will, she will suffer. Fortunately for her, I have confidence that you will be her chivalrous defender and you will go to Stamford as I require.'

I put my hand on the door latch and spoke with as much quiet authority as I could muster. 'You forget, my lady, that I too have been tutored by Roger Bolingbroke. I never thought to emulate his example but I can trade one threat for another. If you repeat that evil menace once more, I shall disclose all I know to Lord Fitzvaughan: your daughter's birth, the killing of the second child within your womb and the fact that, in consequence, you are incapable of bearing him an heir.'

She stared at me and her lower lip began to quiver. 'You could not do it,' she said.

'You underestimate my resolution. I am not the callow youth you toyed with years ago.'

She narrowed her eyes. 'Yes, you have changed. I think someone has hurt you very badly to put this metal in your soul. A woman, no doubt, in Italy. Poor physician.'

This was not something I was prepared to pursue and I opened the door. 'I mean what I say, my lady. Remember that and withdraw your sinful threat.'

She was always adept at recovering her composure. 'I fancy it was one of my more venial transgressions,' she trilled. 'Perhaps you and I will burn together in Hell, Harry, for the viciousness of our mutual scorn. But before we meet that fate, I foretell that we will burn together again in lust, while still in this mortal life.'

'Never!' I slammed the door behind me as I left, causing a passing servant to jump in alarm, scattering a dozen silver goblets from the tray he carried.

When I knelt to help him retrieve one vessel which had rolled against the doorframe, I heard Maud whisper through the woodwork. 'Oh, don't be too sure, physician. You may checkmate one design but I fancy you are less strongly armoured against your own temptations of the flesh.'

My hand was shaking as I replaced the stray goblet on the attendant's salver with a clatter.

*****

If a swarthy villain had crept up behind me as I made my way back to my lodgings he could have garrotted me before I noticed his presence, so absorbed was I in my thoughts. I had dismissed the unpleasantness of my encounter with Lady Maud, although I knew the horror would return to haunt me, because I needed to turn over in my mind all that Suffolk had told me and I was annoyed with myself. I should have been glad to accept that his secret communications with King Henry had not been compromised but I found it impossible. The coincidences of Rollo's violent death, what I had learned in Chartres and the sight of Cawfield with Charpentier fed my nagging anxiety that something was wrong. I speculated that the Earl's message had been intercepted and read before being sent on its way to England as if nothing was amiss. But where was the sense in that? How would it advantage the French nobles who opposed a peace treaty to discover the details on which Suffolk was consulting his sovereign lord? They would be privy already to the conditions the French King was seeking to impose and I could not imagine what else they might be trying to determine. Besides, the letter would have been sealed. Was I reluctant to accept the pitiable truth that I had wasted my time in making enquiries in Blois and Chartres? Had my judgement become so self-serving and petty? I could not shrug off my discomfort.

When I entered the draper's house I could hear the strains of a lute and a melodious voice singing a courtly ballad wafting from the principal chamber used by my host's family. Girlish laughter accompanied applause as the air concluded but I crept silently up the stairs, in morose ill humour, unwilling to be drawn into sociable entertainment. I expected to find our sleeping quarters unoccupied, which would suit my uncertain temper, and was irritated to see a figure crouched beside the crowded pallets. Only as I crossed the room did I realise it was Leone and his face was a picture of misery. He did not look up when I sank down beside him and his appearance filled me with foreboding.

'Is there bad news?' I asked.

He shook his head but did not speak and I was puzzled. Leone was of an equable disposition and not given to sullen moods. 'Do you feel unwell?'

He looked up at me then and gave a mournful smile. 'Not with a malady you could cure, Doctor.'

The sound of a rousing tenor crescendo echoed from downstairs and a glimmer of understanding came to me, despite my preoccupations. 'You're unhappy,' I said and tried not to make it sound like a question for, if my diagnosis was correct, I must deal gently with the unaccustomed emotions he was experiencing. 'I shan't intrude, if you wish to be undisturbed, but if you feel able to think of other matters, I'd welcome your views.'

He gave another wan smile. 'My judgement is all awry, I think.'

'Distraction from what grieves you may give a little respite.'

This jolted him from his self-absorption and he gave a yelp. 'Oh, Doctor, I should have told you at once. The meeting with the French physicians is arranged for tomorrow morning. Everything is organised and I have all the charts and tables that you wanted as well as the phials you ordered.'

'Thank you. You'll come with me I hope?'

'I've nothing to stay here for.'

I suppressed a laugh at his vehemence, pleased to see him get to his feet, but his next words were spoken with bitterness. 'I can't serenade as he does. Where he reels off poetic flattery, I'm tongue-tied.'

'A fine voice and smooth talking are superficial gifts.'

'But ones I'd like to have. Girls seem to like them.' His sheepish grin encouraged me to probe the sensitive issue.

'The draper's daughter has taken your fancy?'

'Her name is Bonne. She seemed happy to be in my company. While you and Rendell were away she let me sit with her while she was at her sewing and she smiled often when I entertained her with stories of my life in Padua and Verona. I thought affection was growing between us and I was happy.' He paused, crumpling the fringe on his jerkin with his fingers, and I did not interrupt for fear of saying the wrong thing. 'Then Matthieu started to pay her attention. I don't think he'd noticed her before he saw us sitting together. Now she only has eyes and ears for him – he's a fine musician. I can't compete.'

'I expect it's a novelty for Bonne to have a musician performing in her honour. Don't think too badly of her. Novelties wear off. Don't show your annoyance.'

He glanced at me with a frown. 'At least you don't taunt me. Thanks.'

'Taunt you?'

'With being a lily-livered lover. Italians are supposed to sweep girls off their feet, enchant them with romantic passion, beckon with a flash of their dark lashes and women fall at their feet. I can't do that. I'm lacking in basic Italian talents, it seems.'

'Who told you that?' I asked, knowing the answer as I spoke.

Leone did not answer but he stood up and held out the bundle of astronomical charts he had collected for me. 'Do you want to check these before tomorrow?'

I took the rolls and studied them, glad that he felt able to talk about my presentation to the French doctors. I let a little time pass before I posed my question as casually as I could. 'Where's Rendell?'

Leone narrowed his mouth. 'He went out. In a huff.'

'Oh dear. Did you quarrel?'

'I wasn't in the mood for teasing. He made a lot of silly gibes and they irked me. I lost my temper and said things I'm sorry for now.'

'Don't worry. Rendell's heard worse, I'm sure.'

I was utterly unconcerned. Even when, hours later, I took to my bed before the boy had returned, I assumed he would creep back, picking his way among the snoring sleepers, grinning at the mischief he had inevitably been involved in, stifling a giggle at the thought of the unsuitable company he had been keeping. Rendell was a rascal, on the border of manhood, and he needed a position more fitted to his temperament than servant to a physician. He was resolved to become a man at arms and despite my misgivings I knew the life of a soldier would suit him. As I drifted into sleep I determined to speak to Suffolk to see if he could be admitted to the Earl's troop of guards.

Chapter 6

Next morning when I realised Rendell had not slept on his pallet, I felt a pang of irritation rather than concern, for I had weightier matters to fill my mind than the peevish moods of my youthful assistants. Fortunately, Leone seemed to have recovered from his inner turmoil and was calmly efficient in the preparations for my presentation. This was to take place in the tower of St. Martin, near the resplendent basilica dedicated to the same saint, and we had not far to walk from our lodgings, with our arms full of papers and medicinal samples. Bonne waved as we left the house and wished us well, which made Leone more cheerful but, sour old cynic that I had become, I hoped it would not reignite the flame of his devotion unreasonably.

I had feared that King Charles's physicians might have invited me to speak to them intent on mocking my upstart ignorance, for I knew I was years younger than most of them and, by comparison, green in the practice of our profession. I was soon reassured and appreciated that my mistrust was churlish, signifying my lack of confidence rather than any justified reservations about their motives. They viewed my period of study in Padua as proof of my worth and the doctorate I held from that university was a talisman to hold their interest and merit their esteem. I began to enjoy my task, outlining the teaching I had absorbed, answering their questions and engaging in scholarly exchanges of knowledge and experience. A wave of sheer pleasure passed through me. This was what I should be doing: exercising the talents I had been trained to use, seeking to broaden understanding of the afflictions which torment mankind, not tangling with the intrigues of great and vengeful men whose pawn I had become. While I relished the congratulations of my peers, at the end of the session I longed for the opportunity to establish myself solely as a valued physician, free to comfort and, where possible, heal without distraction.

'I'd be pleased if you'd take a peek at a patient of mine. I'm off to look in on him now and you might like to come along. It's not a stone's throw from here.'

The speaker was a kindly faced man of middle years with rubicund cheeks, who introduced himself as Master Francisco, physician to Duke René's household, and I readily agreed to accompany him to visit an elderly patient whose condition was deteriorating in a perplexing way. I was flattered and intrigued by what he described and I recalled an old serving woman in Duke Humphrey's household who had withered and shrivelled in the same way. I asked Leone to carry our chattels back to the draper's house and I begged him to be gentle with Rendell who would probably be chastened from whatever excesses he had indulged in during the previous night. Then I set off with my companion across the marketplace towards an imposing mansion built in a mixture of brick and stone, with patterned gables over its narrow, pointed windows.

'Some days he's in much better shape than others,' my new friend told me. 'He manages to play a part in the court when he deems it necessary. It's almost as if, by willpower alone, he can rise to the occasion when he chooses.'

This was wisdom that delighted me for it was rooted in a physician's observation, not abstract divination, and I entered the grand residence in a state of excited anticipation. We were escorted along a passage, although it was clear the French doctor knew exactly where to go, but as we halted outside the door to the sickroom a richly-dressed woman emerged and stood in front of us barring our entrance. I caught my breath in consternation. She nodded to Master Francisco and fixed me with a steely glare.

'You are the English physician from the riverside,' she said accusingly.

69

'Madame, la comtesse,' I managed to say, alarmed that I had come to the house of the unpleasant invalid who had abused me in the court and was known to oppose the truce with my country.

'I invited Doctor Somers to accompany me in visiting the comte de Langeais,' Master Francisco said with a bow. 'He has studied in Padua and may have advice to offer.'

The Countess gave an audible sniff. 'By all means. 'We are obliged by your interest. My husband is unwell today. He slept badly. Give him what assistance you can but it would be inadvisable to reveal that Doctor Somers is English. He is ill disposed towards King Henry's kingdom.'

'Your pardon, madame. I didn't know it was the Count we were to visit. He has seen me at the court. I will leave.'

'No, that isn't necessary, Doctor Somers. Stand in the shadows. His sight is poor. You physicians will converse in Latin, will you not? My husband will have no idea who you are.'

I could not prevent my mouth betraying a flicker of amusement and, to my surprise, the lady responded with a hint of merriment in her eyes which softened her stern expression. I reflected that she was accustomed to balance conflicting interests between her husband's partisanship and her own allegiance to Princess Margaret of Anjou. All the same, I was nervous of agitating the sick man and kept well back from his bedside.

The consultation was a depressing business for the comte de Langeais was both stricken and spiteful. It was troubling to see the tremors in his hands and the stiffness of his neck and I knew he was suffering from a wasting malady for which we could do nothing, except to offer medications which might dull the pain. Master Francisco was more cheerful, stressing that his patient's condition would improve in a few days if he rested, which was perfectly possible as the progression of the inevitable paralysis would not be constant, but he also urged cupping and with this I could not agree. It was not proper for me to voice a dissenting opinion in front of the Count so I stayed silent but the old man was vociferous in resisting his physician's prescription.

'You'll not have me cut again, you useless quack. My arm is scarred enough with incisions of your lancet.'

'Which is why I recommend cupping, my lord, cupping with scarification and a liniment of saltwort to purify the skin. After the procedure, you should drink a preparation of salt water, sage and parsley, perhaps with a little hartstongue to reduce any inflammation. I assure you this treatment will prove efficacious in reducing the excessive build-up of your blood. The sign of Taurus governs diseases of the neck and it is that area of the body which should be addressed. I will send the surgeon to attend you.'

'I'll not have him admitted. You will not conduct your fiendish experiments on my flesh any longer. You imposters are demons from Hell, not Christian men. You, there, the fellow lurking in the shadow, what do you say?'

I did not move but I was bound to answer him in French. I deepened my voice. 'My lord, I am come from Italy. I am here merely to learn from Master Francisco.'

'Bah! Useless, all of you! Get out and don't come again. Get out!' He raised his quivering arms and gave an unworldly howl, like wild animal at bay.

Hurriedly we bowed and quitted the sickroom and I was happy to accept Master Francisco's invitation to share a flask of wine before I returned to my lodgings. The Frenchman drank down a glassful at speed and it was clear he was disturbed by his patient's recalcitrance. I had also found the scene gruelling but for quite different reasons. After refilling his glass, he raised it to me.

'I give you thanks for not disputing my treatment, although it may be that you favour some other approach.'

'I don't believe we can offer any beneficial physic to the poor man, only to try and lessen his suffering. It's true I'm not convinced cupping is helpful in such a case. When I watched dissections in Padua...'

'Sainted Virgin! You've witnessed dissections of the human body?' Master Francisco sounded deeply shocked.

'It's accepted practice at the university and it's revealing. To see how the sinews and organs relate one to the other...'

'No more, I beg you. I'm not persuaded it is God's will we should investigate His creation in such an intimate manner.'

'But surely human anatomy is crucial to our calling. Can it be wrong to seek to understand more?'

Master Francisco was not to be persuaded and we parted, respectful of each other's sincerity but cautious not to endorse opinions which we could not share. Chastened and weary, I walked back to the draper's house and it was only as I turned the corner and saw Leone run towards me from the doorway, that I realised something was wrong. Even then my mind was so filled with medical matters that I did not foresee the cause of his concern.

'Thank Heaven, you're back, Doctor. We don't know what to do. Rendell is still missing.'

*****

It soon became evident that Leone was doing himself an injustice by suggesting he was helpless in the face of Rendell's disappearance. He had already organised a search, sending our fellow lodgers, the musicians, to make enquiries in all the places they could think of where the lad might have strayed. They returned at intervals to report as they visited hostelries, markets and entertainments without finding anyone who recognised the description of my servant. Leone had been very competent but my arrival allowed him to pass over the responsibility he had accepted and the tension this released caused him to blink back tears.

'It's all my fault. I shouldn't have spoken so curtly. He's run away.'

'I'm sure that's not true. He may be in some trouble but I'm sure he's not run away. Have you asked at the castle?'

'Yes and I checked with the town guard. He's not been taken in charge.'

'Well, that's a relief.' I tried to sound jocular but it was not how I felt. Nearly twenty-four hours had passed since Rendell was seen and I had too readily dismissed his absence as due to some boyish mischief. Now I doubted it. I decided that, despite Leone's enquiries, I would go to the castle and question the sergeant-at-arms but before I could set off Matthieu appeared, bounding along the roadway from the direction of the river. It was ironic that it should be the lutenist who brought us the first snippet of information.

'I've found a stonemason who remembers seeing him last evening,' he shouted as soon as we were within earshot.

'Where? Where?'

I put a restraining hand on Leone's arm as Matthieu drew breath.

'Down by the river. There's open ground just beyond the walls. They stage spectacles and amusements there. Not the most salubrious pastimes,' he added apologetically.

'What was going on there last night?' I asked.

'Dog fights. Vicious affairs. The dogs are trained to kill and they set them on each other. Men place wagers. They're rowdy events.'

It was all too likely that a disgruntled Rendell might have gravitated towards such a performance. 'What could the stonemason tell you?'

'Only that a lad fitting the boy's description was there, cheering on the dogs and enjoying the fun – as he called it.'

73

'Did he see where Rendell went afterwards?'

'He didn't notice. It was getting dark by then and people were coming and going all the time. That's all he could say.'

'He might have come to all sorts of harm in such a place.' Leone twisted his hands together.

'Rendell's no fool. He's used to the hurly-burly of street life. We must see if we can find others who might have seen him at these dog fights. When will there be another one?'

'I don't know. News spreads by word of mouth when they're arranged.'

Bonne had come from the house and was listening to our conversation. Shyly she stepped forward. 'Sir, the carter who brings rolls of woollen material on his barrow for my father's use – I think he frequents the dog fights. Sometimes they have other wild animals as well. I've heard him talk of them; though I try to stop my ears for the accounts are horrid. But he may have been at the fight yesterday. He keeps his carts along by the marketplace.'

In a trice Leone and Matthieu set off, side by side at a trot, to find the carter. They returned with a brawny fellow who seemed as much in thrall to the draper's daughter as his escorts. He addressed himself directly to Bonne in a surge of verbiage.

'I saw the boy, mistress. I did. He was quite near me and I noticed him because he was so caught up in the scrap. Shouting and cheering as if his life depended on it. I like to see a youngster entering into the spirit of things. I'd seen him at the house here when I delivered the velvets your father ordered the other day so I knew where he came from. What was strange though was that his behaviour changed. Suddenly went quiet, he did, and pulled back into the crowd as if he didn't want to be seen. I wondered if he'd spotted his master or someone else he didn't want to know he was there. Shame to scare a boy so he can't enjoy a bit of honest sport, that's what I thought. He slunk away before the end – at least I think he did. I didn't see him go but we were all hooked on the kill, when the brown dog got his fangs in the throat of the white one, and when it was over the lad wasn't there any longer. He hasn't come to any harm, has he?'

Without waiting for a reply the carter launched into repetition of his story but Bonne's father had now joined the growing crowd outside his house and he drew me aside.

'A bad business, Doctor Somers. Do you have enemies in the town?'

I was surprised by his question and, thinking of the anonymous swarthy man, uncertain how to reply. 'Not that I'm aware of, monsieur. But I understand some of your countrymen remain ill-disposed towards any Englishman.'

'I don't believe that's it: not casual hostility. I suspect this is a bit more targeted. It happens, I'm afraid, and with all the visitors in town, every ne'er-do-well for miles around would see an opportunity to make a dishonest profit. I fancy your servant has been taken hostage and you'll be receiving a message in a day or two, stating the price they want to release him.'

I was aghast. 'But I'm not a rich man. How could they imagine I'd be able to pay a ransom?'

'It'll be known you serve the Earl of Suffolk. I'd say they could demand a good price for the boy.'

I was not persuaded but the idea was plausible, especially if I was the real object of someone's animosity. 'If that's true, I hope they'll contact me quickly. It would be a relief to know something...' My voice trailed into silence as I pondered the awkwardness of approaching Suffolk for a payment to secure Rendell's freedom – and the very real possibility that such a request would be refused.

'You'd be wise not to create a stir until you've heard from the villains. Don't want to frighten them off: otherwise they might harm the boy. I'd wager they'll contact you quickly if they see you're willing to co-operate. Word from the court is that there's to be a great betrothal ceremony and after that your Earl and all his English followers will depart across the Narrow Sea. Kidnappers will soon find out what's planned and they'll want to conclude their business and make good their escape from the neighbourhood well before then. Don't worry, Doctor Somers, it's a tiresome trouble for you but it'll all come right, mark my words.'

He was a man of the world and he meant well but I did not find his words consoling. Some niggling instinct told me it would not be so straightforward. I thought of Henri Charpentier's murderous intentions towards Rendell and I wondered where he had been the previous evening. I had last seen him earlier that day, conversing with Andrew Cawfield, which was unexpected in itself, and I did not trust him to abide by any promise the captain of the guard might have extracted when he was released from detention. I could imagine he would find pleasure in the savagery of fighting dogs. It would have been Rendell's dangerous misfortune if their paths had crossed at that barbarous entertainment.

*****

Three days passed and I received no demand for a ransom. Nor, despite discreet enquiries, did we obtain any further information relevant to Rendell's disappearance. Gloom settled over the house and even the servants crept quietly about their work as if unwilling to disturb the illusion of calm by making unnecessary noise. The musicians were mostly absent, practising their contributions to the impending ceremonies, along with other entertainers whose programmes were being organised by the royal chamberlain and his lackeys. Hope and despair tussled with each other in my heart. One moment I tried to convince myself Rendell would reappear, recounting some improbable adventure, and the next I would succumb to the inescapable conclusion that he had fallen victim to a horrible fate.

Rendell had enlivened my exile, by turns amusing and exasperating me, and when I was carried off a prisoner from Verona he had attacked and killed the leader of my assailants. He had grown from an untutored rascal, with a rough and ready wit, into a bright lad with precocious skill at swordplay and an indomitable resilience. When I returned to England I would be bound to visit his endearing sister, Grizel, who had married my old friend, Thomas, and I dreaded facing them with news of her brother's demise. Meanwhile my grief was intensified by Leone's misery for he held himself responsible for all that had occurred and rejected attempts to comfort him, even by Bonne. His youthful ardour had been tarnished by its association with Rendell's destiny and he could not exonerate himself from blame.

When it became clear that there would be no demand for a ransom I renewed enquiries to discover what had happened and I paid a visit to the tract of land, outside the town walls, where Rendell had been seen. It was a bleak dusty area, a disused gravel-working, with a deep pit in which the dogs were loosed against each other, and hurdles positioned around it to prevent the animals breaking out into the audience. There was nothing in the place to give a clue as to how a boy had disappeared, nor anyone nearby who would admit to knowing anything helpful.

The only reprieve I found from worrying about Rendell was when Suffolk required my attendance at the castle to treat a minor ailment or injury suffered by one of his retinue. I grasped these occasions to practise my profession with gratitude, for concentration on helping others freed my mind from its miserable obsession. By contrast, when I was summoned to take part in a rehearsal for the English procession which would feature in the betrothal ceremonial, I felt I was participating in a meaningless charade and I longed to absent myself. I could not expect the Earl or Lord Fitzvaughan to comprehend why

I was sorrowful, for they would consider loss of a servant as a slight inconvenience, no more, and these thoughts fed my growing anger.

Frustration at the vain ritual and my volatile mood led me to behave rashly, abandoning my usual caution. This was not the first time in my life I had acted foolishly while giving way to melancholy: my ill-advised engagement in Padua, to a girl for whom I felt no real affection, derived from another bitter period of unhappiness. Now, distress for Rendell's fate drove me to indulge my bad temper in a manner I was to regret and, in seeking to make amends for this, I accepted familiarity with Suffolk's secretary.

When the procession of English worthies broke up I found myself beside Andrew Cawfield and he seemed content to walk with me, sharing his amusement about the way Gaston de la Tour had persuaded Lord Fitzvaughan to send the boy, Bartholomew, back to England. I expressed regret for this because Bartholomew had been friendly to Leone and me on our journey from Italy but I could appreciate that Gaston would not brook him as a rival for his lordship's attentions. Cawfield continued chatting inconsequentially and started to complain about trivial administrative details but this irked me and I let my irritation boil over, turning on him with accusation in my voice.

'You're seeking to divert me with this tedious officialdom so that I forget the dubious company you keep. It won't succeed, Master Cawfield.'

His stride did not falter but he went pale. 'Whatever do you mean?'

'You were consorting with a follower of the French lords who oppose the truce. I can't imagine a valid reason for that, only a despicable one.'

'You're accusing me of treachery?'

'Your word. Intriguing that you choose to use it.'

'I would never betray the interests of my King to his enemies. I did speak with the Seigneur de la Flèche's man, at his behest. I gave him no privy information.'

'Did he ask for some?'

Cawfield stood still and faced me, clutching his gown across his chest as if to protect himself. 'Doctor Somers, I believe you are an honest man and I wouldn't have you think badly of me. I hoped you hadn't observed my encounter with Charpentier and I don't blame you for misconstruing it but I am no traitor.'

'I'm supposed to accept your word, am I?'

'If I tell you what happened, I beg you will not inform the Earl. I know he doesn't trust me and I fear he would choose to interpret my actions as if I was at fault.'

The sincerity in his voice softened my stubborn hostility and I became curious. 'If you convince me you're telling the truth, I'll say nothing.'

Cawfield sighed and his tense features relaxed. 'I'd be glad to share the burden I've carried for the past few days. I'd be glad to count you as my friend. Henri Charpentier had been sent to bribe me to betray my master. Somehow the Seigneur de la Flèche and his cronies had divined that the Earl didn't trust me so they thought I might be disaffected and ready to do him harm. I refused absolutely to consider their request and walked away without listening to whatever else he wanted to say.' He paused and I could see the perspiration on his upper lip and along his hairline. 'I beg you to believe me, Doctor Somers. I swear it's the truth.'

I felt deflated, my anger dissolved, and I was sorry for the wretched man, terrified of carrying blame for what he had shunned. 'I accept your word, Master Cawfield. I'm afraid I've offended you by recalling this unpleasant event.'

'No, no, you had every right and I wouldn't wish you to think badly of me. If this conversation could lead us to a better understanding, to us becoming friends, I'd be grateful it took place.'

We had come to the parting of our ways and I had no wish to prolong our exchange. Friendship with Cawfield did not appeal to me but I appreciated the strain under which he worked and understood why he mistrusted the Earl. I shook his hand when I bade him adieu but, as I set off for my lodgings, all my heaviness of heart returned and I felt I had not behaved well towards him.

Chapter 7

As soon as I set foot in the draper's house Leone hurtled down the stairs to greet me with greater excitement than he had shown for the previous ten days and he quickly shared his news. 'The carter came to tell me there's to be another dog fight tonight. I said I'd go. I wasn't sure if you'd be free.'

'Nothing will stop me,' I said with resolution and for a moment I fancied the saints had taken pity on my distress but this illusion was not to be sustained.

That evening we joined the garrulous porter among the crowd peering down into the insalubrious pit, where a succession of hounds bared their fangs to rip hair and flesh, slobbering blood down their dewlaps. The stench was foul and the frenzy of the onlookers as they placed their wagers seemed to me as bestial as that of the crazed animals. Between each bout I jostled my way through the throng, seeking information, describing Rendell, trying to jog memories and, for my pains, receiving abuse and becoming the butt of unsavoury jibes.

'Shift yourself, arsehole. You're blocking my view.'

'I'll fetch you a boy, matey, if your tastes lie that way. Don't waste time on one who's buggered off.'

'Not surprised he's made off. Your face would turn any boy's stomach. Satan's spawn, you must be.'

It was a long time since I had been scorned for the birthmark on my cheek and, although I knew such language was common parlance, I found it hurtful. I was glad to see Leone, who had left my side, but he was taut as a drawn bowstring and seized my arm.

'Doctor, come. There's a pie-seller here who knows something.'

The man was cadaverous and his pies stank but I bought one and wrapped it in a kerchief as if I would eat it later. If I had entertained any intention of consuming the rancid object, his tale would have driven away the most ravenous appetite.

'I call him to mind, mate. The fucking foreigner took him. Just as the fight got exciting. Everyone was looking at the dogs. He pushed past me, scattered my pies. I bloody shouted but he took no notice. Just swore at me. He had the boy over his shoulder. Unconscious, I think. Must have clouted him, I reckon. He'd got a club in one hand. The other arm looked stiff.'

'You didn't report it?' As I spoke I knew I sounded prissy.

'Report it? Christ, what d'you think, mate? Reckoned he was recapturing his serving lad who'd run away. Weren't going to put myself out for a disobedient bloody brat, was I?'

'Why did you think the man was a foreigner?'

'Heard him swear at me, didn't I? Didn't come from round here. Not English either, heard enough of you lot in the last month. Dark face too.'

'Have you seen him again? He's not here tonight?'

'No. I heard he got hurt. After he set the fucking dogs on the boy.'

'What?' I felt the blood drain from my cheeks and Leone clutched my wrist.

'Seems he followed the dog-keeper back to the farm where he keeps the creatures. Then in the night he let the biggest ones out, to punish the boy for whatever he'd done. Seems he got mauled himself. Maybe served him fucking right, eh?'

'The boy was savaged by the dogs?' I could hardly speak.

'Reckon so. Ask the keeper when they've finished here. I don't know any more.'

I thrust enough money into the man's outstretched hand to buy all his malodorous pies and staggered away from him as vomit rose in my throat. Leone was already on his knees, retching. I dropped down beside him. 'God rest

82

poor Rendell, and damn his murderer to Hell,' I said, letting fury drive away my nausea. 'The minute the fight is over we tackle the keeper.'

*****

The man was disinclined to talk and it took every ounce of persuasiveness I could summon to reassure him that I was not an agent of the town authorities but a harmless physician. I marvelled at my own patience as I humoured him despite my instinct to throttle the rogue for breeding murderous beasts. I was beginning to despair and feared I would do something foolish in my frustration, when he swore abruptly under his breath, indicated to his assistants that they should take charge of the dogs and proceeded to speak in what I thought initially was gibberish.

'No one can say I'm not as good a Christian as any other poor fellow trying to make my living as best I can and I don't know the ins and outs of it. It's a priest he needs, not a physician, but it'll be all one to him, I'm thinking. No way will I take a priest to him, asking questions and spouting anathemas. You'll not get much sense from him but it'd be a good deed to give him comfort.'

As I grasped his meaning I gripped his shoulders. 'Are you saying the boy is still alive?'

'Holy Mother, no. He took off like a bolt from the bow, with the dogs in pursuit. Found the gory tatters of his jerkin. I can show you. No, the dying man's his master. The one who set the dogs on him.'

My suddenly burgeoning hope was shattered, replaced by cold calculation. 'You know where this fellow is? I'd like to see him.'

'God help me, he's in my barn. If he's still breathing, that is. There's nothing you can do for him but I'll take you there, if it's what you want. You'll make it worth my while?'

I held out gold and the man's eyes gleamed.

We clambered onto the keeper's cart and he drove three or four miles downstream to a farmstead across a field from the river. In addition to the ramshackle house there were several outbuildings and we could hear yelping as the dogs were driven into their quarters across a yard. We were led to a smaller shed, beyond the midden, where remnants of hay were scattered on the floor and, on a dusty pallet with soiled sheets, a man approaching death lay groaning and mumbling unintelligibly. His face was drained of colour, except for the yellowish smudge of his eye-sockets, but his skin was olive-hued. On top of the bedclothes the torn remains of his right arm rested, the stump enveloped in a bloodstained bandage. The smell of putrefaction was appalling.

'Did what I could,' the keeper said as he ushered us into the hut. 'Tied the upper arm and applied egg white to stop the bleeding. There was no festering at first but it was a fearsome jagged wound. It looked as if he might recover for a few days but then the flesh started to rot. The stink tells you how bad it is. I'll leave him to you.'

Leone was at the bedside, bending over the man. Abruptly he looked up. 'It's the fellow who's been trailing you. He's speaking Italian.'

At the sound of Leone's voice the man's eyes flickered and focused on me. 'Doctor Somers,' he murmured.

'That's my name. What's yours?' I was not confident that he would be capable of coherent conversation.

'Enrico di Lucca,' he said with the hint of a smirk.

Our arrival seemed to give a faint boost to his fading life and I resolved to take advantage of this even if it was not in the best interests of the contemptible wretch. I had no salves or distillations with me to ease his suffering but I felt entitled to seek an explanation of his actions. 'Why have you been following me? You've tried to kill me.'

'No, that's a lie.' He clamped his mouth shut as a rictus of pain distorted his face and I sank back on my haunches fearing we would get no help from him. After a brief rest, his anguish lessened and he leered at me. 'Not you, doctor.'

'What do you mean?'

'Not you. The boy. The murderer. A life for a life. I've done my duty.' He nestled his head against the pillow and turned away from me.

I wanted to shake him, to beat him until he gave more information, but I was a physician and my calling required me to give succour to friend and foe alike. I struggled to govern my impatience and my temper. Leone, calmer than I was, leaned forward.

'Who are you?' he asked quietly. 'Who did the boy kill?'

There was a moment of silence while the man's mouth twisted downwards. 'Carlo di Lucca was my brother,' he said at length. 'I have my revenge.'

'Carlo di Lucca?' I stared in horror as understanding came. 'Carlo? The mercenary? Matteo Maffei's henchman?'

'The same. Your servant killed him in Verona.'

'He was defending me. Maffei's men abducted me.'

'It wasn't in fair fight. Carlo was assassinated. I was bound to avenge him.'

'The boy was barely thirteen years old when he tried to save me from capture but I'm sure Carlo would have cut his throat without a second thought.' The dispassionate physician in me was losing the battle and my anger was undisguised.

'Old enough to kill. Old enough to die.'

I turned away while Leone took up the questioning once more. 'Did Rendell die when you set the dogs loose?'

'Was that his name? I never knew. The dogs caught him by the river, they told me. I'd hoped they tear him to pieces in front of me but he took to his heels when the stupid animals grabbed my arm.'

'Why didn't you use your crossbow, like you did before? You only just missed when you shot at him from the wood.' While he was speaking I wondered if Leone had always suspected the bolt was aimed at Rendell rather than me.

Enrico di Lucca licked his dry lips. 'Your guards winged me with an arrow in my shoulder when they came after me. That cramped my style for a couple of weeks, without the strength in my arm to wind the bow. Even using a knife would have been difficult. Your party was always well protected, wherever I followed you. It was sheer chance I saw the boy at the dog fight when he was alone. I thought heaven blessed my enterprise and to see him mangled by the beasts appealed to me.'

I clenched my fists, digging the nails into my palms to prevent me striking the diseased man, but the effort of so much speech had become too much for him and his body began to twitch. His forehead was drenched with sweat and his convulsions intensified. 'You are rewarded for your barbarity,' I said with bitter self-control. 'You are near death and should prepare your soul for judgement.'

'You don't need to tell me, physician. I don't fear God's judgement... I've done my duty.' He closed his eyes.

I stood up, desperate to escape from the brute, but Leone wanted more details. By contrast with my brusqueness, his tone was soothing. 'You were in Marseilles when our ship arrived from Livorno. How did you know?'

This was a question Enrico was willing to answer and with an effort of will he rallied himself. 'I was in Genoa when I learned of Carlo's death, weeks after it happened. Maffei knew what I'd do and sent me word you were heading for France. I guessed you'd make for Marseilles so I went there to wait.' His voice faded but his feeble grin registered pride in what he had achieved and he lay back on the bolster peacefully.

So, I thought sourly, Matteo Maffei had triumphed. He had failed to have Rendell put to death by judicial process for killing his right-hand man but he had been confident that Carlo's vengeful brother would hunt down and destroy the boy they both saw as their enemy. Maffei must have had us tracked, content for me to have been eliminated alongside my servant. 'Come,' I said to Leone. 'He's despicable. We'll speak further to the keeper of the dogs.'

Sorrow clouded the youth's eyes as he held my gaze. 'You go, doctor,' he said. 'I'll stay for a bit. A cold poultice on his brow may give a little relief. I'll dampen a rag. Even villains shouldn't die alone.'

Chastened by the lad's charity and guiltily conscious of my own boorish shortcomings, I nodded and left them alone.

*****

The keeper was ready for his bed and loath to talk but I threatened him with denunciation to the authorities and, in my incoherent rage, I must have carried conviction. Later I reflected that it was a foolhardy menace to have uttered, for the fellow needed only to let loose his dogs and two inconvenient visitors would trouble him no more. At the time cautious good sense had been driven from my mind, so consumed was I by hatred.

'Where is the boy's body? Did you give him Christian burial?'

The keeper folded his arms and faced me with a truculent expression. 'What remained was carried downstream. The dogs chased him into the water and ripped him apart in the river. I ran after them but was too late to stop them. When I called them off they didn't come at once but the second time they abandoned their quarry and trotted back, docile as you please. They dropped these scraps of the boy's jerkin at my feet.'

I had no doubt the ragged shreds of material came from Rendell's clothes but for an instant my thoughts were diverted by a resurgence of irrational hope. Although there was blood there was no body, not even a severed limb. Was it possible Rendell had survived, injured perhaps but still alive, capable of recovery? Almost at once I obliterated that thought for, if Rendell had been rescued and was conscious, he would have sent us news. If, on the other hand, his lacerated corpse had been washed up beside the riverbank somewhere to the west, between Tours and Saumur, there was no reason at all why we should have heard of it. Great rivers were often freighted with anonymous cadavers, which were tossed into a common grave with none the wiser. A boy, who had been knocked unconscious by a blow to the head and, shortly after coming to himself, was forced to run for his life, would have been easy prey for ferocious dogs. I bowed my head in resignation.

The keeper retired to his rest and I sat for some time on a barrel in the yard, staring at the brilliance of the stars with their unknowable secrets. Did they really govern our destinies as astrologers insisted? Could Rendell's inevitable fate have been encompassed in the hour and place of his birth? I was not persuaded by that mystic lore but acknowledged there was much in the circumstances of our lives which we could not explain.

The exercise of reasoning calmed me and I regretted the mean-spirited attitude which had caused me to betray my professional detachment and shirk my undeniable duty. When I had composed myself sufficiently, I went back into the noisome shed to keep vigil with Leone beside the pallet where Enrico di Lucca tossed and grunted in mortal torment. We sat mostly in silence, although Leone murmured prayers from time to time as he wiped his patient's fevered brow, and in due course the first streaks of dawn, entering through gaps in the broken roof, gave pallid light to the man's emaciated features. Perhaps the sun's faint warmth brought him a measure of comfort as his writhing ceased and, finally quiet, he departed this life to face the judgement which, I knew with shame, was not for me to anticipate.

Chapter 8

Affairs of state continued inexorably towards their climax, indifferent to personal grief. Throughout Tours preparations were in hand for the auspicious day: triumphal arches decked the entrance to the castle, garlands were hung from balconies and, at every corner on the route of the planned procession, musicians, in their appointed positions, practised welcoming ditties with loud enthusiasm. Our fellow lodgers were seldom in the house during the day but returned each evening to continue arguments started earlier about who had played the wrong note or come in too late and spoiled their harmony.

I was in no mood to tolerate such niceties and hid myself away but I was pleased that Leone was receiving Bonne's attentions while Matthieu and his lute were otherwise engaged. I did not like to see him burdened with unjustified guilt and hoped the resilience of youth would enable him to set aside his heartache more quickly than I could. His temper had become more unpredictable than usual and he railed against Gaston de la Tour, whom he had never met, for securing Bartholomew's banishment from Lord Fitzvaughan's entourage.

'Don't say those things in public,' I advised. 'Gaston doesn't brook slights to his self-esteem or his lord's honour lightly.' Leone looked sceptical and I thought it necessary to reinforce my warning. 'He can be vindictive in the heat of the moment, even if his mood may switch later.'

I did not explain that I had good reason to know this because I sounded sanctimonious and was uncomfortable with my own disposition. I would still be accounted a young man by other people but I felt I had aged by a decade in the last year and doubted if I would ever recapture the gift of uncomplicated joy.

I was surprised to be summoned to meet Suffolk two days before the betrothal ceremony was due to take place. I had expected him to be fully occupied with tailors, furriers, goldsmiths, perfumers and all the other providers of accessories to fit him to stand as a worthy proxy for his sovereign lord, King Henry. As I trudged the now familiar route to Suffolk's lodgings I wondered if he was afflicted by some inconvenient malady and required urgent treatment to save him from spluttering over the vows he must make or needing to rush to the latrine at an inappropriate moment. He might be excused for suffering human frailty at such a time – he was not merely representing his King at the betrothal, he carried with him England's reputation in the eyes of the French court, as the key article of the truce he had negotiated fell into place.

I was prepared for him to look pale and nervy when I entered his chamber, but not for the haunted expression on his face. He dismissed Andrew Cawfield with a flutter of his hand and waved me to a stool, speaking without any exchange of courtesies.

'You have your ear to the ground in the town, Harry? Do you hear anything that might be of concern to me?'

I blinked in surprise, not at all clear what he meant. 'Your name and position are esteemed among the townsfolk.'

He shrugged impatiently. 'About the truce?'

'It's widely welcomed and the French nobles who opposed it seem quiescent, as far as I can understand.'

He sighed. 'There's no gossip about... the implications?'

'The implications of peace, my lord?'

'There must be gossip, speculation. Do you hear nothing that has caused you to question what is being said?'

I felt wholly inadequate in this interrogation. 'No, my lord. Is there something more explicit you have in mind?' It came to me that he might be referring to the unspecified items which had not been finalised when, as Lord

Fitzaughan had announced, the 'main point' was conceded by King Henry.

'Only that I've been made aware there may be mischief in the offing, perhaps not in France – perhaps in England.'

'I've heard nothing at all about events in England.' My definite and honest assertion did not sit comfortably with my growing disquiet.

'No. Of course. There seemed a chance you would have picked up scurrilous conjecture in the town.'

It was obvious he was unwilling to be more exact about his worries, which was irksome and left me floundering. I deliberated whether I should share with him the theory I had developed linking Rollo's murder to the death of the anonymous man in Chartres but I could not see its relevance to possible rumours circulating in Tours about the truce. I was relieved when he abruptly changed the line of his enquiries.

'You've made the acquaintance of the comte de Langeais?'

'Yes, my lord. I accompanied one of the French physicians on a visit to the comte, his patient. He suffers from an unpleasant wasting disease.'

'You've not met the comte de St Benoît?' I shook my head as he continued. 'He is the leader of the French clique opposed to the truce. It would be useful to know what scheme he and his cronies are devising. You should keep alert to discover what you can. I want no last minute hitches.'

'Certainly, my lord, but may I ask where your information has come from? I don't wish to duplicate enquiries which have already been made.'

He grunted. 'That's not likely,' he said. 'My information comes from across the Narrow Sea.'

The unease in my stomach intensified. 'Can you tell me more?'

My persistence angered him and a vein in his throat stood out as he shouted. 'No, Doctor Somers, I can't. These are matters of state. I've already shared more with you than is sensible. Your earlier service justified my confidence in you but I won't have you exceeding your remit and prying into what is not your business.'

This sudden shift in his attitude towards me renewed my annoyance and I felt belittled by his disdain. It drove away any possibility of putting forward my tentative, and probably unwarranted, theory. I bowed and muttered an apology – for what I was not certain - and my mildness seemed to calm him, although he spoke grudgingly.

'Enough. You have my trust, Harry, but you mustn't press me to disclose what I am not at liberty to repeat. You will say nothing to anyone about this discussion. Go now. But we wish you to attend us in our train at the betrothal.'

I was glad to escape but perturbed by our puzzling conversation. I also noted Suffolk's unconscious use of an imperious 'we' when he dismissed me and the inference I drew from this, with respect to the Earl's state of mind, was not reassuring. I hoped the magnificence of his role at the forthcoming ceremony had not distorted his judgement. My mood was not improved by an exchange with Andrew Cawfield as I crossed the outer chamber. He gripped my arm in comradely fashion and it took will-power not to shrug him away, reminding myself that it would be ungracious to rebut his attempt at friendship.

'I expect you found the Earl troubled, Doctor Somers. Did he confide his concerns to you?'

I bit back the rejoinder that I would not share such information with Suffolk's secretary if the Earl had chosen to keep Cawfield in the dark. 'Not in any specific way. He must have many weighty matters to consider at present.'

'Tactful as ever. He wants me ignorant of his most private dealings but he's had wind that his reception in England may not be as joyful as he hoped.'

I was uncomfortable to receive these confidences. 'Surely he's conducted all his business here with the blessing of the King?'

Cawfield chuckled in an unpleasant way. 'Oh yes, King Henry has blessed everything. That's the beauty of it. My lord Earl thinks he's covered his back securely. But the carapace may slip and will his defence be enough then? Don't tie your destiny too firmly to that of great men: that's my conclusion.' He moved away but looked over his shoulder to pose his final question. 'You used to serve the Duke of Gloucester, didn't you?'

I nodded and he grinned as he put a finger to his lips. 'I need say no more, doctor. Fortunes rise and fall, rise and fall.'

*****

The previous day the bells of Tours had rung out to mark the signing of the treaty which inaugurated two years of truce; now they were pealing for the betrothal which sealed the new-found accord. As a member of Suffolk's household I had a good position in the basilica of St. Martin with a clear view of the impressive company processing along the aisle to support the winsome young bride. Despite my gloominess I was dazzled by the array of vivid silks, opulent furs and glittering jewels on headdresses, belts and necklaces. I must have gaped like an ignorant yokel. Unruffled and sophisticated as always, Lord Fitzvaughan, standing at my side, hissed the names of the eminent dignitaries as they passed us and he enlivened his catalogue with less than diplomatic comments.

'The King of France you recognise and you'll remember Princess Margaret's father, decked out in royal robes as King of Sicily – though he'd be ill-advised to set foot there now the throne is securely filled by a rival. Did you know King René has endowed his daughter with the islands of Minorca and Majorca? Pure face-saving humbug! René claims to have inherited them from his mother but he has no influence over them whatsoever. He's sending the girl penniless to King Henry with a make-believe dowry of lands they'll never control. Then we have the Dauphin Louis and the bride's brother, John, Duke of Calabria – another title of distinction and little practical worth; I wonder what those two have to say to each other. By all accounts Duke John is on cordial terms with his father, while the Dauphin and King Charles share mutual loathing. Now here we have the Dukes of Brittany and Alençon and a bevy of Counts – Vendôme, St Pol, St Benoît, Langeais. What a couple of wizened scarecrows the last two are! Swallowing their rancour to attend the celebration they've fought tooth and nail to prevent. I heard Langeais had dragged himself from his sickbed to be present. God knows why. And here comes Constable de Richemont leading the lesser fry in attendance on their masters. I must say that squire at his heels is a charming boy; I'd be glad to make his closer acquaintance. But no doubt you'll find the second procession more pleasing to contemplate. See, over there.'

Walter Fitzvaughan directed my attention to the ladies entering by a side door, led by the French Queen and her sister-in-law, the bride's mother, Isabelle of Lorraine. He droned on, indicating the Scottish princess who was the Dauphine and the Duchess of Calabria, following their respective mothers-in-law, but my attention was diverted by the entry of the bride's personal attendants. Among them I noted the comtesse de Langeais whose height ensured that she stood out among her companions and who swept forward with austere grace and a supercilious smile. She disdained to acknowledge any of the French onlookers but, as she passed our group of English worthies, she raised her left eyebrow and I imagined for an instant that she was giving me a sign of recognition. Immediately I berated myself for so stupid a thought and wondered why I should conceive such a fanciful notion.

Monsignor Pierre de Mont-Dieu, Papal Legate and Bishop of Brescia, moved forward to officiate at the betrothal and I turned to watch the principal participants as they exchanged vows. Margaret of Anjou looked even more radiant and vivacious than when I had seen her at the earlier ceremony but what astonished me on this occasion was the admiring way in which she regarded Suffolk. Of course she would have met him several times since she was first presented as King Henry's intended bride but it had not occurred to me that she might have developed any special rapport with him. For his part the Earl did not disguise obvious fascination with his future Queen and the smiles he bestowed on her seemed to exceed what was required of a congenial proxy.

Momentarily I was seized by a dreadful fear that there was an unseemly bond between them but I rejected the idea, suspecting that Suffolk's interest was not personal but political. If he had succeeded in winning her trust, he could look to further his prospects at the English court beyond what he had already achieved. He would recognise that this forceful and beautiful maiden was bound to dominate her feeble, besotted husband and, with them both reliant on the Earl's support, they could elevate William de la Pole to an impregnable position of prestige and wealth, equal to that which Cardinal Beaufort had long enjoyed. The life of that aged cleric must be drawing to its close and Suffolk was obviously intent on becoming his unchallenged successor at the King's right hand. The Queen's favour would bolster his pre-eminence and I needed to look no further to explain the Earl's swelling pride. It was not for a humble physician to criticise his master but I hoped ambition would not blind Suffolk to the hazards of the dangerous path he had chosen to follow.

As we trailed back to the castle, through the cheering populace of Tours, I lost contact with Walter Fitzvaughan and his exuberant commentary, walking in silence and allowing my mind to drift back to the household I first served. Duke Humphrey of Gloucester had been a generous patron to me and had no part in his wife's ruinous plot to bring about his royal nephew's death through witchcraft. The exposure of that evil scheme had led to the Duchess's imprisonment for life, the execution of her cronies and my exile. Gloucester was not accused of complicity but had lost his influence at King Henry's court and retired to his palace at Greenwich where he spent his time, as he loved to do, in the company of scholars. He had always opposed moves to make peace with France, after spending years fighting across the Narrow Sea and suffering a serious wound on the field of his eldest brother's great victory at Agincourt. He would not relish news of the day's events, the betrothal and truce, and he would regard Suffolk, the grandson of a merchant, as an unworthy upstart. But Duke Humphrey was now of no account in the King's Council. I felt a twinge of conscience that I had abandoned Gloucester's service and joined the household of the coming man but, in truth, no alternative had been open to me after Suffolk contrived my pardon.

I entered the great hall where the betrothal feast was to be held and was looking for a place at one of the lower tables when I was hailed by a friendly French voice. Master Francisco clapped me on the back and bade me sit with him, which pleased me, for the conversation of a congenial professional man was likely to interest me more than the pleasantries of some unknown courtier. We spent an agreeable three hours as course followed course and, lubricated by the excellent wine dispensed from barrels for guests and common folk alike, we admired the extravagance of the entertainment and catering. Pies as tall as towers were lugged into the hall by sweating attendants who set down their loads in front of the principal guests with evident relief, mopping their brows with their sleeves. Next, to an accompaniment of marvelling gasps, doors in the pastry opened and two giants emerged, carrying trees with monstrous fruits which they tossed to the diners. This amusing interlude was surpassed by the arrival of extraordinary living creatures, named to me by Master Francisco as camels, the like of which I had never seen. These strangely shaped beasts carried imitation castles from which men-at-arms debouched who proceeded to exchange blows in a mock battle which risked overturning our benches and the laden trestles. Hilarity grew unbridled.

I was drowsy with wine and overcome with the ridiculously lavish display when we needed to struggle to our feet as the royal party left the hall. After this it was to be expected that behaviour would become more raucous and I hoped I might slip away without discourtesy. I was about to make my excuses to my amiable companion when a crash resounded from one of the higher tables, accompanied by cries of alarm. I peered towards the disturbance and realised it came from the place where I had glimpsed the comte de Langeais seated with his colleagues and at once I feared that the old gentleman had succumbed to the excitement of the occasion. This seemed to be confirmed when Master Francisco seized my arm and pulled me with him in that direction. Only when we pushed our way through the cluster of twittering noblemen did I realise that the man slumped across the table was not Langeais but his neighbour, the comte de St. Benoît.

Langeais sat, stony-faced, staring at what we might have assumed was the victim of a drunken stupor and, as we joined him, he commented succinctly and with entire accuracy. 'He is dead.'

Master Francisco established there was no pulse and servants were summoned to remove the embarrassing corpse from the scene of otherwise uninterrupted festivities. Meanwhile I helped the comte de Langeais to resume his seat and served him a goblet of wine, for he was deeply shaken by his crony's sudden apoplexy and had turned almost as grey as St. Benoît. To my surprise he asked me to escort him from the hall, while his squire ran ahead to prepare a couch where he could rest, and he leaned heavily on my arm as we negotiated the crowded corridors, remaining silent but pressing my hand intermittently as if in gratitude. We made our way slowly to a part of the castle I had not previously visited, where the French noblemen had quarters, and we entered a narrow chamber where a bed had been made ready for him. While I was helping him lie comfortably, a door at the far end of the room opened and the Countess entered, hurrying to his side.

'Guillaume, my lord, this is dreadful news about St. Benoît.'

He reached out a stiffened hand to her as I stepped back. 'My dear, do not fret yourself. It has been a shock but for me it is not mortal. Unlike for my wretched friend. This physician brought me here and I shall rest.'

I bowed and made to leave but the Countess stopped me. 'Doctor Somers, we are obliged. Please wait for me outside while I settle my husband. I should be glad to speak to you.'

I walked up and down the anteroom for several minutes while I pondered what the formidable Countess might wish to say to me and I could not altogether repress the unaccountable excitement that I felt. When the lady came quietly from the bedchamber she beckoned me to follow her into the passageway.

'My husband is sleeping,' she said as we stood in a window embrasure. 'The day would have been challenging for him without this sad event to bring extra distress.'

'Rest is certainly the best prescription for the Count.'

She turned to the window but I did not believe she was surveying the scene outside and I fancied she blinked back a tear. 'It was rash of him to quit his bed at home but he was determined to attend the ceremony.' I waited and in a moment she had composed herself and faced me again. 'I wished to thank you for troubling to care for a man you must know has fiercely opposed peace with your country.'

'I am a physician, madam, and bound to offer help to any who need it.' I knew I sounded pompous but was uncertain how else to respond.

She ignored my pretentiousness. 'I was sorry to hear what befell your young servant. I remember him at the riverside when you tended the page who nearly drowned.'

I must have looked startled. 'My lady, you're kind. I didn't know news of Rendell's fate had reached the court.'

'Princess Margaret and her attendants have been much in the company of the English ladies who have accompanied their lords to Tours. The Lady Fitzvaughan told us of the boy's misfortune.'

I swallowed hard but felt the flush rising up my cheeks. 'The Lady Maud is always well informed,' I said.

The Countess glared at me and her voice cut like steel through my self-esteem. 'The Lady Maud is most loquacious. Injudiciously so. She boasts of her many conquests – before her marriage I trust – and she names you among them, Doctor Somers.'

I closed my eyes and wished the floor would open up and swallow me.

'If it is true, physician, and I note you offer no denial, it is shameful on your part. I do not presume to judge a noble lady.'

'Madame, la comtesse, I accept your rebuke.' I hung my head and longed for her to dismiss me.

'That at least is creditable.' As I looked up her expression softened. 'I had not intended to reprove you, Doctor Somers. There are many who say I have too sharp a tongue. I was concerned to hear you traduced when you had been of service to my mistress, the princess, and my husband. I had not expected that you would concede the accusation.'

'My lady, your frankness is refreshing among the artifice of a court, whether in France or England.'

She gave one of her tight little smiles. 'Will you accompany the Earl of Suffolk when he returns next spring to stand proxy at the marriage and convey Princess Margaret to his royal master?'

'I don't know what I shall be called upon to do. Will you remain in the princess's service when she crosses the Narrow Sea as Queen of England?' The words were out before I thought how presumptuous they were but she did not frown at my crassness.

'My place is with my husband,' she said and moved away from the window. 'I bid you adieu, physician. I hope your fortunes prosper.'

I bowed low as she re-entered the chamber and then sought to find my way out of that unfamiliar wing of the castle. I took several wrong turnings and found it hard to concentrate on the direction I should take, thinking how apt an allegory my wanderings were for the many misguided steps I had taken in my life.

*****

The long train of complacent Englishmen straggled northwards from the Loire Valley, behind the resplendent Earl of Suffolk, fêted by rejoicing crowds in every village. Our stately progress took a month to reach the port of Harfleur and in its early stages it followed the track of my previous journeys. Through Blois and Châteaudun we rode and my sense of desolation grew as I was reminded at every turn of Rendell jogging along on his pony at my side when I last traversed that terrain. We rested for the night at Chartres and, billeted in the very same hostelry we had visited together, I could not resist the urge to seek out young

Jeannot who was still to be found chasing hens from the yard. It was gratifying that he recognised me at once but I should have foreseen his immediate, disconcerting enquiry.

'Is your servant here, sir? Rendell?' He sounded pathetically eager.

I shook my head, unwilling to hurt him. 'He had to travel by a different route. But he'd have wished me to give you greetings. You were very helpful when we came here before, you and your brother.'

He wiped the back of a grimy hand across his face and grinned. 'My brother made another find in the tannery a few days after you went,' he said.

'Not another body?'

'No, nothing so exciting. But he reckons it might be linked to the poor fellow drowned in the vat.'

'What was it?' I held my breath.

'It was at the bottom of a different tank, where they pour the madder, so it was thick with yellow dye. He couldn't tell what colour it had been.'

'A garment?'

'A jerkin. No use, though, because it was stiff with the dye.' He paused so I gave him a coin for his information and ruffled his filthy hair to show my appreciation. He cocked an eyebrow. 'It had a crest on it.'

'I don't suppose you could make out what it was.' It was not a question and I shrugged in anticipation of his reply.

'Couldn't say what colour but the shape was obvious. It was a swan.'

I reeled back from him, trying not to tremble. 'Has your brother still got it?'

'No. He burnt it after it had dried out a bit. We reckoned it was what the man who was stripped naked had been wearing.'

'Very likely,' I said and gave him another coin before returning to the inn.

His theory was possible but there was an alternative explanation – one that accorded with the troublesome idea which had plagued my thoughts in recent weeks. It could have been the livery worn by the murderer before he switched clothes with his victim and, if so, it was clear he might have come, not from the household of a dissident French noble, but from one of the greatest in the land across the Narrow Sea. For, as I knew very well, the swan was a favourite device of my former master, Humphrey, Duke of Gloucester, principal opponent in England of the truce with France. How it might have advantaged him to intercept Suffolk's private correspondence with King Henry, I could not tell but I was left with a gut-wrenching fear of impending disaster.

Part II: England 1444-1445
Chapter 9

It was not the return to my native land that I had dreamed of during my exile. I was not riding with glad expectancy towards those I loved, warmed by a gentle English sun, steeped in the comforting joy of resuming my role as physician in the household I had served until my flight. The dank, cheerless weather matched my gloom as my horse splashed along rutted, muddy tracks to a position of dependence on Suffolk's favour, for which I felt little enthusiasm. I was troubled by the possibility that my old master, Humphrey of Gloucester, would, at best, privately disparage my disloyalty and, at worst, set himself publicly against William de la Pole's new influence with the King. Either alternative would make it difficult for me to visit the friends I had in Gloucester's great Palace of Pleasance at Greenwich, downstream from the City of London. Worse still was the knowledge that, among those friends, were Rendell's sister, Grizel, and her husband, Thomas, my close companion before I fled, to whom I must break the news of the boy's dreadful fate. Moreover I had heard nothing of my mother for nearly two years, and feared to learn that she had died in grief at my disgrace, while I could gain no solace from thoughts of Bess, now Mistress Willoughby, and lost to me forever.

Leone, riding at my side, was not impressed by the undramatic, sodden countryside and he shivered, without affectation, each evening when we entered the cold portals of whichever castle, hostelry or abbey had been required to offer us hospitality for the night. I wondered if it had been wrong to bring him with me from Italy, when he had no need to seek refuge elsewhere, and I felt unworthy of the trust he placed in me as mentor and model – seeing myself as a contemptible pattern for any aspiring physician. I wished I could be sure that Suffolk would agree to sponsor the lad to study at Oxford, as I had done when I accompanied Duke Humphrey's natural son to the university, but I suspected the Earl might not so willingly give patronage to ambitious understrappers, in Gloucester's open-handed way.

My melancholy thoughts did not accord with the jubilant atmosphere of our progress, for, despite the depressing rain, our arrival was celebrated by the damp residents of towns and villages along our route. They lined streets and crowded market squares, to cheer and shout Suffolk's name, while on bridges and at farm gates groups of rustics waved and stamped their feet. We could be in no doubt that the prospect of peace with France, after so many decades of warfare, was popular and even the humblest of the Earl's adherents were made to feel they had participated in a magnificent achievement. It would have been churlish not to smile back at such welcoming scenes and I did my best to appear suitably appreciative, while others in our company doffed their caps and caused their horses to caper gracefully, thus gaining more applause. It was only natural that the greatest impact of this rejoicing would be felt by the man whose personal triumph was being recognised but, when I glimpsed the arrogant gleam in his eyes as he acknowledged his reception, I worried that Suffolk might fail to keep a sense of proportion about the fleeting benefits of fame.

Lord Fitzvaughan and his wife left the Earl's retinue before we reached London. I had been unaware of their departure but I encountered Gaston de la Tour when we stopped on the last full day of our journey and he told me, with a grimace, that his lordship was escorting Lady Maud to their estates in Norfolk before returning to join the court. I had found Lord Fitzvaughan a helpful source of information on our journey, during the long periods when I had no direct contact with Suffolk, so I regretted his absence but, so far as his lady was concerned, I felt only relief that she was no longer at hand. When we approached Westminster Palace it became clear that the Earl intended to call at once upon the King while his followers proceeded to his house in the City. We paused to watch Suffolk enter through the great gateway of the palace and I listened with amusement, and reluctant agreement, to Leone's tactfully worded comments on the antiquated appearance of the royal residence compared with those of the Venetian Doges and Mantuan Marquises.

Suffolk's City house, known as the Manor of the Rose, was a fine crenelated mansion consisting of several ranges and a four-storey tower. I was delighted to find a room was ready for a physician's use but less happy to be told that my master required me to wait upon him, after his return from audience with the King, knowing this might involve fretting in an antechamber while he dealt with more urgent matters and more distinguished visitors. So indeed it proved and my frustration was not lightened by the presence of Andrew Cawfield, at his officious worst, seeming to decide at will whom to admit and in what order. I knew Leone was fully competent to set up my equipment and seek ingredients for my standard remedies, but I wished I could have shared his routine tasks rather than spending the time with sycophantic courtiers. After an hour or so I found space on a window seat, vacated by a cleric who had been admitted to the inner sanctum, and sat squeezed between a bored-looking attorney and a purveyor of fragrances whose aroma was more pleasing than the stench of travellers, to which I had become accustomed, but in its way no less overpowering. My head had drooped towards my chest when at last Cawfield bellowed my name.

The Earl looked tired but self-satisfied, as might be expected, and he wasted no time on pleasantries. 'Your assistant can obtain your physician's requisites, I take it? Can he treat minor cuts and scalding?'

Taken by surprise and only half-awake, I agreed.

'Good. You have leave of absence for ten days to fulfil the commission you have been asked to undertake. You may wish to rest a day or two after our long trek but you should then set out directly for Stamford and return as quickly as you can.'

I blinked, not wishing to believe what he seemed to be saying. 'Stamford?' I repeated dimly.

'Representations were made to me to release you for some purpose which I imagine is known to you. As I have great respect for Lord Fitzvaughan I am pleased to comply with his request.'

'Lord Fitzvaughan asked you to let me go to Stamford?' It seemed inconceivable that Maud's husband would know of her appeal to me.

Suffolk's finely shaped lips twitched with amusement. 'His catamite, that Norman fellow, Gaston, brought me a note franked with his lord's seal after Walter and his lady rode north. I gather it is some delicate matter to which you are privy. I wish to know no more but you are free to oblige his lordship. Ask Cawfield to send in my sergeant-at-arms as you leave.'

When I withdrew I was fully alert, outraged but full of admiration for Maud's ability to get even Gaston de la Tour to carry out her errand – and for her audacity in using her husband's seal to mislead the Earl. She was skilful and unscrupulous; knowing I was disinclined to go to Stamford, she would leave nothing to chance. I found myself grinning at her contrivance and berated myself silently. At least she had been removed to Norfolk so I need not encounter her in person. Whatever the outcome of my visit to the Priory of St. Michael, I would convey it to her in writing. Back in our chamber, where Leone was already stretched out on his pallet, I penned a short letter and before I retired I found one of the Earl's henchmen who promised it would be taken at daybreak to the Manor of Danson.

Danson lay to the east of Greenwich, in the county of Kent, some dozen miles from London. It was a small manor belonging to old acquaintances of mine, Sir Hugh and Lady Blanche de Grey, who had given refuge to my mother and were no doubt still in contact with the household of their eminent near-neighbour, Duke Humphrey of Gloucester. I dared not send a communication by one of Suffolk's messengers direct to the palace at Greenwich but I could be confident Sir Hugh, who was not well-known at court, would forward my enclosure to Thomas Chope, Grizel's husband. The reply from Danson was with me by late afternoon and gave cheering news: my mother was in reasonable health, overjoyed to hear I was returned to England and appreciative that my duties prevented me paying her an immediate visit. To my forwarded missive I could expect no written reply but I prayed that on the morrow my old friend would be at the City hostelry where we had met several times in years gone by. He at least would understand my caution in approaching him.

I arrived early at the waterside inn, ordered ale and peered, against the sun, at a succession of wherries crossing from the Southwark shore but I could not identify Thomas among the passengers. I had begun to fear that my message had not reached him or he was unable to come, when I felt a hand grip my shoulder from behind and span round to be hugged by muscular arms. He had filled out since I last saw him and had the smug air of a man whose fortunes were prospering.

'Welcome back, you recreant. We hadn't heard of you for so long we were beginning to think you'd come to grief.'

'Thomas! I'm glad to see you! You look well.'

'Master carpenter, I am now, Harry Somers. In charge of the team who work at Duke Humphrey's house in London as well as at Greenwich. I came here at dawn to inspect some old panelling at Baynard's Castle; as good a reason as you could find for me to be in the City.'

I laughed at his ready instinct to cover his tracks. 'I'm grateful.' I thrust the jug of ale towards him, reluctant to broach my main business. 'I wish I could have come openly to Greenwich but I'm in Suffolk's service now and need to be cautious.'

'It's wise. Duke Humphrey's lost much of his old influence but there are signs he's beginning to flex his sinews again and he has no love for Suffolk.'

'I'm out of touch with so much. I could tell you more of the struggles between the Venetian Republic and her rivals then I could about...'

Thomas reached out and gripped my wrist. 'You didn't set up this meeting for casual gossip. I read the signs as soon as I got your message. There's bad news, isn't there?' I nodded, unable to speak for a moment and he understood. 'Rendell?'

I choked back tears as I summarised the story, omitting the more painful details, and I watched Thomas's deepening frown. 'I have a task to carry out which takes me north of London for two weeks. When I return I'll contrive to meet you and Grizel so I can tell her as much as she wishes to know. But she has the right to be told and I wondered if you...'

My voice cracked and Thomas held up his hand to stop me. 'Of course; but I won't tell her yet. She's very near to giving birth.'

'Dear God, I didn't know.'

Thomas smiled. 'It's more than two years since our boy was born. It's time there was another in the cradle. We named him after you, did you know that? But we always call him Hal, to avoid confusion. He's a sprightly little fellow.' I shook my head, lost for words, and Thomas went on speaking to divert us from the embarrassment of giving way to emotion. 'We heard you were to marry an Italian girl.'

109

'Misleading information seems to travel with supreme ease. I was betrothed briefly but the arrangement was revoked – it would have been wrong for us both.'

'I can't believe you lived a life of celibacy among the dark-eyed beauties of the Venetian Republic.' His lip curled in a way I remembered: a sure sign he was teasing me.

I met the challenge. 'There was a woman I would have married without a qualm.'

'Your mistress?'

'For a short while. But she was of superior lineage and remained true to her protector.'

Thomas still had the knack of understanding what I did not say. 'She caused you pain.'

I poured more ale, marvelling that I could discuss this so dispassionately. 'It's in the past.'

He winked. 'Let's drink to the future then and pray that God will grant young Rendell's restless soul peace. He lived bravely.'

*****

I journeyed to Stamford in the company of some London cloth merchants who were bound for the wool markets of Lincolnshire. They had hired armed guards to ensure their safety on the road and it was an uneventful ride but I was weary from so many weeks in the saddle and did not relish the prospect of discussing Lady Maud's private affairs with the holy, cloistered woman I had been sent to see. The town appeared prosperous with several fine churches and stone houses and I found lodgings at a substantial hostelry facing the entrance of St. Michael's Priory, where I passed a note through the grille to the convent's gatekeeper for the attention of the Reverend Lady Prioress. Denizens of the Raven Inn told me I would probably have a long wait before I was allowed an audience, or more likely refused one, but next morning I received a message asking me to present myself after midday when the office of Sext had concluded. On hearing that I had been granted an appointment so quickly, my landlord became obsequious and I gathered I was regarded as a person of consequence; but the obvious awe in which the Prioress was held only enhanced my nervousness.

I was shown into a plainly furnished parlour with two doors: one, through which I entered, led to the adjacent gatekeeper's lodge and the other presumably gave access to the main part of the convent. There was no window, only a hatch beside the door to the lodge, and the candles in the wall-sconce were lit, as they needed to be despite the daylight outside. I had scarcely looked round when the second door opened and a tall angular woman of aristocratic bearing glided silently towards me. She extended her hand and I bowed low over it, kissing her ring.

'Reverend Mother, I am grateful.'

'Doctor Somers, you are welcome. I have heard of you. Do you regret leaving the shores of Italy?'

I tried to hide my astonishment. 'I'm overjoyed to have received a pardon for the events which led to my exile and be able to return home.'

She pursed her lips and the creases at each side of them disappeared into the stiff fold of her wimple across her chin. 'That is no answer to my question. You studied at the University of Padua which must bring prestige for a physician.'

'I learned much and hope it will benefit my practice of medicine.' I was feeling my way to find the appropriate way of addressing her.

'Cautious and discreet, that's good. Yet the Lady Maud Fitzvaughan must have some hold over you, which is more worrying. Are you her adherent?'

'No, Reverend Mother, I serve the Earl of Suffolk. I met Lady Maud years ago when we were both at the Duke of

Gloucester's Palace of Pleasance and she presumed on our earlier acquaintance to ask my help in the present matter.'

'Which requires consummate discretion and secrecy. She seems to have made a wise choice. You haven't bedded her since your return to England.'

I felt myself flush. 'No, madam.'

'Well done, physician. You say what is required and don't waste words on vain protests about things you were not asked. You were surprised that I'd heard of you? You expected a Prioress would live secluded from the world, knowing nothing of secular affairs?'

'I confess my ignorance.' I could not suppress a smile.

'The sisters who are my charge must live devout lives of prayer and service, protected from the corruption of the world. In their purity they petition Heaven on behalf of sinful mankind. Within the Priory it is my duty to see that they are supported to fulfil their sacred vows, to the glory of God, and that any backsliding is dealt with fittingly. But my role is wider than governance of this house. I am bound also to promote its broader interests: to seek patrons, increase our endowments, ensure we are not disadvantaged by the quirks of great men who might help or hinder our fortunes. For this reason I maintain contacts who keep me informed of what it is useful for me to know and, with my Lord Abbot of Peterborough, to whom this house is subject, I monitor events that are relevant to our continued prosperity. Many a City merchant would envy me my channels of information.'

'Reverend Mother, I'm impressed.'

'So you should be, you impudent pup!' She gave a low melodious laugh and I knew she was not offended. 'I come of a great family in the north of England, related to the Percys, Earls of Northumberland. I am well connected to scions of church and state and all these relationships, all this knowledge they bestow on me, is at the service of the blessed house I am honoured to lead.'

I bowed my head, conscious that I was in the presence of a formidable woman, and briefly she eyed my humility with approval. Then her expression became sharper.

'Well, what have you come to ask me? What has Maud told you of her past?'

'I know of the child she bore who was cared for at the Priory and that little Eleanor has disappeared.'

I noted that colour had come into the lady's cheeks and she spoke with vehemence. 'Maud Fitzvaughan is a harlot who has endangered her immortal soul but her infant is a sweet child and must be saved from the evil influence of her mother.'

'Lady Maud spoke of her infant as a cherub.'

'Hah! What does she know? She cannot have seen the baby for more than a few minutes before Eleanor was whisked away to the wet-nurse. Later she was brought here for nurture.'

This was harsh but undoubtedly true. 'Lady Maud sees herself now as a bereft mother. I think her concern for the child's welfare is sincere.'

'Does she see herself as a player in the mummers' plays? Wailing for Herod's slaughter of the innocents?' The tone was caustic.

'Years ago Lady Maud told me how she was abused as a child and became the pawn of a malevolent guardian. I find it credible that she wouldn't wish her daughter to suffer a similar fate. She fears Eleanor has been abducted for such a purpose.'

The Prioress fingered the rosary at her waist. 'You are a commendable advocate. You find potent arguments to persuade the uninformed. However, I do not believe that dreadful fate has befallen the child.'

'Lady Maud said she'd received a message from you to that effect. I need to ask you what you know.'

She folded her hands in her lap. 'I've taken no oath of secrecy and I'd be glad to know that my supposition is correct. I will confide in you, Doctor Somers, on one condition: that you keep me informed of your enquiries and what you discover.'

I suspected the Prioress could be as devious as any ingratiating courtier but I could not deny her right to know what had happened to her charge. 'I accept your condition, Reverend Mother.'

'Good, Doctor Somers, we understand each other. So now – I shall explain. From the moment Eleanor came to St. Michael's, regular payments for her upkeep were received from Lady Maud's protector, the late Roger Bolingbroke, until the wretched man met his deserved end on the gallows, as you well know. In the meantime, however – and Lady Maud is ignorant of this – we were given other donations explicitly for the little girl's care. These did not cease until she was smuggled away from the Priory by a woman who claimed to be bringing her a message from her relatives.'

'So you deduce the person making the payments was responsible for her removal?'

'Precisely. And this person has been aware of Eleanor's existence from the time of her birth. There had been no personal contact until the woman who took her visited the Priory twice in the last year – it was cleverly contrived to avert suspicion.'

'The payments continued after Bolingbroke's death?'

'I have said so. You are rather slow, Doctor Somers. Who else might have learned of Eleanor's birth and had an interest in providing for her, perhaps from a belated sense of duty?'

I stared at the reverend lady's wise, unscrupulous face. 'The child's father?'

She smiled with her lips but her eyes were cold. 'It seems plausible. Do you know the man's identity?'

'No. I'm not sure whether...,' I floundered.

'You are not sure Lady Maud knows either. I suspected as much. Find him, Doctor, and I think you will find Eleanor.'

'Why should the father want to take her after so long – and in such an underhand way? Isn't it possible someone else found out about the child and has evil plans to misuse her, as Lady Maud fears?'

'These are questions for you to answer. But the payments made by this anonymous donor have been generous, more generous than I would expect from a villain who planned the child's ruin.'

She was magnificent and new comprehension came to me. The Priory had for some years been receiving double payment for Eleanor's keep, from Roger Bolingbroke and the unknown other. Even after Bolingbroke's death, they had been richly recompensed but now they had lost not just the child but the generous provision for her maintenance. 'How could the payments be made anonymously to the Priory?' I asked.

'St. Michael's attorney deals with such matters. It's not unusual for payments to be made between lawyers without disclosure of the principal involved and I imagine Master Adams would be unwilling to divulge even the name of the brother notary with whom he has dealings. Certainly the notary would not disclose sworn secrets to a third party. It is to Lady Maud you must go to pursue your search. If she wishes you to find her daughter's whereabouts, she must make known to you the candidates for fathering the infant. It's a sordid business, Doctor Somers, but this is the task you have undertaken. I wish you well.'

She rose and I feared our interview was at an end, leaving me with an impossible problem to confront. 'Lady Maud has gone to her husband's estate in Norfolk. Lord Fitzvaughan escorted her there but may have returned to London. I can't simply call on her without a reason I can explain to his lordship.'

She seemed amused. 'Deception is an art you have not yet mastered, Doctor Somers. However, you're right to observe the proprieties. Their manor house is two days' journey from here but it's not an easy route because of the fenland which stretches eastwards beyond Stamford. I will send a message to Lady Maud to seek her guidance on how you are to approach her. Lord Fitzvaughan knows her as a patron of St. Michael's and will suspect nothing. Remain at the Raven until I inform you of her reply.'

Over-awed, I began to thank her for her help but she leaned forward to peer into my disfigured face. 'You are a man of integrity, I believe, Doctor Somers, and you have a respected place in Suffolk's household. Don't put that at hazard. Besides, I'd value any news you might give me from time to time about affairs of state. The Marquis's fortunes rise rapidly.'

'Marquis?'

She patted my shoulder. 'I thought you might not have heard. While you have been on the road from London, William de la Pole has bent the knee before his Grace, King Henry, and been elevated from Earl to Marquis. His success in France is so greatly appreciated. Even your old master, Humphrey of Gloucester spoke courteously in Parliament of his achievement.' She turned slightly so I saw her aquiline profile as she made her next enquiry. 'You have seen the King's affianced bride, this Margaret of Anjou?'

'From a distance. At the ceremonies in Tours. She's a vivid, captivating young woman.'

'Who will turn strong men's heads and make our pious King her slave. You confirm what I've heard. I shall send her the blessings of this house and commend it to her. When she becomes Queen she will no doubt wish to emulate her husband's generosity towards establishments of piety and learning. We shall pray for her benevolence towards the Priory.' She moved to the inner door and put her hand on the latch. 'You are not married yourself, Doctor Somers?'

'No, Reverend Mother.'

'I recommend you should be, very soon, for your soul's salvation and your body's comfort. Don't be afraid of a clever woman who can partner your enterprises. A virtuous and competent widow would suit you well.'

I gulped and she laughed freely as if she had made a witticism. 'You will keep contact, as I suggest, won't you? In return, I will ensure you are informed of anything that may benefit your interests.' She held out her ringed hand once more and I dropped to my knee almost as gladly as Suffolk must have done before his King. 'May Heaven keep you, Doctor Somers,' she murmured and made the sign of the cross over my bowed head.

I reeled out of the Priory gatehouse, scarcely conscious of my surroundings. I had learned so much which I must think about but one thing the Prioress had said brought me great cheer. The Duke of Gloucester had praised the outcome of Suffolk's negotiations and I might reasonably hope that these two important men were no longer at enmity. Whatever the truth about Rollo's fate, the unease I had felt since my discoveries in Chartres must be without foundation.

*****

As advised by the Prioress, I made part of my journey to Norfolk by water along a navigable channel through low-lying fenland, marvelling at the strangeness of the meres and marshes interspersed with fertile ground. Then, back in the saddle accompanied by a local guide, I traversed banked-up causeways until we could ride faster on higher ground, anxious to get this awkward meeting over. Lady Fitzvaughan had replied promptly to the Prioress, with assurances that his lordship had returned to London and, showing admirable delicacy, she had asked that I should not visit the manor house but call at the dower-house, within the same

117

curtilage, where she would meet me, accompanied by the invaluable Marian. I was glad of her discretion.

The Fitzvaughan estates, near to the town of Attleborough, were extensive and provided pasture for large flocks of sheep. I glimpsed several scattered dwellings as we crossed fields and skirted woodland, wondering where the bailiff and his newly-wedded wife might live, relieved that the arrangements for my meeting would keep me away from their vicinity. As we approached the central complex I realised it was well defended, moated and surrounded by a high wall with entry across a drawbridge, and the manor house was dominated by a central tower clearly of much greater age than the other buildings. My guide left me at the entrance where the gatekeeper was expecting me and he dispatched a lad to inform her ladyship that I had come, while I was directed to a pleasant, squat house on the far side of the courtyard with its doorway facing a small garden. I was told the goodwife would bring me refreshment while I awaited Lady Maud and, welcoming that prospect, I relinquished my horse to a groom and walked across to my destination.

A woman was bending over a bed of parsley, leeks and chives, with her back to me. When she heard my boots on the hard-baked earth, she straightened and wiped her hands on her apron but she did not turn until I was beside the low hedge which divided the cultivated area from the yard where hens and piglets roamed. Then she faced me with her beautiful, troubled eyes and dropped a low curtsey.

'Doctor Somers, we are honoured,' she said as my heart somersaulted.

'Mistress... Mistress Willoughby,' I stammered. 'I had no idea... Forgive me.'

She gave a faint smile. 'I have the advantage of you. I knew you were to come here. This is my home. We are privileged to be allowed to live here while no one else has claims on the dower-house. Please come indoors and take some ale. Lady Maud will be here directly.'

I did not move and neither did she. 'Permit me to congratulate you on your marriage.' My voice sounded distant, unreal.

She looked at me sternly but there was no hint of accusation in her statement. 'We heard you were to wed, more than a year ago, but I understand it did not take place.'

'I'm astonished news of that short-lived betrothal reached Norfolk. It was a time when I despaired of ever returning home.'

'Your friend, the apothecary who went with you to Italy, stayed in touch with my lord of Suffolk's household and so in due course the news trickled through to us. Over time and distance it's inevitable mistaken information travels and misleads. It is the way of things.' She took a step towards her house and, separated from her by the hedge, I followed. 'Robin, my husband, will return soon. I should like you to meet him.'

Her calmness annoyed me but I knew I was being unreasonable. Unlike me, she was prepared for our meeting and I could not tell if it was difficult for her to exercise this degree of self-control. She was an experienced lady's attendant, well used to hiding her personal feelings, and I had cause to know how skilfully she could dissemble when the need arose, as it had when she helped me escape into exile. Inwardly I cursed Lady Maud for contriving the circumstances of our encounter but, as I heard light footsteps crossing the courtyard, I was perversely grateful that Lord Fitzvaughan's wife was about to interrupt our conversation. On the threshold of the house I turned and bowed to her.

'Doctor Somers, how kind of you to come,' Lady Fitzvaughan carolled. 'I'm sure you're delighted to renew acquaintance with dear Bess. She has made her home available for our discussion and we are obliged. Come, Marian'.

I followed the three women into a comfortable parlour and accepted a goblet of wine before Bess withdrew and deaf Marian seated herself by the window with her inevitable embroidery. Maud and I faced each other from chairs each side of the fireplace and, as she fingered the rim of her chalice, she giggled like a simpleton.

'Oh, Harry, your face is a study. I wouldn't have missed this moment for the world. Wasn't it clever of me to arrange to meet you here?'

'Cruel not clever, my lady. You trifle with my feelings.'

She raised her eyebrows with mock severity. 'But it's proper for me to act with prudence. I am watched at the manor house.'

'Lord Fitzvaughan has set spies on you?' It seemed improbable.

'No, not Walter. He is most considerate towards me - particularly as he believes I may be pregnant.' I gasped and she gave a disapproving moue. 'Sadly, he will learn in the next few weeks that I have miscarried and we shall both grieve; but he will be encouraged to think I may yet bear him an heir.' She concluded this outrageous statement with a beatific smile, followed by a slight shiver as she continued. 'It's Gaston de la Tour who arranges for my actions to be observed and reported. He's assiduous in ensuring I don't dishonour my husband. He's a meddlesome bore.' She sank back against the cushion on her chair. 'He knows of our old liaison.'

I gave a feeble laugh. 'I'm well aware of that. He tried to have me drowned because of it. But that was years ago and afterwards he facilitated my escape from execution, so I believed he no longer harboured rancour towards me.'

'He is not to be trusted.'

I accepted that conclusion but did not want to be diverted from my purpose. 'I'm not here on my own account, my lady. The Prioress wrote to you.'

She rolled her eyes. 'Is the old woman as fearsome as they say?'

'You haven't met her? She's most impressive.'

Maud gave a grunt of irritation. 'Well, what did she tell you about dear Eleanor? What evidence has she that the poor child is unharmed?'

Determined not to be diverted by sentiment, I countered with my own question. 'Did you know that someone other than Roger Bolingbroke had been making regular donations towards the girl's upkeep at St. Michael's Priory?'

She stared at me. 'For how long?'

'For years. The payments only ceased when Eleanor left the Priory. Can you suggest who might have been doing this?'

'How should I know? Some rogue who learned of my child from Roger Bolingbroke and planned to seduce her when she grew old enough for his purposes.' She clutched herself and began to rock to and fro, wailing softly.

'I don't believe so and neither does the Prioress. Lady Maud, if you are serious in wanting me to trace your daughter you must tell me what I need to know – however unseemly the subject.'

She looked at me suspiciously and pouted. 'What?' It came as a whisper and I was certain she knew what I would say.

'Who is the child's father?'

She shot to her feet and stalked about the parlour, her anger filling the air. 'How dare that dried-up harridan ask such a thing? It's no business of hers or yours.'

I stood to face her. 'In that case, Lady Maud, I must withdraw from the enquiry. Without your co-operation I can do no more. Excuse me, I shall leave.'

Ignoring Marian's gasp of horror, she hurled herself at me, pummelling my chest with her fists. 'No, Harry, no. You're my only chance. You can't desert me.'

I was trembling as I stepped aside but there was no possibility that I would weaken. 'It's your choice, my lady. Either you help me or I can't proceed further. The probability that the child's father is involved must be explored.'

She flounced across the room and subsided onto her chair, scowling. 'I don't know who fathered Eleanor,' she said and tossed her head defiantly.

'Were there so many?'

'You are become brutal, Harry Somers, brutal and callous. Over the years of my girlhood there were several who took me for their pleasure when the chatelaine of my guardian's house traded me as a harlot – under his instruction. How am I to know which of them caused me to conceive? You will tell me, physician, will you not, that they couldn't all have contributed to my condition?'

Her mouth curved in an ugly sneer as I shook my head. 'I need their names.'

'How you enjoy your prurient role! I wish to God I'd never spoken to you of Eleanor.'

'Then release me from the commission and I shall keep your confidence secure.'

She snarled with fury. 'You know I can't do that if my child is to be found. You toy with a mother's broken heart.'

'Mawkish drama will not move me, Lady Maud. The choice is yours.'

She fingered her necklet and tugged it with such force that the clasp gave way and the jewelled chain fell into her lap. She glared at the broken pieces and gathered them in her hand. Then, narrowing her eyes, she looked up and spoke calmly as if naming unimportant members of her household. 'Sir Blakely Dunne was an older man, a wretch who slobbered over me. I believe he lived in Surrey. Master

Edwin Drewman was younger, a wealthy merchant's son in the City of London. I thought him uncouth. I serviced them both at the relevant time.' Her voice became harsh with accusation. 'I was barely fourteen when I bore Eleanor.'

I stared at her tortured expression and could no longer keep compassion at bay. 'Surely you can't believe that either man would wish to subject his own daughter to the treatment you suffered?'

She held my gaze. 'I don't know. My life has taught me to trust nobody.' She rose to her feet, complete mistress of her emotions once more. 'I'm still capable of judgement, physician, and for that reason I recognise the generosity of spirit which Walter shows to me. Does that surprise you?'

I did not answer her question, too obviously intended to switch my attention from the matter in hand. 'Lady Maud, I need to be very clear. Do you wish me to continue my investigation?'

She came close to me, thrusting out her breast and stroking my disfigured cheek with her fingers. Her perfume and her touch revived memories and sensations I had tried to bury but I kept my hands clenched by my sides. She sighed and stepped away. 'Yes,' she said and her voice was steady. 'Do what you must.' Then she beckoned Marian who hurried to open the door and they both moved into the entrance hall. 'See,' she hissed, as a figure emerged from the domestic quarters at the back of the house. 'You are about to meet the stalwart Robin Willoughby. Don't you envy him bedding his incomparable wife?'

As the lady of the manor departed her bailiff came forward and Bess introduced him to me. He was an agreeable, well-set fellow, two or three years older than me, and he was courteous in welcoming my visit. The impression he gave was of a dependable, intelligent yeoman and when he slipped his arm round his wife's waist it seemed a movement of natural affection. It was only to be expected that Bess would have chosen her husband with good sense and, for her sake, I was glad. He invited me to stay for supper but I explained my need to cover as much ground as I could before dusk and he did not press me further. Soon afterwards I left the dower-house amid cordial goodbyes but, as I mounted my horse and looked back to wave, I wished I had not glimpsed the glimmer of moisture in Bess's upturned eye.

Chapter 10

I had much to ponder as I rode back to London but I focused on anything which would put Bess Willoughby out of my mind. Not for the first time I struggled to understand how Lady Maud attracted and repelled me simultaneously. She was a consummate performer, no artifice was too devious for her, no deception too base, yet I sensed that somewhere in her heart there was a seed of sincerity which had never been allowed to develop. Unquestionably she had been misused in her childhood, at the behest of her repellent guardian, and I wondered how different she might have been if she had been nurtured in a loving family. Was that possible or was evil innate in her, her soul possessed by demons? My old Professor at Padua University had emphasised the novel concept of treating the whole person, not merely individual symptoms, but we had never discussed whether external circumstances could moderate or enhance tendencies towards virtue or vice. I reflected that this was treacherous ground, where the role of a physician veered towards that of the priest, and perhaps I would be unwise to pursue questions which could not be resolved but might lead to heretical thoughts.

I tried to concentrate on the countryside through which I passed but away from the fenland causeways it fell into a familiar pattern: interminable woodland, pasture and cultivated strips, occasional moated manors and dreary clusters of cottages outside their walls. I returned to the principal highway bound for London and, journeying south, was once more in the company of merchants, itinerant officials and hawkers, with an armed escort whose presence seemed desirable when we caught sight of roving bands of horsemen with ambiguous intentions. England was an uneasy country where the King's laws had a tenuous grasp on men's minds and the favour of a local baron was viewed as more significant than a justice holding assizes in the vicinity once or twice a year. Most of the towns through which we passed appeared thriving in comparison with the scattered villages but I suspected that their composure owed much to the security of the walls and gatehouses which protected them from the outside world. I had not ridden across my native land so widely since I was a younger and more carefree man; I could not be sure whether the impression I was forming of a depressed and surly populace was something new or the product of my greater powers of observation.

Despite my best intentions my thoughts returned to Bess and the complex feelings I suffered on seeing her again. The loss I felt was undeniable but I was puzzled by a sense of numbness and uncertain whether she still held the attraction for me that she had before I went abroad. I smiled at my waywardness, faced with this conundrum, for there was nothing very surprising in this effect of our changed situations. She was now contentedly married to another and, when in Italy, I had met a woman who filled me with requited passion beyond anything experienced with my first chaste love. How could I have expected that my feelings towards Bess would remain as they had been before my Mantuan enchantress loved and betrayed me? And yet... and yet... was this a deep-seated change or a temporary aberration? I could not tell.

On my return to Suffolk's house I was summoned to attend a young gentleman attendant who had developed a boil in a delicate position which I was able to lance successfully with a handy stiletto I had acquired in Padua and always carried with me in my purse. Thereafter I concentrated on meeting members of the household and learning their ailments. I was bound to undertake the enquiries I had promised Lady Maud but in the meantime I wanted only to practise my skills as a physician. It pleased me to advise on the treatment of abscesses, bellyaches and shortness of breath, to inspect dressings on wounds and worrying growths protruding from necks and behind ears, to give what relief I could to the dying, encourage those who feared they were afflicted more seriously than seemed likely and speak firmly to one or two who, with no obvious justification, believed themselves subject to a myriad of maladies. This was what I had been trained to do and I felt confident using my expertise.

Leone had done well in my absence, visiting a number of apothecaries and sampling their wares on my behalf. The shelves in our chamber now displayed an impressive range of ingredients for potions, poultices and possets, obtained for minimal outlay from vendors keen to secure our regular custom. Leone recommended that we patronise the business of Master John Webber, with premises between Temple Church and Newgate, who had offered his services in a friendly manner and on favourable terms. I was content to accept my assistant's suggestion and resolved to call on Master Webber in the next few days.

The Marquis of Suffolk had gone with the King to Windsor, escaping the fetid air of London during the summer heat when there was ever-present danger of the pestilence. Andrew Cawfield was to join him after completing various commissions but he was eager to spend time in my company before he departed, urging me to strengthen the friendship we had forged in Tours. He invited me to take wine with him and, when I accepted, he regaled me with the latest gossip from the court, seeming in a merrier humour than he had displayed in France, although some instinct made me wary of his motives. He gave an account of the way members of the nobility had scrambled to offer their congratulations to Suffolk on his elevation, though some of them did so with tightened jaws and scarcely suppressed frowns. The Marquis was the man of the moment, secure in the King's approval, and his favour would be essential in the future to ambitious courtiers. I was amused by Cawfield's frankness and hoped he was ready to indulge in unguarded exchanges.

'I heard the Duke of Gloucester applauded the Marquis's achievements. That surprised me as I thought he still opposed peace with France.'

Cawfield beamed at me, flushed with the produce of Bordeaux. 'I'm sure he does but that's the beauty of a truce – a breathing space of two years, no commitment to perpetuate it. Besides, the details of the truce are unexceptionable. King Henry has to pay for the Angevin girl to come to England, even to buy her trousseau, but these are pin-pricks. There was a fear France would impose more stringent conditions. I wasn't privy to such matters, although I confess I was worried by rumours suggesting King Charles would exact onerous terms, but it seems any attempt in that direction was parried by Suffolk – so he is worthy of praise, even by Duke Humphrey.' Cawfield shook his head as if to dispel fuzziness in his thinking. 'I wouldn't take wagers on the truce lasting though.'

'England could do with the respite from fighting, France too, in my opinion. When you travel through the countryside, both sides of the Narrow Sea, you realise how much has been neglected – tumble-down buildings to be repaired, bands of armed robbers to be dispersed, law and order to be upheld more effectively.'

Cawfield guffawed. 'Pigs might fly, physician. You're an idealist. Our great men won't change their inclinations because a truce is declared. Even if we established lasting peace with France, our nobles would sharpen their swords and pole-axes and before long they'd turn them against each other.'

'That's a miserable thought.'

'Realistic, though. Unless King Henry can exert authority in a way he hasn't so far.'

'That's where Suffolk is hoping to influence him? It won't be easy. The Marquis will be seen as an upstart by the grandees from ancient families: elevated from minor nobility because he's secured the King a pretty wife.'

Cawfield sniggered. 'So you're not such an idealist after all, Doctor Somers. It's true our Marquis won't have it all his own way, especially if Duke Humphrey gains his royal nephew's ear again.'

'Is that likely?'

'Straws in the wind, straws in the wind. Suffolk is twitchy about it, I can tell you.' I must have looked surprised and Cawfield lowered his eyes, studying the contents of his goblet. 'He's been particularly irritable with me lately. I fancy I may lose my position. He doesn't trust me.'

I knew this to be true and felt uncomfortable. 'Why shouldn't he? Has he had wind of that approach you received from Henri Charpentier?'

Cawfield snorted. 'Not a murmur and I'm grateful for your silence, Doctor. That's why I can confide in you.'

Inwardly I groaned. 'You've served him for some time, haven't you?'

'Many years. But he knows I have friends with allegiance elsewhere, a cousin who has served Gloucester on his Welsh estates.'

I stared at him, showing my sudden misgivings. 'I grew up at the Duke's palace. He was my patron. Suffolk is well aware of this.'

'While it suits him he'll make use of you but your past service with Gloucester will always be there to justify his animosity when it's timely. Remember that. Don't think you can outwit him. I sense my turn is coming to feel his spite.'

'Can you seek another place?'

'Not so easy when I'm seen as Suffolk's man. It's troubling. I've a wife and three young ones at my house in the City. It worries me what will become of them if the Marquis casts me off.' I nodded silently, surprised to learn of his family, uncertain what to say. 'Be careful yourself, Doctor

Somers. Great men whose fortunes rise seldom retain much gratitude towards their humbler followers. They are consumed by self-satisfaction and arrogance.'

Much as I would wish to, I could not demur as I had already detected this tendency in Suffolk and, to hide my discomfort, I drank deeply.

Cawfield emptied his own goblet and shrugged before grasping the jug again. 'Nothing to be done about it. Have some more wine.' While he was refilling my glass he seemed to remember something and made an effort to steady his hand. 'A ship on its way from France went down in the Narrow Sea last week. No survivors and all the goods it was carrying were lost. Good job it didn't occur when Suffolk was sending messages to and fro, eh? Could have caused havoc with his negotiations.'

This idea provoked painful reminders of Rollo's death and the mystery of whether his message had been intercepted so I simply nodded. Thereafter our conversation became more desultory, but I threw in a casual enquiry about tracing a knight believed to live in Surrey, whom an acquaintance of mine had known years earlier. On my part it was a trifling gesture towards fulfilling Maud's commission but Cawfield relished my appeal to his knowledge of public affairs and said it would be best to put the question to one of the Surrey members of Parliament, whom he happened to know. He undertook to speak to this man about Sir Blakely Dunne but I had no great confidence he would remember the name when he woke from his stupor next morning.

*****

I accompanied Leone to Master Webber's shop and inspected his extensive stock of herbs and ointments with pleasure, quickly confirming the lad's perception of the apothecary's character and honesty. While his apprentices served a succession of customers at the counter, we sat with

130

a flagon of ale in his parlour and exchanged tales of useful concoctions and proven remedies, chuckling over anecdotes about obstinate patients who insisted on receiving mixtures of questionable efficacy for their conditions. I was pleased to have acquired a congenial contact in the City and I took the opportunity to draw on his acquaintance with its residents, asking if he knew of Master Edwin Drewman.

The apothecary beamed at me. 'One of the wealthiest families in London, they are, Doctor Somers, goldsmiths of Wood Street, by St. Peter's Church. The older Master Drewman is most respected.'

'There's a son of the same name?'

'Two sons. It's the second son who's entered the business with his father in the City. The elder, young Master Edwin, is managing their interests across the Narrow Sea, in Normandy. He's a merchant, supplying King Henry's garrison in Rouen with a variety of commodities and services, prospering too from all I've heard, though it's rumoured some of the services he provides might be thought a mite irregular.'

He shook his head sadly and whatever his final words meant, I did not judge it appropriate to press my interest too far. The suggestion of unspecified but irregular services offered to the bored soldiers of the English garrison implied something disturbing, reminiscent of Maud's fears. I told myself firmly that the distance separating them made it less likely Master Drewman had maintained a fatherly concern for little Eleanor but I wondered how long ago he had moved to Normandy. It would be convenient if he could be eliminated from further enquiries.

While Leone and I were walking back to the Manor of the Rose from the apothecary's premises we both caught sight of a scruffy urchin dabbling in a rain-filled gutter and in unison we came to a halt and stared. Then the ragamuffin straightened and scowled at us with unfamiliar features.

131

'I thought for a moment it was Rendell,' Leone said apologetically. 'Stupid, isn't it?'

'No, natural. I did the same. Our minds know the truth but our hearts still can't accept reality.'

Leone nodded and we continued on our way in thoughtful silence, both experiencing the persistent guilt we could not eradicate.

*****

When I saw Andrew Cawfield's luggage being loaded onto a packhorse I went down to the courtyard to bid him adieu as he departed for Windsor. To me it seemed a basic courtesy but he had enjoyed our conviviality two nights previously and embraced me with fervour, which I found unnerving.

'I'm afraid your friend has left it too late to renew his acquaintance,' he said but I was slow in grasping his meaning and must have looked blank.

'Your friend who knew Sir Blakely Dunne. I saw the member of Parliament I mentioned and asked him, as I promised.'

'That was good of you.' I tried not to sound surprised.

'Died three years past, I'm afraid. Sir Blakely, that is. He had lands near Guildford, passed to his son, John. Quite an old man he was, I'm told. Will you tell your friend?'

'Yes, certainly. I'm grateful for your help. I wish you well for your journey. Give my respects to the Marquis. May you have good fortune.'

He swung himself into the saddle and waved as he led his party out of the gatehouse. I stared after him, absorbing the news he had given me. If the Prioress's surmise was correct, that it was Eleanor's father who had taken her from Stamford, it could not have been Sir Blakely. According to Maud this left the younger Master Edwin Drewman and he was in Rouen but I feared her information might not be reliable. The search for the cherubic child was proving complicated but this complexity might offer me a means of escape from my task.

As promised I recorded what I had so far discovered and sent a sealed letter to the Prioress, to be forwarded by whatever means seemed fitting to Lady Fitzvaughan. There could be no question of me travelling to Rouen and I expressed the hope that this meant I had discharged my remit, although some perverse instinct told me it would not be so simple.

*****

It was several weeks later that Andrew Cawfield returned from Windsor and I received a message asking me to call on him, not in Suffolk's mansion but at his own house in the City. Baffled by this request, I presented myself next day at an address in Cheapside and was received at the entrance to a surprisingly opulent residence by Mistress Cawfield, a comely woman who was finely dressed in fashionable attire. Her voice had a faint accent which I could not place but it was clear she was not a native Londoner.

'Doctor Somers, it's kind of you to come. Andrew has taken unwell and is anxious to see you.'

'I didn't realise I was to make a professional visit. I haven't come equipped to administer remedies.'

'Oh, I trust he doesn't need your medicines. He's inclined to be colicky and has cramps in his stomach but I've given him an infusion of pennyroyal and lovage. It's been of benefit to him in the past.' Her expression seemed to challenge me to disagree with her treatment.

'You're wise,' I said. 'The stomach can be agitated by tiredness and Master Cawfield is always busy. A day's rest may sooth digestion.'

She acknowledged my compliment with a smile and opened the door to her husband's study where he lay on a day-bed beside his desk. She did not accompany me into the room and I was glad for I could see at a glance that this was no trivial ailment. His face was grey and he lay with his knees raised, under a coverlet, as if to ease discomfort, but what most concerned me was his agitation.

'Oh, it's you, Doctor Somers. I feared... I didn't feel ready to receive other visitors. I apologise for this weakness. Something I've suffered from before. Forgive me. I'm grateful you could come. Sit down.'

A convulsive pain gripped him and he stopped speaking as he doubled up, clutching his belly, before reaching out for the potion beside him which he sipped. I took the phial from him and sniffed it, confirming it was his wife's remedy, while he lay back, breathing more deeply.

'When did this come on?' I asked.

'Only yesterday as I was riding back from the court.'

'Did you have rich food at the King's table?'

'I suppose so. I had a troubling time there.'

'With Suffolk?'

'And others. I wanted to ask a favour of you, as a friend. I welcomed our conversation that evening we shared a flagon of wine.'

I hid my reluctance. 'How can I help?' I sat on a stool by his side.

'I'm afraid, Doctor Somers. Afraid for my family and myself. I've been threatened.'

I saw terror in his bloodshot eyes. 'Go on. Who threatened you?'

'I don't know. A man accosted me in a corridor of the castle. It was dark, only a flickering wall sconce throwing more shadow than light. He pinned me to the wall as we passed each other and held a knife to my throat. He called me foul names and threatened retribution for what he said I'd done. Then he stamped on my foot with his heavy boot and ran away, while I hopped about with pain.'

'You'd never seen him before?'

'Not to my knowledge. He wore dark clothes, no livery or badge. His hood was pulled forward but his hair looked dark, like his eyebrows. All I noticed was a scar above his left eye. He was acting for others.'

I grunted. 'What had you done to displease them?'

'I can't tell you that.'

'But there had been something? It wasn't a case of mistaken identity or a drunken idiot who didn't know what he was doing?

'He wasn't a drunken idiot.'

'Was it related to the business in Tours – the approach from Henri Charpentier?'

'How could it have been? The Seigneur de la Flèche hasn't infiltrated King Henry's court and I know you've kept my confidence.'

I was becoming impatient with Cawfield parrying my questions. 'Did you tell Suffolk?'

'I dared not.'

'You think the man serves Suffolk?'

Cawfield waved his arm about in denial. 'No, certainly not that.'

'Who then? You obviously know more than you're telling me.'

'I can't say. I shouldn't have bothered you.' He made an effort to rally himself and gave a forced laugh. 'It's foolish of me but I wanted to hear myself tell someone. I can't confide in Jane. It would frighten her and she'd worry. I consider you my friend and it's helpful to have told you. I realise it sounds ridiculous. You must be right. It could've been a mistake.'

'You implied you knew what the fellow was talking about. You took the threat seriously. What did he want you to do – or not do?'

Cawfield drew the coverlet up to his chin but it did not hide his trembling. 'Nothing. There was nothing I could do.'

'That's unusual for a threat,' I said and jumped to my feet as he squirmed in pain, twisting the coverlet in his hands. 'Now you're to set this aside from your mind. I'm speaking as your physician, d'you hear? You need complete rest while the sourness passes through. I'll send my lad round with something stronger than your wife's preparation, a purgative to clean out your bowels. We can talk again if you wish, when you're feeling better, but I think your anxiety will fade when your body is settled.'

He was already calmer and his head flopped against the pillow. 'You may be right, Doctor Somers. Send me the medicine. I'm obliged.'

He closed his eyes and I slunk out of the room to give Mistress Cawfield reassurance, explaining that Leone would deliver a potion which her husband should take without delay. Then I hurried back to Suffolk's house, perplexed by the severity of Cawfield's ailment and wondering if his intense discomfort caused him to exaggerate an innocent encounter and imagine sinister motives where there were none. Mind and body, I reflected, were strangely interlinked.

*****

Leone was waiting at the Manor of the Rose with a letter for me, which I realised had come from the Prioress in Stamford, and as soon as he had set off to the apothecary's I opened it. She begged me to send her the latest gossip from Suffolk's household and enclosed a sealed missive from Lady Fitzvaughan. With reluctance I tore this open and as I read her wild words I could hear Maud's voice becoming frantic with contrived passion. She had adopted the role of wronged mother so completely that she believed her own protestations and I had been cast as a villain who was thwarting her wishes.

What use is it to me to know one man is dead and the other in Normandy? Surely that simplifies the mission I gave you. You must go to Rouen at once, find my beloved child and restore her to the priory where she can be cared for safely. You mock me with your negligence. You fail me when I am distraught with a mother's misery. Go, go to Rouen, I entreat you. Send me no more words until you have fulfilled your task. Do not abandon me, Harry, for all we have been to each other. I implore you to do my bidding.

I flung down the letter, appalled by her recklessness, furious that she distorted the truth of our brief relationship, outraged by the unreasonable expectation that I could abandon my duties and travel to Normandy. The only encouraging point was her warning that I should not contact her until I had found Eleanor; but I had no serious hope she would leave me in peace. In my annoyance I even contemplated revealing her shameful conduct to her husband but I believed I could never behave so basely. Perhaps, despite my exasperation, I recognised something gloriously defiant in her disdain for convention, a way of defying the dishonour others had brought on her.

Later that morning I was summoned to the kitchen where the undercook had sliced the palm of his hand which was bleeding profusely and his colleagues could not staunch the flow. The wound was a nasty one which would need to be tightly bound and dressed with astringent ointment but first it must be cleaned because the knife had imported into the man's flesh a variety of gobbets from the offal he had been shredding. Early in my training, under my first, respected mentor in Duke Humphrey's household, I had learned that cleanliness might help in treating cuts, whether they were received in the lists or the wood-yard, so I took care to extract alien substances from the undercook's hand and I recommended a draught of ale to dull his pain.

That same afternoon I was called to the maid-servants' garret where it was feared a seamstress was afflicted by the sweating sickness but I was able to offer reassurance that her condition was not serious and calm the panic among her companions. I encountered Suffolk's wife, the Lady Alice, in the course of my visit to the women's quarters and was impressed by her charm and good sense as she discussed the health of her attendants. I had been presented to her after my arrival in London but we had not previously held a conversation and I found it pleasing to know that Suffolk had so capable and supportive a helpmate. By the time I retired to my pallet after sundown I was ready for sleep and had set aside annoyance at Maud's incautious letter, boosted in confidence by proving myself useful.

I was not allowed to enjoy undisturbed rest until dawn, however, for while it was still dark I was woken and called back to the kitchen where a sleepy scullion had scalded himself lifting a cauldron from the hook above the hearth after the fire had been kindled. Fortunately the boy was more shocked than badly hurt and I was soon trudging my way back to my chamber but I was surprised to see Leone in the doorway trying to quieten a distressed youth roughly his own age. When he saw me the stranger bounded forward.

'Doctor Somers. I beg you to come. My mother bade me ask for you. My name is Jack Cawfield. My father is dying.'

I blinked as I registered who he was and the unexpected news he brought but I did not hesitate in complying with his request. With Leone at my side, carrying my instruments and remedies, we hastened through the nearly deserted streets to enter the house on Cheapside as streaks of a fiery dawn lightened the sky.

*****

Mistress Cawfield's eyes were red-rimmed and it was clear she been watching by her husband's bedside all night. While she led me through the house she described how Andrew's condition had deteriorated during the early hours, although he continued to insist he was not mortally ill. Her voice was hoarse and cracking with emotion.

'He's been voiding blood and screaming with agony. He says nothing can be done. He forbade me to summon the priest but an hour ago he asked for you and I was glad,' she said. 'I didn't like to disturb you at the Marquis's house. It was Jack here who vowed I shouldn't prevent him going for you.'

'He was quite right,' I answered as I crossed the bedchamber and stared in alarm at Cawfield's stricken face. He looked at me blankly at first but then reached out his hand and motioned to his wife to leave us alone. I moved to touch his fevered brow but he shook his head and seized my fingers.

'Too late,' he said, gulping breath in his determination to speak. 'I know. I beg you, Doctor Somers, see that my family are protected. That's why I asked for you. No one else would bother to help them. I didn't know it would come so quickly.'

I lifted the cover on the pot of night-soil and shuddered. 'This is no ordinary sickness of the gut. When did you know?'

'That I'd been poisoned? I suspected it from the first.'

'Why didn't you tell me yesterday? There might have been something we could do.'

His body convulsed and for several minutes he could not reply but then he lay back calmly and shook his head. 'It's not an accident. It was meant to kill me. It's for the best. They'll be safe from harm when I'm gone.'

'Did the man who spoke to you threaten your family?'

'It wasn't a threat but a promise: a promise that I'd be punished for my failure. I was afraid they'd persecute Jane and the children. They'd brook no excuses or apologies. The fellow said I'd toyed with their goodwill. I took their money but didn't give enough in return. It wasn't my fault but I deserve retribution, Harry. I've sinned.'

Another spasm gripped him and he gave a terrifying shriek which drew Mistress Cawfield and their offspring into the room, the two little ones cowering against her skirts while the older youth stood his ground, fighting back tears. When Andrew ceased to groan he was too weak to dismiss them and I surmised that he knew the time had come when they should be by his side but I was desperate for him to tell me more.

'Who are "they", Andrew? Who does this man serve if not Suffolk?'

He mouthed the words rather than speaking them but his meaning was clear. 'Not Suffolk.'

'Who then?'

'I meant no harm... no harm... poor Rollo...'

Mistress Cawfield had spotted the change in her husband's breathing and she flung herself on her knees clutching his hand and raising it to her lips. 'Andrew, Andrew... don't trouble yourself to speak.'

He made a croaking sound in his throat and I thought the end had come but he fixed me with a horrible stare so I bent down to catch what he was trying to say. His voice was fading but I heard the word 'rogue' and then he mumbled phrases I could not distinguish until, with a final effort, he struggled to speak more clearly and I heard him say, 'Gloucester never knew'.

His head sank back and remained motionless but it took me several moments to realise he had gone and I must perform my physician's duties. I was frozen with fear and disbelief that at his extremity he had named Rollo and referred cryptically to Duke Humphrey. I tried to persuade myself the fever had turned his mind but I must have made a poor show in comforting his bereaved family. Was this to be another death, procured by murderers who could not be identified or ever brought to justice? And what crime had

Cawfield committed that merited lethal retribution? Shamefaced, I wished I had not attended this deathbed or heard that partial but tantalising confession.

Chapter 11

There must be hundreds of men on both sides of the Narrow Sea who bore a scar above the left eye but in the days following Cawfield's death I could not dismiss the coincidence from my thoughts. The whore, Madeleine, from the bawdy house in Blois, had described Rollo's probable killer in this way and the man who threatened Cawfield was similarly marked. Moreover, as he lay dying, Suffolk's secretary had named Rollo and implied he suffered guilt related to his dead colleague. I had never been happy to leave the affair of Rollo's murder unresolved, when there was evidence his assassin was impersonating the messenger he had arranged to meet; and Jeannot, the scamp at the inn in Chartres, had said the jerkin hidden in the vat of dye bore the crest of a swan. I had pushed away the fear that this swan was Humphrey of Gloucester's crest but could no longer ignore the possibility, for Cawfield's last words referred to the Duke. 'Gloucester never knew,' he had said but what my old patron never knew or how he might be involved in these inexplicable events, I could not surmise.

I was convinced Cawfield had been murdered but had little chance of proving this or tracing the occasion when he had ingested some pernicious substance. I felt sure he had known more than he was prepared to reveal to me but he linked his fate to the menacing encounter at Windsor and suggested his removal would safeguard his family from harm. There were ominous implications to this incomplete narrative but I could see no way of pursuing them. It was a relief that Mistress Cawfield had no suspicion of foul play, accepting that her husband had succumbed to the intestinal frailty he habitually experienced and I concluded there was no purpose in aggravating her distress. Instead, I turned to discharging my own neglected responsibilities.

Long overdue, I paid a visit to the manor of Danson where my mother lodged. I went alone, crossing London

Bridge and following the highway which avoided the river at Greenwich and skirted Duke Humphrey's Palace of Pleasance. From the high ground of my route I glimpsed the trees of Gloucester's enclosed parkland spreading down the slope to the riverside and the tops of towers, beside the Thames, catching the sunlight; but I did not linger to study the view. I felt uncomfortable, like an interloper who had no business to be there or, if I was honest, like a man who had abandoned the patron to whom he owed gratitude, even though I had little choice in the matter. I hurried my horse onwards, over the hill and down the sweeping incline to Sir Hugh de Grey's modest estate.

The reunion with my mother was joyful and, to please her, I described various adventures I had during my exile. Inevitably she looked older and frail but she assured me her eyesight still enabled her to work as a seamstress, making small garments for the tribe of young de Greys. It was clear she was a valued member of the household and I rejoiced that she had found a safe haven with the knight and his lady who had reason to be grateful to me for past services. She wanted nothing more than to listen to my tales, to embrace me between each one and to thank God for my return.

'You won't become caught up in great men's doings again?' she asked as she smoothed my brow, brushing untidy hair under my cap.

'I shall be very wary,' I said, without adding that the choice was not entirely mine.

She peered at me from beneath her hooded eyelids and fluttered her hands awkwardly. 'Will you look to marry now you're back with your own folk? You're of an age to think of marrying. I should dearly love to cradle a grandchild before it's my time to go.'

Her expression was wistful and I hated to disappoint her although, with Bess lost to me, marriage was far from my thoughts. 'I'm still new to Suffolk's service,' I said. 'But when I feel settled I'll see what might be done.'

She sighed but did not press me further. 'Tell me again about those cities in Italy where you lived and what you did there.'

So I embarked on another description of buildings and events, carefully omitting all mention of frequent dangers, untrustworthy companions and unsuitable amours. She was content, as were Sir Hugh and Lady Blanche who had never travelled far from their demesne and seemed to regard me as a man with infinite knowledge of the world. It was a pleasant respite from all the burdens which oppressed me, the more so that no one present had known Rendell well enough to enquire as to his welfare.

My grief at Rendell's loss had been reinforced by learning of his sister's anguish when her husband told her the news after she had been delivered of their second son. Thomas continued to meet me occasionally when he was working at the Duke's City residence but he said that Grizel could not bring herself to see me while the pain of her brother's death was so raw. It was obvious she blamed me for failing to protect the lad she thought of as a vulnerable child, even though she knew well enough how wayward and self-sufficient he had always been. At our last meeting Thomas had assured me she was relenting and he suggested she might accompany him to Baynard's Castle on his next visit but I dreaded having to face her recriminations.

This only added to my sense of guilt and, as I returned from Danson, looking down on Duke Humphrey's palace where my friends lived with their growing family, my wretchedness increased to such a pitch that I set my horse into a furious gallop, scarcely caring if I lost control of the animal and was thrown to my mortal injury. When I thundered to the bottom of the hill and remained safely seated on my saddle I concluded I was not to escape so easily from whatever obligations were to be laid on me by

Heaven or Hell's design but I did not find that conclusion in the least encouraging.

*****

Two weeks after Andrew Cawfield's burial, and in accordance with my promise to the dying man, I visited his widow to assure myself that she and her family were not facing difficult circumstances. Mistress Jane received me pleasantly, expressing appreciation for my concern but assuring me she was adequately provided for, due to her late husband's foresight.

She looked down shyly, folding her hands in her lap. 'Andrew was always prudent in his dealings. He cannot have known how cruel a fate awaited him but his affairs were in order and our futures secured, mine and the children's.'

'That's good. You have three children? Jack is your eldest?' I had seen them at their father's deathbed.

She smiled. 'I was a one year's bride when Jack was born and now he's nearly a man. There's nine years between him and the little ones. Suffolk spent long years in France while there was still fighting and Andrew was with him. I seldom saw my husband during that time so I have experience of managing alone.'

'That was hard for you.' Her manner was serene and she was dry-eyed but I felt ill at ease in my unfamiliar role. 'You're not from London, Mistress?'

'My accent betrays my birth in the north of England. I continued to live there while Andrew was across the Narrow Sea and only moved to the City when he was able to return – and we added to our family.'

She must have been some ten years older than I was but her complexion was clear, her modest self-assurance disarming and I warmed to her charm. 'Do you plan to remain in London now?'

She looked surprised by my question and pursed her lips. 'It's too early for me to be sure. I may return to my birthplace but I must ensure Jack's future first. That is my pressing task, the one duty which will be more difficult without Andrew's influence and contacts. It confounds me.'

'Does your son have a particular ambition? Had you discussed it with Master Cawfield?'

She was frowning but she nodded diffidently. 'He aspires to enter the law. Andrew was strongly supportive. He wished Jack to attend the university but I don't know how that can be arranged or whether it can be afforded.'

I felt a surge of relief for here was something I might be able facilitate. 'Perhaps I can help. Would you allow me to consult the Marquis to see what is possible? Master Cawfield served him for many years and his family are entitled to Suffolk's patronage.'

The tiniest twitch of her lip disconcerted me but it was quickly gone. 'That's kind of you, Doctor Somers. I'd be obliged. If Jack were able to go to Oxford next autumn it would be most convenient.'

'I'll do my best.' I had stayed long enough to satisfy the requirements of propriety but I was anxious to reassure myself on one point. 'I trust you've not been troubled by any unwelcome contacts since Master Cawfield's death?' I could not bring myself to mention a man with a scar.

She caught her breath but then laughed, apparently misunderstanding my question. 'Please don't concern yourself. I am too new a widow to attract unwanted advances. I've not been troubled.' Then, after she summoned her maid to show me out, she smiled delightfully and bade me call again if I wished.

*****

It was late autumn before Suffolk returned to his house in the City. I had heard reports of the powerful position he now held at the King's right hand and was not surprised to detect greater arrogance in his bearing and complacency in his voice, yet he listened solemnly to my account of Cawfield's death, expressing regrets which seemed sincere. Knowing that he distrusted the man, I thought this generous and kept to myself the misgivings I had about his secretary's demise. I was particularly gratified when the Marquis enquired as to the circumstances of the bereaved family and willingly answered his questions.

'I don't think they're in hardship. Their house is elegantly furnished with silverware on the dresser and fine tapestries on the walls. Mistress Cawfield has expressed no concerns about their maintenance. She seems a capable woman, well able to take care of her children.'

'Good. Cawfield or his wife must have had money of their own. I doubt he'd have purchased silverware and tapestries from what he gleaned in my service. Still, I'm relieved his family are provided for but I'd be happy to make some gesture towards their comfort.'

It was unexpected but I took my opportunity. 'My lord, there is perhaps one thing you could do. Cawfield's eldest son, Jack, is a bright lad who wishes to go into the law. If you were prepared to sponsor him to attend the university at Oxford it would be well appreciated and, if you did, I could release my assistant, the Italian youth, Leone, to accompany him. It was in this way I undertook my first studies, as companion to the Duke of Gloucester's natural son when he attended Oxford. Many poor students perform such roles, assisting their more fortunate colleagues with their studies and taking advantage of the education they receive alongside their masters.'

Suffolk slapped his knee and burst into laughter. 'You cunning schemer, Harry Somers! Is the Italian's English good enough to profit from the university?'

'It improves daily, my lord, and within the year he will be fluent. His Latin is a good deal better than mine.'

'Then they shall go.' I bowed but Suffolk waved me to a stool. 'You are well thought of in this household and I'm pleased with what I have heard of your services from Lady Alice. You are content here?'

I was surprised by his enquiry and assured him I found my work satisfying but I sensed this was not his real interest, which his next question confirmed.

'Are you still in touch with your friends in Gloucester's household?'

I chose my words carefully. 'There've been many changes at Greenwich. There's only one old colleague I still see, the master carpenter, not a high office-holder.'

'Does he say anything of the Duke's disposition?'

'Why, no. He wouldn't have direct contact with Gloucester very often.' I held Suffolk's gaze, willing him to explain his interest more fully.

'If you could discover any gossip at the Pleasance, or his city house, regarding Humphrey's behaviour, I'd welcome knowing it.'

'Can you be more explicit, my lord?'

Suffolk exhaled. 'When we returned from France he seemed well-disposed, spoke cordially of the truce, but lately he's started to demur, querying details he'd accepted before. I'd like to understand what his objective is.'

'I don't think I'll be able to help you with that. He's hardly likely to confide in a craftsman, such as my friend.'

'Even so, Harry, you are astute and could pick up the inferences if anything was mentioned. Just keep your eyes and ears open, will you?'

Intrigued but discomfited, I had no option but to agree. I was unwilling to spy into my old patron's affairs but as I was in no position to do so the issue did not really arise. Nevertheless, I wished I knew what Suffolk's motives were in giving me this task.

It was only a day or two later when I received a letter from Stamford. I quailed as I slit open the sealed packet,

148

fearing that it enclosed another excited effusion from Lady Maud, but it did not. The communication was from the Prioress of St. Michael's, on her own account, and it made no reference to the child Eleanor or her troubled mother. It referred to information which had reached the Prioress, through the Abbot of Peterborough, concerning matters of state and there was an uncomfortable resonance with the request Suffolk had made to me. She had learned that Gloucester seemed to have second thoughts about the truce with France and was said to be raising pointed questions in the King's Council. She asked if I could throw any light on these rumours or whether I might make unobtrusive enquiries to establish their truth. I was impressed by the channels of communication available to the heads of remote religious houses while the fact that the Prioress thought the Duke's activities worth pursuing reinforced my own curiosity.

*****

The puzzle was not one I could share with Leone as he knew little of Gloucester and, in any case, I surmised he had something else on his mind. He was delighted at the prospect of accompanying Jack Cawfield to Oxford next Michaelmas and thanked me repeatedly for securing him this opportunity but at times he had that dreamy look which I had first noticed in the draper's house in Tours. Then one day while I sat with him at table in the great hall I saw him casting rapturous looks towards the trestle where the maid-servants of Suffolk's household were seated and I understood his preoccupation when a fair-complexioned maiden returned bashful glances. I was pleased to note the modest charm with which she received his attentions, neither simpering nor superficial, and it was clear his suit was prospering. There was no obvious rival for the girl's favours and I wished them well but I hoped they would not

149

commit themselves to each other irretrievably, for I wanted Leone to study and develop his potential as a physician. Yet, I reflected morosely, who was I to pontificate on such a matter, even to myself? I had scarcely made a success of my personal life.

Although I was treated with respect and cordiality within his household I made no close friends among Suffolk's followers and, observing the carefree behaviour of those not much younger than I was, I became conscious of my solitary status. My mother's question rang in my ears and I remembered the sadness in her voice when she spoke of her longing for a grandchild. I wondered if I should set the past aside and seek a congenial wife to give me companionship and, with God's blessing, bring me a family. I concluded quickly that I knew no one suitable but then I pictured Andrew Cawfield's widow sitting tranquilly by the fireside when I had last visited her and, despite our difference in age, the idea of finding her beside my own hearth did not seem unacceptable. Given her bereavement it would be seemly to let some months elapse before beginning a courtship and I found this reassuring, for I had erred in the past through impetuous behaviour while suffering from low spirits, but it cheered me to think my domestic life might be pleasingly settled in due course. In the meantime I would continue to call on Mistress Jane and it might be that our relationship would blossom of its own accord. I was amused that the Prioress of St. Michael's had recommended I take a widow as my bride and this seemed to confirm the boundless wisdom that holy woman possessed.

From his time as an apothecary's apprentice, Leone had acquired a wide knowledge of remedies and I sent him regularly to Master Webber's pharmacy to collect the potions and liniments I required. On a dank and gloomy November day he returned from such an expedition in a state of unusual excitement and I could see him waiting with jittery impatience on the threshold of my room while I

150

dressed a wound on a laundry-woman's arm. As soon as she had gone he rushed in to tell me his news, speaking Italian as he tended to do when we were alone.

'Guess who I met near Temple Church?'

Leone knew few people in England outside Suffolk's household so I was baffled. 'Tell me.'

'Bartholomew. You remember Bartholomew. Gaston de la Tour had him dismissed from attendance on Lord Fitzvaughan in France.'

'Certainly, I remember. Is he well?'

'Never better, he says. He has a position in some great house in the City.' I began to express pleasure at this information but Leone had more to say. 'It's that place your friend, Master Chope, visits when he's in the City. Baynard's Castle, isn't it?'

'Bartholomew has joined the Duke of Gloucester's household?'

'Yes, that's right. He assists the Duke's man of business, Master Gilbert Iffley. He asked how you were but he wasn't very complimentary about Lord Fitzvaughan and Gaston.'

'I can imagine. Are you going to see him again?'

'He suggested it. Said he'd help me improve my English, like he did before. But I wasn't sure you'd approve. You said you needed to avoid contact with Gloucester.'

'True, it seemed tactful, but things have changed and there's no reason to bar you from Baynard's Castle.'

I tried not to sound smug but Leone detected some nuance in my tone and raised his eyebrows. 'What?'

'Suffolk's keen to find out what Gloucester's up to. He's asked me to let him know any gossip I come across but I wouldn't want you to get Bartholomew into trouble.'

Leone tapped his nose in a manner reminiscent of Rendell. 'Don't worry. I know how to be discreet. It's about time we were dabbling in a fresh intrigue. Need to keep our hands in, don't we? Will you go to Baynard's Castle too, when your friend's there?'

I had not planned it but as he spoke I made up my mind to fulfil my outstanding obligation. 'I'm thinking of going to Gloucester's palace at Greenwich. We'll compare notes. Between us we ought to be able to find out whether there's anything to tell Suffolk.'

Silently I added to myself the proviso that I would be the judge whether anything we discovered was inappropriate to share with the ambitious Marquis. The ambivalence I felt in serving my master was matched only by the ambivalence with which I viewed my former patron.

*****

I left my horse at Temple Steps and took a wherry to Gloucester's Palace of Pleasance at Greenwich, asking the boatman to wait for me as I did not expect my visit to take long. My mind was full of dread but it was focused on meeting Grizel and suffering her reproaches for my failure to protect her brother. I was not prepared for the passions which overwhelmed me as I stepped ashore onto the cobbled jetty, remembering the way I had been bundled down it in chains after my arrest, on my way to incarceration in the Tower three years previously. There were tears in my eyes as I mounted the slipway and I wished with all my heart that I had not come. In front of me were ranges of buildings, all built during my boyhood, and the sight awoke so many memories that a lump came to my throat and I trembled. Across the courtyard were the ornate ducal chambers and to one side the wing housing the servants' quarters, where my mother had lived, while facing it were the rooms used by the Duke's group of resident and visiting scholars, which included those where I had first observed the work of a physician. I owed so much to this place and its lord who had sponsored my education. Gratitude for all I learned there battled with the misery of reliving my ignominious removal from its walls when the Duke had been unable to help me and, despite my bold words to Leone, I was relieved to hear that Gloucester was not in residence at the time of my visit.

Thomas must have been looking out for me and he met me at a doorway, pulling me inside and propelling me into their room before I could collect myself. Standing in front of me just beyond the threshold was his wife, pale but with a faint smile, a lovely young woman, no longer the roguish hoyden I recalled. A toddler clutched her sleeve and she held a bundle of shawls enveloping a tiny baby, whom I hailed with due solemnity. At the sight of the gross mark on my cheek the older child, who was my namesake, buried his face in Grizel's skirts, whimpering, but Thomas lifted and consoled him. I felt the only proper greeting for the children's handsome mother was to bow extravagantly and kiss her hand.

'Grizel,' I spluttered but the words I had prepared would not come.

'Cor,' she giggled. 'Courtly manners! Is that what they taught you in Italy?'

I swallowed, grateful that she had lightened the tension of the occasion. 'I'm so glad you're willing to receive me.'

'I didn't want to at first,' she said, 'though I knew deep down you'd done nothing wrong. Rendell would always go his own way. Tom didn't tell me for a while, he's too much of a coward, but I guessed something was wrong, soon as he came back from meeting you in the City. I still don't know the details of what happened. I didn't want to probe and upset myself but I'm ready now.'

Gently as I could I described the circumstances, keeping one eye on Thomas in case he signalled I should stop, but Grizel listened quietly until I had finished. Then she fixed me with a mischievous look and gave a squeal.

153

'Rendell killed a man! You never told me that, Thomas Chope. Lord defend us!'

'He'd already saved my life once before.'

She grinned as cheekily as her brother. 'Then, I'm proud of him and I won't mourn any longer. It won't do no good and I've got this little heap of trouble to think about as well as Hal here.' She nuzzled the rosy face of her newest infant. 'We've called him Dickon.'

I must have looked surprised because I'd expected the child to be named in honour of Rendell, not the murdered archer to whom she had once been betrothed.

She caught my expression. 'There's no one going to match Rendell,' she said. 'To me he's still around, like he always was, causing chaos and achieving great things. Can't lumber one of my boys with having him as a namesake.'

I lowered my head in deference to her instinctive understanding.

*****

I stayed longer with the Chope family than I had expected and before I left Grizel insisted I cradled the baby in my arms. I did so awkwardly for, although I had attended sick children often enough, I was unaccustomed to cosset a healthy scrap with energetic limbs and a raucous cry. I handed him back with an apologetic grin but I was astonished by the surge of emotion I felt at handling this morsel of new life and it came to me that, if this was a modest reflection of what a new parent – or grandparent – experienced, I could better appreciate both my mother's yearning and Lady Maud's distress. I was still pondering this when I said goodbye to my friends and summoned the boatman to untie his craft. At his request, I agreed to share my craft with another man, returning from the palace to the City, who wished to journey beyond my landing stage near the great bridge.

My fellow passenger proved an amiable companion and for most of the journey we engaged in entertaining conversation as we progressed slowly against the turning tide. He spoke knowledgeably of art and scholarship, expressing delight when I described places I had seen in the Italian states, and we compared impressions of towns in France which we had both visited. It was a cold, blustery evening and we sat, side by side, huddled in our capes, with hoods pulled forward, but our amicable exchanges brought warmth to our spirits if not into our bones. At length I risked a more personal enquiry.

'Do you have business at Duke Humphrey's palace frequently?'

'Oh, indeed. I'm in the Duke's service and have been for the past two years.' There was the hint of amusement in his deep voice. 'I'm returning to Baynard's Castle where I lodge. The Duke's due back from court tomorrow. I have much to report to him. And you?'

I was hoping to enquire about the Duke's interests but needed to answer that polite yet tiresome enquiry. 'I've been visiting old friends who serve in his household.'

'You used to serve him as well?'

His face was completely shadowed and I had no idea if this was a casual surmise or an informed assumption. I did not recognise his voice with its melodious accent. 'Some years ago, I did. I've been abroad since then. I'm a physician.'

I hoped he would reciprocate by describing his own role in Gloucester's household but he did not. 'You serve another great lord now?'

It would be risky to attempt to hoodwink him, I thought, and we were now approaching the jetty where I was to be put ashore. 'The Marquis of Suffolk,' I said as I rose to grip the hanging rope which would steady me when I stepped across the gap to the slimy ramp.

'Ah!' He grunted. 'I thought so. You are Doctor Harry Somers, aren't you? I've heard of your prowess in uncovering hidden truths. I'm delighted to have met you.'

'And you, sir, are ...?' A linkman was hurrying down the slope with a flaming torch to escort me.

'My name is Gilbert Iffley. I hope we meet again.'

He lifted his head as the boat moved away from the quay, and light from the torch shone on his features, causing me to catch my breath. There was no mistaking the pronounced scar running parallel to his left eyebrow.

*****

Leone chided me with not establishing Gilbert Iffley's identity earlier in our journey so I could have questioned him more assiduously but he treated the man's scar as a joke. 'I've heard a lot about Master Iffley from Bartholomew and he doesn't sound like a back-street murderer.'

'He's clearly an educated man but that doesn't guarantee a peaceful temperament.'

'Yet he knew who you were? Was that sinister?'

'He'd heard of me somehow. It was surprising.'

'Perhaps Gloucester had mentioned you and was aware you were now with Suffolk.'

That was a sobering thought. 'I hoped I was humbly invisible.'

'Maybe you underestimate your reputation.' Leone must have seen I was uncomfortable with this conversation and he became serious. 'Bartholomew told me Gloucester is awaiting a letter from France, answering some enquiry he'd made, but there's been a disturbance down in Kent and a royal messenger was set on and killed, his packages ransacked, so they don't know whether the Duke's correspondent has never replied or if the reply was destroyed in the riot.'

'Now that is interesting. I wonder what Gloucester is trying to find out and who he wrote to.'

'Bartholomew doesn't know. I pushed him as far as I could. Will you tell Suffolk?'

'I don't think I will. It's probably quite innocent. Gloucester may simply be negotiating to buy some glorious manuscript. He was always doing that when I served him and cultured men like René of Anjou own some beautifully illuminated books.'

Later that evening, after leaving Leone lingering in the great hall intent on snatching a few words with the maidservant he admired, I penned a letter to St Michael's convent in Stamford. I did not want to agitate Suffolk with unjustified suspicions about Gloucester's activities but I saw no harm in sharing my information with the Prioress. Indeed I felt pleasure in communicating with that shrewd woman, whose judgement I would be inclined to trust beyond that of many worldly men, and I told her of my concerns regarding Andrew Cawfield's death as well as my encounter with Gilbert Iffley. It was a relief to be able to write to her without the need to mention Lady Maud. After several weeks of silence from Norfolk, I had come to believe that I was free from that lady's harassment and involvement in her personal affairs – I should have realised this was naïve optimism.

*****

The Marquis and Lady Alice were away at court over the Feast of the Nativity, but a number of guests were accommodated at the Manor of the Rose during their absence and one of these was Lord Walter Fitzvaughan, whom I had not seen since the summer. He arrived, lavishly attended, accompanied by Gaston de la Tour but not, to my relief, by his wife, and I was pleased to spend some time in his company when he invited me to sup with him.

I steeled myself to enquire, in common courtesy, after Lady Maud's health and was immediately embarrassed by her husband's frankness.

'We've suffered a misfortune, Harry. She has miscarried of our first child. She sent me word two months ago but I've been unable to visit her because I've been travelling on his Grace, the King's business.'

I murmured condolences, cursing Maud for deceiving her husband with her fictitious pregnancy and placing me in the unpalatable position of accessory to deception. 'Will you be able to join her soon?' I asked blandly.

'Not before Midsummer but she'll have regained her strength by then. At any rate, it heartens me that my seed has ripened in her maw. Next time I pray we shall be blessed with a live child.'

'Miscarriage of a first child in not uncommon,' I said, trying to sound judicious and not false. 'But are you to journey elsewhere in the meantime?'

He laughed. 'Of course, Harry, and that's why I've come to see you. The Marquis asked me to prepare you, for you're to journey too, in a few weeks. Didn't you expect it?' I must have looked blank because he laughed again. 'We're both to attend the Marquis and his wife as they travel to France to bring back King Henry's bride. The Marquis is to stand proxy at the marriage in Nancy and he will then conduct our future Queen to Paris and on to Normandy where she'll pass into the care of her royal husband's followers. We shall be a party of a dozen nobles, seventeen knights, sixty-five squires, nigh on two hundred grooms and manservants, and all the maids and attendants the Marchioness and her ladies require.'

'I am to be part of this enormous entourage?'

'But you won't get to the ducal palace in Nancy, I fear, or see the glittering festivities at the time of the wedding. The Marquis would like you to be responsible, as physician, for the escort left to prepare the ceremonial entrance into Normandy. He will bring our new Queen to spend Easter in her husband's duchy before they cross the Narrow Sea. There will be processions, feasts, entertainments, deer hunts, endless church services and these have all to be organised before the Marquis and his train arrive. You will have soldiers, musicians, tumblers, versifiers and a multitude of hangers-on to care for. You're privileged to be charged with their welfare.'

Confronted by this undoubted honour, I had only one question and I could guess the answer. 'Where will we be quartered in Normandy?'

'Why, in Rouen of course,' said Lady Maud Fitzvaughan's husband, oblivious of any problematic implications.

There was to be no escape from my foolish, self-imposed commitment but, I reflected, even if I did not relish the enquiries I must make in Rouen, it would be satisfying to solve one conundrum. My failure to identify Rollo's murderer gnawed at my self-esteem but I saw little chance of returning to that mystery, whereas pursuing Maud's unpleasant quest might achieve a result. I smiled to myself, moreover, when I concluded that, on my return from Normandy, a decent interval would have passed since Jane Cawfield's unfortunate husband had been laid to rest and, if fortune favoured me, I could begin to shape a more cheerful future for her and for me.

Part III: Normandy and England 1445-1446
<u>Chapter 12</u>

By the time I arrived in Rouen the proxy marriage had already taken place in Nancy and reports were brought to us of the week-long celebrations there. The marguerite had been adopted as the symbol of the festivities, in honour of the bride, and at the wedding Princess Margaret wore a gown of white satin, embroidered with her nominal flower in gold and silver thread. She had been conducted to the altar by both her father and the King of France, and later these two sponsors met each other at the jousting, which followed the ceremony, where her father triumphed over his royal brother-in-law. I could imagine the satisfaction that gave René of Anjou who aspired so desperately to be a King. Margaret was shortly to be escorted to Paris before making the journey onward into Normandy and the party I accompanied had ten days to prepare her welcome in Rouen.

The activity was frenzied throughout the city and it reminded me of the days before the betrothal a year previously in Tours. This time, however, the artists decorating floral arches, the musicians practising their serenades and the singers warbling their airs were King Henry's subjects, either newly come from England or born and bred in his duchy of Normandy. All were determined to show the magnificence and skill which the new Queen could expect to find in the kingdom to which she was travelling. Nevertheless, there was good reason to have a physician at hand during the preparations, for injuries were not uncommon when carpenters hammered thumbs in their haste to finish elaborate structures and tumblers tumbled too far from platforms and saddles. I had little time to pursue private commissions.

Despite the constraints upon me and my own reluctance, I knew I could not shirk the task I had undertaken and there was no difficulty in learning where to present myself. Along the road leading from the castle to the river, near to a great belfry, was an impressive building which flaunted the golden ball denoting a goldsmith's premises and it was easy to establish that this was the residence of Master Edwin Drewman of London. Accordingly, two days before Suffolk's retinue was expected to arrive, I made my way there and begged half an hour of the merchant's time. When my request was granted straightaway I was aware my purpose had been wrongly interpreted but I was not about to reject an opportunity gained by misunderstanding.

Master Drewman was a well-built man probably in his mid-thirties, exuding an air of smug prosperity. He greeted me obsequiously and poured wine into a finely-chased silver goblet. 'Doctor Somers, you're welcome. I obtained a list of the Marquis's personal representatives who are come to Rouen and recognise your name. I hope I may serve you.'

'I fear I'm not come to make expensive purchases from you although I may take a small trinket, if I can afford one, to take home to my mother.'

He hid any disappointment and smiled. 'Your colleagues have brought me good business. The most ornate decorations in the city are faced with gold leaf and wire from my stock. May I help you in some other way?'

I sipped my wine to strengthen my resolve. 'Master Drewman, my mission is delicate and I apologise if it startles you. I have a confidential enquiry to make on behalf of a noblewoman you once knew.'

His fingers gripping the stem of his goblet blanched. 'I don't understand.'

'I assure you there's no wish to cause you embarrassment but I'm told that years ago you made the acquaintance of Lady Maud Warrenne, as she then was.'

161

To his credit he did not deny it. 'I recall a young girl of that name. I visited her guardian's house on occasion. I know nothing of her fortunes since that time.'

'They have flourished. She is now wed to Lord Walter Fitzvaughan.'

Alarm filled his eyes. 'She's not with Marquis's party, coming to Rouen?'

'No, she's at home on her husband's estate. But my enquiry is made on her behalf. I must emphasise the confidentiality. I hope I may rely on your discretion.'

He frowned and did not answer but I could hardly withdraw from our conversation at this stage. 'Some years ago Lady Maud was delivered of a daughter.'

'Before her marriage?'

'Exactly. May I ask when you met her?'

'What are you suggesting?' His hand was trembling and he set down his goblet.

'I appreciate it may be impossible to establish who fathered the child but she believes that, unknown to her, a man has accepted responsibility and, until recently, made provision for the girl's upkeep.'

Master Drewman breathed out noisily. 'You are seeking to find this man? I can give you my oath it was not me.'

'A year ago the child was abducted from the convent where she had been cared for and the unsolicited payments ceased. The Prioress suggests this circumstance points to her father's involvement.'

'Doctor Somers, I know nothing of this and I'm surprised you've come to me. I admit I was a dissolute fellow before my marriage and when I was introduced to Maud and invited to make free with her, I didn't hesitate to take advantage of her charms. Young though she was she knew how to please a man and seemed content that I should enjoy her favours but it isn't possible I got her with child.'

I raised my eyebrows at this statement and he led me to a window overlooking an inner courtyard of the house. Two small children were playing with a top, watched by their nurse and a pretty woman in expensive clothes. 'You see my wife and our sons. I have a fruitful marriage and am blessed in my heirs. I have made provision for no other offspring and recoil from the thought of having one foisted on me.'

His eyes had filled with tears and I regretted causing him distress. 'I should like to accept your word,' I said, 'but, if you lay with her, how can be sure you didn't impregnate Lady Maud?'

He turned away and his voice dropped to a whisper. 'Doctor Somers, I'm ashamed but the pleasure of bedding Maud lay in the fact she was unable to conceive.'

'Who told you this?'

'The chatelaine of the house, who had charge of her. The woman said Maud had lost a child and become barren.'

I watched him carefully. 'When was this?'

'About six or seven years ago.'

'You're sure of the timing? Surely you'd been visiting her for longer than that?'

'No, certainly I hadn't. For years as a young man in London I had a paramour and was content with her but my father threatened to disown me if I didn't give her up and marry according to his wishes. He paid my doxy generously to leave the City and arranged my betrothal to the woman who is my wife. I submitted to his rule but was irked and during the period of my betrothal I was introduced to Lady Maud. I visited her for only a few months.'

I was appalled by his casual manner but told myself fiercely it was not for me to judge him 'Who took you to her?'

'Her guardian. He found it amusing to encourage my disobedience. My father never knew.'

'Were you aware of others who visited Maud?'

163

'There was an older man who shared her favours.' He paused, searching for a name and I did not prompt him. 'Sir Blakely Dunne,' he exclaimed.

'Could he have been the father of her child?'

'I don't believe so. I understood his visits started about the same time as mine.'

'Did you learn the names of those she entertained before she lost the child?'

Edwin Drewman shook his head. 'I neither heard nor enquired.' He swallowed some wine and stood, pacing around the room until he turned to confront me. 'Maud must know the truth. If she named me she told a vicious lie. Why should she do that?'

Why indeed, I thought angrily and slammed down my goblet on the table. 'I'm not sure what she hoped to achieve but I fancy she gave your name on the instant in order to mislead me. I'm grateful for your honesty. You may rest assured I shall keep what you've told me from all but Lady Maud. Forgive my intrusion.' I bowed and turned to leave him.

'Wait.' He recovered his business-like demeanour and drew open a drawer in a cabinet, smiling slyly. 'You mentioned a trinket for your mother. Pray choose one of these pieces. I shall be glad to make you a gift of it.'

'They're beautiful,' I said, 'but far beyond the resources of my purse and it wouldn't be fitting to accept a gift which might be construed as a bribe. Pardon my bluntness.'

He scowled. 'That's uncalled for. You still entertain suspicions of me.'

'I've heard you offer irregular services, as well as honest trade. I can't dismiss the thought that they might involve girls as young as Maud was – as her daughter is.'

'Dear God!' He gripped my shoulders, staring into my eyes. 'That's abominable! Never would I profit from such vileness. The services you've heard of are purely financial, albeit they result in some losses to the tax gatherers of both King Henry's treasury and those of the French King. Where sales and purchases are registered is sometimes a matter of discretion, you see.'

It had the ring of truth and I grinned. 'The secrets of your commercial transactions are safe with me unless I learn that you've told me lies about Lady Maud's daughter. If you recall anything else I might find interesting, you'd be wise to contact me. Good day.'

Master Drewman's protestations continued to ring in my ears as I left the building, while my gullet filled with bile in disgust at the way Maud had tricked me. She had convinced herself that Eleanor had been carried off from St. Michael's Convent for some vile purpose and when she realised the evidence pointed to Eleanor's father as the person responsible she had panicked. She must have known all along who had fathered her child but she did not wish me to discover the truth.

*****

Two days later I was still furious about the wild goose chase on which I had been sent, for the more I thought about my interview with the goldsmith, the more credible his tale became, so I was grateful for any diversion. Consequently I took up a position, several ranks back on the quayside, to watch the ceremonial arrival as the royal barge glided to its mooring alongside the jetty, after its journey down the Seine from Mantes. I glimpsed the little bride as she was helped ashore and noted she looked weary but, while I listened to a succession of loyal welcoming addresses from civic dignitaries, I could well understand her ennui. For the past fortnight, travelling across France and into Normandy, she had been greeted in a score of towns and in each one she had been bound to endure similar tedious speeches and to respond with grace and freshness. I did not

165

envy her. She was conducted to a magnificent litter, draped with silks and cloth of gold, while the procession formed to bring her through the city. Six hundred archers and a vast assembly of nobles and knights comprised her escort, with Suffolk as King Henry's personal representative riding directly in front of her, and the Duke of York, Governor-General in Normandy, by her side. The Marchioness of Suffolk and other ladies of the English court were also mounted, riding behind the litter, and I was flattered that the Marquis's wife acknowledged me as she passed.

I had never seen Richard of York before but knew of him as the King's distant relative and a friend of my old patron, Humphrey of Gloucester. I noted his imposing figure, his proud deportment and the way he fostered the adulation of the crowd by his gestures and smiles. As he rode past me he leant forward to say a word to his new Queen and I judged from his expression that his tone was probably patronising. That, I thought, would not endear him to the lively young woman but my reflection was shattered by a glimpse, among the swarm of attendants riding in his train, of a man in livery who appeared to be bruised above his left eye and, although I could not be certain I had seen aright, this trivial occurrence diverted my attention.

The crowd began to disperse as the column moved off along the road to the castle but I did not hurry to follow them. I came forward to the edge of the quay to look more closely at the barge, comparing it in my mind with those which glided up and down the Thames and came frequently to the Duke of Gloucester's palace at Greenwich. Attendants were still disembarking from an accompanying vessel and horses were led forward so that a number of ladies could join the back of the procession. From their dress I guessed they were the new Queen's French attendants who would accompany her to her kingdom across the Narrow Sea and I bowed as they passed but, while my head was lowered, I was surprised to hear an exclamation.

166

'Doctor Somers! We did not know you were in Normandy. You should have sent to tell us.'

Her fluttering veil covered most of her face but I recognised the stern voice. I had not expected to see her in the royal party as I thought she had left her position at court and returned to her husband's house. 'Madame, la comtesse,' I said cautiously, uncertain why she was reprimanding me. I wanted to say more but she was already mounted and moving away.

'I pray you call upon us at the castle without delay.'

Her words, spoken with disdain, over her shoulder, caused me to grin foolishly until a groom elbowed me out of the way as he brought forward another horse. 'Mind your back there, physician,' he called and, in my confusion, I gave him an unnecessary gratuity.

*****

I went back to my lodgings at the castle and later that day, while members of the royal party were resting after their journey, I was startled when the Marquis's page announced there was a tradesman to see me. I could only imagine he must be an apothecary or purveyor of remedies with whom I had done business and followed the boy to a small room adjoining the gatehouse. I recognised the prosperous figure of Master Drewman immediately and felt a flicker of amusement to think how insulted he would be by the demeaning designation the page had used. He looked strained but greeted me with thanks for my speedy appearance.

'I hadn't expected to see you here,' I said.

He shrugged. 'I've been turning things over in my mind, delving into my memory, and I may have remembered something useful for you.' His hands were clenched tightly together as if to stop them quivering. 'Before I ceased the contacts we were talking about the other day I did hear some gossip about the lady's past associates.'

I could not prevent a smile. 'Go on. You remember names?'

He spoke rapidly, eager to share what he had to say. 'Not exactly. There was a nobleman, Lord something. I have the name Egerton on the tip of my tongue but that's not right. It was something similar. He came from the north of England. A servant spoke of him as one who would have married the lady. That's all.'

'It's very helpful, Master Drewman. I'm grateful.'

'You will keep my confidence secure – about what I told you?'

'About your commercial activities? I've no reason to involve myself with them.'

He was visibly relieved and held out his hand to shake mine. 'Last year, when there was much coming and going between the coastal ports and the negotiations in Blois and Tours, I was able to serve several members of the English embassy. My customers were well pleased with the private arrangements we made.'

'I'm sure they were.' I did not speak the thought that if they were benefitting from transactions unencumbered by taxes they would have been delighted but it drove me to enquire further. 'Messengers between King Henry and Suffolk called on you?'

'Frequently, and great men too. It would be a delicate matter if their commerce became known.'

'I understand. Have no fear.' It was an unlikely possibility but I pursed my lips as if a sudden recollection had come to me. 'Did you encounter a man with a scar above the left eye? He came to Normandy towards the conclusion of the truce talks.'

Master Drewman looked surprised. 'Humphrey of Gloucester's man? Yes, I was surprised to see him. The Duke was said to be against the peace.'

I rocked on my heels with horror but quickly steadied myself. 'How often did he come to your premises?'

'Only the once. He bought a gold chain for a woman's kirtle. He'd come from Harfleur and was travelling to Blois. I never saw him on his way back. I presume he was in the crowd accompanying Suffolk after the truce was signed. I was very busy when they all stayed in Rouen, I can tell you.'

'I'm sure you were. Did you note the fellow's name?'

'No. Purchases paid for in coin are not recorded.'

All the easier to avoid excise levies, I reflected, but I felt I owed the goldsmith an explanation. 'I was in Blois around the time and met an acquaintance of the man. It seemed likely we'd have friends in common but I never managed to meet him myself. I'm most obliged to you for your help, Master Drewman. I hope I may trust your discretion, in the same way you can trust mine.'

He beamed and relaxed. 'Mutual understanding is good business, Doctor Somers. That's something I understand. I'm pleased to reciprocate your good faith.'

I escorted him through the gatehouse to see him on his way and all the time I was pondering the information he had given me – not about Maud's lover, although that was intriguing, but the nameless man with the scar. The circumstances fitted exactly with what I had learned from Jeannot in Chartres and seemed to confirm that the wretch had travelled from England in his own identity, as Gloucester's henchman, and had then committed murder in order to impersonate Suffolk's messenger and rendezvous with Rollo. I still baulked at the implication that Duke Humphrey was involved in underhand and discreditable activities but, in any case, I was as far as ever from finding a reason for his follower's actions which made sense. If the fellow had intercepted Suffolk's letter to King Henry, how was it possible the communication was delivered safely to its intended recipient? Any tampering with the seal would have aroused immediate suspicion and the King had replied to Suffolk without expressing any qualm.

I could offer no explanation and I now had an extra mystery to consider for I had met a man with the requisite scar, who served Gloucester, but I could not associate Gilbert Iffley in my mind with brutal slaughter and it was scarcely probable that the Duke had acquired a wider following of appropriately disfigured servants. I was uncomfortable with the whole affair and had no stomach for pursuing these ambiguities, concluding it was as well that Suffolk was content to leave them unresolved, as I must learn to do.

*****

I did not comply with the instruction to visit Margaret of Anjou's attendants until the next day and then only after everyone had attended a lengthy service in the cathedral and an even more protracted feast. At that point, fearing to neglect an imperious command but with some apprehension, I presented myself to an official at the door to the French ladies' quarters, giving my name and asking to see the comtesse de Langeais.'

'The Dowager Countess, you must mean, sir. Wait here.' I nodded dumbly.

It was only a few minutes before she came and, now she was no longer swathed in her travelling cloak, there was no mistaking her mourning garb. I felt embarrassed and blurted out my regrets 'I'm so sorry I didn't know of your loss.'

She tossed her head and the heavy folds of her wimple flapped against her cheeks. 'My husband died suddenly two months after my lord Suffolk's company left France last year. It was very similar to the attack which carried off his friend, the comte de St Benoît. I would not be here otherwise.'

'I remember you said you would not accompany Queen Margaret to England because of your husband. Will you now do so?'

'Yes. I have agreed to serve her for a year. My stepson who now holds his father's title will not want me breathing down his neck and my brother accepts that I wish for a period of respite before he arranges my remarriage. But I have not summoned you here to speak of my situation.' The harsh edge had returned to her voice, as when she spoke to me on the quayside. 'Why did you not respond to my letters?'

My mouth fell open. 'You wrote to me, madame? I never received your letters.'

'Ah!' Her little gasp implied disbelief. 'We heard a ship had been lost crossing the Narrow Sea and knew my first letter could have been in its hold. That was why I wrote a second time – in my own hand.'

I searched my memory. 'When was this? Could it have been just before the Feast of the Nativity? A royal messenger was killed in Kent...'

She clasped her hands to her chin. 'Dear God, is it possible? You really did not receive either letter?'

'Madame, I swear, if I'd done so, I should have replied speedily and with gratitude.'

She gave a sigh and for the first time smiled in that enigmatic, delightful way I remembered. 'In a little while I shall present you to King Henry's bride', she said. 'She has granted permission and will receive you but first I have another duty. Wait here a moment.'

She swept from the room leaving me confused and, I acknowledged to myself, excited. The dowager comtesse de Langeais had written to me in her own hand, unbidden, unembarrassed, freely admitting to her solecism. The knowledge that she had defied convention to contact me, a humble physician, stirred me deeply and in my mind I conceded that, however improperly, I felt a wave of desire

171

for this austere but beautiful noble lady. My role could never be more than to admire her at a distance but this would suffice to give me pleasure and I marvelled at my new-found insight.

I had no idea how long I waited for her to return, savouring my revelation, but when she beckoned me to follow her into another chamber I obeyed in blind devotion, oblivious of other attendants around us and their murmur of expectancy. At the end of the room a youth stepped forward as if to conduct us to England's Queen. He was of medium height, smartly attired in Margaret of Anjou's livery, and he bowed low with all the grace of an accomplished French courtier.

'Cor blimey, Doctor, you never bloody knew?' he said with cherubic mischief in his grin as I staggered in disbelief.

'Rendell!'

Chapter 13

'Always thought I were a bad penny, didn't you? You should have guessed I'd turn up.' He spoke cheerily as he let me hug him and I noted the jagged scar across his chin.

'How? How could you have survived?' I was lost in bewilderment. 'I found out you'd been mauled. I managed to track you down to the dog-keeper's farm.'

'The bargeman what dragged me out of the river thought I was a goner. Those sodding dogs had ripped my face open and I'd cracked me head so hard that it knocked me out for a couple of days. Had a fever too. Lost me memory for a bit, hardly knew me own name, and by the time I got me senses back we was nearly at Nantes, by the sea, where the barge was unloading. I'd got no money and weren't up to riding anyway so the only way I could get back to Tours was to cadge another journey on the barge, though I reckoned you'd have left for England by the time I got there. It turned out the bargeman had to go to the castle at Chinon, not Tours, but that was me bit of luck. Her Grace, Queen Margaret and her ladies were there.'

He paused and the Dowager Countess added a quiet word of explanation. 'After the exhaustion of the betrothal ceremonies we went to Chinon to rest. The barge brought silks from the east for Queen Margaret and I went to inspect them. Rendell helped carry the rolls ashore, despite a weak leg and an angry wound on his chin, and to my astonishment I recognised him from our encounter by the Loire – not so much from the sight of him as from his voice. He was still very poorly and in need of a physician's care.'

'Once seen, never forgotten, ain't that right? Madame Yolande saved me, God bless her,' Rendell said with pride, leaving me unsure whether he was referring to some local wise woman, but he squinted at me with a baleful twist to his mouth. 'What happened to the bastard who set the dogs on me?'

'He died of his injuries. I caught up with him just beforehand.'

'Thank Christ! You know who he was?'

'Carlo's brother – Carlo, the man you killed.'

'Yeah, he made sure I knew that. Fancy him being after me all the time he was trailing us through France! We all thought you was his prey.' Rendell gave a rueful grin. 'He pinched all the money I had too before he tried to kill me.'

The Dowager came to my side. 'When we heard the full story Queen Margaret agreed we should provide for your unfortunate servant and I sent my first letter to tell you he was alive. Then my husband died and I went home. After I returned, at her Grace's request, I found Rendell much recovered and serving as an attendant. That was when I wrote to you again.'

'I thought it pretty rotten that you never replied to Madame Yolande, unusual too.' Rendell winked. 'I told her you had an eye for a fine woman.'

'That's outrageous!' I spluttered with indignation and embarrassment while joyfully registering that I had learned the lady's Christian name.

She made no protest but a little colour had crept into her cheeks which was most becoming. 'I'll leave you to talk further,' she said. 'Then I'll conduct you to her Grace.'

After she had gone I upbraided Rendell for his impertinence in addressing the Dowager with such familiarity but I knew it was useless because she had shown no disapproval and he merely chuckled 'She's all right,' he said with an air of superiority. 'She may look fierce sometimes and she don't stand no nonsense but I reckon she's a charmer.'

I took refuge in my professional role and insisted on examining his ugly scar, turning his chin to right and left and running my fingers along the weal. I wished I had been at hand after his mauling, to sew the wound neatly and eliminate its lumpiness but the wound had healed and I was satisfied. Not that Rendell shared my concern for his appearance – he seemed proud of his battle honours and rolled down his hose to display the similar welts on his legs. 'They've been good to me,' he said, 'her Grace and Madame Yolande. They'll take me back to England in their train of attendants but poncing about as a servant ain't no job for a man. I'll come back to you, if you like, but I'm old enough now to go as a soldier.'

'I'll see what can be arranged. Suffolk maintains a large troop of guards.' I noticed Rendell's scowl but had no opportunity to query it.

The Dowager Countess returned and escorted me along the corridor to meet Margaret of Anjou but on leaving Rendell I needed to pinch myself, so dumbfounded was I by the encounter. I could only marvel how he had escaped from the Dance of Death, which wove its trammels round him from the moment the dogs were loosed on the banks of the Loire, and rue the malign fate which had prevented me learning of his survival. The lady noticed my confusion and tried to ease me back to ordinary conversation.

'You are thunderstruck, Doctor Somers. I wish I'd known you did not receive the letters. But tell me, before we meet her Grace, shall we find our sojourn at the English court congenial?'

I concentrated on replying with tact. 'King Henry is a man of pious, sober habits and he will be devoted to his wife.'

'That pleases me. It will be a welcome change from King Charles's court.' I must have smiled and she shook her head sadly. 'I am not a killjoy but while we were in Nancy I found it offensive to observe the way King Charles's mistress flaunted herself before the English embassy. She rode around the lists, wearing silver armour and little else, relishing the ogling of the men and the jealous whispers of the women.' The Dowager's expression was severe.

'The English court will not offer such spectacles, I'm sure. I hope you'll feel very welcome.'

'Not all King Henry's advisers applaud his French marriage, I believe.'

'Opposition has been muted since the truce was agreed. I heard some had feared the terms would be more oppressive.'

She looked at me sharply. 'I see. There were those in France who would have had them more onerous. But come.'

I followed the Countess nervously into the royal apartments, relaxing slightly when I recognised the Marchioness of Suffolk standing at the young Queen's side. She smiled at me while I executed my most formal bow and the Dowager announced who I was.

'We remember you, Doctor Somers,' England's new Queen said graciously. 'You saved the life of our page on the banks of the Loire. We are grateful and pleased to have returned the compliment by aiding your servant. You now serve the household of the Marquis. Lady Alice has told me your services are valued. She has become our Mistress of the Robes and her favoured attendants will be welcome in our chambers. The comtesse de Langeais also has reason to remember your assistance to her late husband. We look forward to your continuing loyalty and dedication to our followers.'

'Your Grace, I'm honoured. I'm at your service and that of your friends and I'm overwhelmed that you have provided for my servant, Rendell, while he recovered from his injuries.' I felt I was speaking as an automaton.

'We owed you no less,' she said. 'He is an amusing boy and has broadened our knowledge of the English tongue. Any youthful gallant who can bring a smile to the stern visage of our dear comtesse has our admiration.'

I trembled at the thought of what unfortunate vernacular phrases England's Queen might have learned but I envied Rendell the sight of the Dowager's smile. My audience was at an end and I made obeisance while King Henry's bride inclined her head with the dignity of a mature and self-assured woman.

The Countess accompanied me to the door. 'My mistress does not speak idly,' she said in a low voice. 'You have won her favour. I trust you will wait upon her in the English court. The Marchioness of Suffolk clearly approves.'

'I will do so with great pleasure, madame la comtesse.'

It seemed to me that her solemn expression softened at my words but I told myself firmly that relief at Rendell's astonishing survival had addled my mind.

*****

Throughout the following week I called on Rendell every day, as if to reassure myself that he was truly living, and I described to him my activities over the past year, omitting all mention of Lady Maud Fitzvaughan's private commission. On the eighth day he told me Madame Yolande wished to see me and when I left him I was conducted to an antechamber where the Dowager joined me. She was flushed and seemed unusually agitated.

'Oh, Doctor Somers, I'm obliged. It's a matter of the greatest delicacy. You may be able to advise us.'

'If it's in my power.' I felt utterly inadequate.

'You will appreciate that Queen Margaret has incurred significant expenditure in Rouen. She has distributed garments and shoes to the poor and must give gifts to the boatmen who will take her downriver to Harfleur. It is expected.' She paused, twisting her hands together.

'Her generosity is much applauded,' I said as understanding came to me. 'The expenses of her journey must have been considerable. Does she have a temporary need for funds?'

177

The Dowager sighed. 'You are discerning, Doctor Somers, and sensitive to her problem. She has already pawned some of her silver wedding presents to the Marchioness of Suffolk but it is not quite enough and she is loath to reveal the extent of her embarrassment. I wondered if there was some trustworthy tradesman you knew of in Rouen, who could arrange a loan. There would be no immediate security for repayment but as England's Queen, her promise might suffice.'

I could not prevent a smile. 'Madame la comtesse, I think I may be able to help. I am acquainted with a goldsmith in the town. If you were to write down what is needed I will ask him to call on you. I imagine he can satisfy her Grace's requirements.'

Her face glowed with pleasure. 'I told her Grace you would be able to assist and I was confident of your discretion.'

'I'm honoured by your good opinion, madame la comtesse.' I bowed and she held out her hand for me to kiss.

'It is an uncomfortable title now I am become dowager and in England it will be cumbersome. If you were happy to call me, as Rendell does, Madame Yolande, I should find it acceptable.'

I bowed again. 'Madame Yolande, you pay me a great compliment.'

As I hurried to Master Drewman's premises I felt an unfamiliar lightness in my heart and knew it was not wholly due to Rendell's safe return.

*****

Our departure from Harfleur was delayed by nine days, so rough was the sea and gusty the wind, but at last, on the ninth day of April, the royal party boarded two broad-beamed cogs and set sail. The Queen, accompanied by Suffolk, his wife and their closest attendants, embarked on the *Cokke John* while the rest of her suite and those of Suffolk's household, including me, were to travel in the *Mary of Hampton*. At the last minute, a message came asking me to transfer to the other ship because Lady Alice had need of a posset I prescribed on occasion to alleviate her woman's pains. As I hastened up the gangway I observed Queen Margaret handing over nearly thirty pounds to cover the pilot's fee and payment for new hawsers deemed necessary for the voyage. I regretted that she was put in this insulting position but did not know who to hold most blameworthy – the grasping English seamen or the lady's impecunious father who had provided so poorly for his daughter's expenses. I averted my gaze in order not to discomfort her but I was glad Master Drewman had proved obliging.

It was a foul crossing and the *Cokke John* lost its mast but we were blown swiftly across the Narrow Sea and arrived on the same day at Portchester Castle. Many of the passengers had suffered sickness, the Queen among them, and they were scarcely aware of the cheering crowds and ringing church bells which greeted our arrival, wanting only to reach dry land. Such was the agitation to get Queen Margaret ashore that Suffolk carried her in his arms, wading through the surf to reach the litter that would take her to her lodgings, and I noticed Madame Yolande lifting her skirts with intrepid resolution to follow them. I helped the Marchioness of Suffolk to make landfall in a more dignified manner after we moored at the wooden jetty but I had no sooner set foot on my native soil than I heard my name called with urgency.

A French page came running towards me and Madame Yolande was close on his heels, white-faced and breathless.

'Doctor Somers, The Queen's physician bids you come at once,' the boy said.

'It is the Queen,' the lady panted. 'She is not merely ill from the movement of the sea. Pocks have broken out upon her face.'

I was delighted to find that the Queen's personal physician was none other than my old friend, Master Francisco, and flattered to join him in supervising her conveyance to God's House Hospice near Southampton where we assessed her condition and administered remedies. The rash which had erupted across much of her upper body was vivid and unsightly so there was great alarm among her followers who feared that she was afflicted with a deadly disease. There was no option but to postpone the formal wedding to King Henry while we physicians conferred and gave our verdict but to our immense relief Master Francisco and I were able to agree that the Queen's ailment was not the dreaded smallpox but the lesser malady of swine-pox. I accompanied my colleague when he made the happy announcement to the Queen and I offered her a pair of soft fabric gloves.

'Your Grace, the pocks will cause you irritation but it is inadvisable to scratch or rub them, especially on your face, in order to preserve your clear complexion.'

She acknowledged my advice courteously and Master Francisco and I shared a jar of ale in celebration after our consultation, enjoying each other's company and exchanging anecdotes. A day later, although the Queen still required rest, she was well enough to receive a visit from a squire bearing a letter from King Henry which she read with delight while the young man knelt before her. Subsequently Suffolk asked her opinion of the squire but she said she had not noticed him and only then did the Marquis tell her that the person dressed in squire's livery was the most serene King of England. It was reported that the Queen was mortified to have kept her husband on his knees while she perused the letter but I thought the episode promised well for a marriage of mutual devotion.

*****

Some ten days after our arrival in England the Queen had recovered sufficiently for the marriage ceremony to be conducted at the Abbey of Titchfield but by then I was on the road to London, with Rendell at my side, bound for Suffolk's house in the City. I had already sent messages to Leone and to Thomas and Grizel with the extraordinary announcement of his survival and I longed to be present at the reunions which would take place. The first was with Leone who met us at the gatehouse and burst into tears, claiming responsibility for all that had happened to Rendell and begging his forgiveness.

'It was my fault. My bad temper drove you out of our lodgings in Tours the night you went to the dog fight. How you must have cursed me.'

'Never crossed me mind,' Rendell said with lordly nonchalance. 'I reckoned you was best left alone, love-sick as you was, but I thought the dogs made great entertainment and won a tidy sum with a wager before that bastard nicked it all and dragged me away. We're still mates, Leone. Got over the draper's daughter, have you?'

The Italian youth cuffed him joyfully and the two lads embraced each other while I felt a glow of satisfaction as we crossed the courtyard but Leone had just remembered what he must tell me. 'There's a person to see you, Doctor Somers. Waiting in the Marchioness's solar. I was asked to inform you as soon as you arrived.'

It was as if an icy hand gripped my heart and I shivered. 'A person?'

'She says she's wife to Lord Walter Fitzvaughan,' Leone said doubtfully.

'Cor, blimey!' Rendell exclaimed. 'Are you sniffing round that bitch again? Lady Maud, ain't it?'

181

Dumbly I nodded as the youths burst into entirely inappropriate belly laughs and I summoned up the anger I had held at bay since Rendell's return.

Chapter 14

You lied,' I said as I entered the solar, giving her no opportunity to speak first.

She rose quickly from the window seat and her mouth dropped open in surprise. It gave me pleasure to see how flustered she looked. Deaf Marian raised her head and stared at us, doubtless trying to read what we were conveying silently to each other. I waited.

It had never taken Maud long to recover her composure and she promptly assumed the offensive. 'I hadn't expected you would go to Rouen.' She spoke accusingly as if I had erred in some way.

'I seem to remember your letter urged me passionately to do so.'

'A turn of phrase. The impulse of a moment. You make no allowances for a mother's anguish. I may have written what I did not mean.'

'So I'm to be criticised for doing your bidding?'

'Your action was crass. The matter is at an end.'

'You no longer wish to find your daughter?' She tossed her head angrily, rippling the fine gauze of her veil but her lip trembled. 'Or are you now confident you know where she is?'

'What did that goldsmith fellow tell you?'

'Master Drewman maintained that neither he nor Sir Blakely Dunne could have fathered Eleanor.' I paused and watched her breast rise and fall rapidly while I tried to dismiss the memories this evoked. She was still damnably alluring. I knew I needed to keep the initiative. 'You'd already lost your second child when they were introduced to you.'

'Introduced! What a charming picture you paint. I was stripped naked and they were brought to my chamber to ravish me.'

She had every right to be outraged but I could not let her escape so easily after the way she had misled me. 'You knew that when you gave me their names.'

'I panicked when you told me someone had been contributing to the child's upkeep. It was unexpected. I sought to throw you off the scent. I knew Sir Blakely had died and the goldsmith was in Rouen. Later I would have rescinded your commission altogether – if you hadn't gone to Rouen.'

There was venom in her final words and it annoyed me. 'So you never wanted me to identify Eleanor's father? A nobleman from the north of England, perhaps?'

She shrieked and gestured wildly to Marian who hurried from the room. Then Maud hurled herself on me. In Norfolk she had pummelled me with her fists and I raised my hands to grip her arms and prevent her blows but this time a small jewel-encrusted knife flashed across the back of my wrist and I jumped back in alarm with a line of crimson bubbles glistening below my cuff. Immediately she attacked again, directing her weapon towards my throat, and while I shielded my neck I had no choice but to use violence with knee and foot to drive her from me. She staggered to the side but kept the blade pointed towards me with murder in her eyes.

'You know too much, physician.'

'Will you kill the Prioress of St. Michael's too? She knows all I've discovered.'

'You shared my secrets with that double-dealing bitch? You betrayed my trust.'

'It was she who suggested Eleanor's father as most probably responsible for her disappearance. You were worried about your daughter's fate as I recall.'

She took a step towards me, holding the knife steady. 'It seems my concerns were misplaced. Her father would cause her no injury.'

'I never thought naïveté one of your failings. It isn't unknown for an unnatural father to violate his own child.' I was shocked at my own bluntness but bemused by her unpredictable behaviour.

'You know nothing.' Her voice cracked and I registered this as a first sign of her weakening. 'I don't understand why Eleanor has been taken from Stamford but she would come to no harm at her father's hand.'

To my amazement I saw her eyes fill with tears and, with irrational conviction, all at once I understood. 'You loved him? You still love him?'

'Curse you, Harry Somers, curse you!'

I stepped towards her and despite her anger she let me take the knife, throwing herself forward to sob against my chest. Hesitantly I put my arm around her and my words sounded lame. 'I have no wish to pry.'

'My life would have been different if we had been allowed to wed.' She seized the hanging sleeves of my gown, clinging tightly as if she would fall without their support and her words poured out with desperate urgency. 'Ralph and I grew up together and were happy that we were destined to marry. Then his father forbade it, preferring a more prestigious match with a rich matron. My hateful guardian encouraged us to exchange worthless, irregular vows and he let us sleep together believing that when I was with child Ralph's father would relent. But he did not. He threatened to disinherit Ralph in favour of a cousin, a scoundrel who would ruin his inheritance. Ralph accepted the betrothal for the sake of the estate but he still came to me, after Eleanor had been taken to the convent, and got me with child once more. That's when the fiendish quack tore the second infant from my belly and made me barren. I was fertile stock before that.'

I had never seen genuine misery in Lady Maud's face before and I put my hand to her brow, stroking aside the curls escaping from her headdress. I had no thought but to offer comfort. 'You needn't say more if it's painful.'

'I want you to understand. No other soul knows the truth. Ralph was compelled to marry a woman nearly twice his age and I heard she bore him two sons. I know no more. He doesn't come to court. By the time Ralph had married I was spoiled goods and my guardian decided to trade me as a whore to recoup some of the expenses he had borne. I was only rescued from that life when he died and I was brought to Greenwich under Roger Bolingbroke's protection. After the defilement I'd suffered it was a blessed relief merely to act as his chattel, obeying his will but not sharing his bed.'

I pressed her hand in commiseration and muttered some inane expression of sympathy. She looked up at me through her lashes, dry-eyed now, pale and rivetingly beautiful. Her breast heaved against me. 'Not all my duties were onerous, as I recall. When I came to your chamber by night I found pleasure in my task to seduce you.'

'We must forget that.' I spoke hurriedly, attempting to release her grip on my gown, belatedly aware that her mood had changed, but when she loosened her grasp on the fabric her fingers stroked my cheeks and drew my face downwards to meet her lips. I did protest but not convincingly and we kissed, gently at first but with increasing fervour, until there was no doubting the urge of my manhood.

'No! No, Maud. This is madness.' I pushed her away with half-hearted vigour but as she skidded backwards she dragged me with her and we landed together on the fine glazed tiles of the Marchioness's solar with Maud spread-eagled beneath me. She giggled with triumph and slid her hand to my groin.

'No! Stop this nonsense.' To my shame, despite my words, I made no move to evade her.

'When you have pleasured me, physician.' Her voice had resumed its accustomed ironic tone. 'I assure you, if you refuse, Marian will swear that you assaulted and raped me. Walter will believe it. He will ruin you – if Gaston does not kill you first.' She wriggled, thrusting herself against me as she untied my points. 'Besides,' she gurgled. 'I have tangible proof you would not be averse to revisiting my privates. Or have you taken a vow of celibacy since losing your Mantuan temptress?'

It went through my mind to question how she knew who my lover had been in Italy but the compulsion of the flesh had become too insistent to dwell on such an irrelevance. She had worked her evil magic on me once more and I succumbed, throwing up her skirt to nuzzle her nakedness. I cannot pretend that my dishonourable action was not gratifying as our rough coupling brought consummation.

'I seem to remember foretelling that we would burn together again in lust, while still in this mortal life,' Maud burbled sweetly as she straightened her stomacher. 'Don't begrudge me one little success.'

'My lady, this must never be repeated. I shall refuse to meet you again unless your husband is present. It will be best.' In the cold aftermath of passion I could speak as I should have done earlier but I still struggled to sound authoritative.

'What a dunderhead you are, Harry.' She stood, rearranging her headdress. 'Besides, I thought you might provide one tiny extra service to soothe my mother's aching heart.'

'What are you talking about?'

'Just to reassure me that Eleanor is safe, would you, on my behalf, write discreetly to Ralph to seek confirmation that Eleanor is unharmed. I cannot expect you to visit him in person but if you could send a confidential enquiry it would calm my anxieties. I shall abide by whatever Ralph has arranged for our daughter.'

Her ingratiating tone infuriated me and I started to refuse but I knew she would threaten again to denounce me as a rapist and I shrugged my shoulders. 'I'll do this and nothing more. You will need to tell me Ralph's full name,' I said coldly.

'Of course,' she simpered. 'Ralph Egremont, Earl of Stanwick.' She had named a distinguished nobleman and I stared at her in consternation as the door was opened quietly. 'See, here is my diligent Marian, come to alert us that our conversation is about to be interrupted. Remember all that has passed between us, dear physician.'

Then she bent down to retrieve a small knife with a jewel-encrusted hilt that had lain disregarded by a table leg for the last half hour and I pulled down my sleeve to conceal a streak of congealing blood on the back of my wrist. She blew me a kiss as she tripped from the room with ineffable grace.

*****

That evening I listened to the banter between Rendell and Leone, trying to divert myself from the shame and irritation I felt at my culpable weakness with Maud. How could I have allowed myself to be beguiled when I knew too well what she was like? How could I have yielded to carnal instinct when I understood the ignominy I would feel as a result of my action? Freed from her enticing presence I wondered if, even now, I could trust what she had told me and I shrank from the thought of framing a letter to the Earl of Stanwick hinting at his paternity of her child. I cursed her deviousness and my spineless acquiescence. I was unworthy of any respectable woman's affection.

Rendell was reciting again all that had happened to him after we imagined him dead on the banks of the Loire, while Leone pressed for more details. I had heard this account before and found it difficult to concentrate until

Rendell sniggered, jumping to his feet, and gestured to attract my attention.

'I never told you, doctor, did I? How I met that bastard, Henri Charpentier, again?'

I stared, wrestling my mind back to what was being said.

'You crossed swords with him a second time?' Leone asked.

'No such luck. He came with his master on a visit to Madame Yolande after her husband died. It was all very solemn and there were lots of other attendants around but we glared at each other across the antechamber outside the room where she received the Seigneur de la Flèche. I managed to spit at Charpentier as they left though. A nice glob of sputum landed on his fine leather boot and he couldn't do anything about it because his master was hustling his bloody men away as fast as they could go. The Seigneur had a face like thunder – maybe the Countess had spat at him. Wouldn't blame her. The gossip afterwards said he'd asked her to marry him but she wasn't having any of it.'

Leone chortled and I could not prevent a grin. I knew I would not choose to incur that lady's wrath and, although I had no right to an opinion on the subject, I was glad she had declined to marry the Seigneur.

'It's a good job you're unlikely to meet Monsieur Charpentier again,' Leone said with a wink. 'He'd slit your belly open after that affront.'

'Let him try!' Rendell sank down on the floor and crossed his legs. 'Did you ever find that fellow with a scar over his eye, doctor?'

I paused before answering. 'I don't think so. I met a man with such a scar but I can't imagine he had anything to do with Rollo's murder.' I hoped I sounded more confident in my assertion than I felt.

*****

I penned a letter of such subtlety that the recipient would probably conclude it came from a madman and I expected no reply but it would enable me to confirm that I had written as promised. Then I attempted to forget every aspect of my encounter with Lady Maud, rejoicing that she and her husband were not to be accommodated at the Manor of the Rose for the forthcoming celebrations.

Over the next few days the Suffolk household was in a ferment of excited preparation for the entry of King Henry's wife into the City of London. Outside in the streets, at royal command, triumphal arches were erected and draped with marguerites while the windows and balconies of merchants' houses were decorated with elaborate banners. Fountains ran with ale and malmsey, to general delight, and onlookers appreciated the sight of maidens, clad as the wise and foolish virgins of Christ's cautionary tale, who accompanied the figure of Saint Margaret to bid her namesake welcome. I watched from the roadside as ladies personifying the virtues waved branches when her procession entered the City but I noted that the cheers of the common people were muted until the King himself appeared. I heard murmurs of discontent around me, complaining that the cost of this French marriage was ruinously extravagant and Margaret's dowry laughable but Gloucester's name was muttered with approval as a counsellor who had opposed the match. It pleased me that my old patron sustained his hold on the affections of ordinary Londoners, who had always idolised him, but the sullen looks on the faces of workmen and fishwives as they stared at the Queen made me uncomfortable.

Three days later Margaret was crowned in the abbey church at Westminster and received the homage of the King's principal advisors. I had no part in that ceremony but it was described to me by others in Suffolk's household who spoke of the elderly Lord Talbot, seemingly entranced by the young Queen's beauty, and contrasted this with the cold courtesy of others whose hostility was thinly hidden. Gloucester, I was sure, would have masked any animosity he felt and shown proper respect but it was worrying to perceive the suspicion with which he was viewed by Suffolk's adherents. After the service concluded Margaret was conducted to the Queen's apartments at Westminster Palace which had been unoccupied for twenty years and appointments were made to complete her personal household. Then, so far as the world outside the royal circle was concerned, life returned to its normal pattern and, to my particular relief and joy, Lord and Lady Fitzvaughan departed to Norfolk without intruding further on my peace of mind.

A few days later a royal messenger brought me a purse containing a generous present of gold to recompense me for my assistance to the Queen in Rouen and in attending her sickbed. A short note accompanying the gift reminded me that I would be welcome to call at Westminster. I was pleased to think that King Henry had made immediate provision to ease his wife's financial embarrassment and I hoped her chamberlain would ensure that Master Drewman's loan was repaid with equal speed, although I doubted a debt to a goldsmith in Normandy would feature as a high priority in her accounts.

Encouraged by this noteworthy boost to my wealth I sought permission to call upon Mistress Jane Cawfield and congratulated myself on receiving her prompt agreement, wondering whether she had guessed my intention and did not object. Accordingly I presented myself at her house that same afternoon, closely observed, to my annoyance, by an inquisitive old woman at the window of the adjoining house.

When I entered Mistress Cawfield's solar, one glance at her troubled countenance corrected my optimism about her motives, but she welcomed me cordially. Her manner was a strange mixture of fluttering hands and steely composure.

'Doctor Somers, I'm glad you are returned. I have great need of your advice.'

'Your servant, Mistress. What's happened?' I rejoiced in this sign of her trust.

She waved me to a seat by the window and offered me wine while she hesitated in framing her question. 'Can you tell me... do you know... why they are enquiring into Andrew's affairs?'

I was nonplussed by this unexpected enquiry. 'What do you mean? I've heard nothing.'

'The officers came and searched his things: three of them – the man in charge and two assistants. They turned out his chest and went through the papers he kept here. I told them all the documents pertaining to his work were at Suffolk's house but they took no notice. I had no means to prevent them. I summoned my manservant but they threatened to beat him and I felt I must comply with their wishes. Jack wasn't at home and the little ones were afraid of the fierce soldiers. Why should they do this?'

I shook my head. 'When did this happen?'

'Some weeks ago while the Marquis and his party were in Normandy.'

'Were these officers Suffolk's men?'

'I imagine so but they wore no livery, just armour and dark cloaks.'

'Did they find what they were looking for?'

'I'm not sure. They took something away with them. I've been so worried since then but they haven't returned and I've heard nothing more. Could they have been royal officials?'

'Royal officials would have worn the King's livery. Did these men have no badges?'

'None that I could see.'

'Do you know what they took?'

She twisted the tassels on her girdle. 'They left Andrew's papers, stuffed back in his chest. I think all they took was a seal. That doesn't make sense. What use is a dead man's seal?'

I caught my breath. 'Are you sure it was his own seal?'

'Why? What other seal would he have? What do you mean?' Her tone was sharp.

I stumbled in giving her a reasonable explanation. 'I thought perhaps... he might have more than one seal... or maybe he kept a copy of another seal here?'

She was intelligent and quickly understood what I was trying not to say. 'Do you mean Suffolk's seal?' I nodded and she bowed her head. 'I don't know if that was what they took but Andrew did bring a copy of Suffolk's seal to the house sometimes. He told me it was so he could deal with documents at home with his family rather than staying to work in his lord's study until all hours. He told me to tell no one as it was irregular. Do you think that was why the officers came?'

'It may well have been. Suffolk would have wanted to retrieve a spare copy of his seal to make sure it wasn't misused.'

'Of course.' She giggled joyfully which I thought misplaced. I attributed her levity to nervousness but did not find this explanation convincing.

'Have you discussed this with anyone else?'

'No. The principal officer said I should not but I couldn't bear the anxiety. I had to consult someone. There are none in the City I know well enough to confide in and Andrew had confidence in you.'

I suppressed a shudder at this ill-founded assumption and decided to risk a leading question. 'Did you get a good look at the officers? Is it possible one had a scar above his eye?'

She gave a start but then shrugged as if to signify it was of no account. 'How sinister! I couldn't see such a mark but the men all wore helmets which covered their brows.'

I decided to tell her what her husband had withheld. 'Master Cawfield had a troubling encounter with a scarred man a little while before his death. I've no notion if it was significant. Probably it was merely the rambling of a drunkard or lunatic. At all events, it's unlikely there's a connection with your visitors.'

She looked at me intently for a moment and when she spoke her voice was a whisper. 'You believe Andrew was deliberately poisoned?'

I was startled but owed her the truth. 'There's no proof whatever but I confess to misgivings.'

'You didn't think to warn me?' Her tone was gentle but I acknowledged the accusation in her words.

'I didn't want to add to your distress. It was only conjecture and I never imagined you were in any danger. Forgive me.'

'Did Andrew know? He said strange things when he was dying.'

I tried to reply with a physician's detachment. 'Words spoken on a deathbed are often confused but your husband did fear he had been murdered.'

She stared at me and I could not read her expression. 'You think I am in danger?'

'No. If your visitors had evil intentions towards you they would have used violence while they were in your house.'

She lowered her eyes and ran her finger over the embroidery on her skirt. 'They may believe I don't know they took anything. Andrew's chest has a small compartment where he kept his seals and a few coins. The money is still there – and one seal. But I looked through the chest after his death, to make sure there was nothing which needed attention, and I know there had been two seals, although I didn't inspect them to see whose crest they bore.'

I could not help smiling at her air of embarrassment. 'Mistress Cawfield, you acted wisely and with entire propriety. But it would be prudent to maintain your silence about this business and I assure you of my discretion.'

She smiled at me. 'I trust you, Doctor Somers, and it's a relief to have shared my concerns. Don't mention anything to the Marquis of Suffolk. The matter is at an end. Poor Andrew was not himself in his later days. Don't trouble yourself about this fellow with a scar.'

I had not said I would pursue the matter but it pleased me that she assumed I might do so on her behalf. Nevertheless, one thing puzzled me and I could not let it pass. 'I'll help you in any way I can, Mistress Cawfield. I'm sorry you don't feel you can confide in your neighbours. Don't you know them at all?'

She sighed. 'We only took this house when Andrew returned from France last year. We were in lodgings near Eastcheap when I first came to London. Then Andrew was fortunate in receiving a considerable sum of money which enabled him to lease this property so we could be together in more comfort. It was a joyful ambition yet I think it has brought me nothing but sadness.'

I murmured my sympathy and, although the occasion was scarcely appropriate for any more personal overtures on my part, I had a contented feeling that she would not dismiss me out of hand when the time was right. More powerful, however, was my sense of foreboding about what she had told me. I had not wished to disabuse her of the idea but I thought it unlikely her visitors had acted on Suffolk's instructions. The interpretation which came to my mind was disturbing and provoked as many questions as it answered.

Suffolk had told me he mistrusted Andrew Cawfield and now I believed he had good reason, for it seemed all too likely that the secretary had betrayed his lord and sold his services to others for unlawful purposes. That could account for his receipt of unprecedented wealth, enabling him to occupy a costly City house, and it suggested that whatever he had done was rated highly by his paymaster. Access to Suffolk's seal would be a prized benefit to anyone seeking to misuse it and it could explain the mystery which bothered me. Suffolk's private letter to the King, taken from Rollo under false pretences, could have been opened, studied and then re-sealed before delivery to its intended recipient, without arousing any suspicion; but some unauthorised person would have become aware of its contents, presumably hoping to make mischief with the information obtained. The existence of a confidential letter, sent with elaborate secrecy, suggested it concerned some matter of great delicacy yet nothing had been revealed, no trouble incited, as a result of its interception. It made no sense.

On his deathbed Cawfield appeared to suffer guilt because of Rollo's murder but he exonerated Humphrey of Gloucester from knowledge of any plot. Certainly the Duke's behaviour at the time of the truce with France had shown no hostility but who else might have profited from suborning Cawfield in the way I conjectured? Moreover, it seemed Cawfield had been threatened and blamed for failing in a task he had been bribed to accomplish, which did not accord with the rest of my supposition – unless he had refused to undertake some further act of treachery.

For all my tantalising speculation, there was no evidence at all that I had divined the truth. If I had solved part of the year-old mystery, I was still without knowledge of the perpetrator and it had spawned a greater riddle.

Chapter 15

I pressed Rendell to make an early visit to his sister at Greenwich but before he did so we received a message saying that Grizel, Thomas and both their infant sons would come to Baynard's Castle for the reunion which I was invited to attend. Duke Humphrey's City house did not evoke memories for me comparable to those of his palace at Greenwich but despite Suffolk's permission, indeed encouragement, for me to go there, I felt awkward entering its portals and contrived that my visit would be brief. At least my excuse of an engagement at Westminster that afternoon was quite true, although its timing was not fortuitous, because I needed to give formal thanks for the Queen's generosity in rewarding my services. Leone accompanied us to the riverside mansion but after paying his respects to the Chope family he went to find his friend, Bartholomew.

Grizel hid her joy at her brother's safe return under a veneer of disparagement, loftily querying the likelihood that he had spent several months at the French court, while Rendell, replying with similarly assumed detachment, recited at length all he had done there. After a while his sister softened her approach to express horror at the barbarous attack which had nearly cost him his life and he responded by describing with pride how his would-be murderer had pursued him across France. Tiring of this familiar recital, Rendell winked at me and introduced another topic.

'Ain't told Grizel yet how I had another enemy in France,' he announced in triumph. 'Fought sword to sword with him: a bastard serving one of the Frenchie lords who opposed the truce. He wanted to cause trouble with the English party.'

'I expect you goaded him into it,' his sister said, unimpressed.

'Bloody didn't! But I fought him fair and square, man to man.' Rendell turned to me again. 'I've been trained by Venetian soldiers and I know my business. I'm old enough now to join a troop of guards, even Doctor Somers agrees.'

Grizel looked disdainful. 'It's true he must be fifteen come Michaelmas. I remember it. Ma couldn't take me to the fair and buy me sweetmeats, though she'd promised, because she was still abed. Nuisance he's been from that day to this.'

'Sodding lie that is! Just jealous, you are.'

Thomas whispered in my ear. 'They'll be at it hammer and tongs for the next hour. You'd best slip away if you're to get to Westminster. Don't wait too long before you come to Greenwich.' He drew me out into the corridor. 'You'd never imagine, seeing them, how happy she is to have him back. Two peas from the same pod.' I slapped him on the shoulder and went to turn away but he gripped my arm 'You'll be without an assistant if Rendell goes a-soldiering, with the Italian lad off to the university. If you need an accomplice, Harry, don't forget your old friend.'

I grinned, remembering our shared adventures a few years previously. 'You're a married man with family responsibilities.'

He spread his fingers in the air, assuming an expression of sheer innocence. 'Might welcome a diversion. Don't forget.'

I gave him my promise but as I walked away I had no expectation of seeking his help for, in spite of continuing uncertainties, I hoped my life would soon attain a plateau of calm uneventfulness.

I had arrived at the water-gate before I heard Leone's call and saw him and Bartholomew hurrying towards me. I had not seen Lord Fitzvaughan's erstwhile companion since we were in France the previous year and I was impressed by his elegance. His handsome features with their prominent cheekbones had matured, his fair hair was elaborately curled and his clothes were of the finest quality. I speculated whether the enigmatic and heavily scarred Gilbert Iffley might take a protector's interest in the young man, beyond that of an employer; certainly it was probable that Bartholomew was receiving expensive gifts from some new patron and I was pleased he had no need to regret his ousting from Lord Fitzvaughan's retinue by Gaston de la Tour.

'Doctor Somers,' he accosted me, 'I'm happy to see you. My master is taking a boat to Westminster and would be glad if you would share it. He'll be here in a moment.'

For an instant I feared he meant Duke Humphrey of Gloucester but I quickly realised he was referring to Iffley, whom I would be interested to meet again, and then that gentleman appeared, holding out his hand in greeting.

'Allow me to return the courtesy of joint conveyance. I understand you also have business at Westminster. How gratifying for me to meet you again.'

It was a blustery day and the water was choppy as we were handed into the wherry and we settled ourselves, side by side, under the flapping canopy at the stern. Then, as we moved off from the bank Master Iffley leaned towards me with a disarming smile. 'I confess, Doctor Somers, my business has been somewhat hastily contrived, as soon as I learned from Bartholomew that you were at Baynard's Castle and intent on travelling to the court.'

'You surprise me,' I said lamely.

'Didn't you enjoy our previous meeting?' His smile was affable and I felt he had put me in the wrong.

'On the contrary. I'm honoured you thought it worthwhile travelling together again.'

'You are not discomforted to accompany the Duke of Gloucester's factotum?' He did not pause to await a reply, which saved me from an awkward choice of answers. 'I confess I wish to take advantage of our meeting to pick your brains on my master's behalf.'

199

My awkwardness was compounded. 'What do you mean, Master Iffley?'

His lips twitched slightly. 'I wondered if you knew the reason for the forthcoming embassy from France and were at liberty to share it with me.'

I shifted position on the thin cushion covering the slats of the seat. 'I've heard nothing of such an embassy.'

'But you are a favoured visitor to the Queen and her ladies, are you not? You might learn something from them?'

'I'm not privy to matters of state and couldn't expect anyone at court to confide in me.' My tone was brusque.

He smiled thinly. 'I think you underestimate your influence, Doctor Somers. But perhaps I should explain my enquiry. Duke Humphrey has been made aware that an embassy from King Charles is expected shortly. Its purpose may be to finalise terms in the truce which were left imprecise at the discussions in Tours.'

From the back of my mind came the recollection of Lord Fitzvaughan's words at the conclusion of the negotiations more than a year previously. 'The main point is conceded', he had said and I had speculated pedantically what remained in dispute. This had been immediately after Suffolk received King Henry's reply to the letter which, I now believed, had been intercepted. That incident seemed suddenly ominous and I tried to hide my instinctive shiver, taking advantage of the rolling boat to draw my gown more closely round me. 'I know nothing of this.'

'Might there have been secret provisions, not mentioned in the public agreement?' he asked with what I was sure was contrived casualness.

My heart was thudding and I struggled to keep my voice calm. 'I've never heard such a rumour but I'm unlikely to have done so. I'm a physician not a courtier.'

My companion braced his feet against the empty seat in front of us as the boat pitched in the wake of a passing barge. 'Duke Humphrey remembers you warmly,' he said. 'I mentioned I'd met you and he expressed pleasure that you were returned from exile. He thought highly of your services.'

I knew this was not wholly true as Gloucester once found enquiries he had authorised me to make too intrusive. 'I have enduring respect for the Duke.'

'The young lord, Arthur, was glad to hear of your pardon.'

I gave a genuine smile for Arthur was Gloucester's natural son whose attendant I had been at the University of Oxford some six or seven years previously. I recalled the spirited lad's exploits, which I had attempted to moderate, knowing it was due to the privilege of accompanying him to lectures that I received my own college education. 'I'm delighted to hear that.'

'The Duke appreciates why it was expedient for you to join the Marquis of Suffolk's household but he would welcome you back in his own service.'

'I'm honoured but King Henry decreed I should serve the Marquis when he granted my pardon.'

'Quite so. The Duke acknowledges your obligation. Nevertheless, you might be willing to obtain information for him without in any way impugning your lord's interests.'

I was becoming uncomfortable in body and mind with the tossing of the boat and the trend of our conversation. I was disappointed to see that we were still some way off the distant towers of Westminster. 'What do you mean?'

'I've mentioned the embassy from France. The Duke would like to know its purpose. He's also heard that Queen Margaret has forged an alliance with the ancient Cardinal which is unexpected and unwelcome news. Any information you could glean on these topics would be valued.'

Belatedly I tried to exert some influence on the direction of our discourse. 'The Duke remains antagonistic to Cardinal Beaufort, I presume. I thought the old prelate had withdrawn from active involvement as the King's adviser.'

'Not entirely. A role of mentor to the young Queen pleases him greatly and, for Gloucester, that could be dangerous: a life-long enemy allied to the French girl whose marriage to the King Duke Humphrey long opposed.'

'I understood the Duke no longer opposed the truce.'

Master Iffley snorted. 'It remains to be seen. He may have been grossly misled'

This could be of crucial importance and I wanted to pursue the comment but Iffley's next words caused me to lurch forward, gripping the side of the boat in an attempt to look as if the rough water was responsible for my movement. 'You conceal your talents admirably, Doctor Somers, when it's wise to do so. I'm aware of the forbidden fruits you have tasted with the beautiful Lady Maud. I confess I envy you that joy.'

'We were both young and reckless when we were in Gloucester's household.'

He looked away with a salacious grin while I prayed it was the events of years gone by to which he referred. Then he swivelled to face me again. 'Ladies find your company reassuring, I imagine. It could be of inestimable benefit if you would seduce one of Queen Margaret's women to gain the insights we covet.'

The palace jetty was in view and I tried to laugh off his suggestion, treating it as a joke, but he patted my arm. 'Think about it, physician. I'm sure Lady Maud instructed you well. I expect you wonder how I know these intimate matters but it is easily explained. The late Roger Bolingbroke was my distant relative and I learned much from him, including the need to act with more circumspection than the wretched fellow ever did himself. I trust we may work amicably in future partnership, Doctor Somers.'

He had named the man who had been my nemesis, whose vicious power over me led to my exile, and that connection made me afraid of Gilbert Iffley. I clambered from the rocking boat anxious for escape as a liveried servant came forward to escort me.

'Doctor Somers, I am commanded to conduct you directly to the Queen's lodgings.'

'How privileged you are,' Iffley said with a slight bow. 'God grant you prosperity and a compliant mistress.'

*****

My formal thanks to the Queen were soon expressed and she acknowledged them gracefully, bidding me remain as long as I wished to converse with her followers while explaining that she must attend the King to discuss various charitable donations they intended to make. I made a deep obeisance, resolved to leave the palace when I could do so with propriety, but as I straightened a richly embroidered skirt in dark brocade glided in front of me.

'May I beg a moment of your time, Doctor Somers. Would you walk with me in the long gallery?'

'Your servant, Madame Yolande.' Inevitably Gilbert Iffley's unseemly proposal came to my mind and it amused me that, although this was the one lady among the Queen's attendants who attracted me physically, she was the least likely to tolerate the merest hint of seduction.

The windows of the gallery gave a view of the riverside where the wind was rippling the water more fiercely and causing some of the moored boats to knock against each other.

'With most un-Christian-like fervour I should be joyful if a gale would drive to destruction one of the vessels crossing the Narrow Sea at this time.'

'Ships from France, madame?' My voice was a whisper.

She nodded. 'Emissaries from King Charles are coming. The Queen of course rejoices that her countrymen will soon be here but one among them is displeasing to me.'

It was presumptuous but my curiosity overcame good manners. 'The Seigneur de la Flèche is one of the French party?'

To my relief she was not offended. 'Rendell has told you of Seigneur Philippe's unwelcome courtship. I guessed he would – otherwise I would not have sought your advice.'

'You're concerned that he will renew his suit?'

'It will be difficult to avoid him at the ceremonies and it seems my brother has given him encouragement to pursue me.'

'Doesn't your brother know the Seigneur's addresses are unwelcome to you?'

'I have told him but my preferences won't rank highly in his judgement. I shall refuse Philippe as a suitor but my dilemma is complicated because Queen Margaret would be pleased for me to accept this marriage.' I must have looked surprised and she beckoned me to a window embrasure where we could talk more privately. 'It would bind the Seigneur more closely to King Charles's supporters.'

'Forgive me but I thought the Seigneur had opposed the truce with my country?'

She sighed. 'He did so, as did my late husband. That you know; but in the weeks after you returned to England last year they were both persuaded to drop their opposition. There were grants of land and money and both were reconciled to accept the truce. I think my husband found this problematic and I cannot dismiss the thought that sorrow at his change of heart played some part in his fatal seizure. Seigneur Philippe seems to have accommodated himself more readily, with the help of increased wealth, but Queen Margaret wishes to reinforce his allegiance to the French King by making me his bedfellow and letting him know it was accomplished at her behest.'

'I'm very sorry for your predicament, Madame Yolande.' I was flattered but puzzled why she was confiding such personal anxieties to me.

It was as if she read my thoughts. 'There is no one at this court with whom I can share my burden, given the Queen's open expression of her views. It is a comfort simply to put the matter into words and I am grateful for your patience in listening to so trivial a story.'

'I don't hold it to be trivial, madame. I wish I could offer help.' I paused, plucking up courage to ask a question tangential to her concerns but central to what I wished to discover. 'Is the visit of the emissaries a goodwill gesture from King Charles? Is the Seigneur's participation a mark of his new position at the French court?'

'Shrewdly discerned, Doctor Somers. They are coming to complete some aspects of the truce which were left imprecise – I know no details – and the Seigneur's presence is not accidental. I am the bait to bind him to his sovereign lord and King.' She moved away from the window, turning back towards the Queen's lodgings. 'If you object to receiving my confidences, please tell me now and I will not repeat my offence.' I shook my head while she was still speaking and she gave me her wonderful, enveloping smile. 'But if you are content for me to trouble you, I beg you to come again to Westminster so that I may divest myself of my foolish, self-regarding worries.'

She held out her hand and I bowed low, brushing her fingertips with my lips. My heartbeats thundered as I watched her re-enter the Queen's apartments and I did not know which facet of what she had conveyed to me was most disquieting.

*****

On my journey back to the City I determined that I would adopt an even-handed approach towards Suffolk and

Gloucester. I would never betray my master but I felt at liberty to share with Gilbert Iffley information which was not explicitly confidential. In fact I was perversely eager to pursue the contact for, although I found the man menacing, he intrigued me. Similarly, if asked, I would tell Suffolk anything of the Duke's activities which were likely to become public knowledge. In this way, I thought optimistically, I could reconcile the opposing claims on my loyalty. Then, on arrival at my rooms, I was given a letter from the Prioress of St. Michael's who had learned, by some undisclosed means, of the forthcoming embassy from France and was anxious for me to enlighten her as to its purpose. I could not repress a chortle of amusement. The idea of becoming not merely a double, but a triple, agent in state affairs was ridiculous but it made me uncomfortable; I wanted only a quiet life in which to attend my patients and, if I was fortunate, establish a contented family home.

Soon after I had read the letter I was summoned to attend the Marquis in his private chamber where I found him sitting uneasily on an upright chair and grimacing. He waved me to his side with an impatient gesture.

'Devil take it, Doctor Somers, I've twisted my back somehow. It's damned difficult to stand straight.' He put his hand to his lower spine. 'I had an old injury years ago when fighting in Normandy and sometimes it returns.'

He allowed me to examine him and I promised to deliver a poultice and a posset to deaden the pain. 'It might be best if you could rest for a day or two,' I said.

'Impossible! It's essential I'm at court. There are important visitors expected. And I don't intend to greet them leaning on a stick.'

I nodded sagely. 'It's possible the embassy from France may have been delayed by the rough weather. I understand they haven't landed yet.'

'How do you know about such things?' He looked annoyed but then he chuckled. 'Of course, I was forgetting your intimacy with the Queen's ladies, ingratiating physician.'

'Neither ingratiating nor intimate,' I murmured, 'but I have garnered some other information, from a different source, which may interest you.' I had his attention and pursued my advantage, diverting him onto the subject of my choice. 'Duke Humphrey's factotum is enquiring why the Frenchmen are coming.'

'Ah! I might have expected it. We must be on our guard. You've made the acquaintance of this factotum?'

I answered his question while registering the implications of his comment. It could suggest that he had something to hide. 'His name is Gilbert Iffley.'

The Marquis nodded but did not say whether he had heard of the man. 'Good, Harry Somers, good. Foster the connection.' He shifted position carefully. 'Perhaps I could afford to spend one day at home.'

'It would benefit you, my lord. I'll fetch the remedies.'

When I returned to administer both dressing and potion Suffolk seemed more relaxed and as I gently kneaded his back he referred to our earlier conversation, asking if the arrangements were complete for Jack Cawfield and Leone to go to the university at Oxford.

'They are, my lord. The boys will leave in two months' time. They and Jack's mother, Mistress Cawfield, are most grateful to you.'

He grunted. 'And that other lad who serves you, the one who tried to emulate our blessed Saviour by returning from the dead, is he well?'

I was amazed the Marquis knew of Rendell's existence, let alone his extraordinary survival. 'The boy is in fine fettle. He'll be fifteen at Michaelmas and has aspirations to be a soldier. He had some training in Italy and can wield a sword with competence.'

'I'd be glad to offer him a place in my troop,' Suffolk said, relieving me of the need to seek another favour from him. 'He's acquired some notoriety and it's always useful to have a guard with a reputation for invincibility.'

I bowed low, expressing thanks, when my patient signalled that his treatment was complete and I should leave him. I returned to my quarters well satisfied with our encounter, both in my capacity as physician and as master to my restless servant but, not for the first time, my good intentions were to prove ill judged.

*****

Leone took my letter to Gilbert Iffley and brought back an immediate response inviting me to call at Baynard's Castle next day, which I duly did although by then I had misgivings about the wisdom of my action. He received me in his study where I told him quickly that it appeared his surmise was correct and French emissaries were coming to finalise details of the truce left incomplete before the royal wedding. I was surprised by the vehemence of his response when he crashed his fist on the desk and scattered papers with its force.

He rose and faced me accusingly, the vein in his neck throbbing. 'Did you have no inkling of these details, this year or last when you were in France?'

I stood my ground 'I told you I wasn't privy to any of the negotiations and I have no information about the new discussions. You asked if an embassy was coming and that's all I've discovered.'

He paced up and down, breathing deeply; then he turned to me in a calmer mood. 'Forgive me, Doctor Somers, you couldn't be expected to appreciate the implications. Yet you may recall something of relevance. Was there no suggestion in Tours of matters still to be resolved, something Suffolk had raised with King Henry but which may have been kept secret until now?'

I tried to show no reaction to a question which could be incriminating, which might hint that Iffley knew of the confidential correspondence Rollo had organised, but I needed to learn more so I drew on the one recollection I had. 'All I can remember is a moment when the lords accompanying Suffolk left his chamber after the King's agreement to the truce had been received. They were celebrating and one said "the main point has been conceded". It struck me as interesting at the time.'

'What?' Iffley seized my shoulders, staring at me with wild excitement and I noticed how his scar had become inflamed as his passion grew. 'Were those the words? The very words?'

'Yes. I confess I wondered if it meant there were other points still to be settled.'

'Wait! Wait here! I'll be back instantly.'

He rushed from the room and, because I was as anxious as him to probe further, I had no option but to contain my patience. I went to the window overlooking the Thames and drummed my fingers on the casement while I concentrated on counting the boats plying their trade along the river until I heard the door open behind me.

'Harry Somers, I am indebted to you.'

I span round at the familiar voice and was startled to see how my former patron had aged in the four years since I saw him last. He had suffered the ignominy of his wife's imprisonment, forfeited his central position in affairs of state and lost his influence with the King, yet his features gave testimony not just to disappointment but illness and perhaps dissipation. Although I acknowledged his claim on my loyalty, my relations with Duke Humphrey had been far from straightforward and I would not have chosen to encounter him again, still less to witness his physical decline. I did not know whether his words referred to my earlier service or my inconclusive conversation with Master Iffley.

'Your Grace.' I bowed.

'Tell me yourself what Gilbert has just repeated to me. The words you quoted which were spoken in Tours. Can you tell me who spoke them?'

'It was Lord Fitzvaughan,' I said, knowing the Duke had always respected his lordship's integrity. 'His words were "the main point has been conceded", as I remember.'

I heard the Duke's intake of breath and he leaned a hand on Iffley's desk to support himself. 'You had no notion what those words meant?'

'No, your Grace, I never knew what the main point was.'

'A capital letter, Doctor, a capital letter which makes all the difference. I'd heard a rumour but the terms of the truce which were made public gave no clue of this scandalous betrayal of my royal brother's heritage.'

I struggled to grasp his meaning, thinking of the victories which his brother, King Henry, fifth of that name, had achieved, the lands in France subsequently lost to the English crown and those the King still held. Then enlightenment came to me. 'The county of Maine? Is that what was meant?'

''Well done, Doctor Somers, you have not lost your flair for solving mysteries. It's now clear to me that a secret clause in the truce refers to the cession of Maine to the French king. A dastardly, cowardly act of treason! If this had been known when the truce was announced the citizens of London would have risen in fury and I should have been at their head. I was intentionally misled, left believing that the rumour I'd heard was ill-founded, that my kingly nephew had rejected the craven suggestion put forward by that renegade Suffolk. Well, it's not too late to create havoc for this French embassy. Thanks to you, Doctor Somers, we now have the truth. You have my gratitude.'

He strode from the room while I was digesting the implications of what he had said: not so much his threat to disrupt the negotiations as the corroboration of my fears regarding Rollo's death and the intercepted letter. Gloucester may not have known of a plot instigated on his behalf but he had been aware of a "rumour" concerning the cession of Maine, although it never appeared in the published terms of the truce. The contentious proposal must have formed the substance of Suffolk's communication to the King, consigned to Rollo and his ill-fated confidential messenger. Henry's reply undoubtedly gave agreement but probably urged secrecy until after the truce had been concluded and his marriage celebrated. The enormity of what I had learned caused me to gawp vacantly at the door through which the Duke had departed until I rallied myself and turned back to his factotum. Gilbert Iffley was smiling at me with bland satisfaction.

'My dear fellow, the Duke is greatly obliged to you. I trust we may rely on your further goodwill.' I was about to demur but he continued hurriedly. 'It will be valuable having young Rendell in Gloucester's entourage. He'll make a commendable go-between.'

'Rendell?' I stared stupidly and bit back the comment that I had obtained a place for him in Suffolk's troop.

'The rascal hasn't told you? He made enquiry when he visited his sister the other day and the master of the guard has agreed. The boy will be joining the Duke's men at Greenwich. You'll be welcome to visit him there – whenever you have news to impart. His welfare will benefit from your interest. Come, Doctor Somers, let us share a stoup of wine and drink to our association, now and in the future.'

His voice was silky, his smile insinuating and for the first time I suspected he was indeed capable of murder.

Chapter 16

I ventured out in public without my doctor's gown so seldom that I felt inadequately dressed when I mounted a horse in the courtyard of the Manor of the Rose, despite the unaccustomed finery of my deep blue velvet tunic and fur-trimmed cloak which had cost me more than I could sensibly afford. It was pretentious and unnecessary to ride the half mile I habitually walked but I felt the occasion justified formality and the dignity of arriving on horseback. I was freshly barbered and my cap with its jaunty feather sat neatly on well cut hair no longer than my ear lobes. I trusted my appearance was every inch that of a successful professional man, worthy the serious attention of any virtuous matron. Nevertheless, I was glad to be spared the mirthful comments of the two young companions who had now left my service. The previous week, at Michaelmas, Leone had ridden off to the west by Jack Cawfield's side and two days later Rendell had embarked on a barge flying Gloucester's pennant, bound downstream to Greenwich. I had engaged a lad to fetch and carry for me while I was working but my rooms were otherwise silent and empty. The time had come for me to create an alternative home for myself so I set out, free from mockery, a hopeful and, I believed, a presentable suitor, ready to claim a new future.

Jane Cawfield had granted my request to call on her and specified the day and time I should come. I had not visited her since Jack left home but she had been so affable and engaging when I last saw her that I believed she suspected the reason for my interest and was content to receive my suit. Accordingly, despite my nervousness, I was optimistic as I turned into Cheapside and approached that impressive doorway which might soon be the entrance to my own residence. The gate into the yard was shut so I tethered my horse to a post in the street but it was only when my second knock went unanswered that I began to worry something was wrong.

The crone who stuck her head out of a window in the house next door did not disguise her amusement. 'Too late, young fellow,' she croaked. 'Got in before you, he did. Didn't stay a widow a moment longer than was decent, that one. She upped and went to the church door as soon as that lad of hers was out of the way. Gone to her new husband's house in the country. She said you'd call and I was to tell you. Seen you before, I have.'

I struggled to control my voice. 'Mistress Cawfield has married? Who is her husband?'

'Lord love you, I don't know who he is, some petty baron. I'd see him call on her, like I saw you time enough. But I'll tell you this, she was carrying his child. Beginning to show it was, no time to be lost. Couldn't hoodwink me, brazen hussy! You're well rid of her.'

I was ill-mannered as I parted from my informant, furious and humiliated by Jane Cawfield's deceit. I untethered the horse, hauled myself into the saddle and without caring where I went, cursing my trustful idiocy, I rode away from Cheapside and into a narrow side alley leading towards the Guildhall. I rounded the corner and saw a crowd collected in the forecourt of the Lord Mayor's headquarters and I realised they were listening to an orator who was arousing their passion. Scrawny and muscular arms waved together in the air, fists clenched, and when the shouts became intelligible I understood that their fury was directed against the French truce and Suffolk who bore responsibility for it. I could not see the speaker as he reached his peroration, raising his distinctive voice, but his words carried along the narrow lane with power and clarity.

'In secret the upstart plotted to serve his own interests: persuaded our pious King that a charming little bride was worth the surrender of his father's inheritance. Only now we learn the county of Maine is the price of this marriage. Damn Suffolk's double-dealing! But Londoners know how to respond. They know who champions their cause. Humphrey of Gloucester has never let you down. Declare for him now and call for him to resume his rightful place at the King's right hand. Get about the work which needs to be done, citizens: make your demands known, carry the message to the gates of Westminster Palace, teach the presumptuous Marquis and his followers they cannot trifle with the City. London has its rights and its defender. Raise your voices for Duke Humphrey.'

Most of the crowd surged forward screaming Gloucester's name but some broke free, running in all directions, brandishing cudgels and axes. A stone crashed against a shuttered window, splitting the wood, and only then did I appreciate how vulnerable was my position: a finely dressed man in the middle of this angry rabble – a man, moreover, whom someone might recognise as Suffolk's servitor. I turned my horse quickly but I had already been spotted and a howl of derision went up from those nearest me.

'Look at this toff. Where you off to, courtier?'

'Who'd you serve then?'

'Pull him down.'

A strong hand grasped my bridle and my horse reared, terrified by the noise and people crowding him.

'I'm not a courtier. I'm a physician,' I spluttered.

They jeered, poking at the fur on my cloak. 'Where's your gown then?'

'Let's get the tunic off his back.'

Suddenly one of the men pulling at the horse's harness pointed to the crest on an engraved plate which decorated the trappings. 'Look at this. It's a bloody leopard's head. He's one of Suffolk's men we're looking for. Drag him off. Cut his throat.'

A distant cheer suggested some other unfortunate wretch had fallen victim to the mob's bloodlust and it gave me the opportunity which I did not deserve. Heads swivelled, grips relaxed and, I thank the saints, I had the presence of mind to urge my restless horse into motion. Two men fell as we hurtled ahead, shaking off their grasp, and I gave full rein to the animal's instinct for escape. A missile hit me as we careered back into Cheapside and towards St. Paul's but I dared not turn south towards Suffolk's house in case a hostile crowd had collected outside its walls. My pursuers were on foot so I hoped I could outstrip them but stray demonstrators tried to halt my progress by hurling sticks and cabbages at my horse's hooves. Somehow he evaded them and we thundered on, until I could see the gatehouse at Newgate, and I prayed that I could flee to Westminster until peace had been restored in the streets. Church bells were ringing by this time and I saw armed men assembling to quell the riot but then I realised that the huge gates had been bolted shut to prevent anyone leaving the City's confines and spreading disorder. There would be no time to explain myself to the marshal-at-arms for half a dozen cudgel-bearing apprentices were close behind me and my horse was tiring. I could think of only one possibility and urged the poor animal into one final dash down an alley parallel to the walls.

Master John Webber was hastily fastening the shutters outside his premises when he saw me approaching with the apprentices at my heels and he needed no explanation of the situation. He flung open the side-gate to his yard and slammed it shut behind us, bellowing through the planks at the young rowdies who seemed to have come to a halt.

'I've seen you, Matthew Tate and William Slater. You'll be beaten until your backs are rutted with gore when you come home – and you'll have nothing but dry bread on your plates for a week. Be off now and take care the guard doesn't put you in a cell. Young fools, the man you're chasing is a good customer and his patronage puts food on our table.'

I slid from my saddle as my saviour led the horse to a water trough. 'They're your apprentices?'

'Two of them. What's got into them this time? Is it this story about secret treaty terms?'

I gulped breath. 'Some rabble-rouser outside the Guildhall.'

'Gloucester's man, I'll be bound. They're right to be outraged by such perfidy but I don't hold with terrorising innocent riders.' He stared at me as I brushed mud from my grimy cloak. 'But you're richly clad today, Doctor Somers. Did they mistake you for a member of the court?'

Unable to speak further I nodded and he led me into his house to the most welcome draught of ale I had ever enjoyed. At least the horror of the incident had driven aside the chagrin I felt outside Jane Cawfield's house but I knew the whole sequence of events emphasised my naïve stupidity. I swore to myself that henceforth I would abjure all pretension, renounce ambition which strayed outside my humble calling and abandon any thought of matrimony. I stayed with the apothecary until order had been restored and the City gates re-opened but, even then, I was grateful to borrow a cloak of well-worn fustian to conceal my inappropriate attire for my return to the Manor of the Rose.

*****

I fulfilled my physician's remit over the following days with earnest dedication, never venturing outside the walls of Suffolk's residence. I saw the Marquis only once when he asked me to poultice his back and I noted he was tense and not talkative but I welcomed his silence. I had no wish to question him about the progress of the talks with the French nobles or the impact of the unrest in the City and I was glad that my task did not take long. Then, as I packed my bag to leave him, he seemed to remember something and tapped my arm.

'The household will be moving to my castle at Wingfield in a week's time. You shall come with us. I think you are not familiar with the county which gives me my title. The air is fresh and invigorating.'

'It will be good for you, my Lord.'

'We'll have a few weeks' respite because the French ambassadors are going home. They're to come back later in the year.' I did not comment and he stretched up one arm tentatively, testing whether the pull on his spine was painful. 'His Grace the King has been beset by contrary advice but I'm sure he will confirm the truce when they return. Queen Margaret will persuade him that further delay will be dangerous. Meanwhile we can breathe good country air and ride to the hunt with no competing demands on our time. I trust you will enjoy our visit, Doctor Somers, and all your patients will be restored to full health.'

The prospect of a visit to the country pleased me and I walked back to my rooms feeling happier than I had since my appalling journey to Jane Cawfield's house but I was not given the opportunity to indulge cheerful thoughts. A squire in royal livery was waiting at my door and the verbal message he delivered brooked no denial. I was summoned immediately to attend the Queen's ladies and, in particular, one lady whose name was not spoken but whose identity was obvious. The immaculate youth accompanied me as I rode, clad in my proper gown and cap, and we were admitted to the Palace of Westminster without the need for any formalities or scrutiny.

I was shown at once to a large chamber where half a dozen attendants sat with their sewing and I had scarcely bowed to them when Madame Yolande drew me aside into a window bay, signalling to a page to pick up his lute and sing. Outside the sky was cloudy and the lady's face was shadowed by moulding on the exterior lintel.

'We will speak softly, Doctor Somers, and not be overheard. I am grateful that you have come but must upbraid you for neglecting us these several weeks.'

Her expression was severe but her voice trembled and the vertical furrows between her eyebrows, which I had never seen before, indicated anxiety. 'Your pardon but I was hesitant to intrude more than was seemly.'

'Doctor Somers, I need counsel. There is no one here in whom I may safely confide. What I say would be fed back to her Grace and she would berate me for obstinacy. I have suffered a gruelling time with Seigneur Philippe's attentions and he insists that we shall be publicly affianced when the ambassadors return. I have been steadfast in my refusal but I cannot hold out against... physical...' She faltered and gripped the window sill as if she might fall without support and I was appalled to see how fragile she appeared, so unlike her usual resolute self.

'He has threatened you, madame?'

She looked away and her whisper was so quiet I was uncertain if I had really heard aright. 'He has molested me.' She paused but then she faced me, gathering her strength. 'He has demeaned me, humiliated me as if I were a common slut.'

I mouthed my question, not daring to speak. 'He tried to rape you?'

She shook her head. 'Not this time but he has pledged that he will, if I do not yield willingly. The Queen permitted him to encounter me alone, except for a frightened little maid, and he called his foul servant to attend him. Charpentier held my arms while his master pawed me, scrabbling at my stomacher as if he would strip it from my dress. He would have gone further but I kicked out and that riled him so he contented himself with slapping me. He knew we would not remain undisturbed and my cowering chaperone could report all.'

'Surely the Queen wouldn't condone this outrage?'

'She blames me for intransigence and says I have no option but to take the aggressor as my husband when the ambassadors return. Otherwise my disgrace will be made known and I shall be proclaimed a harlot. I am defeated.'

I was unable to control my fury. 'You cannot marry this monster. You must not!'

She gave a sad half-smile. 'Dear Doctor Somers, I have no choice. I have been out-witted.'

I thought quickly. 'You must win time. You have promised to serve the Queen in England for a year and it would be dutiful to insist on fulfilling your commitment. Surely she would appreciate that? Write to your brother. Tell him of the assault and beg his protection from the villain.'

'I would not be safe from the Seigneur's viciousness while the embassy is at the court. He will be furious if I refuse to allow the announcement of our nuptials.'

'Couldn't you seek sanctuary somewhere when the French nobles return?'

'I have no means to achieve it, here where I am a stranger. I regard Master Francisco as my only friend at the court and I cannot put him in an invidious position as the Queen's physician.'

Her predicament tugged at my heart. 'If I could help, madame, I am acquainted with a religious house where the Prioress is understanding and wise. Perhaps she would grant you a temporary haven.' As I spoke I recognised that my words could be over-optimistic, for the astute Prioress would not easily forego hope of obtaining the Queen's bounty for the sake of a wayward underling.

The Countess shook her head. 'It would be too difficult, I think. I am condemned to suffer my fate. I am bound to acquiesce.'

Her resignation contained both grandeur and pathos, compelling me to respond, and instinctively I put my hand on hers, withdrawing it at once as I realised the solecism I had committed. 'Your pardon, madame.'

She touched my arm lightly. 'I value your kindness, Doctor Somers, and have nothing to forgive. Kindness is to be treasured; there is so much inhumanity among mankind. The Count was always kind to me, so I found it natural to serve and support him. I esteemed him and my duty was no burden, despite the difference in our ages. I cannot respect a man who would trick me into marriage by abusing my honour.'

I had felt her hand quiver when I clasped it and I was riveted by her graceful response. My compassion welled up so strongly that it was transformed into something rarer, some emotion I had almost forgotten. However futile it might be, I could no more walk away from her than I could stop myself breathing.

'If you were ill, madame, while the ambassadors are here, you could avoid them. Master Francisco is an agreeable colleague and might prove helpful without endangering his duty to the Queen. With your permission I will speak to him.'

She gazed at me and her expression softened. 'He thinks highly of your knowledge. Would you do this?'

'Any assistance I can offer is yours to command. I pledge you my service.' My voice was shaking.

As if to illuminate the revelation which had come to me the sky had lightened and a beam of sunshine fell on her face. Her beautiful grey eyes were filled with tears. 'Your pledge exceeds the bounds of kindness. Am I right to suspect as much?'

I did not hesitate. 'It would be improper for me to say more, given the difference in our rank, but you may judge my sincerity.'

She sighed. 'We are told that in heaven there is no distinction of worldly rank and all are judged on their merits. Perhaps on some other earth men might live so.'

'On some other earth,' I repeated, charmed by her notion. 'On some other earth I might speak freely but not here.'

'On some other earth, Harry Somers, I would claim your love and return it.'

I nearly dropped to my knees before her but laughter at the far end of the chamber brought me to my senses. It was probably not directed at us but our tête-à-tête had been protracted and propriety must be observed. 'I should go, Madame Yolande, but my pledge remains with you. Send for me when help is needed.'

We moved into the centre of the room and the Countess appeared composed as we strolled towards her companions. 'The French embassy is expected to return around the Feast of St. Martin,' she said as if it were a matter of no consequence. 'I shall be happy to consult you again before then, Doctor Somers. In the meantime, I pray you will consider possible remedies for the ailment which troubles me. I am grateful for your advice.'

The page had begun to sing again and, it seemed to me, I had never heard such a dulcet melody.

*****

The pleasure I first felt at the prospect of our expedition to Wingfield in the County of Suffolk had evaporated and I was loath to travel so far from Westminster, although I argued to myself that we would necessarily return when the French nobles crossed the sea at Martinmas. My thoughts were distracted by absurd but beguiling fancies as I packed my instruments, ready for departure, and although they could never be realised I cherished them. I rejoiced that Jane Cawfield had deceived me, leaving me free from guilt to indulge this vain devotion, which I had never felt towards her, and I marvelled that,

221

after so many disappointments, I was still capable of experiencing love.

When a messenger arrived at the Manor of the Rose with a letter for me, I saw it came from Stamford and broke the seal with casual interest, entirely unprepared for its strange contents.

I am given to understand, Doctor Somers, that you will shortly be venturing to the Marquis's residence at Wingfield. This is fortuitous. It would be beneficial to all concerned if you could seek leave of absence to make the journey to Stamford before joining William de la Pole in his titular county. I urge you to present yourself at the Priory in three or four days' time. Matter awaits you which is worthy of your attention. Do not mention this to those it does not concern but you may refer to the good offices of my Lord Abbot of Peterborough if Suffolk queries your business here.

The Prioress's spidery signature completed the epistle, which left me bewildered but reassured by the injunction to tell no one including, I presumed, Lady Maud Fitzvaughan. I supposed the "matter" related to affairs at court and I had no objection to discussing what I knew with the engaging old cloisteress; indeed I welcomed the opportunity to meet her again. Suffolk readily agreed to my request to delay my arrival at Wingfield, seeking no explanation but chuckling over the assignation he imagined I had with a mistress, so within twenty-four hours I was once more on the road north from the City and made good speed to the hostelry of the Raven where I had lodged before.

When I presented myself at St. Michael's I was shown to the parlour where I met the Prioress previously. While I waited I heard birdsong through the door leading to the cloister and the sounds of children's voices – children, probably of irregular but high-born parentage, cared for at the Priory. The Prioress did not keep me long and she seemed pleased with herself when she swept into the room, appraising my appearance but smiling as she seated herself in the single chair beside the hatch to the gatekeeper's lodge.

'I am obliged that you have come, Doctor Somers, and I believe your visit will relieve you of unfinished business. It is not so momentous as the affairs of state, which engage the energies of Marquis and Duke alike and will gain added vigour when the French ambassadors return, but you will find it interesting. Gloucester is spoiling for a fight, I understand.'

'As ever you are well informed, Reverend Mother.'

'Not least by you. I am grateful. But to the matter in hand. There is a visitor to the Priory you must meet.' She opened the hatch and called to the gatekeeper. 'We are ready, sister.' Then she smoothed her skirts and turned to me. 'You have not yet followed my advice to marry.'

I was embarrassed by her enquiry and doubtful how to reply, fearing she knew too much about me already. I cleared my throat but was saved from speaking when the gatekeeper admitted a gentleman, from his dress clearly of high rank but suffering from considerable infirmity. He walked stiffly, leaning on a heavy stick, and his face which still bore traces of earlier good looks was contorted. I deduced that he strove to disguise the pain he endured.

'My Lord,' the Prioress said, 'may I present Doctor Somers who serves the Marquis of Suffolk.' The twittering of birds and children had ceased and her words rang out in the small room.

I bowed, waiting for her to enlighten me as to the gentleman's identity but she did not, leaving it to him to introduce himself. He eyed me severely before inclining his head. 'I apologise for not responding to your letter, Doctor. I suspected it was a trick by the lady we both know and doubted your integrity. I appreciate now I was in error and I regret my negligence.'

223

Fully enlightened but amazed, I bowed again. 'My lord Earl, I'm honoured to meet you. My letter was presumptuous and I was hardly surprised you didn't reply.'

'It did however provoke me to reflect that I had been remiss in leaving the Reverend Prioress ignorant of the welfare of her former charge. Hence we have come to see her and, when she explained your credentials, I agreed to share with you the happy tidings I have brought her.'

The Prioress had risen and she crossed to the door into the main part of the convent, opening it slightly and summoning someone who stood outside. A young girl entered shyly and made obeisance to us all. She was slim, dressed beautifully but without ostentation, and her luxuriant curling hair fell unbound to her waist. I knew, of course, who she must be but it was only when she raised huge violet eyes towards me, before quickly lowering her lashes over them in an intuitive but familiar manner, that I recognised her mother's beauty in her guileless face.

'Mistress Eleanor, I am pleased to meet you.'

'My little charge has blossomed into a fine maiden and prospers under her father's care.' The Prioress put her hand on the girl's shoulder, brushing aside a fluttering curl. 'Would you wish to return to St. Michael's care, young lady? Speak truth now.'

Eleanor gave a rueful grin. 'Forgive me, Reverend Mother, but I like it well at father's castle. I missed the kind nuns at first but now I have many friends at home.'

'Good child. May Heaven bless you. We need not detain you from your recreation but you should be aware that Doctor Somers is your friend. He has been much concerned to ensure your well-being and you should remember him with appreciation.'

Eleanor gave a bob. 'Thank you, sir,' she said. 'You are kind.'

I acknowledged her remark but my throat was constricted as she ran off towards the cloister and my voice was reedy. 'My lord, I'm overwhelmed to have seen your delightful daughter.'

The Earl of Stanwick shifted his position and I thought he grimaced with discomfort but he waved away the Prioress's offer of her seat, too proud to admit his need. 'Now, Doctor Somers, you deserve to hear the explanation for my underhand actions. I have already informed the Prioress. I must ask first that you agree, as she has done, not to share my confidences with anyone else.'

I took a deep breath, sorry to disturb the joyful atmosphere. 'My lord, I owe it to Lady Fitzvaughan to tell her that her daughter is safe. I undertook her commission to investigate Eleanor's disappearance.'

He bit his lip but a fleeting glimmer came into his eyes before he nodded. 'That is proper. I don't object but I request you give Maud no details. Her life and mine would have been utterly different if my father had not forbidden our union but I have long ago faced reality, as she has.' He gave an awkward shrug and propped himself against the casement while the Prioress returned to her chair.

'Doctor Somers,' he began sonorously, 'I admit I was content to leave Eleanor in St Michael's care, depending on my lawyer to see that her upkeep was supported from my revenues. This arrangement would have continued until the girl was dowered and wed but some three years past I suffered great misfortune and it was necessary to review my affairs. My wife, Countess Mary, is now past child-bearing, but God in His mercy had granted us two fine sons after our marriage and I had no concerns for my heritage. Perhaps the sins of my youth required sacrifice, for the little lads themselves did nothing to warrant their fate, but the sweating sickness came into the house and they were both lost to us. Our grief was desperate and compounded by the knowledge that I was bereft of suitable heirs to my estates. Near the same time, I became afflicted with the wasting sickness which you see gradually destroying me. As a physician, you will recognise that my remaining time on earth is limited.

'My cousin will succeed to the title. Nothing can change that outcome, unless the untrustworthy wretch disgraces himself enough to merit the King's reckoning or he is knifed by one he has harmed. That is unworthy of me, I confess, but he is a despicable man. Happily, he doesn't need to inherit all my wealth and it's in my gift to name a different heir for many of my estates. I thank God that the Countess has always been aware of Eleanor's existence and she has been a bastion in supporting my decision. I have publicly acknowledged my daughter, made the necessary provision in my will and, for good measure, petitioned the King to endorse Eleanor's rights as if she were true-born. That is why I took her from the Priory and why I wanted no interference until everything was settled. My cousin remains in ignorance but my lawyer holds documents, certified and sealed, which will safeguard Eleanor's inheritance. She will be a great heiress and I shall die in peace.'

Although I was deeply touched by the ailing man's sincerity, I held stubbornly to the responsibility I had assumed in accepting Maud's assignment. 'Eleanor's mother would be overjoyed to know what you have done. She feared the child had been abducted for some heinous purpose.' The Earl grunted as if he found my assertion improbable and I became annoyed. 'Lady Fitzvaughan was subject to appalling abuse as a girl. Her fears may have been misplaced but they were not capricious. Why are you unwilling to trust her with the truth?'

The Earl leaned forward putting his weight over his stick. 'I have not named Maud as the child's mother. I swore my mistress died giving birth to Eleanor. Maud has a distinguished husband now. I have no wish to bring disgrace on her.'

Humbled, I recognized his wisdom. 'It would indeed be a calamity if Lord Fitzvaughan were to learn the full story. I'll tell her no more than you would wish.'

Only then did he relax and, with a sigh, ask the question he had withheld. 'Is she still beautiful, Doctor Somers? Can she still cause havoc in a man's heart?'

I felt the flush rise from my throat as I tried to sound dispassionate. ''Lady Maud is very beautiful.'

The Prioress gave a slight cough and rose to her feet.

The Earl grunted again and moved away from the wall. 'May God be with her and judge her kindly,' he said and, although he turned from me, I glimpsed a tear on his lashes.

Chapter 17

Before I left Stamford I claimed five minutes of the Prioress's time alone. I hoped the joyful encounter with Eleanor and her father would have put the reverend lady in a charitable mood, so I asked her, with as much insouciance as I could muster, whether she would be willing to provide a haven for a noblewoman who might wish to escape for a time from court life. I should have known better than to underestimate her shrewdness.

Her aquiline nose shot up and she eyed me suspiciously. 'What trouble is she in?'

'She is threatened with a marriage not to her liking.'

'A maiden, under her father's tutelage?'

'No, a widow; but others seek to compel her obedience.'

'She is your mistress?'

'No, no indeed.' I sounded flustered and my cheeks were burning. 'She is far above my rank but she has sought my help.'

The Prioress drummed her fingers on the table at her side. 'Surely she has more suitable friends than you to arrange such matters?' I began to stammer something but enlightenment had dawned and her words soared over mine. 'She is a foreign lady? One of the Queen's French attendants with whom you are acquainted?'

I read her expression and her tone of voice, nodding unhappily as she slapped the flat of her hand on the table-top. 'Doctor Somers, I concede that your good offices in respect of Eleanor merit my gratitude but there are limits to what I will offer in thanks and I will never jeopardise the well-being of St. Michael's for the sake of some wilful French flibbertigibbet. The Queen has lately granted a generous benefaction to the Priory, in answer to my loyal entreaties, and I will not put her future favour at hazard. I presume Queen Margaret herself encourages this marriage?'

I confirmed that this was so and begged her to think no more about my request but it had aggravated her and she would not abandon the subject. 'If this virtuous widow wishes to take the veil, I would be willing to write to a sister house near London where they might accommodate her. I'm confident the Queen would not thwart a pious lady who devoutly wished to enter the cloister. What I will not do is incur royal anger by offering sanctuary to a woman who has no intention of following a holy life. Do you understand?'

'Perfectly, Reverend Mother.'

'The other situation where I feel bound to render assistance to a headstrong sinner is if a child is born of a mésalliance. As in the case of Eleanor, I have a duty before Heaven to provide for such a child in Christian charity. Is your French noblewoman enceinte?' Speechless with embarrassment, I shook my head and the Prioress swept on with her declamation. 'Then she must seek assistance elsewhere and I recommend that you have no more to do with the business. The Queen's favour is worth a great deal more than the smiles of a beguiling schemer – to both of us, Doctor Somers.'

Terrified that she suspected the attraction I felt for Madame Yolande, I blundered into an attempt to mislead her, referring to her advice that I might marry a widow, and mentioning my disappointment with Mistress Cawfield. Her reaction was unexpected.

'You've been preserved from a grievous mistake, Doctor. I know of Jane Cawfield and she would be most unsuitable as your wife. She is kin to the Nevilles.'

My bewilderment was obvious and the Prioress's tone changed to one of patient instruction. 'I've told you of my family link to the Percys. In the north of England their rivals as magnates are the Nevilles. Richard of York is married to a Neville and this Jane is her distant relative. York's lineage may yet prove damaging to the King and it's regrettable that he and Gloucester are close allies. Have nothing to do with their faction.'

I was bemused by her words, nodding blankly, and remained at St. Michael's only long enough to pen a cautious letter for the Prioress to forward to Maud. Then I set out to travel to Wingfield and the castle which was the Marquis of Suffolk's powerbase. I realised it was less than a day's journey from there to the Fitzvaughan estates in Norfolk but I had no intention of venturing further to encounter her ladyship in person.

I shrugged off the unexpected news about Jane Cawfield and tried not to dwell on my failure to help Madame Yolande, although this distressed me, but the happy outcome concerning Maud's daughter reminded me of my inability to unravel fully the other mystery which, after eighteen months, still riled me.

*****

Wingfield's main fortifications were an imposing gatehouse and corner towers joined by castellated walls, behind which nestled a charming manor house embellished by the Marquis's grandfather. Suffolk was treating his visit as an opportunity for leisure, hunting with hawk or hounds, as well as inspecting his lands in the neighbourhood, and he issued no instructions for me. Several noblemen were his guests and I was delighted to see that Walter Fitzvaughan was one of his close companions, with Gaston de la Tour at his side, for their absence from Norfolk would make it easier for Maud to receive and destroy my letter.

The steward at the castle was an amiable fellow who made me welcome and kept me busy with a succession of retainers who were glad to consult a physician about their ailments, as usually they were reliant only on a local wise woman. In fact the advice and remedies they received from her won my approval in most cases but I was able to give some further guidance about their treatments. After a few days I had seen all the patients the steward referred to me but, in company with Suffolk's chaplain at the castle, he begged a moment of my time to speak of a different issue.

'There's an old dame lodged in a cabin outside the grounds who's fading fast and seems greatly troubled in her mind,' the steward said. 'She's served the household well for many years. Father Wilfred calls on her regularly but he's been unable to calm her. He wonders if you could help.'

I probably looked dubious because the priest interjected before I could respond. 'It's not a cure for her bodily weakness that I'm seeking – I appreciate the time is past for that. But she's in spiritual distress and nothing I say seems to console her. I try to distract her with news which might be of interest, as well as instructing her on Holy Scripture in accordance with my calling. I chanced to mention you had come to Wingfield, Doctor Somers, and told her what I knew of you from others. It was when I said you'd been with the Marquis in France last year that she became excited, although she didn't explain her reason, and she asked if you would visit her. I'm reluctant to impose on you but if you could humour her it might bring her some comfort. She's a worthy woman and it's my duty to help her face her end in meek submission to God's will.'

The chaplain seemed as likeable as the steward and I was happy to oblige them although I doubted I could bring solace to a disturbed old woman whose mind was almost certainly wandering. The priest accompanied me to her lodging and I saw immediately the severity of her physical frailty but, after he left me with her, I soon realised that her mental faculties was in no way impaired. She drew up her crooked body on the pallet and reached for my hand, speaking with shrill urgency.

'Father Wilfred told me you were in France at the time of the truce. Were you in Blois, sir?'

I answered cautiously. 'I joined the Marquis in Tours but I visited Blois.'

'Did you hear anything of my son, sir? He died there.

I steadied my hand so that it would not shake in her grasp. 'What was his name, good-mother?'

'Rollo. Rollo Rudd. He wasn't a bad man. I know it. He served William de la Pole loyally. But they tell me he died in a brawl, outside a bawdy house, with all his sins on him. They say he'll go to Hell and I won't find him in God's care when my time comes. I can't bear to think that. It tears me apart.'

I pressed her fingers gently, controlling my own emotion. 'I never met Rollo but I heard much about him from his lord. He died honourably on Suffolk's business and is sincerely mourned. Who told you this nonsense about his death? Was it the chaplain?'

She gave a squeak of irritation. 'Chaplain never knew Rollo. He only repeats what he's heard, same as all of them. Suffolk sent word to let me know Rollo had been killed. He didn't give details, didn't suggest any disgrace. But then the man came to the market at Diss around Midsummer and he bad-mouthed my boy to the landlord at the inn. He said Rollo was a villain and got no more than he deserved. He said Rollo was a base and rowdy scoundrel, asking to have his throat cut.'

'Who was this man, mother? How did he know about Rollo?'

She shook her head wearily. 'No one knew his name but he was a cheery fellow by all accounts, generous, bought ale at the tavern for everyone and drank deeply himself. No one had seen him before, maybe a salesman travelling to the wool fairs. He had a scar.'

I froze, my hand rigid in hers. 'A scar?'

'Over his eye, the landlord said, nasty, angry-looking. Was the man right, Doctor, did he tell the truth?'

232

I bent towards her to be sure she could see my face. 'No, mother, God forgive him, he was a liar. He has caused you needless grief. Rollo was murdered by one who wished to harm the Marquis. Suffolk tried to discover the murderer and bring him to justice. I made enquiries on his behalf but couldn't identify the wretch responsible – only that he had a scar, just as you described.'

She seized my arm, hauling herself into a sitting position. 'Are you sure? Is it true? Blessed saints, have we been tricked? Was it my boy's murderer telling lies about him?'

'I can't answer you, mother,' I said as I eased her back against the straw-filled bolster. 'But I give you my pledge I will renew my search for him. Try to rest your spirits now and put those foul lies out of your mind. Rollo served his master well.'

She closed her eyes and released my hand. 'God be praised for sending me this comfort. Heaven bless you, Doctor. I may hope to see my boy again in God's good time.'

'Amen,' I whispered but there was no peace in my raging heart. Could this evil braggart have been Gilbert Iffley? It was difficult to imagine but evidence was building which might incriminate him.

*****

Within a week we were back in London, expecting the imminent return of the French nobles who were already riding through Kent with strict instructions from their King to conclude the truce on the terms he had specified. Awaiting me, to my joy, was a request from Master Francisco to call on Madame Yolande in a professional capacity, as she was suffering from a disorder on which he would welcome my opinion. The brotherhood of physicians had never seemed so advantageous.

Meanwhile there was another encounter I was determined to have, however rash it might prove, and I presented myself at the gatehouse of Baynard's Castle with the urgent request to see Master Gilbert Iffley, intending to put direct and provocative questions to him. The gatekeeper stared at me as if I was feeble-minded and summoned a guard to escort me from the building when by good fortune Bartholomew approached from the courtyard, leading a saddled horse, and he quickly led me aside.

'Master Iffley hasn't been here for six weeks or more. He left with the French ambassadors and will return with them shortly.'

I was nonplussed. 'He went to France with them?'

'I suppose so. Is something wrong, Doctor? You look angry.'

I tried to disguise my frustration. 'I'd hoped to discuss a problem with him. It'll have to wait. Is Master Iffley often away from the Duke's household?'

Bartholomew grinned. 'I first met him in France when we were there last year, just at the time that rat, Gaston de la Tour, was plotting to get rid of me from Lord Fitzvaughan's household. Since I joined Iffley's service, after we returned to England, he's been away as much as he's at home. I don't complain. I welcome the freedom to work without his oversight. He values my accuracy with pen and counting frame'

'Was he in Tours at the time of the truce?'

'He was representing Gloucester so he kept a low profile but he knew someone in Suffolk's train – his secretary, I think.'

'Andrew Cawfield?'

'Yes, that's the name. I heard he died, poor fellow. Master Iffley used to meet him regularly. They'd known each other for years. I think they had business with some of the French lords who opposed the truce but I never knew anything about it.'

Bartholomew's revelation fed my suspicion that Gilbert Iffley had been responsible for the interception of Suffolk's letter to the King, and it linked Cawfield with him, convincing me the wretched secretary's death was no accident. He had been killed by those who had previously bribed him to betray his master. My impatience to question Iffley was difficult to contain but perhaps his absence was a blessing, I reflected, for I needed to concentrate on other immediate concerns.

*****

The palace was festooned with garlands welcoming the French envoys and I was uncomfortably aware of their presence as I mounted the stairs to the Queen's lodgings. I steeled myself to suppress my emotions, pushing aside the memory of the soft words Madame Yolande had given me at our previous meeting in case they had been a fleeting whim which she regretted. It was a relief to be shielded by my physician's panoply and Master Francisco greeted me jovially, enjoying the masquerade we had devised although he understood little of the circumstances. He led me to the antechamber where the lady was propped on a day-bed, attended by her tiring maid and with a range of potions set out on a table by her side.

As soon as I saw her my heart somersaulted with delight for there was no misconstruing the tender look she gave me, belying the severity of her voice. 'I am in great pain, Doctor Somers,' she said. 'Master Francisco thinks I have damaged my shoulder badly and must rest but I have consented to his request that you give him your opinion.'

I bowed and with trembling hands examined her right collarbone and upper arm while she winced convincingly as I touched her and sank back against the pillows as if in agony. I nodded, assuming some semblance of detachment as I spoke.

'I concur with Master Francisco's judgement. Complete rest is necessary for the injury to correct itself. It is difficult to apply a splint in such a position to hasten recovery but perhaps some strapping would help.'

My fellow physician drew his gown round him and cleared his throat. 'Well thought of. I have advised her Grace, the Queen, that the comtesse should play no part in the activities of the court for some weeks. With reluctance, she has accepted my advice.'

'I will miss the ceremonies in connection with the French embassy,' she said with an impressive show of regret, 'and have been forced to reject all requests from our visitors to wait on me.'

Master Francisco had turned to the attendant, giving instructions about the dosage of various remedies, and Yolande took her opportunity to add the information I longed to hear. 'Philippe de la Flèche has already renewed his suit. The Queen favours it but in view of my illness she has consented that an announcement be deferred. She is touched by my wish to remain in her service until the summer.'

The Queen's physician came to my side and I assumed a solemn expression. 'Doctor Somers, I know you are always welcome with the Queen's ladies and, if the comtesse agrees, I would be content for you to visit, on my behalf, during her convalescence. I have many calls on my time and would find it most expedient. As you appreciate it is a case where nature will heal but the lady should be examined from time to time to ensure all is well.'

I bowed my head and with due solemnity accepted the charge.

*****

Next day I received a message from Bartholomew that Master Iffley had returned to Baynard's Castle and would be pleased to see me. I went without delay but on arrival I was taken to wait in an antechamber and when Iffley joined me he looked unusually worried. He was soberly dressed as usual but some buttons of his tunic were undone.

'The Duke was not himself after the midday meal, complained of a muzzy head and queasiness. He's taken to his bed now and is sleeping soundly so I was free to leave him. I'm glad to see you, Doctor Somers.'

'He has his own physician in attendance?'

'No. The fellow's at Greenwich. He doesn't accompany the Duke everywhere. I can't believe it's a serious ailment. Gloucester's been very busy, rushing to and from the court. He complained of tiredness this morning. Just needs rest, I expect.'

'Well, as I'm here, if there's anything I can do.' It was incumbent upon me to offer although I had no wish to be involved with Gloucester's health. 'I hear you've been in France.'

'I crossed the Narrow Sea in company with the French nobles, when they went home two months ago, but I was bound for Normandy. I had business with my cousin who commands a garrison in King Henry's lands. I returned direct from Harfleur.' He gave one of his winning smiles. 'I've missed some of the excitement in the City streets but now the Frenchmen are returned to England it will doubtless intensify.'

Doubtless, I thought, if Gloucester's henchmen are provoking it, but I did not comment.

He poured wine and held out a glass. 'It occurred to me that you had taken the advice I gave you when last we met. You remember I suggested you might seduce one of the Queen's ladies. It seems one of them has thwarted her mistress's plans by taking to her bed. Margaret is mightily displeased, they say.'

'I've seduced no one,' I said, ignoring his raised eyebrow. 'Did you visit Rouen in your recent trip? I wondered if you'd encountered a goldsmith there who did me service in the summer.'

'Good Master Edwin Drewman? Yes, indeed, and he mentioned you. He's grateful for the opportunity you gave him to ease the Queen's financial embarrassment.'

'I don't know if the loan was ever repaid.'

His laugh was cynical. 'From the royal coffers? Unlikely. But having her Grace in his debt is a comfortable position for a rich man. It brings favour and facilitates further trade.'

'You'd met Master Drewman when you were in Rouen before?'

Iffley nodded. 'We've had dealings in the past. But do you have news for me, Doctor Somers? The King hasn't yet sworn to the final terms of the truce, I hear. There's to be a crucial meeting with him tomorrow. Gloucester and Suffolk will eyeball each other across the throne and Duke Humphrey is hopeful he may yet persuade his royal nephew to reject the demeaning requirement to cede Maine to France. What does Suffolk think? Does he sense that his influence is waning?'

'He gives no indication,' I said and broached the subject I had come to raise. 'I went to his castle of Wingfield recently and learned that a travelling fellow, in the neighbourhood, had been gossiping about the murder of one of the Marquis's closest attendants, last year in Blois. The fellow appears to be scarred above the left eye.'

Gilbert Iffley held my gaze and then burst into laughter. 'My dear Harry, are you suggesting I am a cut-throat?

I never answered that tendentious question because even while he spoke there were shouts and running feet before a frantic banging on the door and the eruption into the room of a wild-eyed serving man. 'Pardon, Master Iffley.

Please come at once. The Duke has collapsed. He tried to get to his close-stool but fell. His eyes rolled in his head and he's unconscious.'

There was no option but to accompany a white-faced Gilbert Iffley hurrying along the corridor and I was alarmed when I entered the Duke's bedroom and saw my unwelcome patient. His attendants had lifted him onto his bed and his head lolled to one side, his cheeks grey and leathery. As I examined him, to my relief, he came to himself but his speech was laboured.

'Black shadows. Behind my eyes. Emptiness.'

'Are you in pain your Grace?'

'Not now. Across my forehead, a band of iron. Gone now.' He showed no sign of recognising me.

'Good. Can you lift your arms?'

Slowly he did as I asked, although it seemed more ponderous for him to raise the left arm, and he managed to wiggle his fingers. So too he could move his legs. His pulse was restless but his breathing had eased.

I addressed the principal attendant. 'Bring me a mild solution of foxglove and chamomile for him to drink – well diluted with wine – and send for the Duke's physician from Greenwich. I will administer the medicine. Then, your Grace, you must rest completely until this episode has passed. It is imperative you do not stir from your bed until you have regained your strength.'

Gilbert Iffley accompanied me from the room when I had done all I could and Gloucester was sleeping peacefully. 'How serious is it, Doctor Somers?'

'I make no promises but I think he will recover. It's fortunate the apoplexy was not more severe. He needs to take care because these attacks may recur and can prove fatal. Make sure he follows the directions of his own physician.'

'It's fortunate you were at hand, Harry.' He sighed and it was the first time I felt confident Iffley was speaking with sincerity. I did not have the temerity to return to the subject of Rollo's murderer.

*****

As I walked back to the Manor of the Rose my mind was filled with the implications of Gloucester's illness and the admission Gilbert Iffley had made of previous dealings with Master Edwin Drewman. More and more connections were being revealed which linked Gloucester's factotum with events in France the previous year but although he had not explicitly denied it, I could not see Iffley in the guise of Rollo's murderer.

I was summoned to attend the Marquis directly I set foot in his mansion and found him, looking tense, with Lord Fitzvaughan at his side.

'What do you know about the Countess de Langeais's illness?' Suffolk barked. 'They say you attended her sickbed.'

'The Queen's physician invited me to accompany him. Master Francisco is a good colleague. The Countess has injured her shoulder and is in great pain. She will be unfit to play any part in activities at court for some weeks.'

The Marquis grunted. 'One of the French ambassadors is furious and likely to play merry hell in the discussions tomorrow. It may disrupt proceedings. It'll be a key meeting. The King is to give his decision on the final terms of the truce and Gloucester's already trying to undermine what we agreed in Tours. We hope to settle everything but Henry's vacillating, listening to his uncle more closely than I like. We can do without unnecessary annoyances.'

I considered what I might properly disclose and then I said quietly, 'Gloucester won't be at the Council tomorrow.'

They stared at me and I enjoyed the moment. 'I've just come from Baynard's Castle and while I was talking to my contact there I was called on to attend the Duke.'

'He's ill? Gravely ill?' Suffolk's voice shook with eagerness.

'A temporary indisposition, I believe – but he won't be able to travel to court tomorrow.'

Suffolk raised his hands. 'Merciful Mother of God, I give you thanks. Gloucester's absence is what we need to strengthen the King's resolve. Well done, Doctor Somers. I hadn't realised how well you'd ingratiated yourself at Baynard's Castle. If the King gives his word to the French tomorrow, I'll see that you are rewarded for giving us this news. I'll return at once to Westminster to speak to the Queen. She will have her husband's ear overnight and, without Gloucester's intervention, I've no doubt she will prevail.'

He hurried from the room, shouting for his squire, leaving Walter Fitzvaughan eyeing me quizzically. 'Well done, indeed, Doctor Somers. You are a man of many talents. Maud asked me to remember her to you.'

'I'm honoured.' I lowered my head to hide my flush. 'Lady Maud is well, I trust.'

'But persistently barren. However, I worked her hard before leaving Norfolk and there is still time. Remember us in your orisons, physician, if you offer any to the Almighty.'

*****

There was no mistaking the rejoicing that accompanied Suffolk's return from the meeting the following day. The King had given his solemn word to the French nobles that Maine would be ceded. A public declaration would be made and he would issue written orders to the governors of all castles in the province to ensure they were surrendered. There were great celebrations at Westminster and, although one member of the visiting embassy glowered, Queen Margaret seemed to have forgotten the misdemeanours of her errant lady in waiting. I heard dissident catcalls in the street outside the Manor of the Rose and shouts for Gloucester to appear in the City and rally the opposition but the Marquis's men spread a rumour that Duke Humphrey was detained in some trollop's bed and his disillusioned followers sullenly dispersed.

Soon after his return Suffolk sent for me and I attended him, hoping for modest recognition of my services, but I was completely astounded by what awaited me. The Marquis rose from his desk and held out a roll of parchment with seals hanging from its lower edge and his own signature visible above them. His delicate mouth was pursed, his hauteur undisguised.

'Her Grace the Queen is delighted with your service and has directed that I reward you with fitting generosity. I am pleased to obey. This is a charter giving you the right to occupy the small manor of Worthwaite, held from me, in the north of Suffolk not far from my estates at Wingfield. It's in the charge of an elderly steward and servants, who will continue to care for the farmland and house, but the revenues are yours and the residence will provide you with a home where you may keep a wife and family in respectable comfort. It's time you gave thought to marrying, Doctor Somers.'

I was dumbfounded and stammered thanks, not wholly comfortable with the manner in which I had earned this lavish reward. I cheered myself by thinking how proud my seamstress mother would be to know I had risen to such dignities. Yet in my heart I grieved at how inadequate they were to fulfil my secret longing and how puny my rank remained when set beside that of a noble lady.

Chapter 18

The French nobles departed, the court prepared to adjourn to Windsor and a veneer of normality returned to life in the City. Elements of the populace inclined towards disruption were disheartened by Gloucester's absence and deterred by the chill wind whipping through the streets. I called at Baynard's Castle and learned from Bartholomew that the Duke had been taken to Greenwich to complete his convalescence, accompanied by Iffley.

Bartholomew was busy attending a cadaverous but prosperous-looking merchant, on his master's behalf, and he was unable to spare me more than a few minutes of his time. Nevertheless, he told me he had received a letter from Leone describing life in Oxford, which interested him although he did not relish the idea of so much studying. Then he bustled back to his visitor, exuding an air of courteous efficiency. I was happy to see him deputising so effectively for Gilbert Iffley.

I too had heard from Leone and was pleased with his progress but I regretted that he would not be returning to London for the Feast of the Nativity because he and Jack Cawfield were to visit a friend's family in Hampshire. There was a cryptic reference to Jack's unwillingness to spend time at his mother's new home and to encounter his new-born half-sister. This reminded me of Jane Cawfield's strange behaviour towards me and, on a sudden impulse, I wandered towards Cheapside. The Cawfield house had new occupants and a hanging sign to indicate that a silversmith now lived there but, as I expected, the crone next door was still sitting by her window observing the world outside. I hailed her.

'I remember you, physician. Found a bride yet, have you?'

I ignored her question. 'There's something you might be able to tell me, good-dame, as you keep so careful a watch on what happens in the street. When Mistress Cawfield lived here did you see when a troop of soldiers came to her house and caused her some distress?' I fumbled inside my gown and drew out a handful of coins.

She held out her hand and clenched her fingers over my gift. 'Bless you, where'd you get that idea from? I never saw such a thing and I would've done because a troop of soldiers would've clattered and brought me to the window. Mind you, there was the time her fancy man – the one she married none too soon – came with a couple of guards. Usually he came alone. But they didn't cause that stuck-up cow distress. She welcomed them in and waved them off with a smile on her face.'

'Were the guards in livery? Or armour?'

'Just leather jerkins and tin-pot helmets. They carried pikes. There was some badge on their chests but I couldn't make it out. He was in his usual furred robe and a silk turban coiled round his head with its end draped over his shoulder. Always wore that when he came a-courting. That's all I know, physician.'

I thanked the old woman and turned away, more puzzled than ever by the way Jane had lied to me, unable to fathom her purpose. Had she invented a hostile visitation by men in unmarked jerkins or was her neighbour mistaken? Why should she seek to mislead me? I could not dismiss the thought that her fabrication was designed to hide something but I had no idea what.

*****

I did not dwell on these mysteries for long because I was due to call at Westminster that afternoon for my regular "consultation" with Madame Yolande, continuing the pretence we had devised with Master Francisco's blessing. She was always attended by her maid, Berthe, and servants passed to and fro through the room so we were scarcely private. In any case our behaviour was entirely correct although some looks we exchanged suggested depths of meaning which we never expressed in words. Each time I saw her she poured out her gratitude for my part in foiling the Seigneur's design to carry her back to France as his bride.

'I have written to my brother,' she said when no one was near to overhear, 'and made complaint of Philippe de la Flèche's boorish conduct. I have entreated him to find me a husband more worthy of my respect. It is agreed I shall remain with Queen Margaret until summer and the Seigneur expects our betrothal will be announced when I leave her but I have asked my brother to arrange my secret conveyance to France before then.'

I vanquished the ache in my heart. 'That's very proper, madame. Shall we test how your injury is progressing? Will you move your arm as far as you can without causing pain?'

She performed the simple exercises we had developed as if to show ease of movement returning to her shoulder and then she took up the book she had been reading when I arrived.

'The Queen has allowed me to borrow this history of the great King Alexander's exploits. It is beautiful. See this illustration of the warrior and his men confronted by a fearsome dragon.'

The manuscript was richly illuminated and I marvelled at the artist's skill in rendering a miniature scene full of lifelike animation. I bent my head to view it better and she leaned forward beside me so close that our cheeks almost touched. I breathed in the fragrance on her skin and drew back quickly. 'It's very fine,' I said.

'All great soldiers have to overcome a dragon to validate their prowess, don't they? But it doesn't seem that Alexander had to rescue a princess. True champions come to the rescue of distressed maidens in my opinion.'

Her eyes held mine and I had no doubt of the message she was conveying. It drove away the fleeting memory of a mural in a Veronese church portraying Saint George and another dragon. There had been a princess in that picture, modelled on a woman who had caused me immense suffering, but that was far in the past and no longer had power to hurt me.

Yolande's features resumed their habitually austere expression. 'True champions do not need to be men of war,' she said. 'True valour lies in a generous spirit.'

*****

Next day the full force of winter made itself felt and, even in the City streets, snow drifted against walls and doorways. At the Manor of the Rose several members of the household were troubled with the rheum and other ailments so I was kept busy and sent to Master Webber for fresh supplies of the remedies he prepared according to my prescriptions. I was aware of the commotion as a party of travellers was admitted to the house, flecked with frost on their chins and foreheads, weary from battling through the near-impassable roads outside the City gates, and I learned that the party was led by Lord Walter Fitzvaughan. I was not eager to seek his company but in common courtesy could not refuse his invitation to take wine together after the household had dined. Gaston de la Tour was scowling by his side.

'You look well, Harry,' Lord Fitzvaughan greeted me, 'and I'm pleased to share my good news with you. Can you guess?'

My heart sank but I gave no hint of understanding his meaning, dreading further complicity with his wife's deceit, daring to hope that she could not have repeated her masquerade.

He waved his hand as if dismissing my obtuseness. 'I have letters from Norfolk. Maud is with child again and more than three months have passed. Her body is already thickening. This time there will be no misfortune. Rejoice with me!'

I mumbled congratulations, wondering if her serving women were complicit in this illusion of pregnancy and recognising that her husband was unlikely to have seen her naked since her supposed conception.

'I'm to cross the Narrow Sea once more,' Lord Fitzvaughan continued. 'King Henry bids me go to his fortresses in Maine to ensure our commanders understand their instructions and deliver up those lands to the French by the end of April in accordance with his pledged word. When I return to England in early summer Maud will be near her time and, with God's blessing, I shall soon have an heir.'

'I pray all will go well, my Lord.'

He put his hand on Gaston's arm and smiled. 'In every way we shall be glad to be done with it.'

Gaston's face by contrast was contorted with malevolence and I suppressed a shudder on Maud's behalf. I had many reasons to resent that seductive woman with her schemes and allurements but I could not wish her ill. I was relieved to listen as Lord Fitzvaughan moved on to other subjects and began to speculate about Richard of York's growing ambition. I remembered my obligation to report to the Prioress of St. Michael's about that nobleman's activities but what I heard were only vague assertions with little substance.

*****

Within the week Lord Fitzvaughan had departed and the Marquis returned to his house. The snow storms had abated but there were still mounds of hard-packed, filthy snow piled each side of the roadway and I was not tempted to take the air beyond the confines of the courtyard. The wind crept through cracks in shutters, coiling its way down staircases and along passages, so warmth was only to be found close to the hearths in the principal rooms where fires were kept blazing. I wore two gowns in an attempt to generate some heat in my body and the ailments I was called on to treat featured growing numbers of chilblains. I yearned for the weather to break and for the sun to remind us that somewhere its benign rays still existed to lighten my way when I next visited the Queen's ladies at Westminster.

Early one morning I was summoned from my bed and required to attend the Marquis at the front of the house. I threw on my ice-cold clothes and was appalled when I realised he wished me to accompany him into the street but he had the decency to offer me a cloak as the great oaken door was opened for us.

'There,' he pointed. 'This is what we've been called to see. The watchman spotted it.'

To the right of the entrance, straddling a decaying drift of snow, lay a body, face-down, naked, rigid, with a bluish tinge in the pale light of dawn.

'I assume he is dead,' said the Marquis with unnecessary caution.

'He could scarcely be otherwise,' I said as I crossed to inspect the unedifying object. 'And as even a drunkard would baulk at venturing out unclad in this weather it seems likely we have a victim of foul play in front of us.'

I crouched beside the corpse and felt the man's motionless pulse. I looked back to the Marquis. 'My lord, why did the watchman trouble you – to come in person to see this wretched fellow?'

The Marquis held out a sodden paper. 'This note was under the man's hand. The sergeant-at-arms read it and sent for me. "A gift for de la Pole", it says. I could hardly ignore such an intriguing offering.'

I forced my arm into the compacted snow and with difficulty turned the solid body so that its head fell sideways. Then I sank back on my haunches drawing breath. 'Come, my lord, and see what it means.'

Before he reached me he understood and stood still as I traced my finger along the line of the prominent scar above the left eye. The battered face beneath it was entirely unfamiliar to me.

'I assume you have been presented with the carcass of Rollo's murderer, my lord. I only wish I could claim some credit in identifying him.'

'How strange. Who could possibly know about it?'

'He may have boasted of his activities to others who decided to impose their own rough justice but I suspect he'd become an embarrassment to the person who employed his services to steal your letter to the King. If so, his vicious principal shows a warped sense of humour by presenting you with the corpse.'

'The fellow must have been lured to his doom outside my house.'

I straightened the body on the ground and stood. 'He wasn't killed here. He suffered a knife wound to the heart but there's little trace of blood on the snow. He was brought here after he'd been executed. As the note says, it's a gift to you, my lord.'

Suffolk gave a roar of laughter. 'A gift I'm ready to accept. Poor Rollo. I'd long ago given up hope of exacting a penalty from his murderer. Now the matter is neatly closed.' He moved to the doorway. 'I must go about the day's business. Do what is needful, Harry, and then we can set aside the whole unhappy incident. I have more weighty matters to concern me than a serving man's death in a street brawl nearly two years ago but it's satisfying to see this scoundrel done to death.'

I watched him re-enter the house and reflected sadly how he had changed from the man in Tours who seemed genuinely upset by his retainer's murder. Now, in the context of his rise to wealth and influence, Suffolk regarded it as a trivial episode of no lasting significance and he was unconcerned that whoever had been behind the attack remained free from retribution. I could not shrug it off so easily. I had been thwarted in the investigations I conducted and I wondered if the "gift" was intended to taunt me with my inadequacy rather than give pleasure to the Marquis. I could not dismiss the thought that this event followed the abortive conversation I had with Gilbert Iffley and my ill-judged reference to Rollo's murderer.

I arranged for removal of the body and studied the discoloured, rutted snow where it had been flung. Cart wheels had carved their way through the frozen surface of the road and recent horse manure smudged the ground nearby. I thought it possible this had been deposited while the animals stood still as their burden was removed from the cart and, if this was true, the position suggested they had approached from the direction of the river.

Drawing my wrap around me more tightly, I followed tracks which might have belonged to the makeshift hearse until they reached the street which ran close to the Thames. The discoloured snow was so churned at the junction that it was impossible to tell whether the cart had come from east or west and I could not hope to discover more by peering at the disordered pattern of furrows. It might have come from the quays and warehouses stretching towards London Bridge or, I acknowledged miserably to myself, it might equally well have travelled the short distance from where the towers of Baynard's Castle rose starkly against the wintery sky. I had no doubt which seemed more probable.

*****

It was on Twelfth Night that I next visited Westminster where Madame Yolande remained in the nearly deserted palace. She had returned to her duties among the Queen's ladies, although excused from any lifting and Master Francisco had advised that travelling to Windsor with the court for the Feast of the Nativity might aggravate her injury. I was amused by the enthusiasm with which the Queen's physician developed the saga of Yolande's supposed injury, enhancing its credibility, and in no way did I object to his fabrications.

It felt strange crossing empty courtyards, passing along bare corridors denuded of sentries, through rooms stripped of their furnishings, until in a small chamber, beside a crackling fire, I found Yolande waiting, attended by her faithful Berthe. For a moment, seeing her in radiant health, I felt uncomfortable about the deception in which we were engaged, although with far more benign intentions than Maud's play-acting, but I swiftly rallied myself to resume the physician's part.

Solemnly I agreed that the strapping could finally be removed from Yolande's shoulder and, with the assistance of Berthe, I uncoiled the binding around her neck and armpit. It was then incumbent upon me to run my fingers over her collarbone to satisfy myself that all was well while Berthe moved away, folding the bandages. As my trembling digits glided across her silky flesh Yolande shivered and the heel of my hand jerked, coming to rest on the swell of her breast above her low-cut stomacher.

I gulped but the apology froze on my lips when I saw the happiness in her eyes and for an instant she stroked my straying fingers before we both controlled our wayward instincts. I stood back from her and bowed.

'There's no need for me to make further visits, madame,' I said. 'The damage to your shoulder is repaired.'

'Yet I hope you will still come. I have enjoyed our conversations while confined to my chamber and would be happy to continue them. We have only a little time before I must return to France and my allotted role. Do not deprive me of what we have together.'

This was unambiguous and I glanced anxiously towards her tiring maid but Yolande shook her head. 'Berthe has served me since girlhood,' she said. 'She knows the secrets of my heart. We commit no sin, Doctor Somers. Let us cherish the time remaining to us.'

I bowed and kissed her hand with knightly courtesy although my voice was thick as I replied. 'I want nothing more, my lady.'

But that was not true.

Part IV: England: 1446-1447
Chapter 19

So began a strange period, in the months following the season of the Nativity, when transitory joy was shadowed by abiding regrets, despite the satisfaction I found in my physician's duties. I attended patients in brew-house, stables, pantry and solar while the Marquis and Marchioness were absent on royal progresses to Windsor, Coventry and Woodstock. I extracted splinters with my invaluable stiletto, dealt with innumerable cuts, burns, sprains and twisted limbs, watched half a dozen retainers die from old age in the cruel grip of winter, and could do nothing to prevent three newly-delivered mothers succumbing after childbirth when the midwives sought my advice. When a highborn page fractured a bone in his arm I sent for the bone-setter but he arrived drunk and swaying, so I splinted the injury myself and gained in confidence from the success of this operation. It saddened me to draw the sheet over five infants under a year old as the croup spread round the servants' quarters but, under my ministrations, two survived and that gave me cause to rejoice.

I should have been content but every week I fed my hopeless passion when I called at Westminster, whether or not the court was in residence, conversing in earnest, decorous terms with my love while we both indulged far from decorous fantasies. Sometimes Yolande coaxed me to examine her shoulder again but whether I touched her or merely looked into her eyes, our encounters were suffused with intense sensuality. It was a tantalising but hopeless reverie which we knew must end. I did not question the inexorable fate which required her to return to France and marry a man whose rank was commensurate with hers; nor would I insult her by taking advantage of our undoubted but futile mutual attraction.

I had other entertaining diversions, sharing jugs of ale with Thomas when he visited Baynard's Castle, sometimes accompanied by Rendell. I learned from Thomas that the Duke was restored to good health while Gilbert Iffley had departed on his travels once more. It was several months since I had seen that disturbing, enigmatic man and I could do no more to challenge him until he returned but this knowledge only heightened the burden I felt whenever I thought of Rollo's murder. Due to his friendship with Gloucester's master-at-arms, Thomas had learned more about Iffley than I had ever gleaned and what he told me was thought provoking.

'They served together in the wars across the Narrow Sea,' he said. 'You wouldn't think Iffley was a swordsman, would you? But it seems he was a doughty fighter and got that wound above his eye in battle. He's a bit of a dark horse. I hear he holds land at Glasbury in the Welsh Marches, though he doesn't advertise the fact.'

'Is that where the Duke met him? Gloucester conducts assizes in Wales, doesn't he?'

Thomas put a finger to his mouth. 'Iffley is Richard of York's man. He holds his land from that royal Duke, not the King's uncle. He's the matchless tool that links the two of them together with confidential communications and surreptitious meetings.'

'Put beside other things I know, that makes me uncomfortable,' I said and Thomas chuckled.

'What are you up to, Harry, prying into great men's business? I can tell something is brewing. Don't forget I'm ready to take part in any adventure you have in mind.'

I demurred on grounds of his family responsibilities, but knew there was no one I would rather have at my side if danger confronted me, although I could not envisage the circumstances. My imagination in that regard was to be stretched to breaking point before long but during those deceptively placid months I nurtured my innocent delusions.

*****

The first disturbance to my peaceful existence came from an unexpected source when Jack Cawfield and Leone paid a visit to the Manor of the Rose just before Eastertide. I was delighted to hear how they were both profiting from their studies and to appreciate that they treated each other as equals and friends but I could not resist introducing a contentious matter into our conversation when I asked Jack if he had news of his mother.

'I've broken all contact with her,' he said with truculence. 'Her remarriage was a disgraceful slur on my father's honour. All for the sake of a barony in the Marches.'

It was as if a cold hand clasped my brow and I stared at him. 'The Welsh Marches?' I repeated with incredulity at the coincidence.

Jack nodded. 'Some place called Glasbury. She queens it there now while her husband does his dubious business around the country on behalf of his paymasters.'

'Who are they?' I asked, dreading the reply.

'He's Richard of York's man but he serves Gloucester now. You may know him. He uses a different name away from his barony.'

'Gilbert Iffley.'

'What!' Leone's explosion of amazement rang through the room. 'He is your step-father? I never dreamed it. Did you know who Iffley was, Doctor Somers?'

'I'd no idea he'd married Mistress Cawfield.' I turned back to Jack. 'Your father must have met Iffley at court?'

'Of course he did. The bastard was entertained at our table sometimes but I don't think my father liked him. Yet my mother opened her legs to the dirty swine as soon as Father was in his coffin. Filthy bitch!'

Leone began to protest at the way Jack spoke of his mother but he caught my eye and dropped the subject while

255

I was glad to let the conversation drift on to safer topics, with Jack taking the opportunity to tell me how popular Leone was among the serving maids in Oxford. Even so, long after my visitors had left I pondered the implications of what I had learned about Baron Glasbury.

I remembered how Cawfield had been threatened by the ubiquitous, unknown man with a scar and how he feared he had been poisoned. In my head I repeated his dying words, naming Rollo and exonerating Gloucester from wrongdoing. It all fitted together with impeccable logic. Iffley was a seasoned killer, albeit nowadays using underlings to carry out his orders, and it probably amused him to employ a man with a similar scar to his own – a man who had subsequently become dispensable, perhaps no longer trustworthy. I felt certain he had bribed Cawfield to obtain Gloucester's seal in order to intercept Suffolk's confidential letter and then forward it to the King, resealed, as if nothing was amiss. Later he must have tried to suborn Cawfield for some other heinous purpose but the remorseful secretary had refused to co-operate and therefore had to die. Whether the opportunity to wed Jane Cawfield was an essential part of the scheme was unclear and I was reluctant to think she could have been complicit in her husband's death but I felt sullied by the contact I had with her and the naïve fancy I had cherished for a future at her side.

I concluded it was as well that Jack had broken with his mother for his own safety could be at risk with such a man as step-father. Yet this entire surmise was circumstantial and there was little chance of proving any of it. Suffolk was no longer concerned about Rollo's murder and he would have no interest in Cawfield's fate. I could only nurse my notions privately but they reinforced my misgivings that Iffley was bent on serious mischief as the cat's-paw of two royal Dukes, Gloucester and York. I must be vigilant in my dealings with him; yet I had perhaps already put myself in a dangerous position by hinting that I suspected the plausible wretch capable of murder.

After my conversation with Thomas I had written to the Prioress at Stamford telling her what I had heard about Gilbert Iffley and his dealings with the two Dukes, as it seemed to be germane to her interest in Richard of York. I knew she would wish to be given this information about Iffley's personal life but I found his liaison with Jane Cawfield too sensitive a matter to share with a woman whose withering look, when she learned how I had been deceived, was easy to imagine.

*****

The very next day Madame Yolande received the long-awaited response from her brother. He had relented, accepting that the Seigneur de la Flèche had shown himself unworthy of her hand, and he now proposed her marriage to a widowed Count, known to her for many years. On receipt of her agreement he would arrange for a ship to convey her from London to France. Yolande looked down at her hands, rigidly clasped in her lap, when she told me this match was acceptable to her but she added she would not reply hastily as her brother must appreciate she had given his suggestion careful thought. Nevertheless, this incursion of reality into our dreamlike world made us more circumspect in the way we spoke and gazed at each other although my visits to Westminster continued uninterrupted. We had no thought that affairs of state were about to disrupt our lives utterly.

The unexpected and ominous news came from Normandy only a few days into the month of May, carried by a sweating, terrified messenger who announced that King Henry's solemn undertaking to cede Maine by the end of April had been thwarted. The Governor of Le Mans and the captains of other towns had refused to obey their orders, barring the gates to the French troops sent to occupy King

257

Charles's new possessions. At the English court Queen Margaret raged against her husband's disobedient subjects but the citizens of London poured onto the streets in jubilation and Gloucester's name was on their lips when they cheered. I heard that Gilbert Iffley had returned to the City and I remembered that after the terms of the truce had been made public he visited a cousin who commanded a garrison across the Narrow Sea. It did not take great powers of deduction to see Iffley's hand in these dangerous events but I was unwilling to accost him until I knew Yolande was safely away from the English court.

Another acquaintance of mine had crossed to Normandy, charged to secure compliance with the King's command, and it was no surprise when Lord Fitzvaughan also returned to England. He appeared briefly at the Manor of the Rose, making no secret of his anger, but he did not linger and set off for Norfolk nursing frustration at the failure of his mission. Only one other person understood his lordship had more than one cause for displeasure and a glowering Gaston de la Tour informed me that Lady Maud had suffered a second miscarriage, speaking spitefully of her inability to carry a child to term. I chose my words judiciously in offering sympathy.

Gaston had other news which I found far more disconcerting.

'The French King has already despatched his envoys to protest at English duplicity. They will arrive in a few days to demand King Henry enforces obedience to his commands and cedes the county of Maine. It's a token of King Charles's fury that his ambassadors are led by a man with no love of England: the Seigneur de la Flèche.'

I swallowed hard, reading into this news far more than King Charles's wrath.

I knew I must warn Yolande, who would be in renewed peril of assault, but I was bound to wait until she had returned from accompanying the Queen on a visit to the aged Cardinal Beaufort – and the French embassy could well have arrived before then. Yolande's safe removal to her native land was the single objective towards which all my ingenuity was directed and, in near desperation, I resolved that there were measures I must take to safeguard her in case the worst happened. My purpose was only precautionary, but I wrote letters, sent messengers and confirmed I would be able to obtain a loan from the money-lenders in Goldsmith Row against the security of my manor in Suffolk which I had not yet visited. Perhaps, I reflected, I was reacting with unnecessary alarm but it seemed prudent to be prepared, and if my precautions were not needed then so much the better.

I learned from the Marquis when the Queen and her attendants were returning to Westminster and I set out in an unseasonably chilly dawn to ride to the palace. He also told me that the French party had already arrived and I was riven with anxiety in case I was too late to prepare Yolande for the inevitable ordeal confronting her. I had no sooner ridden through the great gates at the entrance to the palace yard when my fears assumed physical reality as a mounted figure loomed and a hated voice bellowed at me.

'Christ Almighty, it's that louse, the English quack!'

I stared at the hostile, brutal face. 'Monsieur Charpentier! I bid you welcome to my country once more.'

'The Seigneur has business to conclude with your worthless King and I have accounts to settle for myself in this stinking midden, England.'

'I wish you well in any honest enterprise.'

I could not disguise my revulsion and my words were provocative. He leaned towards me, grabbing the sleeve of my gown. 'You're likely to bear the brunt of my enterprise as you call it. I suspect you had to do with a certain lady's antics, disdaining her betrothed husband, sending him home to France without her by his side. Mark you, she's none too careful with her reputation, that one, shameful

259

bitch. Let the Seigneur into her bed before their betrothal was confirmed. What do you think of that? She'll go back with him this time or her disgrace will be trumpeted throughout the court.'

I contained my rage, knowing I must give no sign of indignation on Yolande's account. 'This is nothing to do with me, excuse me.'

'Maybe, maybe not, but I hear you've attended her sickbed. If I find you helped her evade her lawful lord, when we were here before, I'll slit your gizzard, physician. Seigneur Philippe will know how to tame her peevishness when he has her under his roof.'

I tasted blood as I bit my inner lip to prevent any response, even as he prodded my chest and bawled at me. 'But you're central to my own business, Doctor Somers, and can give me an answer. Where is that slime-bag who served you? The boy who slighted me and should have died by the Loire? What have you done with him?'

I kept my composure. 'He serves a master of greater rank than me now and I don't know his movements.'

A groom had appeared and I dismounted but Charpentier jumped down beside me, grasping my shoulders. Attendants looked askance at the way he was manhandling me and a burly guard approached, showing little respect for his royal master's guest. 'Get out of here, French scum!' he shouted, 'or you'll be thrown out.'

Charpentier rounded, his hand on the hilt of his sword, but as the guard beckoned colleagues the Frenchman contented himself with a snarl. 'We'll meet in a more auspicious setting, Doctor Somers. I don't give up a grudge until it's satisfied. Tell that former servant of yours, he won't escape my reckoning and neither will you, quack.' Then he pushed his way through the onlookers and I smoothed my gown as if nothing of significance had happened.

I gave silent thanks that Rendell was well protected from Charpentier's enmity, secure in Gloucester's palace at

Greenwich, but I almost ran towards the Queen's apartments to reach Yolande.

Inevitably she already knew of the Seigneur's arrival and she shook with emotion as she welcomed me, obviously afraid for her own safety. There was nothing to be gained by trying to hide the full horror that faced her and I told her of my encounter with Charpentier, hinting as delicately as I could at the fabricated allegation he had made about her sullied virtue. She stared at me aghast.

'My brother must not hear this lie or he will compel me to wed the wretch whatever protest I make.'

I pressed her hand in reassurance. 'I don't think Charpentier will spread the slander more widely while he believes you will travel to France with his master. You must foster that illusion for a day or two until your escape can be organised.'

She shivered but her eyes were wide with trust. 'You will help me, Harry?'

'Of course. If you're willing to take the risks involved, and they are great. I have a plan to ensure you can slip away from the court and travel to your brother without the Seigneur de la Flèche tracing your movements. When your brother hears the reason for your flight from your own lips he will surely dismiss any slander the villain spreads.'

She nodded slowly. 'Is it possible for me to escape? The Queen insists that I obey her will. She sees my marriage as a gesture towards restoring shattered relations with the French since the shambles in Le Mans.'

I took both her hands in mine. 'You were right to fear there would be difficulties in finding you refuge in a convent, unless you wished to take the veil, but I have devised a plan to rescue you from Westminster and provide you with a haven until the French have left these shores. You would be accommodated safely with a worthy knight and his lady, with no damage to your honour, but it's for you to judge if you are ready to incur Queen Margaret's anger at thwarting her wishes.'

Her response was unwavering. 'I will never bind myself to the Seigneur de la Flèche and must accept the consequences. In the last few hours I have even dallied with the notion of consigning my body to the waters of the Thames but am afraid to offend God's law. Oh, Harry, your help will be the more precious to me for your selflessness in offering it.'

I had no wish to dissemble. 'You are courageous, Madame Yolande,' I said, 'but I am not selfless in wanting to save you from misery. Your happiness will bring me joy.'

'You will put yourself in danger?'

'I shall try to avoid it. I think the plan is secure.'

'Oh, Harry,' she repeated and her whole body shook so that I thought she might faint but then she drew herself upright. 'And you will help me to go to my brother in France?'

'Joyfully,' I said but it was far from uncomplicated joy that I felt in my heart as I outlined the details of my scheme.

I welcomed her calm intelligence as she listened attentively, asking questions and making suggestions. Only when all was concluded and it was time for me to leave her, did she reveal her feelings again and in so wonderful a manner that I could hardly credit the reality of the lingering kiss she imprinted on my mouth. It was unwise, for both our sakes, but the token had been given and I was bound to her body and soul as strongly as any chivalrous warrior in the old romances who pledged his devotion to an unattainable highborn lady. For such a foolish fantasy I was ready to hazard all my prospects and peace of mind.

*****

Neither of my accomplices was inclined to dissuade me from the escapade for both revelled in the chance of a dangerous diversion but I was culpable to encourage their enthusiasm, knowing I had no right to expose them to deadly risks. For me, however, there was no choice – everything was subsidiary to saving Yolande de Langeais from a fate she abhorred.

There were several circumstances which favoured execution of my plan. Gloucester's old enemy, Cardinal Beaufort, had accepted the Queen's invitation to make a rare visit to the court to attend a celebratory feast in honour of the French guests. Everyone of significance at Westminster Palace would be occupied in the great hall for much of the afternoon and evening. Moreover, Queen Margaret had acceded to the request of a newly acquiescent Yolande to be excused from the festivities, so that she might prepare herself prayerfully for her betrothal next day to the jubilant Seigneur. Then, when I arrived at the unusually peaceful jetty and asked that my waterman be permitted to remain there with his boat until I was ready to leave, the guard raised no objection, recognising me as a familiar visitor to the Queen's lodgings who often carried some sort of bundle under my arm.

I made my way round the edge of the courtyard where a crowd of mummers was gathering before being admitted to the great hall to perform in front of the assembled dignitaries. No one paid attention to my shabby figure as I slunk past and the Countess and Berthe were waiting in the chapel as we had arranged. Berthe was already wrapped in a servant's travelling cloak, which did not appear out of place on a raw spring evening, and she impressed me with her calm good sense. Madame Yolande was plainly dressed, as befitted a suppliant before the altar, but I was embarrassed to see her shrouded in the threadbare mantle I had brought with me from Suffolk's mansion to disguise her as a serving maid. The guard at the jetty showed no interest in us but I made a point of telling him that I was taking the two women to their mother's bedside in the City, as she was gravely ill, and I gave him a generous gratuity. He nodded and handed Berthe into the boat while I assisted the Countess and we settled ourselves on a plank bench under a flimsy canopy. I noticed that Berthe was carrying a roll of cloth, probably concealing a box, which she transferred to her other arm when giving her hand to the soldier, and I admired her calmness.

We did not linger but Madame Yolande eyed the boatman with anxiety, as he pulled on the oars in slack water and took us into the middle of the river. I waited, grave-faced, until we were out of earshot from the bank before smiling at her as I spoke.

'Don't be alarmed, madame. He's not the most accomplished waterman on the Thames but he's my oldest friend, Thomas Chope, Master Carpenter. You may trust him unreservedly.'

'Your servant, my lady,' Thomas said. 'Rendell has horses at St. Mary's Steps across the river, near London Bridge, and he's taken a room for you and your attendant at a respectable Southwark inn. Well, what passes for respectable in Southwark.'

'Thomas was always a wit,' I said, fearing she might not have recognised the irony in his voice. 'It would be dangerous to travel further by night and the hostelry is used by honest pilgrims setting off for Canterbury. 'We'll be on our way at first light and Rendell will escort us to Danson. Sir Hugh and Lady Blanche will make you welcome and ensure your safety.'

There were few other boats on the river in the moonless dark and the small lantern at our bow acted as warning of our presence rather than lighting our way. I caught glimmers of rippling water when occasional ferries crossed our path and a barge slid quietly past in the opposite direction but Thomas, facing back towards Westminster, reported that there was no sign of any vessel pursuing us. We rounded the curve of the river as we approached the City and the Countess drew the mantle around her more closely when the blustery cross-wind caught us. We were now out of sight of the palace so I slipped off my physician's gown and donned a workman's jerkin lying under our seat. 'Mind you take care of my gown, Tom. I'll collect it when I'm back from Danson. Now we look like two worthy craftsmen taking our fair companions to sample the entertainments of the southern shore. Forgive me, madame, but that's how we need to appear – not meriting anyone's attention. To my delight the Countess giggled and for an instant leaned her head on my shoulder.

'Southwark has a dubious reputation, my lady,' Berthe said. 'I've heard it is a place frequented by rogues.'

Thomas chuckled. 'That's why we need to appear as humble folk with nothing to attract footpads and cut-throats. Don't worry ladies. Ordinary folk from the City go to the alehouses and bear-baiting on offer in Southwark without running any danger.'

The tide was beginning to turn and it became more difficult for him to row against the current so I slipped forward and took up a second pair of oars, sitting in front of him facing our passengers. We could make out flickering lights in buildings at the western end of the City and I knew that on my right, hidden in the gloom, were the walls and towers of Baynard's Castle. Men were moving with torches on the quay by the water-gate and I heard the rhythmic swish of many oars as a barge pulled out from the bank. It occurred to me that Gloucester might be setting off to return to Greenwich but the possibility did not concern me as we would be putting in to land just before we reached London Bridge. The barge soon pulled in front of us, tossing our boat in its wake, and Madame Yolande gasped in momentary alarm as she was jolted to the side. I grinned at her in reassurance and hoped Thomas could not see how radiantly she returned my smile.

I knew the lights of houses on London Bridge must be in view when Thomas, glancing over his shoulder, began to turn the boat, making for St. Mary's Steps, and I took up his stroke. I thought the barge had raced ahead of us but Berthe leaned forward and called that it was turning across our path and making for the landing place. She fidgeted with the bundle on her lap as she settled back in her seat and a beam of light from the shore fell on her.

'Have to wait our turn,' Thomas said with a shrug. 'I'll keep my head low in case I'm seen. I reckon they're some of Gloucester's men out for amusement in the Southwark stews. Oh, pardon, ladies. They won't disturb us at any rate.'

I glanced at the bank above St. Mary's Steps and made out a group of men in the shadows standing by some horses. Probably they were waiting for the revellers from the barge but I wondered if Rendell was among them, impatient for us to land and get on our way. We were paddling the oars to hold our place against the tide when two small skiffs appeared from the darkness behind us and made straight for our boat. Thomas shouted an angry warning but they did not change course and suddenly a missile whistled past my ear and a woman screamed. I dropped my oars, pulling the Countess from her seat into the narrow space below it, and hurled myself over her until I realised Thomas was tussling with a fellow trying to board us from the foremost skiff. Jumping up, I heard the whack of his oar as it caught the interloper on the skull and the splash as his assailant hit the water. Without compunction, I drew my small dagger and leapt over the bench to join my friend. Behind me one of the ladies was whimpering softly.

Just as I landed beside Thomas our boat was rammed by the second skiff and, off balance, I was flung sideways, cracking my head on the gunwale. I dragged myself up, blinking away dizziness, amidst much shouting, and plunged my dagger towards the arm of a ruffian who tried to pass me and reach the women. I could not have done him great injury because he hurled himself on me, wielding a cudgel which struck the dagger from my hand as another villain raised his own knife to cut my throat. While I struggled vainly in the first man's grasp I was amazed to see my would-be murderer crumple to his knees with a howl of pain and I recognised my own dagger as it was driven into the shoulder of the man holding me. I staggered aside, not comprehending what was happening as the injured attackers were dragged over the stern into a vessel lying low in the water behind us. Thomas had been similarly delivered from the aggressors but was clutching his wrist as blood welled up through his sleeve.

A familiar voice cut through the cacophony of shouts. 'Christ, Doctor, you'll need to do better than that if you're ever on the battlefield. Madame Yolande's a damn sight more skilful with a weapon.' Rendell vaulted into the boat and slapped me on the back. 'Good job I were waiting with some of me mates. We saw them thieving bastards making for you and guessed what they intended. Commandeered this cockle boat moored by the steps to get to you, we did.'

He stepped over the rowing benches to where the Countess was kneeling beside Berthe and I followed him. She was still holding my dagger in one hand and the gory drips from the blade had stained her dress but her other arm was round her serving woman who was white with pain. 'The rock they threw to frighten us hit Berthe,' she said. 'There's a cut on her temple and she is confused.'

I knelt to inspect the wound, glad to resume my role as healer rather than an unwilling and incompetent belligerent. Two of Rendell's companions had taken up the oars and were pulling us towards the steps as the barge moved away upstream. 'It's not serious,' I said to the Countess, 'but the cut needs treating with suitable balm and Berthe should rest until she regains her full wits'. Madame

Yolande nodded and handed me my soiled dagger. 'It was you who saved me from those cut-throats.'

'The dagger fell beside where I was crouching so I picked it up and thrust it into one wretch's shin and the other's shoulder. I pretended they were Philippe de la Flèche and Henri Charpentier. That made it quite easy.' Her eyes were shining.

'Here we are, Doctor, at the steps. Up you go.' Rendell tugged at my arm.

Thomas had joined us and I insisted on examining his wrist which had been badly slashed. 'I'll bind this tightly,' I said. 'Then you must get back to Baynard's Castle and have the wound treated with oils. You're not coming to Danson like that. Grizel would never forgive me if it putrefied.'

'One of me mates'll row you across to Gloucester's house.' Rendell had assumed an air of authority. He pointed at Berthe. 'This lady could go with them so she can rest. She's unfit to ride. You'll be all right, Madame Yolande, you'll still have me and a couple of other soldiers, as well as Doctor Somers, to take you to Danson.'

Berthe had risen unsteadily on her feet. 'My place is with my lady.' She swayed and the Countess grasped her arm.

'You'll do what Rendell suggests.' Yolande took the bundle which Berthe had gripped throughout the whole episode. 'That is my order.'

'I'll bring her to Greenwich in one of the Duke's barges tomorrow,' Thomas said. 'I'll get a horse litter to fetch her on to Danson.'

'That's all organised then.' Rendell spoke to one of his companions at the oars and both Thomas and Berthe were settled in the boat to cross the river to Baynard's Castle. Then he escorted the Countess and me to where the horses were waiting. 'What I didn't understand was why them rogues thought it worth their while to attack you. You didn't look a likely target. Most unappealing, I reckon.'

268

'I thought they must be the Seigneur de la Flèche's men,' I said, 'not simple ne'er do wells. I feared our escape had been foiled.'

Yolande de Langeais lifted the cloth covering the box she had taken from her servant. The silver casing glinted in the torchlight. 'It contains my jewels and what money I have,' she said. 'The thieves must have been lurking, watching those landing from the river, to spot likely prey. Berthe let the wrapping drop when she leaned forward in the boat and for a moment light from the shore fell on it. She quickly covered it again but it must have been seen. Your Southwark scoundrels are remarkably sharp.'

'True enough,' Rendell said with pride. 'Born in Southwark, I were. Me and me sister. Now we'll go to a Southwark inn where you'll be received like the noble lady you are, Madame Yolande. Nothing bad'll happen to you there.'

*****

I escorted the Countess upstairs to the room Rendell had reserved for her and Berthe. I was pleased to see it was tolerably clean with fresh rushes on the floor, a serviceable counterpane on the narrow bed and a servant's pallet at its foot. I held the door open while she looked round and nodded her satisfaction.

'I'll bid you goodnight, madame. We'll leave at first light but I'll have them send up some food to break your fast before then.' She nodded again but as I took hold of the door-handle she glided forward and looked at me, visibly trembling. 'There's no need to be nervous, Madame Yolande. You'll be quite safe. We've three armed soldiers downstairs.' Her lips were parted and they quivered. 'It's no surprise you're distressed after what we've been through. To give you extra security, I'll take the pallet left for Berthe and put it across the door. I'll sleep there, on the landing, within call. Will that reassure you?'

Gently she released my fingers from the handle and let the door close behind me. 'Stay with me,' she whispered. 'Here, in the room.'

It was my turn to tremble. 'That would be unwise, madame. It would be misconstrued. Your honour would be damaged.'

'Oh, Harry, you are more chivalrous than any belted knight. Heaven has given us this night, I'm sure of it. I'm not concerned for my honour, only for the unbidden opportunity which will be lost forever if we spurn it.'

My mouth was dry. 'What are you saying?'

'You know my history, Harry. I have never experienced passion and, although I hope for a second marriage as agreeable as the first, I do not expect to find fleshly joy in it. We spoke once of what might be for us, on another earth... Why should we not create that paradise for a single night?'

I did not hesitate any longer, captivated by her need, yielding to my own desperate desire, freed from all thought of status and propriety, and we lay together on that bountiful, narrow bed until dawn brought its blush to the Southwark sky.

Chapter 20

I rode to Danson in a stupor, pointedly ignoring Rendell's raised eyebrow, aware only of Yolande's arm around my waist, as she sat to the side behind me, and the occasional pressure of her fingers when she gripped me more tightly. Our escort, sporting Gloucester's colours, ensured that we had an uneventful journey and before noon the Countess was received with fitting respect by my old acquaintances, Sir Hugh de Grey and Lady Blanche.

Lady Blanche, with a clutch of small de Greys at her skirts, was unaffectedly welcoming and I was touched to see Yolande lift one of the infants to examine the toy horse he was holding. Sir Hugh's eyes were round with admiration of his guest's beauty but I was confident he would not attempt to indulge in his habitual philandering with a lady so much his superior in rank. When the Countess had been taken to her chamber I slipped across the courtyard to the servants' lodgings where my mother sobbed to see me again and I was happy to find her in good health.

As common courtesy demanded, I accepted the invitation to stay the night and shared a garret with Rendell. Despite my exhaustion I slept little, yearning for Yolande lodged in the same modest manor house yet inaccessible to me. Her hosts must never know how we had transgressed and I must relinquish the foolish dreams which tormented me with their unreality.

Sir Hugh undertook to send a messenger to her brother at once to explain the reason for her flight from the English court and it was to be hoped she would hear by return what arrangements had been made for her journey to France. She would then marry this suitable widower who she believed would prove a gracious and kindly husband while I was left with a treasured memory, beyond imagining, which must suffice.

Next morning I made my farewells, forcing my lips not to smile too happily as she pressed my hand when she thanked me for my assistance. Then I was mounted and on the road again, with Rendell at my side and three soldiers escorting us. My brief idyll was at an end.

My immediate duty was to warn Rendell about Charpentier's presence in London and the threat he had made but the young warrior merely shrugged.

'Scant chance for him to harm me when I'm in the Duke's service,' he said in his newly deepening voice, 'but thanks for letting me know he's around, filthy swine. He'll get his come-uppance, I can tell you. I won the swordplay exercise for new recruits at Greenwich last week but that's no surprise considering the training I had from the Venetian soldiers. You did the right thing, choosing me as bodyguard. Ready to oblige, any time.'

Rendell continued to chatter in his usual animated manner but I took in very little until he protested at my lack of interest. 'Reckon you're sweet on Madame Yolande, ain't you, Doctor?'

'I admire her certainly,' I said with inane severity.

'Don't worry, I won't never let on about where you spent the night at the inn.'

He winked and tapped his nose and I knew it was useless to contradict him. He sniggered at my silence but then he rode forward to speak to the soldier leading our party. He had become a man, I thought, at ease in his comrades' company, self-confident and skilful in his chosen trade of arms; however much I might regret it, he was suited to his calling. I glanced back at the pair behind me. Naturally they were not wearing full armour for our expedition, but quilted jerkins, strengthened with metal rivets, and helmets with the visors open, exposing their weathered, hardy faces. They made an impressive troop and Humphrey of Gloucester could be proud of them.

From somewhere in the depths of my disordered mind a recollection came to me – of Jane Cawfield dismissing my question whether any of the men who raided her home bore a scar above his eyebrow. She had claimed that their helmets hid their brows but how could that be? She had not said their whole faces were covered and it was hardly likely they would have had their visors down while they trawled through her husband's possessions. Simple pot helmets, mentioned by her observant neighbour, had no visors at all and Jane's lover had been fashionably dressed. I strained my powers of recall further. I had told Jane of the scarred man who terrified Andrew at Windsor and she had deduced straight away that I might think he had been intentionally poisoned. Why had I not thought that strange at the time? She tricked and humiliated me and I cursed my inadequate scrutiny of her behaviour. I had been beguiled by my own stupid fancies and missed the fact that she was testing me, seeking to establish how much I knew or suspected about her husband's death, feeding me misleading information about Suffolk's seal to implicate Cawfield and throw me off Iffley's track.

It was shortly after Jane confided her imaginary fears that Iffley had contrived to meet me when I visited Baynard's Castle and began to inveigle me into helping Gloucester. Now it seemed probable he had identified me as a risk needing to be neutralised. He and his intended wife had been hand in glove. It was not a comforting thought.

We called at Greenwich and found Thomas and Berthe, already arrived from the City, ensconced by Grizel's fireside and subject to her ministrations of ointments, broth and upbraiding. I expected to receive her rebuke myself and was not disappointed. She put her arms akimbo and faced me squarely.

'You should know better, physician as you are, than to put this good lady and my husband in peril of mortal injury. Can't rely on my brother to rescue you every time you do something daft. Tom has a family now and isn't a feckless bachelor like you, Harry Somers. You should be ashamed.'

I hung my head but when I looked up her mouth was twitching. 'Mind you,' she said, 'I haven't seen Tom look this cheerful in a long while. Maybe a bit of excitement's what he needs. Just don't put him in danger. A carpenter's not much use with a damaged hand. You can see I'm expecting again so he'll have four of us to provide for soon.'

Suitably chastened, I settled to enjoy the meal Grizel prepared and to listen to the gossip she and Thomas shared. I learned that the Duke was now in residence at Baynard's Castle, in order to take a more active part in meetings of the King's Council, and the mention of Gloucester evoked in me that familiar mixture of nostalgia and discomfort. I asked if they knew anything of Gilbert Iffley's movements.

'You can be sure he's close at Gloucester's side.' Thomas helped himself to another helping of his wife's thick potage of cabbage, beans and oats. 'Do you want to see him? You might be lucky and catch him if you take the wherry this afternoon. You can leave the horses at Greenwich – they all belong to the Duke – Rendell will see to them.'

*****

In retrospect, I doubt whether I was in a suitable frame of mind to confront the man I suspected of several crimes and he wrong-footed me as soon as I entered his study.

His greeting was urbane as he rose lifting his hands towards the ceiling. 'It's so long since I had the pleasure of your company but I scarcely expected to welcome you here today, Doctor Somers, with all the court in turmoil about one of the ladies you've attended.'

I quickly rallied my wits and tried to look blank. 'What do you mean?'

'One question is on everyone's lips. Where is the comtesse de Langeais? Has Suffolk got her in his mansion?'

'I don't understand.'

Iffley gave a short chuckle. 'No. Surely the Marquis wouldn't risk offending the Queen in so intimate a way? Haven't you come from the Manor of the Rose?'

'I've been at Greenwich with my friends. One of their infants is sick and they asked me to cast an eye over him.' This was the explanation for my absence from the City I had agreed with Thomas and Grizel.

'So you really know nothing of the uproar about the Countess's disappearance? Perhaps it's true the poor lady has flung herself into the river to avoid a displeasing marriage.'

'I'd be sorry to think so.'

'Indeed, so would we all. I've never made her acquaintance but she was to have been betrothed to a Frenchman of notable unpleasantness. The Queen favours the match and is incandescent with rage. Gloucester was at court yesterday and no business could be transacted because of her ranting. Our gentle King has no control over her when she's angered.'

It did not seem likely that Iffley had any specific reason to suspect my involvement in Yolande's flight and I resolved not to be deflected from my purpose in visiting him. 'This isn't why I came. I've learned that since I first met you I've failed to address you by your proper title, Baron Glasbury.'

'Ah!' He sat down and waved me to the window bench. 'That peevish stepson of mine has been talking, I gather. My role in serving Humphrey of Gloucester requires discretion and I choose to remain in the shadows. My background is of no consequence.'

'You've married Jack Cawfield's mother.'

'And he resents it. This is true. But I do not apologise. I met Jane many years ago when she was not free

275

and I've admired her with patient constancy. I admit that when Andrew Cawfield died I seized my chance with indecorous speed. There, that's my confession. Does it satisfy you?'

'Cawfield's death was fortuitous, I suppose?'

'What are you suggesting? I seem to remember that on the day the Duke was taken ill you hinted I might be a cut-throat. You have an overwrought imagination, Doctor Somers.'

'I don't see you wielding a knife yourself, although I believe you've been a soldier.'

He chortled. 'So you've been making enquiries about me. That's unwise.' He tossed back the skirts of his gown and crossed one muscular leg over the other. Listen to me, Doctor. I should like us to be allies in the events which will transpire. Our King is a noble but fragile soul and he needs a sound, dispassionate adviser by his side. Suffolk is not the man for this role, he is conceited and self-serving, and Queen Margaret is a fractious, unreliable Frenchwoman. It's in the interests of the English realm that someone more suitable should play this part.'

'Gloucester?'

'Duke Humphrey is admirably suited to guide his nephew, as he has done in the past, but you and I know, as do few others, that his health is unstable. While he remains well, I'll do all within my power to support his cause but it's prudent to recognise an alternative possibility.'

He paused and I knew his meaning but would not prompt him. We held each other's eyes until he gave way.

'Gloucester himself approves my strategy. Duke Richard has his trust.'

'York?'

'Quite so. These are high stakes, Harry Somers, but our country would profit from the success of our enterprise. The struggle to gain the King's ear is joined and the outcome is of supreme importance. You're intelligent. Don't ally yourself to a losing competitor.'

'You told me once that the late Roger Bolingbroke was your relative. He used threats to persuade me to play a part in his enterprise and it led me to a cell in the Tower of London and the threat of execution.'

'Roger was a foolish necromancer. I don't intend to indulge in witchcraft or treason.'

'But you don't cavil at shedding blood in pursuing your objective?'

He stood up and turned away from me. 'Don't think you can coax an admission of murder from me, physician, but many a philosopher has held that petty functionaries can be treated as expendable for the greater good.'

I rose and bowed. 'I suspect some would consider your scheming tendentious enough to merit the executioner's axe if it fails in its purpose.'

'You exaggerate. As I told you, I am circumspect. Remember what I've said.'

*****

I had much to ponder after this encounter but I was glad to be forewarned about what awaited me and was not surprised to be summoned to attend on Suffolk when I returned to his house. My fear was that the guard at the Westminster jetty had reported my presence on the evening of Yolande's flight and my pretence of taking two serving women to see their dying mother. If this had happened I was in serious trouble.

My first surprise on entering Suffolk's room was to see Walter Fitzvaughan by his side but his lordship expected this and came forward to greet me.

'Your eyes do not deceive you, Harry. I am returned after the briefest of visits to Norfolk. I have to cross the

Narrow Sea once again to berate those recalcitrant captains in Maine who have refused to obey their King.'

Suffolk laughed. 'King Henry cannot bear to be parted from his beloved wife but his servants must sometimes endure long separations from their spouses.'

I looked from one to the other, trying to determine whether this joviality hid a darker mood. Then Suffolk held out a glass of wine.

'You've heard about the Countess de Langeais, Doctor Somers?'

'I've heard the Countess is missing.'

'Has he been up to his tricks again?' Walter Fitzvaughan guffawed. 'Wouldn't be the first time he took a titled lady to his bed.' This indelicate reference to his wife was embarrassing but his lordship looked remarkably cheerful.

'Nonsense,' Suffolk said, to my relief. 'No one imagines the unsmiling Countess has dishonoured herself certainly not with a mere physician, but she has absconded and one of the French envoys is furious. It's assumed that she and her maid slipped out of the palace with the company of mummers who'd been performing in front of the court. I suppose she never mentioned her intention to you, Harry? You've attended her, I believe.'

I put on the most serious expression I could manage while rejoicing at the stroke of luck the presence of the mummers had brought us. 'Master Francisco asked me to oversee her convalescence after an injury. It eased his burden. The lady never made me privy to any plot she had devised.'

I knew that my cautious words would be judged dissembling in any academic debate but Suffolk was not interested in unpicking my meaning. He put his hand to the small of his back and grimaced. 'Of course not, no one would suppose otherwise. But I've sent for you as my physician. I'm plagued with this pain again. I want you to treat it.'

278

'Certainly, but I haven't brought my poultices. With your permission I'll fetch them at once.'

Suffolk nodded and Lord Fitzvaughan accompanied me from the room, chatting affably. 'I should have liked to stay longer on my estate,' he said, 'to ensure Maud was with child again before I left her but the King's will must be obeyed. Still, she seems to have no trouble conceiving, only in sustaining the infant in her womb. I fear she may not have taken sufficient care of herself on the previous occasions so, in case she is ripening once more, I'm leaving nothing to chance. Despite his reluctance to be parted from me, Gaston has remained in Norfolk to watch over her and he will ensure her every action is monitored to prevent anything endangering her health.'

I murmured approval of Lord Fitzvaughan's good sense but I felt momentary sympathy with Maud for it was doubtful that she could contrive a credible miscarriage while under Gaston's assiduous and unfriendly scrutiny. Presumably she would not embark on a pretended pregnancy in these circumstances.

'Gloucester is flexing his muscles again in the King's Council,' Lord Fitzvaughan said. 'He's revived his old antagonism to Cardinal Beaufort, no doubt because the aged cleric has the ear of the Queen and Suffolk. I've always had respect for Duke Humphrey, as you know, but it behoves us all to be wary of dissension in high places.'

We reached a staircase where we would part and to my surprise, as he slapped me on the shoulder, his lordship winked at me. 'By the way, Harry, he said, 'the Marquis is less observant than me. Is that a love-bite on your throat?'

*****

After two weeks I heard that the French nobles had left England, satisfied with King Henry's pledge to secure the cession of Maine. A few days later Sir Hugh de Grey wrote to me enclosing a letter from Yolande, short and formal in its wording as was proper. She thanked me for my services but made no suggestion that I might visit her before she left England and, although this was only to be expected, I found, as I read it, that tears were spilling down my cheeks and I acknowledged my desolation.

I made it my business to visit the apothecary, Master Webber, in person from time to time and to distract myself from miserable thoughts I set out to walk to his premises. It was one of those rare days in England when the heat was a tangible presence, inhibiting movement with its oppressive weight, reminding me of my first summer in Padua when the luxurious warmth fostered lassitude and caused me to nod over my studies. Londoners, ill acquainted with such weather, made no concessions and scurried about industriously but there was tension in the air as if their overheated discomfort might lead to disorder on the streets. I mentioned this to Master Webber as we sipped our ale at the back of his pharmacy.

'You're right,' he said, 'and there's mischief afoot. I'm grateful for your patronage on behalf of Suffolk's household and there's something you should know.' He rose and put his head round the screen separating us from the area where the public were served. 'Matthew Tate and William Slater, come here.'

Two lanky lads in splattered aprons responded to their master's call and, although I did not recognise them, I knew they had been among the rabble chasing me when I took refuge at the apothecary's.

'You know Doctor Somers,' Master Webber said. 'Tell him what I extracted from you under threat of the whip yesterday.'

They shuffled their feet and would not look me in the eye but the younger of the two was evidently frightened. ''There's a call for all true citizens to rally at the London

Stone and declare for Humphrey of Gloucester and Richard of York in protest against the jumped-up Marquis.'

'The damned apprentices always assemble at the London Stone when there's a riot brewing,' the apothecary said. 'You'll be aware there's little love for Suffolk in the City.'

I nodded. 'Do you know who issued this summons?'

Two pairs of lips clenched but the elder apprentice was prepared to be defiant. 'Don't know their names,' he growled. 'One's a bonny orator, nothing much to look at, tall and skinny. The other doesn't say anything but stands by, smirking; he's got a scar over his eye where he was injured fighting for the King.'

That was no surprise. 'Why in particular are they calling out the apprentices to riot against Suffolk?'

'They say the Marquis is bedding the Queen, French harlot that she is.'

Their master slammed his fist on the table. 'Shut your mouth, you young fool. That's treasonable.'

'And I'll swear it's most unlikely,' I said, thinking how tame my rebuttal must seem. 'But thank you for your frankness. If the call to riot is being bruited abroad, you can be sure the City Guard will be out in force and you've small chance of putting Suffolk in danger.'

'May be not this time,' the older apprentice said. 'But he'll not escape the people's justice forever.'

That evening I penned a letter to the Prioress of St. Michael's telling her what I had learned and within a week I received her reply. It was brief and recorded her gratitude but it concluded with a strange injunction to me.

Study the forebears of the royal house and be well advised of the possibilities.

I had no idea what it meant.

*****

Soon afterwards I received an invitation from Master Francisco to visit him at Westminster and I appreciated it would look peculiar if I declined. I had not been to the palace since Yolande's flight but I was bound to appear there at some point so I decided to put it off no longer. It proved to be purely a social call, with inevitable physicians' gossip about unusual maladies, and no one looked askance at my presence in the Queen's lodgings. I parted from my friendly colleague in a contented frame of mind and collected my horse from the groom, ready to ride out through the great gateway but holding back as a posse of courtiers entered from the road outside.

I recognised that some wore the livery of Cardinal Beaufort's followers but there were others in assorted colours and one, who flaunted a pennant with the arms of France, whom I had hoped never to see again. I drew back into the shadows as the troop passed through the archway to the stables. Then I beckoned a guard I knew by sight.

'I thought the Frenchmen had returned to their own country,' I said, pressing a coin into the man's hand.

'All except that bad-tempered bastard, Doctor. The story goes his master left him here to find the lady what ran away to avoid marrying him. Good luck to her, I say: if his master's as crabby as his servant.'

I went on my way shivering with foreboding and, for the first time, wishing that Yolande had already left England. Each day I expected to learn of her departure but as yet I had heard nothing more from Danson and it puzzled me. I knew I must alert her to Charpentier's continued presence and urge her to expedite the arrangements for her departure. Rendell must also be warned in case the Frenchman sought him out, still avid for revenge.

I sent a message to Rendell and met him at the riverside hostelry so I could stress in person the importance of restraining his natural hot-headedness if he should encounter Charpentier. He listened to my pontificating without interruption but his look was disdainful and I guessed he would act exactly as he wished. He was no longer a boy in my service but a member of Duke Humphrey's guard at arms and it was stupid of me to think I could control his behaviour.

'No unnecessary bravado, that's all I'm saying,' I concluded weakly.

He shrugged and quaffed his ale. Then he grinned. 'That's not why I came here, not to hear you maundering on about Charpentier. I've a letter for you, from Danson.'

I gasped with delighted surprise. 'You went there?'

'Yeah, didn't want Madame Yolande to leave England without saying goodbye. I thought she must be going soon. She was glad to see me too. Though she looked a bit peaky. Expect that bugger, Sir Hugh, had been pestering her.'

I protested at Rendell's impudent suggestion and tried to appear unconcerned but it worried me because Sir Hugh's lecherous nature was all too well known. I shared a meal with the lad and then walked with him to Baynard's Castle, to make sure he went safely on his way, boarding the wherry to Greenwich. I had done what I could to protect him but he would make his own choices now.

Back in the Manor of the Rose I retired to my room and broke the seal on Yolande's letter, expecting to learn of her imminent departure, recognising this would bring me mingled joy and grief. I noticed it bore no superscription or signature but I knew her writing and the message rendered protocol redundant.

I beg you will not rebuff me. I cannot remain at Danson much longer and I dare not return to France. I am with child.

Chapter 21

At first it had been difficult to persuade Sir Hugh and Lady Blanche that they need not accompany Madame Yolande to the vessel at Deptford. They had grown fond of her and were anxious to fulfil their duties by seeing her safely aboard ship for her return to France. Fortunately, although unpleasant for the infant, the youngest de Grey child developed a mild fever and the concerned parents accepted that they should stay with their family in case the invalid called for them. Thomas had come from Greenwich to accompany me in escorting the French ladies and, after tearful farewells at Danson, two of Sir Hugh's men rode with us until we were within sight of the dockyard. Satisfied that they could report our successful arrival at the quay to their master, these fellows were then happy to accept my gratuity and made their way to a tavern to spend it.

What it would have been inauspicious for anyone from Danson to see was the humble fishing ketch on which the ladies embarked, looking for all the world as if it would be casting down its nets in the Thames estuary. Even more questionable in the eyes of an onlooker who knew the parties involved would have been my presence at the lady's side as we stepped on deck and cast off from the shore.

Snugly wrapped in her travelling cloak, Yolande insisted on staying out in the air as we sailed downstream, sending Berthe to stow their possessions in the tiny cabin put at their disposal. It was the only time we had been alone together since a surreptitious conversation when I paid a visit to Danson a week previously. That was when we had constructed a plausible story to convince her hosts that there was nothing untoward in her departure.

'If I am sick now', the Countess said, breathing in deeply despite the smoky air, 'it will be put down to the waves. These last few days it has been difficult to conceal my nausea.'

'Thank God, you've been able to get away without incurring suspicion. If the wind holds we shall dock at Ipswich within two days.'

'Heaven has favoured us. Suffolk would be astonished to know how timely his generosity was to prove.'

'I pray the manor is fitting for your sanctuary. I wish I could have visited first and met the steward and his wife who have charge of it.'

We held each other's eyes and I knew I must put into words what tore at my heart. 'Yolande, sweet love, I grieve that what gave me such joy has brought you suffering. I dare not insult you by offering you my hand and my home. They're yours to command but the future which is rightfully yours will await you in France next year when your travail is over, far removed from the modest comforts of a physician's hearth.'

She gave a wistful smile. 'Dear Harry, I'm touched beyond belief. I wish the world would permit our lawful union without the retribution it would bring us both. Your life would be considered forfeit by powerful men, for defying the distinctions God has set between us, and I would be condemned and dishonoured without the hope of bringing up our child in tranquillity. The solution we devised is the only realistic one.' Tears flooded down her face despite the clear-headed formality of her speech.

'Once I've seen you settled at Worthwaite Manor I'll ride on to Stamford to make my plea to the Prioress of St. Michael's. Our child will be well cared for by the sisters in her house and I give you my pledge that I'll provide for the infant's welfare as long as I live. You've written to your brother to explain that your return to France will be delayed?'

'Yes. I have told him I am going to rest in the country to regain my strength after an ailment. My recovery will prove to be slow but, God willing, I shall find myself well enough to cross the Narrow Sea in the spring. I don't know how I shall bear parting from our child.'

I lifted her fingers to my lips and felt the quiver which passed through her body in harmony with mine. 'We must be practical,' I said. 'It's the only way to safeguard your honour.' Yet I knew that thenceforward my own life would be changed for ever.

*****

While I stumbled through a halting explanation of my situation, the reverend lady did nothing to ease my awkwardness but as her understanding grew her lips began to curve into a slow smile.

"You are confessing to a shameful sin, Doctor Somers,' she said. 'But it is not my role to impose penances. I recognise your honesty in seeking to provide for your bastard but I would ask you to satisfy yourself that the child is yours. Women of easy virtue are adept at identifying a man who would more readily accept responsibility than another.'

I tried not to show my indignation as I was determined not to mention Yolande's name. 'The circumstances are not as you suppose. There's no doubt the child is mine.'

She was unconvinced. 'If we took every by-blow offered to our care, even by the nobility, we would be knee-deep in mewling infants. I can see no good reason to take yours, physician, although I acknowledge the services you've provided in supplying me with information. Pay the mother to succour her brat.'

'Reverend Mother, I beg you to help. It isn't possible for the mother to acknowledge the child.'

'So,' the Prioress pursed her lips, 'she is a married woman whose husband is to be deceived about his wife's shame?'

'No!' The exclamation came before I had considered its implications.

'A maiden you have seduced or ravished?'

I spread my hands on my thighs and shook my head. 'I cannot give you details.'

She rose, interlacing her fingers at her waist. 'I do not accept "cannot", Doctor. Either you disclose the mother's name, or I refuse absolutely to assist.'

'You helped Lady Maud,' I blurted, 'without knowing the father of her child.'

'A misguided and misused noblewoman. Not a common slut, nor a humble squire's daughter.' She eyed me in silence for several moments as I attempted to keep my expression bland. 'Is it possible? Can you have so far forgotten yourself that you have bedded a highborn lady? How can she hope to conceal her predicament from her family?'

'That can be arranged. It's the child's upbringing which concerns us.'

I should have known better than to underestimate the Prioress's perceptiveness. A light came into her eyes and she resumed her seat, leaning towards me attentively. 'You've told me of your gracious reception at the Queen's court and I've learned that a distinguished member of her entourage is missing from her duties. Could it be there is a connection? Can you really have tupped the famously austere but, I understand, beautiful comtesse de Langeais?'

I was trapped and said nothing, bowing my head in a vain attempt to hide my flush. She chortled with glee.

'Now, Doctor Somers, we are nearing the truth, aren't we? And, I should add, engaging my interest. Is the Countess Yolande your mistress?'

Unhappily, I faced her and said I must take my leave. 'I was wrong to hope you would be willing to help in Christian charity without speculating about the lady's identity and naming a woman of virtue and honour.'

She waved imperiously in my direction. 'But I am most ready to assist, now I appreciate the position, Doctor Somers. I shall be delighted to shelter the Countess's accidental infant. How have you accommodated her until she is brought to bed?'

'That needn't concern you.' I hesitated, unclear whether I could rely on her change of heart. 'The baby will be brought to you directly after the birth.'

'And Countess Yolande will return to France? You need not answer. It's all clear to me. You will of course incur obligations beyond the payment of the child's upkeep. I shall expect your more active attention to the interests of St. Michael's – sometimes at the expense of others who retain your services. You understand me, I think?'

I began to demur but she spoke over me. 'You are not in a position to object, Doctor Somers, and I ask nothing unlawful. Merely timely and explicit information and occasionally the fulfilment of a commission on our behalf. You accept? Good.'

I should have foreseen the bargain she would require and it was useless to argue. She fingered her knotted girdle delicately.

'You may start by telling me what you know of the circumstances in which Suffolk secured the King's sworn promise to cede the county of Maine to the French. How did it come about that Gloucester was absent from the meeting of the Council?'

'I understand he was unwell.'

'It must have been a serious ailment to keep him from so crucial an occasion. Yet I hear he has recovered.'

'So I believe.'

'Is the affliction likely to recur?'

'I am not the Duke's physician.'

'But you know more than you are admitting. I can tell from the contraction at the corner of your mouth. There's camaraderie among medical men, I assume, and you've heard their gossip.'

At least she did not know I had attended Gloucester on his sick bed. 'It's always possible illnesses may recur.'

She tossed her head and the folds of her wimple fluttered. 'The Duke's way of life is not conducive to his good health. He is a libertine.'

'I owe much to his patronage, reverend lady.'

'My family has no love for him or his crony, the Duke of York.'

'I know little of Richard of York except that he is the King's lieutenant in his lands across the Narrow Sea.'

'I advised you to study the antecedents of the royal house. Haven't you done so?' I shook my head and she continued. 'King Henry's grandfather took the throne from childless Richard who was ill-suited to wear the crown. They were cousins, the sons of brothers born to the great King Edward. Do you know how Richard of York is related to them?'

'Isn't he descended from a younger son of King Edward?'

'On his father's side, yes. But on his mother's side, his forbear was Edward's son, Lionel of Clarence, senior in birth to King Henry's ancestor.'

I stared at her. 'You mean York could advance a claim to the crown?'

'Hush, Doctor Somers, never speak the idea. Such a claim would involve inheritance through a female in two generations and it is moot whether it would have substance. Duke Richard has had the good sense never to make it but he offers support to Gloucester who remains next in line to the crown until the Queen produces an heir. However, in the event of Duke Humphrey's demise, who can say what might happen.'

She clasped her hands and bowed her head as if in prayer while I digested the implication of this lesson in genealogy and it came to me that it threw light on Gilbert Iffley's devious intentions. She looked up and noted my expression with a fleeting smile. 'I take it that Humphrey of Gloucester's condition will not improve if he's put under strain?'

'A quiet life is generally beneficial to health.'

She gave a delighted cackle. 'How judicious you are, Doctor Somers. 'Make it your business to find out more about contacts between the two dukes. This Gilbert Iffley is an unscrupulous go-between: alias Baron Glasbury, you say. Is he married?'

I shuddered but dared not hide the answer she sought. 'He has taken Jane Cawfield to wife.'

'What!' she shot to her feet. 'How long have you known this? I told you the woman was kin to the Nevilles, to York's own wife. Don't you recognise the faction which is being formed? The seeds of rebellion are being sown.'

This seemed far-fetched to me and she registered my scepticism. 'You will see, Doctor Somers, you will see. Meanwhile it's enough for the present. Remember our agreement. Return to your French strumpet and give her my compliments. I shall arrange for a wet-nurse in Stamford to care for the child until it is weaned and then the Countess's bastard will be reared at St. Michael's. Your unblushing lady will be able to resume her place among King Charles's courtiers without any perceived blemish on her honour and you will gain misbegotten progeny of rare but undisclosed distinction.'

I clenched my fists in anger at the epithet she applied to Yolande but I knew better than to protest. I understood that the price of the Prioress's co-operation was my acquiescence.

*****

I returned to Worthwaite Manor in a state of anxiety for I scarcely knew its custodians and feared they might resent the task I had imposed by asking them to serve a pregnant stranger. Yolande had been introduced as a recently widowed lady from Normandy and, although I suspected they gave no credit to this story, I hoped the steward and his wife were astute enough not to query it openly. It was a relief when the Countess confirmed that they were treating her with deference and Berthe was working cordially with them.

'Your steward keeps his distance,' she said, 'as is correct, but his wife, Dame Elizabeth, is delightful and knowledgeable about childbirth. I shall be content here, Harry, and I am deeply grateful.'

I was uncomfortably aware that the Fitzvaughan estate, in the neighbouring county of Norfolk, was less than twenty miles distant from my house. I dreaded the possibility that Lady Maud might discover I held the manor and the identity of my secret guest, although I had no intention of alarming Yolande with such a thought. 'The servants understand there must be no public acknowledgement of your presence?'

'They have been informed and I trust them but it is too much to hope that news of a foreign woman staying at the manor will not seep out in the neighbourhood. I've suggested to Dame Elizabeth that she give the impression I am the Marquis of Suffolk's paramour and you have been commissioned to provide me with accommodation for my lying-in. That would be a fitting role for William de la Pole's physician, would it not?'

She gurgled with amusement and I admired her contrivance although the innocent reminder of my humble status pained me. To hide my unease, I told her that the Prioress had agreed to take the baby at St. Michael's but I hesitated to ask what I most wanted to know, until she pre-empted my unspoken question.

'Will you come again to visit me before my time is due?'

'You will permit it?'

'How can I bar you from your own manor?' She smiled mischievously. 'And indeed I do not wish to deprive myself of your company. You have marked my soul as well as my body and both have need of you.'

Her words granted me permission and I took her in my arms. 'I'll seek Suffolk's consent for me to travel here around Michaelmas.'

'Michaelmas? I shall long for the weeks to pass and by then I will be big with child, our child, Harry.'

She nestled against me and we embraced, lost in natural joy which ignored the constraints of worldly prohibitions. That night and the next, after the servants retired and Berthe had tactfully withdrawn into the antechamber, I crept into Yolande's room and we lay together in mutual happiness, never referring to the conventions and morality we flouted.

By day I assumed my expected role as keeper of the manor and inspected its pastures, fishponds and stands of woodland, taking in little of the husbandry which the old steward explained in tiresome detail and longing for dusk. Then, on the third morning, against the urging of my spirit but complying with my unavoidable duty, I left Worthwaite Manor and my love to return to London and the physician's work I had too long neglected.

*****

It was a pleasant surprise to find Leone at the Manor of the Rose, on vacation from the university while Jack was visiting an elderly great-uncle in the country. He had already made himself useful in the Marquis's household, dressing burns and cuts suffered by the servants in the kitchen, and he was eager to consult me about the warts on a scullion's fingers. He was well aware, however, that the news he had to give me would be unwelcome.

'I went to see Bartholomew,' he said and he frowned, alerting me to the significance of what he was about to say. 'A man was leaving Baynard's Castle as I approached the entrance and I couldn't believe my eyes. I ducked into a doorway so he wouldn't see me but, to make sure, I asked Bartholomew if he knew his identity. It was Henri Charpentier.'

I took a deep breath. 'I wasn't sure he was still in England. Did you find out what he was doing at Gloucester's house?'

'Bartholomew said he'd called several times recently and Gilbert Iffley always sees him in private.'

'It's worrying that he's infiltrated the Duke's household. Rendell must be warned in case the wretch turns up at Greenwich.'

The Italian youth grinned. 'I saw Master Chope while I was at Baynard's Castle so I asked him to tell Rendell.'

It amused me that Leone referred so respectfully to Thomas but I praised his quick thinking. I mulled over the implications of what he had told me and my anxiety went beyond any possible danger to Rendell. Perhaps the contact was not so surprising. I knew Gloucester had dealings with the dissident French nobles while the truce was being negotiated in Tours two years earlier and Charpentier could have been a go-between then. I was also certain that Gilbert Iffley employed ruffians to carry out violent deeds and Charpentier was admirably fitted to be another of his hired thugs. The Frenchman was ostensibly in England to trace the whereabouts of the comtesse de Langeais but the link between him and the man I suspected of instigating two murders was ominous.

I gave Leone a summary of the reasons for my absence from Suffolk's house and, as I expected, he asked no indiscreet questions but he gave me a penetrating look so I felt certain he understood more than I had explained. He had known me in the throes of passion for my Mantuan lover and, although he was now a grown man able to judge for himself, I did not want him to view masculine inconstancy as creditable.

I sent a message to Thomas and met him at the inn by the river a few days later. After I had assured him of Yolande's safe arrival at Worthwaite Manor and dodged the further lubricious questions he was tempted to ask, we turned to the subject of Henri Charpentier and it was clear he had already taken steps to safeguard Rendell as far as possible.

'I had a useful chat with the master of the guard at Greenwich. We're quite friendly. He's a good fellow and thinks highly of Rendell. He doesn't hold the same opinion of Master Gilbert Iffley. It seems the Duke's man of business has been known to interfere with matters beyond his remit. He's tried to borrow members of the guard for his own purposes and give directions to the sergeant-at-arms. My friend resents that intrusion into his concerns so he's very ready to view any mate of Iffley's as bad news. If Charpentier makes any effort to enter the Palace of Pleasance, he'll be removed by the guard without ceremony.'

I laughed but quickly became serious. 'I hope Rendell has the sense not to come to the City and walk into a trap.'

'I'm sure he finds the chance to be provocative enticing but he's under instructions from the master of the guard. Let's hope he respects his officer's wisdom.' Thomas swirled the ale in his beaker and stared down at the pattern it made. 'There's no doubt there's something afoot in the Duke's private council-chamber and Iffley's at the heart of it. You'd best be careful of blundering into affairs of state. You did that once before and...'

'It led me within inches of the gallows.' I finished his sentence. 'I'm not likely to forget. What do you know about these secret discussions?'

'Hearsay only of course but my mate's got his ear close to the ground. Gloucester's had enough of being pushed aside. He sees the King led astray into unwise actions and he's no longer prepared to sit on his hands and bite his lip in silence while his enemies smear his name with slanders.'

'I've heard some of this gossip in the City. Iffley's been stirring up the apprentices to riot in support of Gloucester.'

'Londoners have always liked the Duke and they've never warmed to being foisted with a French Queen. Especially when she's evading customs duties, with crafty rackets run for her benefit, exporting wool and tin without paying the proper dues.'

'Is that true?'

'It's not just at Baynard's Castle I've heard it. Merchants I meet on the riverside wharfs are full of complaints about her privileges. Unfair trading, they call it.'

I remembered how I had invoked Master Drewman's help in Rouen to save Queen Margaret from ignominious penury. 'She grew up in a family rich in titles but with scarcely a groat between them. I can imagine she's become a canny businesswoman.'

Thomas grinned impishly. 'Well, you're not the most neutral commentator, are you? Got a taste for the French ladies, I reckon.'

I cuffed him lightly and he put a finger to his lips. 'Not just French ladies either, according to Rendell's tales about your time in Italy. Who'd have thought it when we were lads? You were the prissy one – and now I'm the solid craftsman mired in matrimonial responsibilities while you've been intimate with who knows how many beauties. Not just attending the bedsides of great ladies but jumping into them too.'

'That's a great exaggeration,' I said pompously but Thomas slapped me on the back and called for another flagon of ale.

'Here's to my friend, the philandering physician,' he laughed. 'God bless him and all his patients.'

'Amen to that,' I said with complete sincerity.

*****

I was resigned to resuming my usual way of life and, as always, found satisfaction in practising my craft among my patients. When I next examined Suffolk he reported a considerable improvement in his back, with only occasional twinges of pain, but as he pulled down his shirt his brow was furrowed and I could see something troubled him.

'Will you be moving from the City during the summer, my lord? Some respite on the hunting field might refresh you.'

He shook his head. 'I'll travel on progress with the King, wherever he goes, but I'll not be journeying to Wingfield. I can't risk leaving the court as things stand. Old rivalries are being revived and I need to be at Henry's side.'

'Gloucester's men are agitating in the City, I believe.'

'More than that. Gloucester's dug up all the old allegations he made against the Cardinal years ago, accusing him of misusing the King's jewels and enriching himself at the expense of the royal treasury. The Duke seems to have made a remarkable recovery from the ailment which disabled him. If anything, he's more vigorous than ever.' The Marquis glared at me as if it was my fault Humphrey of Gloucester had not succumbed to his seizure the previous year.

'Unaccustomed physical frailty may exercise a man's mind and encourage him to take action over matters which seem important, while strength remains to him.'

'You mean Gloucester's time may be limited and he's trying to gain an advantage while he can?' Suffolk's eyes lit up but I did not admire the sneer in his voice.

'Such things are in God's hands, my lord.'

Suffolk nodded solemnly and became calmer. 'You're right. You're a good man, Harry Somers. The fact that I'm unlikely to visit Wingfield for some time doesn't mean that you shouldn't travel to your manor once more. On the contrary, I think you should. You need to familiarise yourself with your possessions. You have my leave to go, when it pleases you.'

'Thank you my lord.' I bowed my head, concealing a treacherous smile. 'I was thinking that I might journey there around Michaelmas.'

'By all means. You'll be welcome to call at Wingfield and I shall envy you the sight of my favourite castle.'

I helped him into his gown and left him with a spring in my uneven step as I hurried back to my quarters. My mind had wandered, as it so often did, to that sanctuary in Suffolk where the woman I had no right to claim was nurturing my child in her womb. I made silent petition to the Lord Christ for her safety but I could not still the churning in my unquiet heart where exhilaration and misery did constant battle.

Chapter 22

I travelled with a company of petty traders and hawkers to Saint Edmundsbury where we lodged at an overcrowded inn in a side street as the main hostelry was full with prosperous wool merchants attending the market in the town. I was uncomfortable in the fetid atmosphere, anxious to be on my way at first light to complete my journey to Yolande, scarcely controlling my impatience, but I was forced to satisfy myself with a night's rest where it was available. I looked enviously towards the spires and towers of the massive abbey, where I imagined the guest accommodation would be more salubrious than mine, but I gathered there was no room within its hospitable portals for humble physicians or their like.

Before the last trace of pink-tinged cloud disappeared at dusk I went into the yard to breathe more freely but found it no great improvement, pungent with the stink of horses instead of sweaty men and equally sour to the throat. I walked out into the square and watched the stallholders dismantling their booths until I needed to draw back to permit the passage of a small party of haughty riders, with their escort, who approached the Abbey Gate with confidence. The leader of the group appeared to be a wealthy fellow, clad in costly riding clothes but lean-faced and with a disagreeable expression. I fancied I had seen him somewhere before but could not place the occasion and guessed I had merely crossed his path in the City, perhaps at Master Webber's pharmacy. He paid me no discernible attention.

During the night I woke in a panic. I had no recollection of a nightmare but was seized with a sense of horror which I immediately associated with Yolande and I lay, close-packed between two portly clothiers, quaking with terror at the thought that she would not wish to see me, although this possibility had never troubled me before.

There was no light in the room but the air was filled with wheezes and snorts of a dozen sleepers and in my disturbed state I imagined them the reverberations of monsters from Hell. I longed for dawn, unable to summon sleep into my disturbed mind, and when it was time to rise I was muddle-headed and afraid.

I left my fellow travellers in the town and hired a guide to escort me across country to the property I held from Suffolk, while all the time my dread increased. When I presented myself at Worthwaite manor-house, in a ferment of nerves, Yolande greeted me with courteous formality which only exacerbated my anxieties. We stared at each other warily while I tried to fashion words which would enable her to sever our ties without rancour. I had determined it was my duty to make clear I could place no claims upon her and would not burden her with my presence, leaving forthwith for Wingfield, but I struggled to express these loathsome yet virtuous sentiments. She lowered her head as I stammered nonsense and I imagined her embarrassment at the situation.

'You must not feel compelled to stay,' she said softly, 'but it is your house and I am the interloper, not you. If you wish me to leave...'

'No, no, you misunderstand. The house is yours to use but if you would rather I did not visit...'

'The decision must be yours, Doctor Somers...'

'Holy saints grant them a modicum of good sense! Take her in your arms, master physician, and feel the swelling of her belly where your seed ripens.'

We both turned, open-mouthed, to stare at the normally reticent Berthe who grinned broadly at our consternation. 'The two of you are frightened of your shadows, or perhaps each other's. Don't be alarmed. I can see you are longing to embrace but afraid the other has changed. Stuff and nonsense! Kiss her, Doctor Somers. See how she'll return the compliment. Begging your pardon, my lady.'

I swallowed and my voice was feeble. 'Is it true, madame? Is Berthe speaking the truth?'

Yolande said nothing but in a moment she was pressed against me, her arms round my neck as I held her, and the foolish fears we had both suffered dissolved in the certainty of each other's loving presence.

We spent a night of joyful harmony and next morning while Yolande rested I agreed to make a tour of inspection, escorted by the steward who was eager to secure greater interest from me than I had shown on my previous visit. Berthe followed me into the yard and begged a word in private before I set out so we moved to the shelter of the dairy while I was turning over in my mind what news she had to impart.

'Is your lady's health of concern?' I asked.

'Not at all, Doctor. Since her sickness passed she's in bonny health. But her occupation here has not gone unnoticed.'

'Gossip is inevitable.' I shrugged with relief that Yolande's pregnancy was uncomplicated.

'That's so and mostly there's no reason for concern.' Berthe paused and I held my breath. 'But ten days ago a gentleman called at the manor and asked to see the lady staying here. As you suggested, we'd spread the word that Madame Yolande is a lady from Normandy and it seems this caller also comes from King Henry's Duchy across the Narrow Sea. He wished to pay his respects.'

'Gaston de la Tour!'

'You know him, sir?'

'He serves Lord Fitzvaughan whose estate is only twenty miles from here.'

Berthe nodded. 'Near Attleborough, he said.'

'Was he admitted to the house?'

'He was given refreshment as hospitality demands but I explained my lady was indisposed and he accepted my word. He was properly polite and made no awkward enquiries but I sensed there was more behind his visit than neighbourly courtesy.'

'Your intuition is unfailingly accurate, Berthe. Does he know I'm in possession of the manor?'

'I don't think so. He seemed to have heard the rumour that my lady is the Marquis of Suffolk's mistress and was intrigued.'

'Inevitably. But he's close enough to the court to have learned that the Countess has disappeared from the Queen's lodgings and shrewd enough to develop a theory he wishes to test. I've reason to know he can be dangerous.'

'I'll have it given out that my lady's health is fragile and she can receive no visitors. As it is, she doesn't venture far from the house when she takes the air but I'll make sure she never leaves the manor grounds. I haven't told her of the gentleman's enquiry.'

I agreed these sensible precautions but insisted Yolande must be told that Gaston de la Tour was residing not far away and was not to be trusted. She would probably remember seeing him by Lord Fitzvaughan's side in France, for both the royal betrothal and the marriage. I had no doubt he would recognise her. It was an uncomfortable coincidence but we were forewarned to avoid unnecessary risks.

I re-joined the steward, ill at ease but concentrating assiduously on his descriptions of fine quality fleeces and the yield to be obtained from my flocks of sheep. I realised for the first time how it was possible to enjoy a steady income from Worthwaite's contribution to the wool trade and listened with interest to an account of English weavers producing their own worsteds. We were no longer dependent just on sales of raw wool to the cloth-makers of Flanders and I understood why merchants were pounding the roads between London and East Anglia in such numbers to negotiate purchases and place orders.

The steward led me across some scrubby heathland behind the manor house, reminding me that the northern boundary of Worthwaite's land was formed by the River Waveney. I peered ahead, discerning where the land rose slightly but unable to make out a watercourse in the intervening depression. I had grown up beside the Thames at Greenwich and in recent years had become familiar with the Adige in Verona and the Loire at Tours. The humble stream which confronted me was far from being their watery equal.

'The town of Diss lies three miles yonder on the Norfolk side,' the steward said. 'It's our nearest market and the hostelries are good. You should visit it, sir.'

I agreed that I would go there but something at the back of my mind irked me until, much later in the day when I sat at table with Yolande, the memory came back and I felt a wave of guilt. My lady noticed me shiver and expressed concern but I assured her I was not ailing, only rueful, convicting myself of negligence, and I described Rollo's frail bereaved mother at Wingfield.

'You must visit her while you are here,' Yolande said with a sweet smile.

'I will but first I'll go to Diss to find the landlord who encountered a scarred man spreading disgraceful lies about her son.'

'You must do what you feel is right, Harry, but don't entangle yourself in matters best left alone.'

She reached out to touch my hand and the natural affection of her gesture drove aside any thought that her words might carry a portent of calamity.

*****

My horse splashed through the leaf-strewn waters of the Waveney and trotted obediently up the steep slope to the centre of the town where the market square nestled below a church of flint and stone, mellow in the morning sunlight. There were two inns flanking the square, one apparently more popular than the other from the townsfolk milling around its entrance, so I went there to make my enquiry. The landlord was a genial fellow and remembered at once the incident I referred to; he was willing to expand on what I had heard and my only difficulty was in interpreting his unfamiliar dialect.

'I mind that villain well,' he said, 'though it's more than a year ago I saw him. He was drunk when he came through the door and I told the potman to put him out if he caused trouble but we were that busy and Scarface was quiet at first so he slipped our attention. Then half a dozen men from Wingfield came in, regulars they were, wearing the Marquis's livery, and the bugger recognised the crest. Suddenly he was on his feet and taunting them about their comrade's murder in France. I'd heard nothing about it before but I sensed there was violence in the air. The name of the murdered fellow escapes me...'

He paused and I prompted him. 'Rollo Rudd.'

'That's right. They all knew this Rollo and when that foul-mouthed sot started to insult his memory, the Wingfield men rounded on the bastard and though he drew his sword he was too unsteady to use it. They flung him out through the door.'

'So he lumbered off after that, did he?'

The landlord rubbed his stubbly chin. 'To tell the truth I was afeared he'd broken a limb – he crashed down on the ground so hard – and I didn't want the town beadle claiming I ran a disorderly house. I went outside and got him to his feet, helped him into the saddle and sent him on his way.'

'Did he say anything to you?'

'He did. He swore a lot about his master, said the ungrateful rogue had threatened to cast him off, despite all the jobs he'd done for him. He started to tell me some pretty unsavoury things, I can tell you, knifings and poisonings he carried out. I didn't want to hear.'

'Did he say why he was in Diss?'

'He'd been sent on an errand to some estate up near Attleborough but he'd been beaten and robbed there – so he said. At any rate he was travelling back to London in a filthy mood and he'd taken to the bottle which made him more cantankerous.'

One unexpected phrase registered in my mind. 'The estate near Attleborough – was it Lord Fitzvaughan's?'

'Might have been. He didn't say. That's all I know. He rode off without a word of thanks and I remember thinking the ungrateful bloody drunkard would come to a bad end, like enough.'

'He did,' I said, pressing money into the landlord's open hand. 'I'm very grateful for what you've told me.'

As I rode down the hill I knew my gratitude was constrained by alarm because, a year previously, Gilbert Iffley's minion must have been sent to see Walter Fitzvaughan, making a connection which horrified me. Fortunately it seemed that the fellow had been rebuffed, which suggested his lordship would have nothing to do with Iffley's devious schemes, and that was consistent with my belief in Fitzvaughan's integrity.

To my surprise I soon found myself beside an expanse of water, roughly circular in shape, bordered in part by cottages straggling down the slope from the church, but mostly fringed by scrub and bracken, in the midst of which, on the side away from the town, were a few shabby huts. I reined in my horse, realising I had missed the track I needed to follow back to the Waveney and was startled to hear my name called from behind me.

'It's Doctor Somers, isn't it? I thought I recognised you at Saint Edmundsbury.'

The sour-faced merchant rode to my side wafting a velvet-clad arm in the air and I struggled again to remember where I had seen him in London. His resonant voice also struck a faint chord in my memory. 'Your servant, sir. You have the advantage of me, knowing my name.'

'Boice, Doctor, Stephen Boice. We've never been introduced but you were pointed out to me once. You're staying at Wingfield, I presume. You serve the Marquis, do you not?'

These apparently innocuous enquiries were unwelcome. 'I do. I'm bound for Wingfield now.'

'Of course.' He smiled thinly. 'Myself, I conduct business on behalf of the Brotherhood of Drapers – among other patrons. I'm often in these parts. You've discovered the mere. Remarkable, isn't it? They say it's fully sixty feet deep, maybe bottomless in fact. What do you think of that?'

'As you say, it's remarkable. I didn't know of its existence. You will excuse me. I must be on my way.' I bowed my head and turned my horse but a gloved hand grasped my bridle.

'You'll need the trackway to the east of the town if you're bound for Wingfield. I expect you came by that route.'

'Of course,' I said, cursing my stupidity. 'Perhaps our paths will cross again in London.'

'Or anywhere. How does the vulgar saying go? Upstairs, downstairs, or in my lady's chamber? Ah, if only, don't you agree? Good-day to you, physician.'

He set his spurs to his horse's flank and shot away up the hill leaving me trembling with uncertainty as to his meaning. Who was Stephen Boice? What did he know of my affairs? Where had I seen him first? These were questions I could not answer.

*****

I arrived at Wingfield muddy and unkempt after riding with unwise haste but, I as I entered the gatehouse, I rejoiced to see the chaplain emerging from one of the towers carrying a fine tapestry cope.

'Father Wilfred,' I hailed him. 'I'm not sure if you remember me.'

'Doctor Somers, of course I do. You're most welcome. I'm forever in your debt for the way you brought comfort to that sad bereaved mother. The old dame passed from this life in blessed peace when, without your intervention, she was at risk of incurring the pains of Hell for her recalcitrance.'

'Rollo's mother is dead?' My voice was flat with disappointment and guilt. 'I'd hoped to give her reassurance that her son's murderer had himself gone to face God's judgement.' I did not admit what a laggard I had been in delivering this message.

'His will be done. I'm bound for the chapel. Will you join us? Are you are staying the night here or are you visiting your manor? We were pleased to hear the Marquis had bestowed Worthwaite on you.'

I should have known the household at Wingfield would be aware of my good fortune but it worried me. 'I fear I must journey on before dusk falls,' I said vaguely, 'but I'll gladly come with you to Mass before I leave.'

The chaplain patted my arm and I followed him into the chapel, feeling myself in urgent need of Heaven's protection and guidance, for everything that had happened since I left Worthwaite that morning seemed freighted with danger.

*****

I found Yolande sitting with Dame Elizabeth, the steward's wife, sorting through a pile of household linen and, as she dismissed the old woman, she smiled up at me.

'You have a good stock of embroidered napery, Doctor Somers, and it has been well stored. It is free from mildew and needs only a day's airing to make it fit for use.'

I grinned to see the Countess immersed in household duties but her expression was serious. 'You do not mind me involving myself in the affairs of your household? It is something in which I have experience.'

'Of course I don't mind. I'm flattered by your interest but I'm afraid the simple inventory at Worthwaite hardly matches the range of possessions with which you've been familiar.'

'No matter, I am glad to find an occupation. I have also introduced the kitchen to some savoury sauces which you may find enriching your meat.' She leaned forward to take my hand and frowned. 'But you look troubled. What has happened?'

I had not wanted to distress her but her perception encouraged me to share my concerns and, sitting beside her, I poured out my anxieties, describing not only the disconcerting events of the day but the background to Rollo's death, my conviction that Gilbert Iffley was behind his murder and much else. I told her more about Lord Fitzvaughan and emphasised Gaston de la Tour's capricious nature but I said nothing of Lady Maud's private history and the perilous charade she enacted, for that was a confidence I was bound to keep in accordance with my promise.

'I underestimated the power of gossip. I'm afraid for your safety here if rumours are spreading.'

Yolande looked at me thoughtfully. 'Tell me again what that merchant said to you in Diss.'

I repeated his words exactly for their provocation had lodged them in my memory. 'Upstairs, downstairs or in my lady's chamber. I'm afraid he has wind of your presence here.'

'Maybe, but perhaps not with accuracy. You quoted another comment before. Can you repeat it?'

'He added something like "if only, don't you agree?" What are you thinking?'

She sank back in her chair and raised her feet onto a footstool. 'That he did not believe you were the foreign lady's lover, only her physician. Have you forgotten the hint I gave Dame Elizabeth as to my child's paternity? May God forgive me: I had not thought what harm the falsehood might do. These people believe I am Suffolk's harlot.'

I jumped to my feet. 'Heaven forbid that idea doesn't spread to the wrong ears.'

'To Iffley's ears?'

'There's been contact between him and Lord Fitzvaughan's household.'

'And between Iffley and Henri Charpentier, you said.' The misery on Yolande's face reflected where her deepest fear was rooted. 'If Charpentier learns I am here...'

'We must pray he doesn't but I'll write to the lady Prioress at Stamford and implore her to grant you sanctuary. She has no love for Duke Humphrey of Gloucester and if she realises you are in danger from his acolytes she may relent and offer help.'

Yolande smiled and when I knelt by her chair she took my hands and placed them on her stomach so I could feel the vibrations of the infant she carried. I buried my head against that precious swelling and blinked back tears that she must not see. Despite the terrors we faced, in my heart there was joy at the sweet accord between us, such as a man and wife might share from day to day; but I knew I must not indulge such hopeless fantasies.

Chapter 23

A week later I returned to London and resumed my duties at the Manor of the Rose, nervously waiting for a response from the Prioress and fearing to receive a cry for help if Yolande's security was further threatened. Yet I heard nothing from either and when a month passed I began to hope that the silence from Stamford mattered less if all was well at Worthwaite. I was content to care for my patients quietly, grateful that the Marquis's troublesome back seemed not to require my attention but relieved that he greeted me in friendly fashion when we encountered each other about the house. I began to reckon the days until I could return to my manor, after the Feast of the Nativity when Leone would be at hand to cover my absence, but my increasing confidence was soon to prove misplaced.

The cloying mists of November filled the City streets but did not deter aggrieved citizens from congregating and shouting abuse at the Marquis and his cronies. Gloucester's name was once more on the lips of those who berated the King's current advisers and I heard from Thomas that the Duke was often at his London house and made frequent visits to the court. Thomas had been commissioned to install new panelling in the principal rooms at Baynard's Castle and so was regularly in the City to join me in a jug of ale at the hostelry overlooking the river. One day he seemed unusually agitated and it was never his way to beat about the bush.

'Bartholomew has told me Gilbert Iffley is spreading a rumour that Suffolk is sheltering the Countess of Langeais on his estate and has made her his mistress.'

'But he hasn't linked me or Worthwaite to these events?'

'It seems not but it may only be a matter of time. Why should Iffley be interested in Suffolk's bedfellows?'

'Only in this hypothetical case.' I drew a circle with my finger in some liquid split on the table-top. 'It's a ploy to undermine Suffolk's influence at court and trap him in clever lies. The Queen is his most ardent supporter but she would be furious if she believed he had carried off her errant attendant, prevented Yolande from making the intended marriage with the Seigneur de la Flèche and bedded her himself.'

'I've heard it said the Queen and Suffolk make the two-headed beast together.'

'Don't repeat that, Tom. It's treason. But if there's a crumb of truth in it, the Queen's anger would be the greater.'

Thomas whistled and promised to keep his ear to the ground for more gossip. 'You're wise to steer clear of Iffley these days'.

'I'd be happy if I never had dealings with him again. I'm satisfied he's an evil schemer who'll destroy anyone in his path if he judges it necessary. I wish Gloucester had a more worthy counsellor at his side.'

I returned to the Manor of the Rose in sober mood, despite the ale I had quaffed, determined to write once more to the Prioress and beg her help before the Countess's condition made it impossible for her to journey to Stamford. I was unprepared to be clapped on the shoulder and hugged by an aristocratic arm as I walked along the corridor to my room and astonished to see Lord Fitzvaughan's sunny face beaming at me.

'I've just returned from France, Harry, and have soothed the ruffled feathers of the French King as required. I'm rewarded by the happiest news I could imagine. A letter awaited me here from Norfolk.'

'From Lady Maud?'

'From Gaston who has watched over her as bidden and reports she is now big with child.'

I stared stupidly at him, trying to hide my incomprehension. 'That's joyful news, my lord. Are you travelling there?'

He laughed. 'There's no need and I have business at the court. Suffolk and Gloucester are squaring up for a battle royal – literally so, a battle for the royal ear. Suffolk intends to indict the Duke for his past misdeeds but Humphrey has defended himself brilliantly before the Council. I need to see how matters go and take steps to seek my own advantage. I shan't need to journey to Norfolk until Maud has been delivered of my heir. She's well advanced in pregnancy this time and all should be well.'

I expressed my pleasure and privately pondered whether it was possible Maud could be carrying a child, whether after all the loss of her second baby had not rendered her barren. Perhaps all along Maud had been misled by false information and if this was so I could genuinely rejoice for both her and her husband.

At long last I received a letter from Stamford but its contents were not what I had hoped for and troubled me. The Prioress expressed sympathy for Yolande's predicament but advised that it would be inadvisable for her to leave Worthwaite. She had received an account of the rumour spreading in London about Suffolk's alleged role in the Countess's disappearance and she believed that his enemies would have spies in the vicinity of Wingfield, snooping for news of a pregnant noblewoman. If it was thought such a lady was being conveyed out of the district in a closed litter she could be in the utmost danger of capture. The Prioress's fears were horribly credible and I remembered my strange encounter in Diss with Stephen Boice, whose interest in my affairs for no convincing reason disconcerted me.

Brawls in the City streets became a daily occurrence but in December events took a more serious turn when Suffolk brought before the King's Council one William Catour, apprentice to John Daveys who was armourer to Richard, Duke of York. With a calm demeanour Catour avowed to the assembled dignitaries that his master had spoken seditious words, claiming that King Henry had no legitimate claim to the throne which rightfully, by descent, belonged to York. Daveys fiercely denied the accusation but, whatever the truth of it, Richard of York was wrong-footed by this untimely assertion and became vociferous in demanding that his armourer be rigorously punished. The judges, as was customary in such a case, ordered recourse to the judgement of God and the two base-born men were required to fight a duel with single-sticks on the open ground at Smithfield outside the City walls. Counting houses, workshops, market booths and slaughterhouses duly closed their shutters and proclaimed a holiday so all could enjoy this public spectacle.

By all accounts it was a notable occasion, attended by the King and Queen and the whole court, to say nothing of the vast throng of citizens avid for blood-curdling entertainment. I was not present, loathing the idea of the uneven contest which pitched a young and vigorous apprentice, presented as virtuous upholder of the King's cause, against his older and less agile rival who was widely vilified as a traitor. I never doubted the outcome and shook my head in resignation when colleagues who were present described how the armourer was struck down by his opponent, promptly declared guilty in the eyes of God and hanged on the spot, to an accompaniment of whistles, cat-calls and obscenities.

There was much speculation in Suffolk's household that the episode had harmed both York and, by association, Gloucester, for their enemies could portray them as plotting to betray the King, ready to sacrifice an underling in order to sow the seed of suspicion in men's minds. To question Henry's legitimate right to the throne was treasonable and the hostilities between great men at the King's side were becoming hazardous for their minions – among whom I could count myself particularly vulnerable.

*****

312

It was more than six months since my last uneasy conversation with Gilbert Iffley and I was determined to avoid further contact with him. I suspected the influence of Baron Glasbury in both the mounting unrest on the streets and the escalating quarrels between King Henry's counsellors and I was resolved to have nothing to do with his plots. I even took circuitous routes when I left Suffolk's house in order not to pass Baynard's Castle and risk meeting him; but in all my contrivances there was a weakness which I shrank from admitting to myself but which Iffley knew.

The sealed packet was delivered by a servant apparently wearing royal livery and I opened it with clumsy fingers, fearing a summons to submit to the King's justice for my misdeeds. When I realised the letter came not from King Henry but his uncle, I gave a momentary sigh of relief, quickly replaced by a shudder as I speculated what Humphrey of Gloucester wanted with me. I recognised his seal and handwriting and, reading his kind words about the service I had rendered him the previous year when he was taken ill, I grew calmer and smiled to see how my old patron respected my medical skill. His invitation to join him for a glass of wine in his London house on the Eve of the Nativity gave me pleasure but also caused consternation for it seemed probable I would encounter Gilbert Iffley. Nevertheless, I persuaded myself that Iffley's malicious influence would be neutralised in the Duke's presence and the baron might in fact be enjoying the Feast of Yule in his own house, with his alluring wife, lately Jane Cawfield, at his side.

As I entered the courtyard of Baynard's Castle I noticed a small troop of Gloucester's guards drawn up by the archway to the stables but I paid them no closer attention, welcoming the sight of Bartholomew who bounded down the steps of the great hall to greet me. Then, unexpectedly, I was trembling with alarm as I remembered another occasion when I had stood on that very spot and I cursed my deficient memory which had failed to stir into action earlier. In Iffley's absence, Bartholomew had been conducting business with a cadaverous merchant who meant nothing to me at the time but whose identity I now knew. What a fool I had been not to make the connection when I saw Stephen Boice in Saint Edmundsbury and then met him in Diss. He was another of Gilbert Iffley's cronies, possibly one of his agents, and inevitably his presence in East Anglia might signify danger to Yolande and to me.

I hardly heard what Bartholomew was saying as he conducted me through the hall to an antechamber, served me with wine and then left me to await my host. It was a beautifully furnished room and I admired the new panelling covering its walls which was doubtless the product of Thomas's craftsmanship. I took a sip from the jewelled goblet and prized the richness of the wine's fragrance. I sat down on an upholstered bench and drank more deeply, reassured that only two drinking vessels had been set out on the table suggesting that the Duke would receive me alone.

I was not surprised by the lengthy delay before the door opened but the unaccustomed relaxation made me feel drowsy so when I heard the handle squeak I jumped to my feet in sudden confusion, embarrassed by weakness in my knees. Gilbert Iffley, Baron Glasbury, stood on the threshold and bowed with mocking flamboyance.

'We are obliged that you have come, Doctor Somers.'

'I expected to meet the Duke.' My voice sounded curiously unfamiliar.

'The Duke is at Greenwich for the festivities.'

'He sent me an invitation.' As I spoke I understood I had been tricked and again cursed myself for an idiot.

'Our hands are similar, aren't they? I've perfected an imitation of his writing style and of course I have access to his seal.' He sounded irritatingly complacent.

'I don't appreciate the joke. I shall leave.' I took a step forward but the room seemed to spin beneath my feet and I was forced to steady myself by clutching a chair-back. Only then, as I began to feel sick, did I realise I had been drugged. 'I demand to leave.'

'When we have finished our conversation, Doctor, not before. Sit down.' He put a hand to my chest and propelled me back onto the bench while I struggled to combat the lethargy which seized my limbs. 'I fancy you've not encountered this fine concoction before. One of your apothecary friends could tell you about it – poppy, columbine and I don't know what are in it. The correct proportions are crucial or you would pass out completely and that would render our meeting worthless.'

'This is outrageous. Let me go.'

He grasped my gown, bunched it up beneath my chin and glared into my face. 'All you need do is tell me where the woman is hiding and confirm that she is Suffolk's whore. Then you will be taken back to the Marquis's mansion and a short sleep will restore all your faculties.' He felt me tremble when he referred to Yolande and a cruel smile twisted his mouth. 'She's at Wingfield, is she not?'

'I don't know what you're talking about.'

'Don't you? Then I'll refresh your memory for it was you helped her escape from Westminster, on Suffolk's behalf, and arranged for her to be hidden somewhere. I've found a witness who will swear you took her and her attendant by boat from the palace on some spurious excuse. Then you went to Wingfield a few months ago to check for the Marquis that she was in good health. Is she carrying his bastard?'

'Rubbish. It's all nonsense.'

He dragged me to my feet and I felt limp in his grip. 'Don't be stupid, Doctor Somers, why should you defend William de la Pole? Your heart still serves Humphrey of Gloucester, doesn't it? That's why you came so readily in answer to the message I sent you. You only need to tell me the truth. I want to be certain before the Duke publicly accuses Suffolk of seducing the Countess. The Queen's anger will do the rest. If she deserts the Marquis and persuades the King to cast him off, he'll be destroyed.'

'I'll tell you nothing of the sort.'

He flicked my chin in a derisory manner. 'You needn't worry on your own account, Harry. If you co-operate your name won't be mentioned and Gloucester will be happy to take you back into his household at any time. Your friends already serve him, don't they? Did any of them help your audacious escapade?'

I registered the veiled threat and felt him tighten his hold on my gown. I lifted my hands to resist but he pushed them aside. 'It's all lies,' I said as firmly as I could.

With abrupt violence he smashed my head against the wall and I felt the corner of a panel imprint itself on my scalp as my cap fell to the floor. 'I've no time for heroics, physician,' he snarled. 'You try my patience. You'll tell me what I need to know now or you'll be handed on to one who'll treat you far more barbarously than I will. This is your last opportunity. Tell me.'

'No.'

He punched me in the mouth and I tasted blood while, despite my effort to stay upright, I crumpled to the floor as he let me fall. 'Henri!' he called and, at his summons, I shut my eyes.

I did not need to see the Frenchman's vicious face as he dragged me out of the antechamber and down a flight of stairs before flinging me into a dimly lit chamber where a range of fearful instruments decorated the wall.

'So, little physician,' Henri Charpentier said, kicking me in the belly as I lay on the floor, 'at last I get my reward for all the trouble you have caused me and the Seigneur. You will tell me what the Baron wants to know or you'll taste the refinements I have to offer.'

I shook my head without speaking and he dragged me to my feet. 'Very well, stubborn dolt, first I shall crush your fingers.'

He forced my hands into manacles fixed to the top of a shelf while I cringed, struggling to maintain some semblance of self-control. With a laugh he unfastened a rope from the wall and I looked up to see two huge weights dangling high above my fingers. 'When I let go, they will fall,' he said with a smirk. 'I'll give you a taste of how heavy they are. Then I'll peg your fingers in position so you can't wiggle them or screw up your hands when I drop them a second time. You'll not manage much doctoring with your fingers mashed into a pulp. You won't even be able to amputate them yourself – maybe you'll bleed to death.'

In my muzzy mind I knew that this man would enjoy torturing me and whatever I told him would not prevent his cruelty. He wanted to hear me squeal with pain, to see me spew in terror and, whether or not I swore Iffley's allegations were true, he would have his entertainment. I was not made for heroism but I thought of Yolande and clenched my teeth. 'I've nothing to say.'

Still holding the rope with one hand, he twined his fingers in my hair, twisting my head with painful force, and spat into my face but the moment it took to satisfy his spite with this personal offensiveness saved me from worse injury. The sounds of the door flung open, shouts, swords drawn from scabbards and the screech of the falling weights all happened simultaneously. Instinctively I tried to clench my fists, jerking them backwards in the manacles as far as I could, but I heard myself cry out as the side of my left hand took a blow. Around me there was hubbub but I was too stunned to take in details.

Someone in half-armour released me from the wrist-irons and called for a bandage to bind my wound while another offered me wine from his own flask and I drank gratefully.

317

'Why the Hell did you come here, Doctor? You knew Iffley is a villain.'

I grinned at Rendell stupidly. 'Walked into a trap. How did you know I was in trouble?'

'Saw you in the courtyard. I told the master of the guard to check with Bartholomew why you'd come. We was just off to Greenwich to join the Duke and I didn't think you'd come willingly to meet Iffley. Bartholomew said he'd told you the Duke wasn't here but you didn't seem to take it in. If I'd known that bastard Charpentier was here I'd have gone for him with my dagger but he was too quick when we burst in.'

Blood was seeping from my left hand and pain shot up my arm as I touched it gingerly, extending and bending my fingers. 'There's a bone broken in my little finger,' I said. 'It needs strapping to a splint. Thank God it was no worse. I'm in your debt again, Rendell.'

'What's all this maudlin twaddle, then?' Thomas, in his work clothes and carrying a chisel, ran through the door. 'I could hear the commotion where I was working up in the solar. Christ, Harry, what's happened?'

Explanations were given and I was helped upstairs. I learned that Iffley had left the house after Charpentier took charge of me, which was no surprise for the fastidious Baron would be careful not to be present when I was put to the instruments. I was more troubled that the Frenchman had escaped, fighting his way past the soldiers on the stairs and knifing one of them while everyone's attention was on my predicament. Bartholomew had seen him seize a horse and ride away before anyone in the yard knew what had happened.

Rendell and his companions departed for Greenwich but Thomas insisted on accompanying me to the Manor of the Rose where, to my relief, we found Leone had arrived from Oxford for the Feast. He immediately and competently assumed the role of my physician. He set my hand in rigid binding, gave me an infusion to dull the pain and ordered me to sleep until the full effects of the drugged wine had worn off. I was ready to obey the novice practitioner and Thomas helped me to my bed but when we reached the pallet I saw a sealed packet on the pillow.

'Where did this come from?' I turned to the page who served me.

'Let it lie until you've rested.' Thomas made to pick up the package but I took hold of it before he could.

'It was delivered with letters from Wingfield, sir' the boy answered. 'The messenger said to say it was pressing.'

I ripped off my steward's seal and tore open the enclosure, written in Yolande's hand. I knew the contents would be hateful to read.

Dear love, I beg you to come if it is possible. A dire event has occurred and I need your counsel. I am asked to give my response by Twelfth Night to a proposition on which you must be consulted. I am in good health but anguish of mind. Forgive me.

I dismissed the page and read Yolande's message to Thomas. 'I must leave at once,' I said. 'She's in danger.'

I reached for my travelling garb but sank down on the bed as my head swam and Thomas put his hand firmly on my wrist. 'You'll sleep the night first, Harry, or you'll collapse on the road. And I'm coming with you. You're in no state to ride alone. I'll send to tell Grizel and order fresh horses.'

I could not argue with him as Leone's potion took effect and, still clasping Yolande's letter, I lay back and shut my eyes. I was soon lost to the world but demons infested my dreams.

Chapter 24

I over-estimated my powers of recovery from Iffley's devilish potion and next morning felt feverish and weak, reluctantly complying with Leone's order that I spend a further day in bed. Thomas fetched Grizel and their children from Greenwich to share a modest celebration of the Nativity in my chamber and, despite my longing to be on the road, I was glad I had not separated the father from his family at such a time. The lively infants provided us with entertainment and by the evening I began to regain my strength, heartened by Grizel's insistence that Thomas must certainly accompany me to Worthwaite as I was not to be trusted to protect myself without him.

Grizel also brought interesting news from Greenwich that Humphrey of Gloucester intended shortly to decamp from his palace there, with his immediate supporters and four hundred armed guards, to take up residence in his strongly defended castle at Devizes in the south-west of the country. His sister was particularly proud that Rendell was to ride out as one of the party but I was interested in the inference that Gloucester saw himself under threat. Whether he was seeking protection within the walls of his stronghold or assembling his soldiers there in order to march out in force against Suffolk were not questions I could answer but both possibilities were unsettling.

At last Thomas and I were mounted and away from the City but our progress was frustratingly slow. My friend had engaged the services of two sturdy retainers carrying lances, who gave us confidence against the risk of attack by vagabonds, but the weather was bitterly cold and the rutted tracks were filled with ice which necessitated picking our way with care. In the fields standing water lay frozen, with grasses swept by the wind bowed under its surface in wintery obeisance. We slept five nights at indifferent inns and spent nearly twice as long in the saddle as the journey would ordinarily take. My anxieties grew with every extra hour while the ache in my useless hand provided a throbbing counterpoint to my fears. When at last we arrived at the manor I was prepared to find Yolande carried away by Iffley's men and my steward slaughtered on the threshold but both were at hand to greet us and, although she looked worried, the Countess appeared in excellent physical health.

As soon as my companions had been accommodated and refreshed I joined Yolande, accompanied only by Berthe. I apologised for my delay in responding to her cry for help and explained my injury, while I held her in my arms, conscious of her pounding heart as she nestled against my chest.

'Has Gilbert Iffley discovered your sanctuary? Is he threatening to proclaim you as Suffolk's light-o'-love?'

She smiled. 'No, not that. I know nothing of the man. The matter does not concern my honour so much as the well-being of our child.'

'Something is amiss with your pregnancy?' I cradled her face with my right hand.

She took hold of my fingers and kissed them. 'I thank the Saints, all seems as it should be in my womb. The problem concerns the infant when born.'

My agitation grew. 'The Prioress has changed her mind and will not take the child? Why has she approached you and not written to me?'

Yolande put a finger to my lips and made me sit at her side. 'You must be calm. Be assured I have not heard from the Prioress. It is another proposal entirely that has been put to me. A lady has visited me. A lady known to me who lives not far from here.'

My blood ran cold as understanding came. 'Lady Maud Fitzvaughan?'

'Indeed.' Yolande wrinkled her nose. 'She is a good deal too free in speaking of your past intimacy with her, Harry, but I am bound to sympathise with her predicament.'

'She has told you...,' I faltered.

'Of the constraints in her marriage and her inability to bear a child, although her husband believes she is enceinte. She has implored me to allow her to take our child and present it as her own.'

'What!' I sprang to my feet. 'How dare she?'

'It would be a prodigious deception to practise on her husband but it is not for me to judge, if she can reconcile her conscience to the falsehood. The child would be cherished as Lord Walter's heir and brought up in a noble family.'

'As befits its mother's status but not its father's!' I could not hide my pain. 'She is taunting me.'

Yolande put her hand on my arm. 'She doesn't know you are the child's father. She has heard the gossip about Suffolk and doesn't question it. She believes you have a care for my health under his authority.'

'You didn't disabuse her of the idea?'

'It seemed unnecessary.'

I tried to control the rage building inside me. 'How does she think she can contrive such a monstrous trick? Lord Fitzvaughan has put her under surveillance by his friend.'

The Countess gave a half-smile which seemed strangely patronising. 'Oh, Gaston de la Tour is party to the ruse. I think it may have been his suggestion. He escorted her when she came here.'

I rounded on Berthe, sitting quietly in the corner of the room. 'Why were they admitted? I thought you understood he was dangerous.'

Yolande's voice became imperious. 'I ordered that they be admitted. The lady suffered a fall while riding outside the manor grounds. Monsieur de la Tour was merely accompanying her as squire.'

'Another trick.'

'I expect you are right but she has reason for her ploys. She has been cruelly misused in the past.'

'She is a scheming bitch!'

Yolande's face froze. 'That is hardly courteous.'

'You remind me that I am a baseborn peasant and you and she are noble ladies. Nevertheless, she's an unscrupulous seductress concerned only for herself.'

Yolande's tone became tart. 'I don't imagine she has seduced Monsieur de la Tour from what I understand of his attachment to Lord Walter.'

'He is equally unscrupulous. Their interests coincide because if she bears a child her husband will have no reason to visit her bed again. I imagine Gaston accused her of pretending to be pregnant and she wheedled him into working with her to acquire a child conceived out of wedlock. How did you respond to their fiendish proposal?'

'I said I would consult the child's father and we agreed to meet again on Twelfth Night.'

'If they try to set foot here I'll hurl them from the door. You can tell them the father is not worthy to have his infant reared in their renowned household, being a mere physician.'

'Am I to address them while they sit in the mud where you have hurled them?' Her sarcasm was biting. 'For your sake it seems imprudent to let them know the truth.'

'For your sake more likely because you're ashamed to admit you let me into your bed. I understand. Forgive me, Madam, for intruding where I have no business to be. In the morning my companions and I will remove ourselves to Wingfield and trouble you no more. Do as you think fit; barter our child in return for their silence and forget you ever met me.'

I strode from the room and slammed the door.

*****

It was Berthe who sought me out an hour later when I was slouched at table with a flagon of ale after I had told

323

Thomas to leave me on my own. She approached timidly and begged my pardon for her failure to prevent Gaston de la Tour encountering her mistress. My anger had already been replaced by misery and I knew I owed her an apology.

'I was wrong to blame you. I ask your forgiveness, Berthe.'

'It's freely given, sir, but it's you and my lady need to be reconciled, if you'll excuse me saying so.'

'The Countess made clear how little she respects me.'

'So why has she been drowning in tears since you left her? She's sobbing so hard I begin to fear for the child.'

I was wary of this comfort. 'Are you sure she's not mourning her lost honour in coupling with an ignoble underling?'

'Oh, Doctor Somers, you should know her better than that. She loves you as she's never loved another. You were at odds through misunderstanding each other. She thought you might prefer the child to be nurtured in a great house rather than confined in a convent and you would be absolved of responsibility for the infant's upkeep, freed from a lifelong encumbrance. She gave no indication to Lady Maud of what her answer might be. She only said she must consider and consult.'

I peered at Berthe with watery eyes. 'I don't regard my child as an encumbrance.'

'She would weep with joy to hear you say so.'

'Did she send you to me?'

'No, Doctor. She would berate me if she knew I'd come. She is a proud lady.'

'I've no doubt of that but a humble physician has his pride too. That might surprise her.'

Berthe ignored my tendentious comment. 'May I tell her you will call on her before you leave for Wingfield tomorrow? It would calm her and give her hope.'

I looked into Berthe's open, honest face and felt tears trickling down my cheeks. 'If she will receive me in the morning, I will call,' I said and pushed the ale aside. 'I'm not hopeful it will result in any change of plans.'

I did not sleep that night, fearful of facing Yolande's austere superiority without the carapace of anger to shield me, for my fury had dissolved into desolation. Perhaps, I reflected, she would refuse to see me and that might be for the best, saving us both from another hurtful exchange, but Berthe brought me word that I should call after breaking my fast.

The Countess's face was as grey and drawn as mine and a wave of tenderness passed through me. I did not want to add to her pain. She gestured to Berthe to leave us as I opened my mouth and I was encouraged by her willingness to be alone with me. I had prepared what I hoped was a judicious statement.

'The shock of your announcement yesterday caused me to speak unwisely, my lady. I wouldn't wish to go from you with hostile words. May we part on friendly terms?'

She shivered and twisted the fringe of her mantle, sitting in silence for several moments before she spoke softly. 'I do not wish us to part at all, Harry. I was thoughtless and crass. I misjudged and hurt you. Do not go to Wingfield on my account. This is your home. It has become one for me also.'

I was stunned and searched her face to understand what she was saying. 'It would give me pleasure to stay if I can do so without offending you.'

'The offence is mine: to have dismissed the possibility that what my heart is telling me is true. Our child should not be a pawn in the hand of others but reared by its parents in their own home.'

I was shaking uncontrollably. 'What are you saying, Yolande?'

'That if you were to ask for my hand in marriage, Harry, I should agree.'

We held each other close in desperate happiness, knowing there were huge obstacles to our future life together, uncertain where we could find safe refuge from her enemies and mine, but content to defer the resolution of those challenges. Only immediate concerns needed our attention. We would keep our secret until after Lady Maud had been given her answer but I would then go to Wingfield to seek the good offices of Father Wilfred who I hoped would marry us secretly. If Thomas was able to remain with us that long he would serve as my groomsman. It would be necessary for me to travel to London after our nuptials but I promised to return within two months when Yolande would give birth to our child. In our joy we blanked out from our thoughts the many impediments which threatened the success of our plans and the reactions we might expect when those plans became known.

*****

I stood behind Yolande's chair when Lady Maud Fitzvaughan swept into the room. I knew Gaston de la Tour had accompanied her to Worthwaite but he had not sought to climb the stairs and was taking refreshment in the kitchen. The sight of Maud wearing padding under her dress to create the impression of pregnancy filled me with a mixture of annoyance and compassion but there was no time to dwell on my feelings. She saw me at once and frowned.

'Countess, it is fitting that we discuss matters alone, woman to woman. There's no need for your physician to attend you.'

Yolande replied in her haughtiest tone. 'It is my wish that Doctor Somers should remain. Our conversation will be brief. I have consulted my child's father and your proposition cannot be accepted.'

Maud's face distorted with anger. 'The Marquis is prepared to face the Queen's vengeance and pain the wife he is said to cherish?'

I had advised Yolande not to prolong the meeting by responding to provocation of this nature but I recognised she would make her own decisions. 'The Marquis is not the father of my child,' she said.

Maud looked surprised and bit her lip. 'But the father is unable or unwilling to offer you marriage?'

This was dangerous and I coughed in order to catch Yolande's attention and divert her from this subject.

'On the contrary,' she said, 'the child will be born in holy wedlock.'

'Ah!' The exclamation faded and Maud became very still, staring at us. She was no fool and I could detect understanding coming to her.

'Surely it cannot be... my lady, forgive me, but is it possible this licentious quack has lain with you? He is a notorious libertine and if he has forced himself on you, you have my condolences. All the more reason to accept the offer I've made and conceal the shame he has brought on you. There's no necessity for you to demean your noble birth by taking him as husband.'

Yolande rose and spoke with icy contempt. 'Lady Maud, my marriage will be for love, not convenience. Our meeting is at an end.'

'You French trollop, how dare you treat me with condescension and disdain! I shall proclaim your disgrace to the whole world.'

'Then your own ignominy will be likewise proclaimed. Can you contemplate that?'

Yolande moved quickly to the door and I made to follow her but Maud seized my arm, squeezing the wrist above my bandaged hand. 'You vile snake, Harry Somers, I'll make you pay for this.'

'Because my relationship has thwarted your disgraceful scheme?'

'Because you have made that scornful noblewoman your loving slave!'

She swirled away, leaving me clutching my sore hand and marvelling that the emotion which directed her actions was not just anger at the foiling of her plan but straightforward sexual jealousy. I experienced a presentiment of disaster which was all too credible.

*****

I resolved to ride to Wingfield to see Father Wilfred without delay but next day a message was brought to tell me the Marquis was to arrive there imminently and he planned to remain at his castle for a fortnight. Prudence dictated that, although courtesy required me to visit Suffolk, I must not speak to the chaplain of my personal affairs while William de la Pole was in residence. The deferment of our marriage was irritating but did not seem of critical importance.

Some nine or ten days after Lady Maud's visit I received a request to call at the principal hostelry in Diss at a specified hour to meet an acquaintance who wished to see me urgently. I suspected a plot but was wary of ignoring the appeal, in case this resulted in some form of retribution. I did not want to distress Yolande by telling her but I shared my concerns with Thomas who had agreed to stay at Worthwaite until our wedding, although he was growing fretful to return home. He and I agreed that the most likely originator of the message was Gaston de la Tour and it could be dangerous to meet him alone so Thomas insisted that he would come with me, which I welcomed wholeheartedly.

The landlord at the inn remembered me and told me with a wink that the woman was awaiting me in an upstairs room. I looked at Thomas in alarm.

'I refuse to meet Lady Maud again,' I said.

Thomas nodded and told me he would convey my message but I followed him up the stairs and stood to the side when he opened the door. I heard his yelp and rushed forward, fearing he had been attacked, but his cry was one of astonishment which, in a moment, I echoed.

'Bess! Mistress Willoughby.'

The young woman whom I had truly loved with all the innocent devotion of my first passion stepped forward and curtsied. She was very pale and, although not in so advanced a state of pregnancy as Yolande, was clearly carrying a child. 'Doctor Somers,' she said, 'I am so grateful you've come.'

'What can I do?' I asked inanely, suddenly aware of appalling possibilities.

'Lady Maud has spoken to me. She says you are in a position to help her but have refused. I know no details but I think she has asked you to procure a baby from some unfortunate woman who does not want her child. I appreciate your reluctance to do so heinous a thing, if it means deceiving Lord Fitzvaughan, but if you do not help she is threatening to take my infant when it is born.'

It was not like Bess to be so gullible. 'That's ridiculous. How can she take your child? Surely your husband wouldn't allow it?'

Tears welled up in Bess's eyes and she wrung her hands. 'They have imprisoned him: Lady Maud and Master de la Tour. They say that he's guilty of theft – that he's stolen wool from their flocks and profited from its sale. None of it is true but he's in danger of execution for such offences. He can only be reprieved if I give up our child.'

'Does Robin know what they are threatening?'

'I don't think so. They won't let me see him. He's to be kept in prison until my time is due. When I have surrendered my baby, he will be released and then I am to tell him I bore a dead infant.' Her voice broke and tears flooded down her cheeks. 'Oh, Harry, if you can bring yourself to help, however distasteful it must be to you as an honest man, I beg you to save Robin and our child.'

I steadied myself against a table. 'By Heaven, Bess, I swear they won't succeed in this foul plan.'

'You will find a foundling for them?'

I cleared my throat. 'That's not what they've asked me to do. The child Lady Maud wants is mine. It will be born in a few weeks, around the time her pretence of pregnancy would come to fruition.'

Bess staggered to a chair. 'I didn't know you were married. How can they possibly expect you to give up your child?'

'The child will be born in wedlock but complications have delayed the ceremony. Affairs of state have caused difficulties.'

She bowed her head. 'Forgive me, Doctor Somers, I had no idea of your position. I can't understand why they thought I could persuade you to save Robin – if your own happiness is the cost. Surely there are abandoned infants, left at the church door, who would serve their wicked purposes.'

'They don't want a baseborn child. I don't' think they really want yours. They are using you to put pressure on me.'

She understood what I did not want to put into words. 'Your wife-to-be is of noble blood?'

I nodded and saw the slight tightening of her mouth. My hatred for her tormentors increased but I knew I was not defenceless against their pernicious threats. What I must do would compromise my integrity, which I held dear, for it required me to break a sworn promise, but I had no doubt I would do what was necessary.

'Dry your tears, Bess, and be brave. I believe I can save your husband and safeguard your child. Go back to Lady Maud and tell her I am considering whether I can assist you in your predicament – buy time for me to act.

Trust me, I will do whatever I can to frustrate her evil schemes. She's gone too far in threatening you.'

'I trust you with my life,' Bess said and sincerity shone through her tearful eyes, 'with Robin's and the child's. I shall pray for you.'

'I beg that you will,' I said for I knew I was embarking on a hazardous enterprise.

*****

Yolande gave me her blessing, after I had told her everything, and I set out for Wingfield with Thomas at my side. I thought it possible that Lord Fitzvaughan was with the Marquis but I discovered he was still in attendance on the King at Windsor. Even so I did not hesitate in my intention to see him and made plans to leave next morning and ride south. At least this would permit Thomas to return home to Greenwich when we neared London.

I paid my respects to Suffolk while at the castle and was glad to find him in cheerful mood, unconcerned at my lengthy absence from the Manor of the Rose. He had received good reports of Leone's abilities as my locum and was content for me to remain at Worthwaite for a few weeks more. Nevertheless, he asked me to pummel the irksome muscles in his back which I was forced to do with my right hand alone, while we conversed, and he pronounced himself better for the treatment.

'The King has summoned Parliament to assemble,' he said, 'and it'll be a critical meeting at which antagonisms are to be resolved. Gloucester is called, as are we all, and there will be straight talking about our differences. I imagine we shall all arrive with large companies of armed followers for self-defence and tensions may run high. It's essential that you are present in my train at this occasion in case my back causes me trouble. I can't afford to show the least weakness in such a gathering.'

'Certainly, my lord, I'll present myself at your London house in good time.' By then, I thought with solemnity, I would be a married man and, with God's grace, I would have averted the dangers threatening both Yolande and Bess.

'There'll be no need for you to travel to London,' the Marquis said as I helped him put on his gown. 'Parliament is to meet at Saint Edmundsbury so you'll have but a day's journey to join me there.'

That suited me well but I quickly realised the reason for the location. The abbey at Saint Edmundsbury was a retreat favoured by the King and it lay centrally in East Anglia where Suffolk had his powerbase. This Parliament was designed as a direct challenge to Gloucester's influence and he would be well advised to bring his armed retainers, as the Marquis expected.

Next day Thomas and I were on the road again but when we reached London we parted and I continued alone to Windsor where I sought an immediate and private meeting with Walter Fitzvaughan. He had returned from the hunt shortly beforehand and was bathing but he agreed to see me, so when I was called into his chamber he was fragrant with aromatic oils.

'I know you well enough, Doctor Somers, to appreciate that you wouldn't seek an urgent meeting unless there was good cause. Have you come from Wingfield? Do you bring word from Suffolk?'

'I have and I've seen the Marquis but I come on my own account. What I have to say won't be welcome to you and I beg your forbearance. It isn't easy for me to break a promise I've given but the wellbeing of people dear to me is at hazard and I must speak out. It will be hurtful for you to learn the truth but I'm bound to tell it.'

He sank into a cushioned chair and indicated that I should sit on a bench but I preferred to stand. His expression was stern as if he had prepared himself for

332

unpleasant news and it did not alter as I told him the history he should have learned years earlier, at the time of his marriage, and went on to outline the deception his wife and his lover had jointly planned. I did not name Yolande but spoke of her as a lady of gentle birth under my protection.

I had been uncertain how he would react and readied myself to be flung from the room for my impertinence. I respected his judgement and his moderation in dealing with others – which had earned him the King's trust on diplomatic embassies – but the information I was giving him touched him personally and might unleash hidden passions. When I had finished my account he sat without moving, exactly as he had while listening to me, and I began to fear the effect on his mind. At length he rose and strode about the room, halting beside me.

'She cannot bear a child you say?'

'Sadly, she cannot.'

'But she has a daughter who is in the care of the girl's father?'

I confirmed this but doubted whether I had the right to disclose the man's identity.

'He is a nobleman? And they had hoped to wed when the child was conceived, when they were both young and free?'

'I understand so.'

'Gaston is helping her?'

'He escorted Lady Maud when she put her proposition to the lady I mentioned.'

I held my breath as Lord Fitzvaughan stomped past me and resumed his patrol up and down the room. After several minutes he turned back to me. 'I am obliged, Doctor Somers, for your honesty. I wish I had been informed earlier but you are not to blame for that omission. You may rest assured this little game is over and the ladies who have been threatened will hear no more. They had no right to imprison my bailiff.'

I thought it strange that it was the fate of Bess's husband which evinced the first hint of emotion from his overlord but I remembered that the working of the human mind is impossible to predict. I wondered if Walter Fitzvaughan's extraordinary self-control in the face of my revelations was healthy and dreaded a deferred eruption of his fury.

I watched in silence as he sat down again.

'I hadn't realised I'd pained Gaston so badly,' he said. 'I'm touched that he wishes to secure me the heir I need and longs for me to return to his side. He means well and I bear him no ill will. I shall leave for Norfolk in the morning.'

'Lady Maud has been greatly abused in the past,' I said, filled with guilt at betraying her secret and fearing for her safety.

'I shall not thrash her, Doctor Somers, don't worry, although I have every right to chastise a scheming liar. Don't you realise? If what you've told me is true it may be that she has never been my lawful wife for she was pre-contracted to another, the father of her living child. This gives me pause for thought and I shall consider what to do – I see more than one possibility. Say nothing of this to anyone while I come to a conclusion.'

'I give you my word. But you will prevent harm to the two pregnant ladies?'

'Of that you can be confident. Leave me now, Doctor Somers. You go with my gratitude.

I left Walter Fitzvaughan with a tumult of conflicting feelings, satisfied that I had prevented horrific injustice to Yolande and Bess but nervous of the repercussions when Maud discovered that I had broken my word. I relied on her husband to frustrate her malign intentions but it had not occurred to me that I was handing him a weapon with which to shatter their marriage. Even as I rejoiced at my success, I was overwhelmed with remorse.

Chapter 25

As soon as it was light next morning I went to the stables to collect my horse, noting with apprehension that there was snow in the air. The ostlers were already busy, saddling a number of fine animals and I saw a troop of men assembling in the courtyard ready to ride out with their lord. Only then did I realise that their pennants bore the crest of the Fitzvaughans and in a few minutes his lordship was at my side.

'Ride with us, Harry. We leave at once for Norfolk and will pass near to Wingfield. I have a strong troop of men and we'll make good progress.'

I was happy to accept this protection on the road from the customary risks but I also had in mind that if Henri Charpentier was still at court, he might have discovered I had come to Windsor and could waylay me. Undoubtedly he considered there was unfinished business between us – and so did I. In fact the journey was free from danger but we did not make the rapid progress Lord Fitzvaughan foretold. Before long we ran out of the desultory snow showers but, in the countryside north of the Thames Valley, winter had settled with an enduring frost. The ground was hard and icy so there was no question of spurring our steeds into a gallop. It took two days longer than expected to reach Saint Edmundsbury where I accepted with reluctance that we must spend the night, remembering the unsavoury inn where I had stayed previously, but the inconvenience was mitigated because I was invited to accompany his lordship into the guest chambers of the abbey.

Vast though their resources were, the hospitality of the monks was stretched by our arrival for many other noblemen and their entourages were established in the guest house, come early to secure their places in readiness for the meeting of Parliament the following week. Among the throng I recognised Stephen Boice whom I had seen before at Saint Edmundsbury and, although he nodded to me cordially enough across the room, the sight filled me with disquiet because of his association with Gilbert Iffley.

Lord Fitzvaughan indicated that he might spend a second night at the abbey but I resolved to set out next day however difficult the conditions. By then a cold swirling mist enveloped the land and it took me until nearly dusk to reach Wingfield, mostly on foot leading my horse. This exertion wearied me and I was tempted by the suggestion of a pallet overnight so I despatched a servant boy to Worthwaite with a scribbled note to announce my impending arrival in the morning. I also benefitted from a brief word with Father Wilfred who agreed to conduct the marriage ceremony which would bind me to the woman I loved and gave me great contentment.

Because my exercise had made me hungry I accepted food and wine beside the kitchen hearth and watched as a handful of other wayfarers were given nourishment and offered shelter for the night. The undercook exchanged banter with some he obviously recognised.

'What happened to that Norman fellow who came in with you two nights ago? He wasn't local.'

A scraggy man in a ragged cloak cackled. 'Reckoned himself a cut above us, he did. Went off early in the morning on his own. Haven't seen him since.'

'That the one who tried to go upstairs in the castle?' The pantry-man set down a bundle of candles on the table.

'Yes. I fancy he'd have been up to no good if he'd had a chance.'

'A likely thief if ever I saw one.'

'Fat chance he'd have here, with all the Marquis's household at hand.'

They chuckled and the conversation turned to other things but my heart was hammering with a premonition of catastrophe. It was inconceivable that Gaston de la Tour would have posed as a beggar to gain access to the castle and

I knew of no-one else from Normandy in the vicinity but a Frenchman could pass as Norman. I leapt to my feet.

'Your victuals have refreshed me and I'm anxious to be home. I'll be on my way after all.'

'It's black as hell and foggy outside,' one of the travellers said, holding his hands to the fire.

'I'll head north to the river and follow the bank. I've been that way before.'

They shrugged and turned back to their chat while I hurried to retrieve my horse and continue my journey. From something as inconsequential as that light-hearted exchange, everything which was to follow resulted.

*****

In the two miles along the track to the river the mist thinned sufficiently for a faint glimmer of the quarter-moon to show intermittently and that speeded my progress. I wondered if I was inventing dangers when there were none and began to hum tunelessly to myself. Then, as I skirted one of the innumerable meanders in the river's course, I saw the dark shape, half in and half out of the water, and a cold tremor passed through me.

I dismounted and led my horse to the water's edge where the atrocity was fully visible, confirming the impression I had formed at first glance. On the frosted grass of the bank and the thin ice fringing the river splatters of blood were frozen where they had fallen and among them lay the boy's body, spread-eagled. His throat had been cut with such violence that the wound gaped open and his head hung at a grotesque angle. There was nothing I could do for him but his murder was an appalling outrage for he wore the de la Pole livery. It conveyed a fearful message and I knew that my note had never reached Yolande.

I have no memory of the next six or seven miles until I saw the dull glow in the sky ahead and hurtled forward like a madman fearing my whole manor was ablaze. As I neared the building I could see that only the stable-block was burning but I tumbled from my saddle in ungainly fashion in my panic to find out what had happened. My steward rushed to meet me.

'Doctor Somers, oh my goodness! We didn't know you were coming. It's the stable roof. We've got it under control. The lads with the buckets have done well. They got the horses out too.'

'Is anyone hurt?'

'Not to speak off. A few singes perhaps. A spot of butter will see to that – they won't even need your attention.'

'The Countess?'

'She's' indoors with Berthe. We called out there was nothing to worry about. Dame Elizabeth was going to them. Good job the stable-block's freestanding.'

I felt a wave of relief. 'How did it happen?'

'I fancy some careless fool took a taper into the loft. We let a couple of pedlars sleep there because of the weather. Luckily one of the stable-lads woke up just as the straw was catching. Their speedy action...'

'Holy Saints!'

I raced to the house and collided with Dame Elizabeth as she staggered over the threshold, her face as white as the hoar frost. 'Oh, sweet Mother of God!' she gasped and clung to my gown. 'Heaven's sent you but it's too late.'

Despite my usual halting gait I mounted the stairs two at a time and through the open door of Yolande's room I caught sight of Berthe, on her knees, sobbing into the counterpane. I did not need to be told Yolande was gone.

I flung myself down beside Berthe. 'What happened?'

As she turned to face me I saw the angry weal across her cheek and the ropes which had bound her wrists slipped from the bed. 'He's taken her, Doctor – Charpentier. He broke in when the men rushed out to the fire.' Her eyes were wild with horror. 'He had her slung over his shoulder.'

Dame Elizabeth had followed me into the room. 'I met them at the foot of the stair. He pushed me into the larder and put a chest in front of it.'

'How long ago?'

'It took a while for my shouts to rouse the kitchen-maid to let me out.'

Berthe dragged herself upright. 'I took a blow to the head and when I came to myself they were gone.'

'He'll have a horse. There'll be tracks.'

I tore my way down the stairs, shouting to the steward as I seized my horse from a groom. 'The Countess has been abducted. I'll follow the tracks. Send men after me as soon as you can. Make sure they're armed.'

My horse was weary but he seemed to sense my urgency and pricked his ears as I took a lantern from a hook and led him round the outside of the house. As I suspected, beyond the postern gate leading to the riverside, the frosty grass had been disturbed by trampling hooves and the prints led straight down to the river. We forded the partly frozen water and I spotted where the ice had been cracked on the other side as they scrambled up the bank. At the top of the ridge the line of hoof-prints stretched as far as I could see beside the river.

On the outskirts of Diss the trail began to climb the hill and it seemed likely that the villain was making for a house in the town. I urged my reluctant horse up the slope but he was panting and I could not force him beyond his strength so we paced more slowly and this enabled me to distinguish that, from a certain point, there were hoof-prints in both directions.

I peered at the tracks and after a short distance saw that they diverged, with those climbing the hill turning off to the right across open ground where the slope was less acute. Over to my left I was conscious of a more intense darkness

339

and, as the sliver of moon cast a beam towards it, an oily glow of liquid. I knew then that I was looking down on the mere, from the side away from the town where, I remembered, there were three or four probably deserted huts. Fortunately this recollection made me cautious and I spotted the tethered horse while we were downwind so it did not discern our presence. With my heart pounding I looped my reins over a bush and crept forward on foot, keeping behind the alien horse, trying to identify which of the shacks was occupied. This at least was not difficult. A pair of footprints led to the most substantial hut and beside them, I recognised with agonised understanding, was a line of scuff-marks in the frost, suggesting someone had been dragged towards the door.

It was not bolted and it gave surprisingly easily to my touch, affording me a view of the interior before I pushed the door wide. All my self-control was required to stop me screaming out in abhorrence as I drew my dagger.

I saw Yolande first and thought her dead. She was face downward, like the murdered messenger boy, although because of her condition her body was twisted to the side. Her mantle lay discarded by her side and her dress had been ripped. Her pale thighs caught the light from a lantern and a smudge on her buttocks glistened with the foul slime of her abuser.

No longer cautious, I flung the door open as Henri Charpentier turned, his points still untied, and seeing me, roared with laughter. His sword belt and scabbard were on the ground a few feet from him.

'I didn't expect you until morning, physician, but you're most welcome. Look at your whore! She spurned my noble master but was content to lie with a common leech. My cock's exacted reparations on the Seigneur's behalf. I've had her, Doctor Somers, and I'm minded to have her again once I've disposed of your troublesome presence.'

With a rapid movement he bent to his left to recover his sword but somehow I managed to dart forward and kick the scabbard before he grasped it. This infuriated him but we were both well aware that, with his physique and training, he could destroy me with his bare hands, despite the puny dagger in my fist. He threw himself on me, kneeing me in the belly, and we crashed to the ground. I jabbed with my dagger towards his neck and produced a trickle of blood on the yoke of his shirt but in an instant my weapon had been wrenched from me and his own poniard was brandished above my face. I seized his wrist with both my hands but one was still feeble from my injury and he taunted me with weakness, grabbing my good right hand and crushing it to the floor with his left while he heaved himself half on top of me.

'I intend to amuse myself with you, little physician. You've led me a dance. Pretending the whore was serving the Marquis in his bed. You escaped the refinements available in Baynard's Castle but Gilbert Iffley was always finicky. Now I can devise my own torments.'

He drove the tip of his dagger into the soft flesh of my shoulder where I had an old wound and I understood that the pain was intended to inhibit my resistance to worse indignities. Then he thrust the weapon through the thick material of my loose sleeve, pinning it to the ground so close to my wrist that if I tried to move it the blade would slice my flesh. He moved both his hands to my throat and leered.

'I'm going to castrate you, Doctor. It seems fitting. But first I'll choke you until your eyes are popping and you can scarcely breathe. Don't fear, I'll leave you strength enough to feel my knife in your vitals before I grant you eternal release.' His thick fingers began to press on my windpipe.

To struggle would only increase my agony, I thought, and resigned myself to death, hoping I would become unconscious more quickly than he intended. In a quirk of mind I remembered poor Rollo murdered outside the brothel in Blois where his mistress, Jeanne, could not see him. My mistress, who should have been my wife by now, was lying dead across the room.

Suddenly, as if responding to my thought, I heard a faint moan and realised with amazement that Yolande was living, battered and abused but living. The knowledge roused my laggard intelligence and as the slow, calculated pressure on my throat continued, I burrowed surreptitiously across my stomach with my injured hand until it found the purse hanging on my belt. I heard the gurgling in my throat as my fingers slipped under the flap of the purse and eased out the Paduan stiletto with which I had conducted many minor operations. Now it – and I – faced our greatest challenge.

With all my fading energy I forced the bodkin into Charpentier's groin and the cruel unexpectedness of my response took him unawares. He lurched to the side and released his grip on my throat while I, coughing and retching, clutched at his poniard on the floor and plunged it into his guts. As he squirmed, screaming profanities, I withdrew the dagger and stabbed him with it a second time. Blood spilled from his mouth and belly and he was helpless before me, his eyes staring with appalled surprise. There was no need to repeat my acts of violence but the rabid animal inside me could not be stopped. Again and again I knifed him and then, barely sensible of my actions, I dragged his carcase from the hut and let it roll over the shiny coating of the frosty slope to splash in the deep waters of the mere.

As my victim subsided within a ring of bubbles I fell to my knees, sobbing, and when the Worthwaite men found me soon afterwards I was still grovelling on the icy ground, babbling incoherently.

*****

It was Dame Elizabeth's kindly face I saw as I came to myself and she held out a posset for me to drink.

'God bless you, Doctor,' she said. 'We thought you were lost to us when they brought you home.'

I registered that there were dressings on my shoulder and arm and my head was thudding but I rallied my senses. 'Yolande?' I asked.

'The Countess lives and still carries your child but her condition is perilous. I do what I can to sustain her and we pray.'

I valued that combination of reassurance and honesty. 'I must go to her.'

Dame Elizabeth started to protest but the steward, whom I had not noticed standing by the door, hurried forward to support me as I staggered from my bed and half-carried me into Yolande's room. Her eyes were closed but the movement disturbed her and when she saw me they brimmed over with tears. The steward set me down by the bedside and withdrew as I reached out to kiss her. There was no colour in her cheeks and she looked exhausted.

'I am defiled, Harry,' she said. 'That brute...'

'Shush, my sweet, there's no need to speak of it. You're safe now and must recover your strength.'

She spoke urgently, as if forcing out the words. 'The child still moves, though I fancy more feebly. I have set my mind to bring it to timely birth but I fear it may come too early.'

I tried to exude calmness I did not feel. 'You must do nothing to endanger yourself. God has preserved us both and we must cherish each other. As soon as the chaplain can come from Wingfield we must marry.'

A strange and unsettling expression came into her eyes. 'God may wish for a sacrifice to repay his bounty.'

'The Lord Christ does not ask for sacrifices,' I said but the conviction I asserted was not echoed in my heart, for I was troubled by a gnawing fear of my own.

'You killed the villain?' There was a note of wonder in Yolande's voice.

'In that I'm sure God guided me.'

I pressed her hand but was unwilling to say more and, understanding how weary she was, I left her to sleep.

After the steward had helped me back to my room he produced a packet which he said had been delivered that morning from the Marquis of Suffolk. 'I told the fellow to inform the Marquis of your injuries,' he said, 'but it seems you were expected at Saint Edmundsbury yesterday and William de la Pole will brook no further delay.'

Only then did I realise I had lost two days while I lay in a fever under Dame Elizabeth's care. 'I'm bound to go,' I said, almost grateful there was a duty for me to fulfil. 'Is there a groom who could ride with me? I'm not sure I can handle the reins at the moment. Thank Heaven, it's only a day's journey and I can return quickly if I'm needed here.'

'Not before tomorrow morning,' said the steward's wife as she bustled towards me. 'It'll be foolish enough then, but I know you'll be chafing to go, doctor though you are. Men!'

And so it was arranged.

*****

The ground had thawed in the last two days so the journey was muddy but straightforward and, despite the throbbing of my wounds, I rode pillion in reasonable comfort. By contrast my thoughts were distinctly uncomfortable as my memory recalled the scene of Henri Charpentier's death. With shame I visualised myself repeatedly stabbing a corpse, giving vent to despicable vindictiveness: I whose calling was to heal and succour. Self-defence was any man's right but to glory in killing, even when I had every cause to wish the lout dead, was to indulge my basest nature. Never before had I imagined I possessed

344

such barbarous instincts and the newly-won knowledge terrified me.

Chapter 26

Saint Edmundsbury was swarming with people: peers with liveried entourages of clanking men at arms, prelates – each with a chancel-full of clerics in attendance, knights of the shire trying to outdo each other with displays of affluent gravitas and all the riff-raff that customarily accompany such an assemblage. In the noisy chatter of the marketplace I detected excitement and a hint of danger in the air. People were waiting for something, even if they were not clear what.

I presented myself at the abbey where the Marquis was residing, in close attendance on the King and Queen, and sent in a message to announce my presence. I had feared I must then seek a bed in the insalubrious hostelry I remembered but an officious monk produced a list and told me I was to be billeted in a private house which Lord Fitzvaughan had taken for the occasion. This was good fortune but I was nervous of encountering his lordship after his confrontation with Lady Maud.

I was turning to leave the abbey gatehouse when another monk, who had heard me give my name, summoned me to attend at once upon the Marquis and I was hurried through the fine guest quarters to a still more palatial mansion. This was where the royal party and their principal advisers were accommodated in far from monastic simplicity. Suffolk came without delay, anxious for me to massage my unguent into his back, and he was disconcerted to see the bandages on my left shoulder.

'Holy Mother, Doctor Somers, last time it was but a broken finger, now it appears you've been engaging in sword play.'

'An unfortunate accident,' I said with an attempt to sound casual. 'Is Parliament now in session?'

The Marquis frowned. 'The main business cannot be conducted until Gloucester comes. We're told he is coming but he's already behind the due time. Ouch!'

'Pardon, my lord, but you must try to lie still while I knead your muscles. You're well supported by retainers in the town. I saw dozens in your colours while I rode from the gate.'

'More than three thousand armed men attend me and every baron is similarly accompanied according to his status. We're wise to be wary for it's been reported Gloucester is coming with hundreds more.'

'Surely there'll be no violence within the abbey precincts and in the presence of the King?'

'We will not be the first to draw our swords.'

I did not pursue the implication that Gloucester's men might initiate hostilities. It seemed improbable but I found it telling that Suffolk was sufficiently agitated to consider the possibility.

'Duke Humphrey's men are spreading malicious lies that I have seduced the Countess of Langeais and secreted her at Wingfield. I've been hard put to it to convince Queen Margaret this is not true. I shall demand that Gloucester retracts the vile allegation.'

I was pleased I did not falter in rubbing his back but my heart missed a beat. 'There's no news of the missing lady?' I enquired as nonchalantly as I could.

'Her body's at the bottom of the Thames, if you ask me. Well done, Doctor, I feel relief already. Have this as your fee.'

He handed me a generous bag of gold and I took my leave with a promise to attend him again whenever required. I suspected that my relief of mind at escaping this conversation was at least as great as his physical relief.

A page conducted me out of the abbey and pointed the way to Lord Fitzvaughan's house, a merchant's substantial residence from its appearance. I had scant opportunity to admire its proportions, however, for on the threshold, in close dialogue, were two men I least wanted to see and as I approached they turned and hailed me.

'Doctor Somers, how pleasant to meet you again,' said Stephen Boice with a sardonic smile and in that moment I recognised his silky voice as that of the orator who had incited the citizens of London to riot.

'Welcome,' echoed Gaston de la Tour, waving his companion away. 'You're expected. Allow me to show you to your quarters.'

I was troubled by the Norman's show of affability, which was as unnerving as his antagonism because either disposition was liable to be false, but I followed him into the house. When we were alone he put his hand gently on my sound shoulder and spoke with apparent sincerity.

'I've reason to give you thanks, Harry Somers, and I'm sorry to see you've been injured. You've done me great service although I realise I wasn't intended to be the main beneficiary.'

His words seemed ominous and in a flash I feared that Walter Fitzvaughan had slain his wife as bestially as I had dealt with Charpentier.

Gaston de la Tour smiled. 'The Lady Maud is banished from his lordship's bed forever and will moulder at his Norfolk manor, unloved and unvisited, while he decides her fate. I am most obliged. By the way, his lordship asked me to tell you that Willoughby, the bailiff, is restored to his position and his fertile helpmeet – although that perhaps is not the outcome your secret heart would wish for.'

'On the contrary...,' I began but did not continue.

'And the Countess, whom you, most impudently, have impregnated, is similarly free from the harassments we devised when it seemed we had no alternative.' He caught my look of horror and slapped me more heavily on my shoulder. 'Don't worry, Harry, I owe you my silence. Have you actually married her?'

I mumbled vaguely and Gaston de la Tour laughed. 'You may be wise not to, physician. If you do, you'd best flee the country. You've done that once before, as I recall.

shouldn't care to have Queen Margaret as my enemy. She's becoming a rare termagant as she grows into womanhood: a right royal bitch, you might say.'

I was glad to escape both his fulsome gratitude and his dangerously provocative observations but as we reached the door of my room he remembered another message he had for me.

'You're in demand by church and state alike. The Marquis you've seen, I take it, but the Abbot awaits your attendance.'

'The Abbot of Saint Edmundsbury?'

'No, no. The Abbot of Peterborough – he's here with half the notable clerics of the realm. You're to call on him at the abbey. Tomorrow will do. I'd no idea you were so well connected. Lord Fitzvaughan will see you in the morning too. He's dining with the Earl of Stanwick this afternoon.'

'What?' I could not control my astonishment. I had never named Maud's former lover to her husband.

'Ah, of course, you didn't know, Harry. The Earl is present in Saint Edmundsbury for the Parliament, despite his indifferent health. Walter is tempted to cast off the Lady Maud, claiming they were never lawfully wed because she was pre-contracted, and he forced her lover's name from her. If Walter's marriage to the barren sow is shown to be invalid, with the Earl's cooperation, it can be speedily annulled. You'll have his undying gratitude as well as mine.'

Gaston de la Tour bowed and withdrew while I stood gaping after him.

*****

Each day that I heard nothing from Worthwaite meant there were grounds for hope that Yolande was recovering and had not lost the child. Accordingly I set out for the abbey next morning feeling more cheerful than I had been since Charpentier's attack, although still suffering waves of guilt for the ferocity of my response to him and the harm I had caused Lady Maud. I remembered the significance of the Abbot of Peterborough, not merely as the head of a major religious house with many dependencies, but specifically as the superior and confidant of the Prioress of St. Michael's, Stamford, but I was intrigued as to why he wished to see me.

At first sight he was unprepossessing – short and dumpy with hooded eyes – but when he spoke his voice resounded with authority and he wasted no time on pleasantries.

'I know all about you, Doctor Somers,' he announced. 'The Reverend Mother keeps me fully informed.'

I did not find this reassuring.

'I'm merely her messenger boy, you understand.' I bowed my head in acknowledgement of this unlikely assertion. 'There's going to be trouble here before the end of the week.' He paused, expecting me to say something.

'In what way, my lord Abbot?'

'If we could tell that, we could avert it. But if Gloucester comes at all he's expected to bring a private army with him, which will look like treasonable defiance, and if he doesn't come he'll be disobeying the King's command and putting himself at hazard.'

'Are you suggesting he's walking into a trap?'

The Abbot threw back his head and chortled. 'She said you were shrewd. In my opinion that's exactly what it is: a trap to obliterate Duke Humphrey's influence once and for all.'

'I'm sorry to hear that. The Duke was my patron. I owe him my education.'

'No time for sentiment, young man. Don't throw away the advantages you've gained by backing the wrong man at this stage. By all means keep your options open as long as you can but make sure your skills will be sought after by all parties.'

'That's exactly what I aim to do,' I said but I did not add that once my marriage to the Countess became common knowledge I would have lost the goodwill of almost everybody.

'You're thinking you've lost the luxury of choice, eh, Doctor? That's what the Reverend Mother surmised. So I'm to give you another lifeline. That's my message. If you find yourself in a dilemma, as you may, claim the protection of the Church – as a faithful servant and physician to the Cardinal.'

'Cardinal Beaufort! He's Duke Humphrey's lifelong enemy.'

'Quite so. But he's now of a great age and ailing. It may be in your power to give him ease in the final phase of his illustrious life. I've recommended you to him. There's no need for your immediate attendance in Winchester but if you find yourself in disfavour at the court, perhaps at risk of arrest, proclaim your duty to the Cardinal. Even the Queen would not challenge his holy authority.'

'I'm astonished. I don't know what to say.'

'Just take this token and keep it safe. It shows the Cardinal's personal crest. No need to make known that you have it but don't be afraid to invoke its power if you're in peril.'

He lifted my hand and put the small badge into my palm, folding my fingers over it. 'I can't guarantee it'll help the wretched Frenchwoman you've bedded so you need to get her back across the Narrow Sea as soon as the child is taken to Stamford.'

I inclined my head. When Yolande and I were married the child would never be placed at St. Michael's but I owed it to the Prioress to tell her this news directly and not through the Abbot. I appreciated there would be limits to the protection offered by the Cardinal's token in those circumstances but in any case the idea of calling on his good offices repelled me and I pushed aside the possibility.

*****

Expectation grew in Saint Edmundsbury as rumours spread concerning Duke Humphrey's intentions. He was reported to be on the road with a thousand warriors at his back, then an hour later this was disputed and he was said to be holed up in his castle far away in Devizes, quailing for his life. It was wise to believe nothing without the evidence of one's own eyes but some witnesses were more credible than others and when Bartholomew appeared in the town I quickly made contact with him.

'I didn't know you'd be here, Doctor Somers.' He seemed ill at ease, looking over his shoulder at other drinkers in the hostelry where I had taken him.

'Don't worry. I'm not working against Gloucester. But I'm anxious to get away from here on my own account and I can't do that until Suffolk's business is finished – which depends on the Duke arriving. I'd like to know if he's coming or not.'

Bartholomew lowered his voice. 'He's coming.'

'From Devizes?'

'No, he's been at his palace in Greenwich for the last few days. I've been sent ahead to make sure everything is ready for him at St. Saviour's Hospital where he's to lodge. He'll be here tomorrow.'

'Is he coming with a great army at his heels?'

'Not a bit of it. I've been told to ensure there's room for eighty-five followers. Maybe he should have a bigger escort. I was surprised to find Suffolk's patrols guarding the road into the town from the south.'

'Is Iffley with him?'

'I think so but they argued about the arrangements. Iffley wanted a huge army in attendance and the Duke wouldn't have it. He doesn't believe he's in any danger from his nephew, the King. I've never seen Iffley so angry with the

Duke. He was threatening to withdraw from his service. I could hear them shouting at each other.'

I thought Gloucester would be well rid of such a devious adherent but I doubted Iffley was likely to abandon everything for which he had been working.

'Where would he go?'

Bartholomew mouthed the single word. 'York.'

I let the youth return to his duties but advised him to be careful while he was in the town. 'Gaston de la Tour is here,' I said by way of explanation and he spat onto the rushes underfoot.

*****

I watched from the shelter of the Abbey Gate as Gloucester proceeded from the south gate to his lodging at the other side of the town and I observed that Gilbert Iffley rode some way behind him, tight-lipped and frowning. The Duke also looked strained and I was reminded that he was now over fifty years old and beginning to show his age. His had been a turbulent life, on the battlefield, at court and, it was widely rumoured, in the bedchamber. I was glad I managed to escape his and Iffley's notice and turned to enter the abbey precincts when I heard my name called by a familiar voice.

'Oi, Doctor Somers. I hoped you'd be here. What d'you think of me, all rigged out like a proper man of war?'

Rendell did indeed look the part, in half armour with his visor raised, and he rode in step with his colleagues displaying accomplished precision. It was more than six months since I had seen him. I waved.

'If you get leave from your guard duties, I'm lodged with Lord Fitzvaughan by the butter market.'

He winked as he passed. I was impressed by his presence in Gloucester's personal escort but I reflected that the inclusion of such a young and relatively inexperienced soldier in the bodyguard confirmed what Bartholomew had said about the Duke's confidence in his own security.

I attended Suffolk who required further treatment to his back but was unusually taciturn while I eased his muscles. As I was finishing, the Marquis received a summons to attend the King and Queen and he bounded out of the room with agility for which I considered I could take credit. I was then free to return to my quarters and did so unmolested although I was puzzled to see so many men in Suffolk's livery patrolling the streets.

In the lobby of the house where I was staying a lad was waiting whom I recognised, a lad who served the steward at my manor. He bowed and held out a letter which I snatched from him rudely. I broke the seal and caught my breath as I read the childlike writing.

Doctor Somers, your son is born before his time. He is frail but living. The Countess is also weak and begs you to come when you are able. Your servant, Berthe.

I shouted for my horse and ran to my pallet, collecting my mantle and trying to contain the mixture of excitement, joy and terror which engulfed me. In only a few minutes I was riding to the north gate of the town as if all the demons of Hell were driving me before them. Then I came to a clattering halt in front of crossed halberds.

Suffolk's soldiers barred my way to the gate and the portcullis had been lowered. No one was to pass, in or out of the town, I was told. Deceitful in my alarm, I protested that I was the Marquis's physician and he would be content for me to go to Wingfield but the sergeant shook his head.

'No exceptions, Doctor. By the King's command.'

I saw then that there were royal guards beside their de la Pole comrades and knew I could not argue myself through the gate against this sovereign prohibition.

'How long will the proscription last?'

'Till we get orders otherwise.'

I cursed under my breath but at that instant the chain of the portcullis creaked and the grille began to move. The mad thought came to me that I might dash through the opening and escape but then I saw the party of nobles re-entering the town and recognised the Duke of Buckingham and the Earls of Salisbury and Dorset, some of the highest in the land, all with royal blood in their veins. I would be cut down before I passed the gate if I tried anything foolhardy. Through the raised barrier I saw an impressive building beyond the town walls and a fearful thought came to me.

'What's the building?' I asked the guard, dreading his answer.

'St. Saviour's Hospital,' he said as he sprang to attention while the noblemen rode past us.

I retreated to my lodgings in great unease and handed my horse to the groom. I intended to return to the abbey and seek Suffolk's authority to leave the town but as I approached the entrance I met Lord Fitzvaughan and Gaston de la Tour who confirmed my worst suspicions.

'Duke Humphrey is arrested, charged with all the ancient offences the Cardinal alleged against him years ago. The King has ordered he be held prisoner in his lodgings while a full enquiry is conducted into the validity of the claims. His gentlemen attendants are likewise confined to their quarters.' Lord Fitzvaughan looked shaken by the news and mopped his brow with his sleeve.

I had other concerns and risked sharing a confidence. 'My lady is brought to bed of a son but both are weak. I'm fretful to go to Worthwaite.'

'You've no chance at the moment. Suffolk's as twitchy as a bedbug in a beard. When he's had Gloucester dragged off to a dungeon cell he'll relax. Give it a day or two.'

I had no choice and strove to be patient but next day I presented myself at the Abbey Gate with a request to see the Marquis – only , as I feared, to be sent away. My desperation grew and I wondered if other messengers had been sent from Worthwaite but denied access to Saint Edmundsbury. At least if this was so, Yolande would learn of my predicament. But I dared not speculate what further news a messenger might bring.

I knelt in earnest prayer in half a dozen chapels, I played at chequers with Gaston de la Tour and I welcomed the need to examine the rotund merchant, who was the landlord of our lodgings, when he tumbled down the stairs, the worse for liquor. Any diversion was helpful to stop my mind drifting into miserable speculation, for I dreaded that my guilt would reap its punishment at the expense of those I loved: double guilt as a man forsworn and a brutalized killer. Morning and afternoon I went to the abbey only to be dismissed but then, in the early evening of the third day, Suffolk sent for me and it seemed that after all Heaven was granting me the opportunity I craved.

I took a variety of potions and lotions to the abbey, ready to treat whatever condition troubled the Marquis, but I was not allowed to broach the subject nearest my heart before he held up his hand.

'Harry, I've summoned you on a matter of state importance. Gloucester is arraigned to come and answer charges before his peers and the members of his household are under arrest. But his man has brought a message that the Duke is taken ill and lies unconscious. He has his personal physician to attend him but I suspect a plot and a fabricated malady. It presents me with a problem. If Humphrey is genuinely sick he is entitled to receive physic and I would not wish to deny him or be portrayed as churlish towards my enemy but I wish to have his condition confirmed independently. I've decided you should be escorted to St. Saviour's to examine him and approve any necessary medicaments. You must go there at once.'

He swept from the room and two guards escorted me downstairs to where the Duke's attendant was waiting. I experienced a frisson of displeasure but no surprise when recognised this person was Gilbert Iffley and he bowed to me with cool courtesy.

'Suffolk is a pitiless brute,' he said, 'but at least in sending you he is providing a physician who has knowledge of the Duke's affliction. I judge his condition serious.'

I gave a brusque nod of acknowledgement but did not reply.

'You are offended to have dealings with me, I fancy, after our contretemps when last we met.'

My temper was brittle. 'Contretemps! You assaulted and drugged me and consigned me to the torturer.'

'You were foolish, Harry. If you'd sworn as I'd asked you, we'd not be where we are now.'

'You were asking me to swear to a lie.'

'I'd have thought a trivial lie was the least of your transgressions. I didn't know then that the Countess was your bedfellow.'

I gnawed my inner lip to prevent any response, horrified that Iffley had discovered the truth, and we marched the rest of the way through the town in silence.

*****

The Duke was lying in a narrow bed, piled high with blankets, and he looked a puny, shrunken figure, his face haggard and slightly crooked. He was in a deep coma.

Gloucester's physician gave a curt bow and scowled at me.

'Suffolk ordered me to come but I'm sorry to intrude. When was he taken ill, Doctor?'

'Three hours ago, maybe more. He was struck down while he sat at table. He hasn't changed since we laid him in his bed. Iffley insisted Suffolk was to be informed. I saw no such necessity.'

'Has he been given any medicine?'

357

To my surprise it was Iffley who answered. 'I specified that a mild solution of foxglove and chamomile be prepared before Doctor Woodman could come. Just as you prescribed when you treated the Duke at Baynard's Castle.' His voice was clipped and apprehensive.

'I doubt he could have been coaxed to drink it. But you acted correctly.'

'I spooned a little between his lips.'

Doctor Woodman muttered under his breath but Iffley ignored him, smiling thinly and addressing his question to me. 'Is his condition mortal?'

'I can't be certain and must defer to his own physician but I'd say he's in a critical state. If he rallies by morning, there'll be hope of some recovery.'

'Some, Doctor Somers?' Iffley pushed his cap back from his forehead. 'What do you say, Woodman?'

'It's possible,' the physician said with a shrug.

I thought it sensible to explain further to Iffley. 'The seizure has been extremely powerful. If he survives he may well suffer some lasting incapacity.'

'Humphrey of Gloucester will not be himself again?'

'I'm afraid that is my diagnosis.'

Iffley lowered his head. 'We are obliged to you, Doctor Somers. I'll have food sent to sustain you and Doctor Woodman. In order to satisfy Suffolk it will be fitting if you both watch over the Duke.'

'I shall observe carefully what my colleague eats,' I thought ungratefully, 'in case you have tampered with food for my nourishment'. Then fleetingly I wondered if Iffley had sought to speed Gloucester out of this life, as I was sure he had poisoned Andrew Cawfield. Nevertheless I dismissed the idea, because I could think of nothing he would gain by losing his patron, whose fortunes he had sought for so long to manipulate and foster.

I had no option but to remain at St. Saviour's, barred from travelling elsewhere, fretting at my impotence, praying silently in a mixture of reverence and frustration for the health of Yolande and our little son, longing to escape to visit them. For two days and nights Doctor Woodman and I sat by Gloucester's bed, taking turns to rest, and in all that time we exchanged few words. Independently, we checked the patient's pulse, lifted his eyelids and listened to his breathing but we did not share our diagnoses, although I imagine we were in agreement that the end was near. Then, on the third morning, we both rose from our stools as Gloucester moved an arm, moaning faintly, and opened his eyes to stare at us vacantly. In unison we sent for the priest and withdrew while the Duke made his confession and received the last rites. I was glad Heaven had accorded him that opportunity to acknowledge his sins and be granted the hope of remission for his failings. Although it was not for me to judge, in my heart I believed his flaws were outweighed by his virtues.

That afternoon, after the sun had risen to its zenith and a wintery beam shone through the high window above us, I stood to close Humphrey of Gloucester's eyes while Doctor Woodman folded the dead man's arms across his chest. Then, together, we drew the sheet over his wizened, cultivated face. The youngest of great King Harry's brothers, doughty warrior in his youth, wounded at Agincourt, impulsive, arrogant courtier, dedicated foe to those he hated, educated sponsor of learned scholars, curious seeker after knowledge, lover of beauty and inveterate womanizer had breathed his last.

Chapter 27

Standing by the priest, while other members of the household entered the room, I said a silent prayer for Gloucester's soul and then, seeing he had not come, I called for Gilbert Iffley. When there was no response I called his name again and Bartholomew appeared, blanching when he saw the covered figure on the bed.

'Is Iffley coming?'

Bartholomew twisted his hands together. 'He's gone. He left the house during the night.'

'How could he escape the guards?'

'I suppose they were less zealous than they might have been, knowing Gloucester's condition, and Iffley always had gold to ease his passage.'

'Do you know where he's gone?'

'I'd guess he's fled to join Richard of York. He told me before I went to bed that Duke Humphrey was dying. He left with Master Boice.'

'Stephen Boice? I didn't know he was here.' I took off my cap and ran my fingers through my hair, feeling confused.

Bartholomew raised his eyebrows. 'Didn't you know? Master Boice is Iffley's good-brother. His sister is Mistress Iffley.'

My expression must have reflected my astonishment. 'Boice is brother to Andrew Cawfield's widow and therefore kin to the Nevilles?'

'And a staunch follower of the Duke of York.'

'I wish I'd known earlier.'

I felt inadequate to consider the implications of this information and had more immediate priorities. 'I must speak to the captain of Suffolk's guard. Will you take me to him?'

The young man held open the door and I spoke quietly as we went along the corridor. 'The game has changed, Bartholomew, now the Duke is dead. You should look to your own best interest when you have the opportunity, although you must decide where that lies.'

'It won't rest with Iffley, of that I'm sure,' he said and silently I applauded his wisdom.

The captain of the guard trembled at the news of Gloucester's death but was briskly efficient, sending a messenger to Suffolk and ordering reinforcements to stand sentinel over the Duke's principal attendants, so there was soon a swirl of activity in St Saviour's and I concluded, conveniently, that my continued presence was redundant. By rights I should go directly to the Marquis to make my medical report but it was possible that, in the hurly-burly, I might slip out of the building and take my way wherever I chose. I crossed the guardroom, peering around me, and it reinforced my rebellious instinct when I saw a group of Gloucester's less exalted followers, stripped of their arms, throwing dice, with Rendell among them.

He looked up and came at once when I beckoned.

'Gloucester's dead,' I said, putting my finger to my lips. 'Can you get me a horse, do you think, before discipline is restored among Suffolk's men? Get one for yourself if you can. There's no guarantee what will happen here when the news gets out.'

Rendell tapped his nose in a familiar manner. 'They ain't bothered about us ordinary hangers-on, only the highborn gents they've already locked up. Come on, Doctor, let's get you out of here quick. Did you give Gloucester something to help him on his way? Was that the reason you was sent here?'

Only then did it occur to me that Rendell's jesting innuendo could be repeated by others with far more malicious intent and I contemplated the painful possibility that Suffolk had sent me intentionally to bear the brunt of such accusations.

*****

When we had ridden out of sight of St. Saviour's I reined in my horse and leaned across to Rendell.

'I have business to the north of here but I suggest you make for London. Gloucester has no heir and all his lands and goods are likely to be seized – the palace at Greenwich and Baynard's Castle among them. Thomas and Grizel will need to have a care for themselves and their family. Get to them as fast as you can and help them.'

I thought Rendell would protest but after a pause he nodded and wheeled his horse, wishing me Godspeed, while I gave Heaven thanks that he need not come with me to Worthwaite. He believed Yolande had returned to France months previously and he had no knowledge of our continuing liaison. When we were married, Rendell would be among the first to know but until then I was in too fraught a state of anxiety to cope with his mock outrage and ribald jests.

It was a clear night and the moon was full so I rode for as long as I could, resting sleeplessly for an hour in the shelter of a byre, in order to arrive at Worthwaite at first light. The last few miles in the chill of dawn were a torment, both to my weary body and more especially to my mind, for I could not dismiss a growing fear of disaster. By the time the rooftop came in view, I sensed an evil hand was laid upon my manor. A stable lad, rubbing his eyes, stumbled across the yard and I flung him my reins without a word; then I entered the house to find my world changed irreparably.

I stared at the figure in black crossing the vestibule before I recognised Father Wilfred and realised what he was carrying. He stopped and regarded me with compassion before advancing slowly and he held out his tiny, swaddled burden.

'I'm so sorry, Doctor Somers. The little mite struggled bravely but he came too soon. It's a week since he was born and but an hour ago he died. I wish he could have lasted longer for you to hold him breathing.'

I took the bundle and looked down on the miniature face, perfectly formed, free from any blemish such as that which disfigures my cheek. I was very familiar with the distortions death can bring to stiffened features and the rictus which fixes itself on a silent mouth but my son's icy lips were formed into the resemblance of a smile and I caught my breath. A cherub's smile. Maud Fitzvaughan's description of the baby she bore came to me in that instant of agony and I comprehended the grief she had felt when Eleanor was taken from her. A tear fell from my eye onto the infant's forehead and instinctively I put my finger onto the moisture.

'I've given him Christian baptism, Doctor,' the priest said. 'The lady directed he be given your name.'

I struggled to speak clearly. 'Thank you. I'm glad you were here.'

'I'd come several times from Wingfield, hoping to conduct your nuptials as you'd asked. But then the child was born and it was clear he was unlikely to survive.'

I rallied myself as best I could, dreading what would come next. 'The Countess?'

'She's weak but Dame Elizabeth says she will grow stronger. She's sobbed herself to sleep. The boy died in her arms.'

I shut my eyes, reeling from the joy of hearing Yolande would recover, for in my desolation I had feared she too was dead.

'Sadly, it's necessary for her to leave your house. I've sent for a litter from Wingfield to convey her safely to sanctuary.'

'What danger is she in?'

The priest looked at me squarely. 'The Marquis of Suffolk has been told where she is staying. It's imperative she isn't here when he sends men to haul her before the Queen.'

'Who has betrayed her? Who found out? Did Charpentier tell someone before he died?'

'I don't know who you mean but the person who discovered her refuge is a man I've met before. I believe him to be a spy and an enemy to the Marquis. His name is Boice.'

'Stephen Boice.' I repeated the name and my tears welled up again. 'Pray God, the Countess can be conveyed to sanctuary quickly. Fortunately Suffolk has many other preoccupations at present so he may not send to detain her immediately. Gloucester is dead.'

The priest pursed his mouth and made the sign of the cross. 'That's news indeed. God have mercy on him. Go to your lady now and help her prepare for departure. I'll conduct her and her maid to sanctuary and they will be well cared for until it's safe for her to emerge. If you agree, I'll also take your little son for Christian burial.'

I hugged the small corpse to me. 'Not at Wingfield. I beg you not to bury him at Wingfield on Suffolk's land.'

Father Wilfred looked surprised but nodded. 'The priest at the Church of Saint Mary the Virgin in Diss is my friend. He will consent to accommodate a tiny grave.'

'That's fitting.' I said, choking over my words.

I could not tell Father Wilfred how fitting I thought it that the resting place of my doomed son would look down on the spot where his father had mutilated a dead man with shameful brutality. In my mind his fate and my guilt were inseparably linked. I kissed the deceptive, smiling face and held him out for the priest to take from me forever.

*****

I stood at the door of Yolande's room, hesitating to enter in case I disturbed her sleep and fearing what I must endure for, from the first sight of the priest carrying my son

I knew what to expect. Then I heard movement and she called my name. I opened the door and Berthe bobbed to me, with downcast face, as she slipped out, carrying a pile of dresses. Yolande was lying on her bed, propped on cushions, swathed in a heavy travelling cloak. Her cheeks were sunken but had a hint of colour. Her eyes were swollen.

'I heard your voice. You have seen Father Wilfred?'

'Yes. And I've seen our beautiful son. Oh, I'm so sorry I was prevented from coming earlier. I had no choice but to stay in Saint Edmundsbury at Suffolk's command.'

'You could have done nothing to save the boy. I knew he could not live from the moment of his birth. Dame Elizabeth knew it too.'

Her words sounded cold but they were at odds with the misery on her face. Briefly she glanced down and I saw the empty cradle beside her bed, its blanket still showing the shallow depression of a tiny body. I went to her side and knelt, forcing myself to speak steadily.

'Father Wilfred has told me you must seek sanctuary to save yourself from the Queen's anger.'

Her voice strengthened and acquired an edge of disdain. 'The man Boice deceived us. He announced himself as your friend, come from Saint Edmundsbury on your behalf, so he was admitted to the house. He had some inkling I might be here but he had never seen me so he employed a ruse to confirm my identity. He had heard the rumour I was a lady of Normandy so he spoke to me of Rouen and mentioned Master Drewman, the goldsmith who aided Queen Margaret. I foolishly said too much and...'

She had begun to weep and I clasped her hand. 'There's no need to explain. Boice is a subtle villain and he's hand in glove with Iffley, both of them agitators fomenting riot in the City of London. They've plotted our downfall for their own purposes; they aim to discredit Suffolk.'

Yolande tossed her head and in this gesture I recognised the proud, intimidating Countess I had first encountered in Tours three and a half years previously.

'These English gentlemen and their petty manoeuvrings are nothing to me,' she said and I knew my fate was sealed. I had no strength to waste in useless protestation.

'The Queen and Suffolk have other preoccupations. You won't need to stay in sanctuary for long. You'll be able to evade their notice and cross the sea unnoticed in a few weeks.'

She looked at me closely, puckering her brow. 'You understand? I shall return to France when it is safe. Father Wilfred says it can be arranged in the spring.'

'To your brother's protection?'

'It is best. He believes I have been suffering from some dire malady and will be joyful I have recovered. Rumours may follow me across the Narrow Sea but false rumours abound and, when I am by his side, my brother will discount them. He will not see it as in my nature to behave so – unchastely.'

'You know my truest wish is to marry you,' I said, with no hope of altering her intention. 'I shall mourn little Harry all my life but we would have other children and could build a life of shared happiness for us and them. I'd willingly brave the world's disapproval and travel to some far land to achieve this.'

'But I am a coward, Harry, and must fulfil the duties of my rank, as you must fulfil the duties of your calling. God did not intend us for each other and has taken the child which bound us. Forgive me, my love, but I must obey His will and discharge the obligations He has placed on me.'

We both heard the sound of horses in the courtyard and glanced towards the window. 'The litter has come,' Yolande said. 'Forgive me, Harry, for causing you such pain

Your dream entranced me but dreams are unreal in this burdensome world.'

I smothered her hands with kisses but our moment of emotion was disturbed by a shout.

'Christ, Doctor Somers. You've led me a bloody dance! I've been to Wingfield looking for you.'

'Rendell!' Yolande and I exclaimed together as the lad burst through the door, red-faced and dishevelled. He halted in amazement when he saw us and gulped as he took in the details of our pathetic scene.

'Madame Yolande. I didn't know you were here.' His testiness increased. 'I didn't know the Doctor had this poncey manor come to that. Kept right in the dark, I've been.'

'I am about to leave for a place of safety,' Yolande said. 'I have been ill and Doctor Somers granted me a resting place to recover.'

Rendell glared at the cradle but, remarkably, he did not comment on our relationship. 'It's the Doctor who's most in danger at present,' he said. 'It's probably too late to get you away before they arrive but you might prefer to be caught outside rather than in a lady's bedchamber.'

I stood up, registering the maturity of his judgement. 'Who is coming for me?'

'Christ knows who they are, half the nobs from the court, it looked like from a distance. They've got authority from Suffolk to arrest you.'

'On what charge?'

'Smothering the Duke of Gloucester on his sickbed.'

'Of course.' I bent to kiss Yolande. 'You're right, sweet love. I'm snared in great men's intrigues and can offer you nothing. God bless you and take you safely to your brother and a worthy husband.'

'God keep you, Harry. I beg you to save yourself. Look after him, Rendell. He is the core of my being.'

Unimpressed by mawkish sentimentality, Rendel seized my arm, dragging me through the house and into the courtyard where Father Wilfred was waiting with the litter and harnessed horses.

'Wait until we're clear of the manor,' I said to him 'then set off with the Countess. There's a troop coming to seize me and I shall ride to meet them. The chances are they'll be satisfied once they have me in charge and you'll have the opportunity to cover a good few miles before they think of impounding the manor.'

I hauled myself into the saddle, shouting thanks to my steward and Dame Elizabeth who had come from the house to see what was happening. Then, with Rendell riding flank to flank, I headed along the track leading south towards those sent to execute Suffolk's warrant and to face the trumped up charge which could lead me to the gibbet.

*****

Rendell had been rightly impressed by the party sent to arrest me and I was amazed by the sight, not so much by the posse of men at arms but the nobles they escorted. It was strangely encouraging to see Walter Fitzvaughan leading the group for I had faith in his honesty and trusted he would have no truck with the imposition of rough justice without trial. What astonished me was recognising the person at his side, who appeared in more robust health than when I had last seen him, and I noted a bevy of clerics in the rear surrounding an uncomfortable-looking Gaston de la Tour.

I drew rein and halted in front of them, doffing my cap. I was unafraid, not from enviable courage or foolish bravado but because I was drained of feeling after the scene I had experienced at Worthwaite.

'My lords, you are seeking me, I believe.'

Lord Fitzvaughan grunted and cleared his throat as if to say something but his companion rode forward, peering into my face.

'It is you, Harry Somers, I couldn't credit what they told me. I'd stake my life, you're no murderer.'

'My Lord Earl, you do me honour and I swear I did not kill Humphrey of Gloucester. Who lays this charge against me?'

'Complaint has been made by members of the late Duke's retinue. The Marquis is bound to investigate impartially, especially as you are of his household. I trust you will not be confined for long.'

The Earl of Stanwick gave me a smile of reassurance and I had no doubt of his sincerity. He was an upright man and it was no coincidence he held aloof from the intrigues of the court but I understood it might suit others very well for me to be pronounced guilty. The Duke of York's faction would claim I acted at the instigation of the Marquis and Suffolk, to protect himself, would throw me to the wolves in the same way York had abandoned his armourer who had spoken with untimely enthusiasm on his master's behalf.

I saw Walter Fitzvaughan's sombre expression and recognised that he understood the reality of the situation as I did. 'We are here to take you to prison, Harry,' he said. 'The manor of Worthwaite and all the goods you've received from the Marquis are forfeit. You are to appear before him to answer the capital charge of murder.'

I had no spirit to dispute or plead and when the Earl leaned over to whisper something to Fitzvaughan I diverted myself fleetingly by wondering what the extraordinary rapprochement between those gentlemen might mean for Lady Maud's fortunes; but that was not my concern. Very little concerned me anymore – only the memory of a tiny swaddled cherub bound for a grave in the churchyard at Diss and his aristocratic mother lost to me by his death.

Lady Maud's husband shook his head and it was clear he could not accede to his companion's request. Instead he clicked his fingers and the captain of his guard rode forward to shackle my wrists. I bowed my head in readiness but at my side Rendell coughed and frowned at me, presumably expecting me to accomplish a miraculous escape. Then I realised he was gesticulating for me to look in the direction of the clergymen ranged behind the nobles and for the first time I recognised the Abbot of Peterborough in a central position. His eyes were blazing and when he saw I was looking at him he raised his hands as if in prayer.

My movement was half-hearted because I had resigned myself to my wretched destiny but the Abbot's insistent glare and Rendell's impatience impelled me to take what I thought was a futile action. As the captain of the guard produced his fetters, I delved inside my pouch extracted the embossed token and held it out for Lord Fitzvaughan and the Earl to examine. My voice sounded distant and reedy but it held their attention. It brought a beam of satisfaction to the Abbot's pudgy face and earned an admiring gasp from the Earl. While Rendell gave a squeak o delight, his lordship folded his arms, turned his head to wink at Gaston de la Tour and guffawed.

'I claim the protection of the Church,' I said with growing confidence, 'as a faithful servant and physician to his Grace, Cardinal Beaufort. I am required to go to Winchester without delay to attend him. In his name and in the interests of his failing health I crave passage to obey.'

370

HISTORICAL NOTE

Most characters in *The Cherub's Smile* are fictional but the main events which provide the background to the story are factual. The negotiations for a truce with France in 1444 leading to the betrothal and, in 1445, the marriage of Henry VI with Margaret of Anjou; the emergence later in 1445 of 'secret' clauses in the conditions of the truce which aroused the opposition of Humphrey, Duke of Gloucester, uncle to Henry VI, and the City of London; Gloucester's long-term antagonism to Cardinal Beaufort and, later, to William de la Pole, Earl (subsequently Marquis) of Suffolk; and the events at Bury St. Edmunds (Saint Edmundsbury) in February 1447 are all to be found recorded in the annals.

The Cherub's Smile continues the story of the young physician, Harry Somers, which began in *The Devil's Stain,* followed by *The Angel's Wing,* and several characters in it (both factual and fictional) appear in the earlier books.

THE AUTHOR

Pamela Gordon Hoad read history at Oxford University, and the subject has remained of abiding interest to her. She has also always loved the drama and romance of characters and plot in historical fiction. She tried her hand at such creative writing over the years but, due to the exigencies of her career, she mainly wrote committee reports, policy papers and occasional articles for publication. After working for the Greater London Council, she held the positions of Chief Executive of the London Borough of Hackney and then Chief Executive of the City of Sheffield. Later she held public appointments, including that of Electoral Commissioner when the Electoral Commission was established.

Since 'retiring', Pamela has been active in the voluntary sector and for three years chaired the national board of Relationships Scotland; she continues her involvement with several voluntary sector organisations. Importantly, during the last few years, she has also been able to pursue her aim of writing historical fiction and she published her first two novels, *The Devil's Stain* and *The Angel's Wing* in 2016. These introduced the young physician, Harry Somers, whose story is continued in *The Cherub's Smile;* a fourth book in the series is planned for publication in 2018.

Pamela has also published short stories with historical backgrounds in anthologies published by the Borders Writers Forum (which she chaired for three years). She continues to chair or be a committee member of various local organisations concerned with the creative arts and history.

Other Mauve Square books:

For adults:
The Devil's Stain by Pamela Gordon Hoad: *'A tense fifteenth century English murder mystery, full of twists and turns'*, which introduces Harry Somers, physician and investigator.

The Angel's Wing by Pamela Gordon Hoad: *'The action and drama of the first book continue in this compelling sequel as Harry gains a reputation for his medical skills whilst becoming embroiled in the politics of fifteenth century Italy...'*

Crying Through the Wind by Iona Carroll. *'...Sensitively written novel of love, intrigue and hidden family secrets set in post-war Ireland... one of those books you can't put down from the very first paragraph...'*

Familiar Yet Far by Iona Carroll. Second novel in *The Story of Oisin Kelly* trilogy follows the young Irishman in *Crying Through the Wind* from Ireland and Edinburgh to Australia. *'The author has a genius, bringing you into whichever country she is writing about. You can smell the rain in Ireland and the dust in the Outback...'*

The Manhattan Deception, The Minerva System, Seven Stars and ***Bomber Boys*** by Simon Leighton-Porter. *'...Fast paced thriller with a plot which twists and turns.' 'I loved it...' 'As soon as I picked this book up I knew I wouldn't be able to put it down...'*

Voices by prize-winning author, Oliver Eade: a tale of murder, family love and child abuse seen through the eyes of a grandfather, father and young girl.

For young readers:

***Shadows from the Past** series* by Wendy Leighton-Porter. '*...Wendy has written a fantastic series of books (Shadows from the Past) filled with mystery, suspense, and adventure.*'

Firestorm Rising** & **Demons of the Dark by John Clewarth '*...Children learn that there are far more terrifying things in the universe than they ever learned at school, as a terrifying monster is awakened from a long hot sleep.*'

For young adults:

Golden Jaguar of the Sun by prize-winning author Oliver Eade: first book of a trilogy, spanning the USA and Mexico: a story of teenage love and its pitfalls and also a tale of adventure, fantasy and the merging of beliefs.

The Merging by Oliver Eade is the second book in his *Beast to God* trilogy and continues the story of the young protagonists in *Golden Jaguar of the Sun*.